ALSO BY E.E.

CITY OF THE FORGOTTEN

THE GATEWAY TRACKERS BOOK 9

E.E. HOLMES

FAIRHAVEN PRESS

Fairhaven Press

Townsend, MA

www.eeholmes.com

ISBN 978-1-956656-10-7 (Paperback edition)

ISBN 978-1-956656-09-1 (Barnes & Noble edition)

ISBN 978-1-956656-08-4 (Digital edition)

Cover design by James T. Egan of Bookfly Design LLC

Author photography by Cydney Scott Photography

This one's for Missy, because everyone needs a friend who always says "yes" when it counts and, more importantly, one who won't let you say "no."

1

CHANGES

"No."

"Come on!"

"Absolutely not."

"Well, now you're just being unreasonable."

"*I'm* being unreasonable? *Me*?!"

"Yes. And frankly, uncooperative."

I yanked open the bedroom door and glared out into the living room. Two exasperated faces turned to look at me.

"Sorry, Jess, did we wake you up?" Hannah asked, somehow managing to look frustrated and apologetic at the same time.

"Whatever gave you that impression?" I mumbled, rubbing at my face beneath my nest of sleep-tangled hair.

"Probably the yawning, the slurred speech, and the fact that your eyes are still basically closed," Milo suggested helpfully.

I shuffled out into the living room, closing the door a little harder than was strictly necessary, and fumbled my way toward the coffee maker. "And here I thought I was doing a good impression of a conscious person."

"We're sorry," Hannah repeated, throwing a look at Milo as she said it. "Why don't you go back to bed?"

"There's no point. My alarm is going to go off in twenty minutes anyway.

Waking up once was bad enough; I don't want to do it twice," I sighed. "What are you two fighting about anyway?"

"What else?" Hannah replied with a roll of her eyes.

I nodded knowingly. There was only one topic of conversation that could cause this level of consternation before eight o'clock in the morning, and that was...

"Wedding plans," Milo finished my thought for me. He was perched on the couch surrounded by what appeared to be a mountain of white fabric samples and every bridal magazine printed in the last six months.

"All right, I'll bite," I said as I waited for the coffee to start brewing. "What's the issue this time? Table linens? Passed hors d'oeuvres?"

"Dresses," Milo answered, pouting.

"I thought she already agreed to let you make her dress," I said.

"Oh, she did," Milo replied. "And now she's decided to break my heart instead."

Hannah groaned and dropped her head into her hands. "Milo, for the hundredth time, I still love you, you are the most talented designer on the face of the planet and I adore everything you do, but I am NOT going along with this."

"Along with what?" I asked. I was still missing something, my brain too gummed up with sleep to work properly. "Hannah, whatever style of dress he makes, it's going to be gorgeous on—"

"No, not dress. *Dresses*. Plural."

I blinked. "Oh."

"That's right. Milo has decided that in order for my wedding to be a success, I need to wear not one, not two, but *three* different dresses over the course of the evening," Hannah said. I had to admire how she managed to get the words out given that her teeth were clenched so tightly that she more closely resembled a rabid dog than my mild-mannered twin sister.

"Is that... a thing?" I asked. "Costume changes at weddings?"

"Oh, it's not just *a* thing, it's *the* thing," Milo chirped, sounding quite manic with excitement at the prospect. "All of the celebrities are doing it. One dress for the ceremony, one for the reception, and a third one for the after-party!"

"What after-party?" Hannah gasped. "I'm not even... wait, am I having an after-party?"

Milo grinned sheepishly. "I may have mentioned it to Karen. She thought it was a great idea."

Hannah groaned and tipped over on the sofa, burying her face in the cushions. The only person as excited as Milo about Hannah's upcoming wedding was Karen. She had shrieked like an overexcited toddler when she heard the news, and immediately went into planning mode. It turned out that our family estate had money set aside for things such as this.

"But I thought our mom was cut off when she ran away?" Hannah had asked when Karen informed her the wedding was paid for.

"She was, but your grandmother's will had stipulations that specifically allotted money for the weddings of future granddaughters, and that money was doubled if those granddaughters were Durupinen," Karen explained.

"Doubled?" Hannah gasped. "But why?"

"Because your grandmother would rather have spent every penny our family has than risk that one of our rival clans might throw a more impressive wedding than our clan," Karen admitted.

Hannah had turned to me in that moment, panic dawning on her features. "This is going be a nightmare, isn't it?" she'd whispered.

"Oh, undoubtedly," I'd whispered back, even as Karen started gushing about posh London venues.

So now, any hopes Hannah may have had of a small, intimate ceremony somewhere had been crushed to dust. Add in the unfortunate fact that Kiernan's family was likewise desperate to make this joining of two powerful clans the most anticipated event of the Durupinen social calendar, and she had completely lost all control over her own wedding. Now she and Kiernan sat like two deer in headlights every time the topic of their impending nuptials came up, despite the fact that it was well over a year away—the one victory they'd managed to win was staving off the event until after Hannah had finished her thesis.

"Finn has a pilot's license. Just say the word and it's off to Vegas," I muttered out of the corner of my mouth.

Milo let out a gasp worthy of a telenovela climax. "How dare you even utter the 'V' word!" he hissed at me. "Keep it up and I will refuse to make your maid-of-honor dress!"

"Promise?" I asked, grinning.

Meanwhile, Hannah, the least Vegas-y person I could think of, seemed to be lost in genuine contemplation of a drive-through chapel wedding performed by Elvis. Milo cleared his throat to interrupt her rhinestone-studded thoughts, but she held up a hand to stop him.

"Milo, I can't talk about this anymore or I'm going to have a meltdown," Hannah said in a voice of forced calm, "and I don't want to have a meltdown today because I have an important presentation to give for class this afternoon. So, while I dearly love you and your enthusiasm, can we please discuss the ludicrous number of dresses some other time?"

Milo lifted his chin, looking as dignified as he could while half-buried in scraps of white fabric, lace, and ribbon. "Yes, we can discuss the completely reasonable number of dresses later," he replied. "But not too much later, because I have to get sketching."

Hannah managed not to roll her eyes. "Fine."

"Vegas," I mouthed.

"I'll think about it," she mouthed back.

Milo glared silently at us.

I took my cup of coffee to the couch, shifting the bridal textile mountain so that I could sit down. "Any new internet theories about who you really are?" I asked Milo.

The change of topic instantly brought a grin to his face. "Someone this morning suggested that I was Gianni Versace, who faked his death to escape the paparazzi and reinvent himself," he said. "I mean, that's twisted and bizarre, but I'm flattered by the comparison."

Ever since Milo's most recent runway show, the internet had been working overtime to figure out who he was and why no one ever saw him. Milo's website explained that he was very private and reclusive, but that wasn't nearly an interesting enough explanation for the conspiracy theorists of the world. There was even a website dedicated to "sightings" of Milo, which included grainy cell phone photos of everyone from other celebrities to random name-less pedestrians who happened to be in the right place at the right time. Strangely enough, as ridiculous as the theories had become, no one had guessed he was a ghost/spirit guide living out his dream of fashion notoriety. The whole thing lent a mystique to Milo and his designs that had sent his popularity through the roof, and he couldn't have been more gleeful about the whole thing. After all, it was the kind of celebrity drama he would have lapped up if it had been about someone else.

"Are you ready for today?" Milo asked, the grin fading from his face. "Are you nervous?"

I took a sip of my coffee, considering the question. "No. I don't think I'm nervous. I've made up my mind. I just... I want to get it over with, y'know?"

"Yeah, makes sense," Milo said, nodding sagely.

"If it helps, I think you're doing the right thing," Hannah said.

I shrugged. I wasn't convinced one way or the other. I just knew how I felt.

Ever since we had returned from Castle Island three months ago, I'd spent more time at Fairhaven than ever. We'd had to debrief with Catriona and the Trackers, testify before the Council, fill out report after report, and attend disciplinary hearings for the students involved. And when it was all over, Catriona sat me down and asked me, formally, if I would consider becoming a Tracker again. And surprisingly, rather than laughing all the way out of her office, into the grounds and off into the sunset, I'd told her I'd consider it.

I know, I know. But, trust me, no one was more surprised to hear those words come out of my mouth than I had been myself.

But the truth was, the events at Castle Island had revealed the true state of the Durupinen world to me in a way nothing in the past couple of years had done. Part of it had been my willful ignorance; I didn't want to believe that we were in as much danger as ever, and so I didn't. I simply refused to acknowledge it. I'd had enough of danger, enough of mad dashes across the globe, enough of prophecies and betrayals and apocalyptic-level stakes. I'd decided I'd done my part—more than my part—and it was someone else's problem now. I was done cleaning up other people's messes.

But it turned out that we couldn't count on other Durupinen to protect us from danger, when other Durupinen *were* the danger. We were splintered and divided, and it was going to take all of us who fought for the Reckoning to ensure we could move forward from it, even if we had no more desire to fight.

That didn't mean I was ready to sign back on to become a Tracker. But it did mean I would have to consider very seriously what my role would be going forward, because bowing out was not an option. That much was abundantly clear. I'd been wrestling back and forth with my answer, and told her I'd decide by today. I'd run out of time to avoid it any longer.

"What time are you heading out?" Hannah asked.

"Soon," I replied. "As soon as the morning traffic lightens up."

"And how about packing?" Hannah asked, voice tentative.

I looked over at the pile of boxes in the corner and sighed. The events at Castle Island had thrown our lives into such disarray that our plans for moving closer to Fairhaven had been delayed as well. But as spring loomed around the corner, so did the impending move out of our Notting Hill flat in London and into south Cambridgeshire, which meant I really needed to pack. But packing meant accepting that we were moving back into Fairhaven's orbit, and there was a part of me that was still fighting that reality. And so I had been staring at the same pile of broken-down cardboard boxes for a solid week, and hadn't placed even a single item in any of them.

"I'm actively avoiding it," I said, "until I inevitably have to throw everything I own haphazardly into containers at the last possible moment in a fit of panic."

"That sounds like a healthy and mature coping strategy," Milo said.

"Yeah, I like it so far," I replied, sipping on my coffee unconcernedly.

"Future Jess might not like it very much," Hannah pointed out.

"Maybe not, but that sounds like a problem for future Jess, now doesn't it?" I said.

Hannah just shook her head, smirking. She had been diligently wrapping things in bubble wrap, and tucking them neatly into labeled boxes for two weeks now, and I couldn't blame her for trying to motivate me. After all, she'd be the one who'd have to help me in those final days when I'd at last sunk beneath the crushing weight of my own procrastination, and so she was really just exercising self-preservation.

We weren't all moving together—at least, not technically. Once Hannah and Kiernan had gotten engaged, it seemed obvious that they would want and need their own space, but it was too difficult to think of not living near each other. After all, we'd spent so many years missing out on being sisters, we weren't ready to compromise our time together. And so Finn found us a real estate agent and she found the perfect solution: a pair of semi-detached cottages on a quaint village high street, barely an hour from London, and less than fifteen minutes from the gates of Fairhaven. They shared a garden enclosed by a hedge, as well as a modified shed in the back which the previous owner had converted into a sort of tiny-house office, but which we all agreed at once should be Milo's studio. It was in every way ideal, but accepting that we were really moving there meant change—my sister married, my boyfriend and I officially living together, and, most intimidating of all, Fairhaven and all it encompassed looming very close by. If I started packing those boxes, I was admitting that all of this was actually happening, and my brain wasn't willing to make that shift yet.

"I'll pack a box when I get home tonight, okay?" I said, crossing my heart.

"I'll believe it when I see it," Hannah murmured, not bothering to look up from the bridal magazine she was now casually perusing.

I shot a glance at Milo, who snorted disbelievingly.

I just shrugged. After all, I didn't believe me either.

I arrived at Fairhaven shortly before the midday lunch break. Students were still in classes, and the hallways were fairly deserted. I congratulated myself on my timing—it was always easier to avoid outright staring and pointing if I could get myself settled at a table before the students flooded the hallways. Hannah and I were already infamous around Fairhaven when the school year had started, but since we'd been responsible for the discovery of the coven several months before, our reputation among the students had grown to near-celebrity status. Apparently, you couldn't de-throne the queen bee of the academic social scene without achieving a certain amount of notoriety. I slipped into the still empty dining hall, glancing at the table over which Aisling Porter, aforementioned queen bee, had held court each day for meals, and felt a pang of sadness for the girl.

Aisling was still recovering from the disastrous flirtation with witchcraft that had nearly caused a catastrophic spiritual event on Castle Island. She had yet to fully regain her ability to speak, though she was conscious now and making rudimentary attempts to communicate. Her mother, Geraldine Porter, had been a highly influential member of the Council until the shame of her daughter's actions had driven her to resign. Hannah said that the word floating around the Council room was that she resigned to avoid an inquiry into her own involvement in the scheme; it was rumored that Geraldine Porter had known more about her daughter's plans than she had admitted to.

This didn't surprise me in the least; the most powerful of the Durupinen were still desperate over their perceived loss of power in the Reckoning, and the lengths to which they'd gone to recover it had bordered on mutiny. Celeste had been forced to up her security, even within Fairhaven, and Council meetings had become nothing less than a circus. The only person happy about this was Milo, who hovered in the corner of Council meetings with his mouth hanging open, drinking up every barbed word and dramatic exit. It had reached the point where missing a Council meeting was akin to missing an episode of his favorite reality television show.

"It is the Real Housewives of Fairhaven and I am here for it!" he declared every time he showed up to dish all the details to me.

I swung through the buffet line just as the workers were removing the covers from steaming trays of food, snatching a cup of coffee and a muffin before they cleared away the remainder of the breakfast pastries. Then I found a table in the corner of the room and settled myself at it to wait, turning my back on the room in an effort to reduce the gawking when the students flooded in. I'd barely swallowed my first bite when someone dropped into the seat across from me.

"Hi, Jess!" said Gemma Dawson with a tentative smile.

I returned the smile, glad as always to see this new, happier Gemma. When first introduced to my mentee in the fall, I'd worried that she'd never open up enough for me to get to know her. But several months and one extremely hard life lesson later, I could confidently say that we were friends. It was a friendship that almost didn't have a chance to grow.

One of my biggest fears, upon returning to Fairhaven after our mad dash to Castle Island, was that Gemma would be raked over the coals for her part in the scheme. On the one hand, she had been extraordinarily foolish—getting caught up in something so dangerous. On the other hand, the social pressure had been intense, and her life of isolation, followed by relentless bullying, had ill-prepared her to stand up to the other girls involved. I stood before the Council and testified on her behalf. I didn't believe, as some Council members did, that the girls should be expelled and possibly even sent to a *príosún*. What good would it do, I had asked, to ostracize them from the Durupinen world, when we had the opportunity to teach them, to help them grow, to learn from their mistakes, even the astronomically big ones, and to pave the way forward for the next generation of Durupinen who would only ever know the true way of things? There was some intensely spirited debate on the subject; but in the end, it was agreed that Gemma should be suspended for a period of two weeks, during which time she would complete a lengthy and thoroughly researched assignment about a Durupinen's true calling. This she would have to present in its entirety to the Council, who would have to approve it in order for her to resume classes as an Apprentice. Then, when she finally did return to Fairhaven, she would volunteer at the castle, working in the library and occasionally with Fiona and me to give back to the community she had so endangered. She did all of this gratefully, for Gemma had never truly bought into Aisling's fever dream of power and privilege. She had wanted only to be accepted, to no longer be persecuted. Aisling's actions had been an attempt at self-aggrandizement; Gemma's, an attempt at self-preservation. The Council, thank goodness, was able to recognize the difference.

"I've finished these for you," Gemma said, sliding a set of papers across the table.

"Wow, already?" I asked, taking them from her.

"Yes. The Scribes had a conference on Saturday, so I had some extra time," she replied.

"Yeah, but this must have taken you hours," I said, flipping through the papers. It was a painting categorization system that Fiona had been avoiding for almost a year, until she realized she could foist it off on someone else instead. I looked up at Gemma, narrowing my eyes. "You're staying on top of your schoolwork, right? All this penance paperwork won't mean much if you flunk out."

Gemma laughed and gave me a girl guide salute. "My homework is all done and my marks are tip-top, cross my heart. My mother wouldn't accept otherwise."

"Nor your grandmother," I said darkly.

Gemma gave a delicate shudder. "Too true."

"Is everything okay there?" I asked, keeping my eyes carefully on the papers in my hands. Gemma's grandmother, the matriarch of the reclusive Clan Reibiliúnach, had been very severe on Gemma when she discovered what her granddaughter had taken part in on Castle Island. So much so that she'd had to be talked down from banishing her own granddaughter from the house. I knew Gemma was sensitive on the subject, so I avoided her gaze so that she could arrange her expression and tone however she chose.

Sure enough, she sounded just a little too breezy when she replied, "Oh, coming along, you know."

"Glad to hear it," I said, chancing a glance upward. But Gemma wasn't looking at me; she had caught the eye of someone over my shoulder and was giving a tentative wave. I turned to look and saw Orla Campbell walking past our table, a tray in her hand and a ruddy flush of embarrassment on her cheeks. She dropped her eyes when she saw me catch her gaze and sped up to find a seat several tables away from us.

"How is Orla doing?" I asked Gemma, lowering my voice.

Gemma gave a sort of half-shrug. "All right, I suppose. She's still barely said two words to me, but she's not trying to be mean. She hardly speaks to anyone."

Orla and Ciara had been offered the same choice as Gemma. Orla had taken it, her clan having been truly shocked at her behavior and desperate to cling to their position. Ciara's family had opted to pull her from Fairhaven and end their bid for an open Council seat. It seemed they were unwilling to swallow any more humiliation than they had been doled out already.

"Are you still able to help Fiona and me this afternoon?" I asked Gemma, once we had watched Orla take a solitary seat in the corner.

"Of course!" Gemma said, her voice and expression brightening. "I've got class until two, but I'll join you as soon as I'm done."

I smothered a smile. Against all odds, Gemma had taken a shine to Fiona. Perhaps living with her formidable grandmother all her life had inured her against intimidating authority figures, but when Gemma met Fiona, she barely flinched at her cursing and flinging of any object unlucky enough to stray into her path. If I considered the matter, I had to admit that there was a sort of comfort in being with Fiona. If she had something to say, she simply said it, with no regard for the feelings she might trample in the process. But at least you always knew she would never bullshit you. Watching Gemma and Fiona together gave me hope that, even if I couldn't be at Fairhaven as frequently as Fiona needed me, she would have all the help she could want in Gemma's quiet and earnest obedience.

Gemma, meanwhile, leaned eagerly forward across the table and lowered her voice to a conspiratorial whisper. "Do you suppose it's possible that Fiona could have found the right Casting?"

"It's possible," I answered carefully. "But honestly, I don't want to get my hopes up. We've been searching for close to six months, and it's always been a bit like looking for a needle in a haystack."

"Even so, we're bound to find it eventually!" Gemma said brightly.

I looked at her, cocking my head to the side. "What's it like, to be young and full of hope?"

She rolled her eyes. "Oh, come off it, Jess. You're not old."

I grinned. "That's the nicest thing you've ever said to me."

Gemma just laughed. It was nice to see her laughing, after the start to the school year she'd had. "So are you going up to see Fiona now? You won't attempt the Casting without me, will you?"

I shook my head. "I've got to go see Catriona first. There's something I have to do."

My expression must have been grim because Gemma's eyes widened. "My goodness. That sounds rather serious."

I sighed. "Oh, it is."

~

The walk to the Trackers office felt a hundred miles long as I trudged the long stone corridors. I'd been dreading this moment since I'd made my decision, but I knew I couldn't put it off any longer.

The door to the Trackers office was open when I arrived, and the bustle inside was typical of what I'd seen every time I'd been near it over the last year. There were several Caomhnóir who had applied to join the ranks since the Reckoning, and so now there were harried-looking women and men flitting around inside it like harassed bees in a hive. Catriona wasn't to be found in the outer office and my query about her whereabouts was met with shrugs and blank stares. I walked through to the larger inner office and found her in the back corner, a cell phone jammed between her ear and her shoulder as she dug through a filing cabinet.

"Look, I don't see how that's my problem, Yvette," she said into the phone. She looked up and saw me standing there, and beckoned me forward with impatient but perfectly polished fingers, even as she continued her phone call. "Yes, I'm sure you're quite overwhelmed, but it's not my fault you've allowed your team to dwindle to almost nothing. I've got no one to spare for you, I'm sorry." She held the phone away from her ear as the woman on the other end shrieked so loudly I could hear her strident tones from where I stood. "Lovely speaking to you, too, au revoir!" Catriona shouted over her before abruptly ending the call, cutting the woman off mid-curse and tossing the phone away in disgust.

"Imagine trying to pilfer my agents because you couldn't be bothered to properly staff your own office. What a parasite," Cat muttered, before finally looking at me with narrowed eyes. "If you're here to report another pack of students casting ill-advised hexes I swear to the Aether—"

"Don't worry, Cat. No additional covens to report at this time."

She heaved a sigh of relief and dropped into a chair, half hidden by a huge stack of file folders.

"How's it going, boss?" I asked her.

Catriona snorted without looking up from her mountain of paperwork. "How does it look like it's going? If I wasn't so short-handed, I might be able to crawl out from under it before next century, but as it is..." Her head snapped up and I watched with grim satisfaction as the meaning of my words finally sank in.

"You called me boss."

"Yes, I did."

"You never call me boss."

"I do now."

She leaned back in her chair, looking positively thunderstruck. "I don't believe it."

"Neither do I," I admitted.

"I was convinced... I *never* thought... You're not having a laugh, are you? I am begging you not to joke with me. My blood pressure is through the roof as it is."

"I am decidedly *not* having a laugh," I grumbled. Rarely had I felt less like laughing. *Crying* maybe, but...

"So then... are you telling me you're back?"

"I'm back," I told her, and crowned the announcement with a sarcastic salute. "For better or worse, I'm a Tracker again."

2

BLOOD OF MY BLOOD

"A TRACKER? AGAIN?"

Fiona was staring at me across the chaotic wasteland that was the top of her desk with an expression that could only be described as disgusted. I felt the color rising in my cheeks as I gritted my teeth.

"Yes. Again."

"I thought you were done with all that nonsense!" she barked.

"So did I, but I guess we were both wrong," I said, just managing to keep the bitterness out of my voice.

Until this point, everyone I'd told about my return to the Trackers had been supportive. If any of them doubted my decision, they'd kept it to themselves, especially when I told them how hard-fought the decision had been. And honestly, it had been all that support and encouragement that had enabled me to put one foot in front of the other and drag myself to that Tracker office to accept Catriona's offer. It was a good thing I hadn't told Fiona about the decision beforehand, or I probably would have lost every bit of my nerve under her withering glare.

"This is a good thing," I said, trying to convince myself as much as her. "I'll be at Fairhaven much more often."

"Yes, but I'll have to share you with that ruddy Trackers office, and they'll likely take precedence and ship you off to goddess knows where. No one will care about cataloging sculptures or restoring paintings when there's a bloody Necromancer wreaking havoc in some corner of the globe. I reckon I'll see less of you than ever."

For the most fleeting of seconds, I thought I heard a note of sorrow in her voice, but it was gone again before I could be sure. Still, it took me a moment to find my next words, and when I spoke them, it was with a healthy dose of Fiona's own gruffness.

"Well, good then, seeing as I annoy you so much. And anyway, that's why I've been training Gemma. She'll be a good set of hands to have when I'm off cleaning up after Necromancers."

Fiona snorted. "She's greener than green, that lass. Hardly any help at all. Suppose she's coming today to get under our feet, is she?"

"Yes, she'll be up as soon as her last class is over," I said, smothering a smile. Fiona could complain about Gemma all she wanted, but the truth was that she'd taken a shine to her—well, as much as Fiona could take a shine to anyone. In many ways, they suited each other. Gemma was quiet and hard-working, and she didn't complain or ask too many questions. Fiona practically had to invent reasons to throw things, which was frankly always amusing to watch.

As if on cue, a knock sounded at the door, timidly at first, then gaining in confidence.

"Well, come in then, if you must," Fiona barked, and Gemma slipped through the door, an unmistakable gleam of excitement in her eye. She was breathing heavily, a sure sign that she'd taken the tower stairs at a run.

"Sorry... got here... as quick... as I could," she gasped, stowing her book bag neatly against the wall and clutching a stitch under her ribs. "Have you... did you already...?"

I laughed. "Catch your breath, Gemma. I told you we wouldn't start without you."

Gemma's answering smile was more of a grimace as she tried to control her breathing again.

"What's she in such a tizzy about?" Fiona asked, jerking her thumb over her shoulder in Gemma's direction.

"She wanted to be here when we tried the Casting you found. I told her not to get her hopes up, but what can I say, she's young and you haven't crushed her spirit yet," I answered.

A mischievous smile tugged gently at the corner of Fiona's mouth. "Oh, I don't know, Jess. A bit of hope might be in order this time."

I stared at her. "What do you mean?"

"I mean this isn't just another wild stab in the dark, lass. I think I bloody well found it."

Before I could reply, Fiona took off around the corner of the desk, maneuvering through the madness with impressive speed until she reached a pile of boxes I recognized as the ones that filled the shelves of the archives in the back rooms of the library. She pulled one off the top of the stack and scurried back to her desk with it.

"Clear a space!" Fiona barked at us, and Gemma and I leaped into action, trying to stack Fiona's chaos neatly into piles.

"I said clear it!" Fiona snapped, and with one sweeping gesture of her arm sent the entire contents of the desktop tumbling, fluttering, and crashing to the floor. That done, she placed the archival box into the center, pulled on a pair of latex gloves that had been hanging out of her overall pocket, and lifted the cover off the box, setting it aside.

I leaned over the box eagerly, my heart thumping. I'm not sure what I was expecting to see, but after such a dramatic unveiling, I felt a pang of disappointment when the box was revealed to be full of old books.

"I thought we'd been through every book in the library," I joked feebly.

"We damn near had," Fiona said as she carefully extracted a book from the pile, "and that's when I realized we were looking in completely the wrong place altogether."

This pulled me up short. "The wrong place?"

"That's right. It came to me last week, as I was headed through the Gallery of High Priestesses. Do you remember when the secret in Agnes Isherwood's tapestry revealed itself to you when we were restoring it?"

Seeing as that secret had set into motion the most important events in the Durupinen world in the last several centuries, I wasn't likely to have forgotten. "I think I might vaguely recall something of the sort," I said; sadly, my expertly delivered sarcasm was utterly lost on Fiona, who plowed right on as though I hadn't spoken at all.

"Right well, I got to thinking; this all goes back to Agnes Isherwood. If not for her, the Gateways may never have been taken from the Geatgrimas. She knew they would need to be restored, and I reckon she did everything in her power to ensure that would happen. As more time passed, and the Gateways remained in Durupinen bloodlines, she must have known how important it would be to have a way to find all the Geatgrimas again, when it was time to restore them. She would have made sure of it. And so I thought to myself, why not look in her writings for the answers?"

I looked back down at the books in the box, my heart springing into an excited gallop. "So are you saying... did these books actually belong to her?!"

"Not as such, no," Fiona said. "They aren't original copies—those would never have survived this long if people were allowed to simply handle them. But they are transcriptions of her diaries, notes, and other papers, copied over and preserved for posterity, and even they are amongst the oldest documents in our archives. I had to send for them from Skye, and they finally arrived earlier this week. I've been digging through them ever since."

"Why didn't you tell me?" I asked her, almost indignantly. "I could have helped you!"

Fiona shrugged, determinedly not looking at me. "Didn't want to get your hopes up. And, in light of everything you've been through regarding Agnes... well, I thought there was a chance it might be unpleasant for you."

I started. Fiona was keeping her voice carefully nonchalant, but I'd caught an edge in it nonetheless. "Are you saying you were trying to... protect me?" I asked, incredulous.

Fiona snorted. "I said exactly what I meant to say," she grumbled. "Call it what you like, it makes no difference to me."

The sentiment was so decidedly un-Fiona that I suddenly had to swallow down a lump in my throat before I could answer. "Thanks, but I... I think I could handle it."

"Well, that's good to know, as I doubt this is the last we'll need to consult them," Fiona went on. If she'd noticed my moment of sentimentality, she was pretending she hadn't. But I knew Fiona's diminished eyesight, though better than it had been, still made tasks like reading a formidable challenge. To have faced down such a pile of it herself just to spare me a few pangs of pain or discomfort... well, she would have rolled her eyes if I'd said it out loud, but I was more grateful than I could express.

There was no more time to dwell on it though, as Fiona steered the conversation away from sentimentality faster than a getaway driver in a high-speed police chase. With a grunt of satisfaction, she extracted the book she was after and gingerly turned the pages until she found what she was looking for. Eagerly, Gemma and I leaned over her shoulders, peering down at the faded, spidery writing.

"That's the tapestry!" Gemma whispered, a reverence in her voice as she lifted her eyes from the drawing on the page to the genuine article now hanging on the wall of Fiona's studio.

"Well-spotted," Fiona said witheringly. "A regular detective, you are. It's the words we're after, not the illustrations."

Our eyes roved eagerly to the words on the page. The first few sentences seemed to outline a sort of record of the tapestry: who had designed it, who had helped in its creation, how long it had taken to weave, and so on. It was interesting, but not exactly helpful. Then, down at the bottom of the page, was a strange little poem, with several cross-outs and corrections that suggested Agnes had struggled with it. It could have been mistaken for a doodle, or a simple bit of wordplay, but I knew better than to take anything Agnes put on paper for granted. Still, it explained why others might have overlooked it, or thought it unimportant. I read it out loud, and even as the words fell from my lips, I could feel that there was power in them.

"When all seems lost, look to the southwest,
There a glimmer, a key to a lock,
Blood of my blood, reveal the trail
A map, a guide, that will lead all home."

"What does it mean?" Gemma whispered.

"No bloody idea," Fiona admitted. "That's what we've got to find out."

"When all seems lost, look to the southwest..." I muttered, turning to look at the tapestry. Could she be referring to the Geatgrimas themselves? They were certainly lost at the moment—or, at least the map was. Could Agnes possibly know that it would take so long for the Gateways to be returned? She must have realized it was possible.

Gemma was already running for the window. "This is the south tower, right? So southwest would be in... this direction?" I met her at the window and we both looked out over the grounds. We could see the trees of the forest, the little dell where the crumbling graveyard was located, and beyond it, the border wall in the distance.

"There a glimmer, a key to a lock..." I repeated the second line, but though the sun shone brightly down on the grounds, nothing glimmered at us from that direction.

"I don't see anything, do you?" Gemma asked, her voice full of disappointment.

"No," I admitted, "But basing the clues on the grounds seems risky. Who knows how the landscape has changed since Agnes' time here?"

"And who's to say that Fairhaven would even remain under Durupinen control?" Fiona added, still poring over the book. "The Necromancers were a dangerous force in her day—that's what got us in this mess in the first place."

I turned back, letting my eyes rest on the tapestry again. "I wonder..."

"You wonder what?" Gemma asked eagerly, her excitement reigniting at once.

"Well, the tapestry is meant to be a map in itself. Which means... southwest would be the bottom left part..."

I crossed the room as quickly as I could without tripping over anything, and dropped to my knees in front of the tapestry. Gemma followed, coming to rest beside me. We both stared at the terribly faded old threads, our eyes scanning... searching...

"What are we looking for?" Gemma whispered.

"A glimmer..." I murmured, my eyes coming to rest on the bottom edge of the tapestry. It was hopelessly frayed; some of the threads looked like a gentle breath could have disintegrated them. I scooched closer, folding in on myself until my nose was an inch from the fabric. My exhalation caused the slightest of ripples. It was enough for the light in the room to fall upon the threads just right, so that it produced the tiniest glimmer... like the most minuscule of flames. If I had blinked, I would have missed it altogether.

"There you are," I whispered and, with the gentlest touch, I parted the frayed edges of the threads to reveal a single golden thread, iridescent despite its antiquity, tucked in amongst the faded tans and faint blues and greens.

"What have you got there?" Fiona asked, excitement creeping into her voice now in spite of herself.

"It's a golden thread," I told her. "Just the edge of it, poking out where it's all frayed here at the bottom."

Gemma looked up at the tapestry, frowning. "I don't see any gold thread in the design," she said.

"Neither do I," I said, and yet its very absence caused a feeling of anticipation to unfurl in my stomach. A hidden golden thread... now, where did it lead?

I joined Gemma in a minute examination of the tapestry, looking to see if the ravages of time had revealed that glimmer anywhere else, but if it ran anywhere else through the tapestry, it was still carefully hidden from the outside gaze. Finally, I gave up and shifted the weight off my protesting knees and came to a rest sitting cross-legged in front of the little glimmer we'd managed to discover.

"Another dead end, is it?" Fiona asked, sounding somewhat defeated. "I might have known."

"I don't think so," I said. "What was the next part? Can you read it to me again?"

Fiona bent low over the book again and barked out, "Blood of my blood, reveal the trail;

a map, a guide, that will lead all home."

"Blood of my blood," Gemma repeated. "What do you suppose that means? It sounds like a ridd—*what are you doing?!*"

"Taking it literally," I said. While Gemma had been mulling the words over, I'd pulled a safety pin from my shredded jeans and opened it so the point gleamed just below my upheld finger. Over Gemma's cry of protest, I jabbed it into my fingertip and withdrew it at once, watching with mild interest as a bead of blood blossomed there.

"You... you think it means actual blood?" Gemma gasped. I looked over at her and saw she was looking rather queasy.

"You aren't gonna faint on me, are you?" I asked her with a mild chuckle.

"No, I... I don't think so. Just warn me before you stab me, would you?" Gemma said, shaking her head as though to clear it and regaining a bit of her color.

"Oh, I won't be stabbing you, or anyone else for that matter. Well, I suppose we could always try Hannah, if mine doesn't work."

Gemma's eyes went wide as the realization hit her. "Oh!"

"What's happening?" Fiona snapped.

"Blood of my blood," I repeated. "A direct ancestor. It's the only thing that makes sense. Agnes couldn't be sure that she would still be around if and when the tapestry was needed, so she had to have a contingency plan." I held up my bleeding finger. "It would seem that I am that plan."

"Well, even if that's true, what are you meant to do with the blood?" Gemma asked, looking doubtful. "Smear it on the tapestry?"

"Dirty that tapestry and I'll have your head on a pike!" Fiona shouted. "It's too old and delicate to be cleaned!"

I rolled my eyes. "I'm not planning on fingerpainting it," I said, though I allowed myself a moment to imagine the look on Fiona's face if I'd gone ahead and drawn a smiley face on the damn thing like a deranged toddler before she could stop me.

Gemma's voice dropped to a hushed whisper. "Do you suppose... just the gold thread?"

I nodded, though my attention was focused on the thread in question. I extended my finger toward it, the blood still quivering on the tip. There was no other instruction, no incantation. I could think of nothing else to do but touch the blood to the very end of the thread and see what happened. I looked back at Fiona, asking silently for permission.

"Well, go on then!" she urged in a whisper.

Reassured that she wouldn't murder me if this didn't work, I took a deep breath, held it, and then ever so gently touched the bead of blood to the very end of the golden thread.

Three things happened simultaneously. First, a feeling like a bolt of lightning shot through my body, freezing me like a statue. Secondly, the bead of blood vanished, as though the thread had absorbed it. And thirdly and most alarmingly, the tapestry burst into flame.

Gemma shrieked and fell backward. Fiona howled and hopped on the spot, clearly fighting a desire to fling herself on the tapestry and try to put it out. I could do nothing but sit frozen exactly where I was, connected to the tapestry as though we were part of the same circuit. But it was this connection that, after a few frenzied seconds, made clear to me what was really happening.

"Stop! Just stay where you are! It's okay!" I shouted to the others.

There truly was no cause for alarm, because what we had taken to be smoke was simply the collected dust of centuries exploding from the fabric in great billowing clouds. What I was sure had been flames was the blinding light of the golden thread as it burst to visibility, snaking all through the tapestry like a fuse that had been lit in the bottom corner with just a taste of the blood from my veins. My mouth hanging open now, I watched through half-averted eyes as the catalyst of my blood set off the centuries-deep Casting hidden inside the tapestry. It burned so brightly it might have been the sun.

"Well, I'll be damned to the depths," Fiona whispered as the last flash of golden light faded away, leaving us in a dim, dusty silence. Gemma broke that silence a few seconds later with a cough.

"It... it worked, d-didn't it?" she sputtered.

I didn't answer her. I couldn't speak. I was staring, agog, at the tapestry on the wall, which had utterly transformed. I heard the astonished gasps of the others when they, too, saw what had transpired.

In place of the faded, moth-eaten, dust-covered hanging that we'd been agonizing over for months was a gleaming tapestry threaded with gold, revealed like a vibrant creature bursting forth from an egg. It looked entirely new and somehow, entirely alive. It wasn't just the light reflecting on the shimmering gold threads, though that was certainly a part of it. There was a wild thrumming kind of energy as I looked at the new patterns that had emerged, as though the design itself was imbued with a tiny portion of the power of the Gateways. It was at once beautiful and disconcerting, but that didn't stop me from rising to my feet and getting a closer look.

Clear at last was the map of the world—its borders ancient and inaccurate now, but still recognizable as the world we lived in. Dotted upon it were hundreds of gleaming triskeles marking the places where Geatgrimas stood... or, in some cases, I was sure, once stood. A braided golden trail ran through it all, connecting the triskeles to each other like beads threaded onto a fine chain.

"Blast it all, you did it, lass. You bloody well did it!" Fiona murmured and then, in an uncharacteristic show of excitement let out a sound like a whoop of joy. I tore my eyes from the tapestry just long enough to enjoy the sight of my mentor jumping up and down like a kid before a strange rumbling sound began.

For one wild moment, I thought we were having an earthquake. The walls and floor were vibrating. Several paint cans tumbled from their shelves, and there rose from the halls of the school the frightened cries of students and staff. The rumbling grew louder, drowning out our voices as we called out to each other. Gemma ran to me, her face white and terrified. I opened my mouth to try to reassure her, but before I could form the words, the rumbling stopped.

"What the actual f—" I began, but Fiona cut my expletive short with another whoop of excitement. Before I knew what was happening she was practically running for the door. When she reached it she turned around and snapped her fingers impatiently at us.

"Don't just stand there gawping, get a move on!" she shouted, her tone so commanding that we hurried after her without really thinking about it.

"Do you know what's going on?" Gemma cried as we ran after her.

"Not a damn clue," I replied.

"Come on! Get a shift on!" Fiona shouted over her shoulder.

"Are you going to tell us what the hell just happened?" I gasped as we hurtled down the stairs.

"No, I'm going to show you!" Fiona called back. She was moving alarmingly fast for a woman with compromised vision, and my heart was so in my throat that she might fall, that I didn't realize where she was taking us until we were standing in front of the door.

"The Léarscáil?" I wheezed, bent over with a stitch in my side.

"That's right!" Fiona said, and inexplicably, she was grinning. Without further explanation, she flung the door open and Gemma and I, throwing one last startled glance at each other, followed.

The first thing I registered was that the room was full of a thick cloud of dust. A high-pitched whimpering sound was emanating from the far side of the room, and when enough of the dust had settled, I saw that it was the new Keeper crouched and shaking beneath her desk.

"Fiona, what are we—" But the question died in my throat as I spotted the tower floor for the first time. The map painted upon it looked brand new, just like the tapestry, with a gleaming golden map identical to the one that had revealed itself upstairs.

"Is *that* what caused all the rumbling and shaking?" I asked, pointing a trembling finger down at the map.

"Seems so," Fiona said, sounding unabashedly proud despite the fact that our accomplishment had scared the crap out of the entire castle.

"Did... did you know that was going to happen?" I asked.

"I knew that the tapestry and the Léarscáil were linked together. I thought *something* might happen. I didn't know it would be quite so... violent." Fiona said with a shrug. Then turning over her shoulder, she called in an offhand voice, "Maeve? You all right down there?"

"Tolerably well, yes," came the reply, a slightly shrill edge of hysteria still clear in her voice.

"Brilliant," Fiona said, then pointed to the great pendulum, drawing my attention to it for the first time. "And look at that! It's already working!"

The Léarscáil itself was straining against its chain, pointing like a compass at one particular Geatgrima, though I wasn't close enough to see exactly where it was located, except that it was somewhere in the vicinity of Europe. I started down the first few steps and then another sudden noise behind me elicited another shriek of surprise. This time, the sound was a voice, and I knew who it was before I even turned around.

"My God! Is it... have you finally... bloody hell!" Catriona stammered, staring down at the transformed Léarscáil map with wide, reverent eyes.

"It looks like we did, yes," I said, gesturing weakly to the room below.

Catriona let out a triumphant whoop not unlike Fiona's and shoved her way past Gemma and me, flying down the stairs in a pair of heels that would absolutely have sent me tumbling to my death. She paused for only a moment at the edge of the map, staring up at the chain of the Léarscáil for any sign of movement, but it was pulled taut still, quivering with tension. Then, keeping to the perimeter of the room, she approached the pendulum closer and closer until she was crouching down beside it to examine its target more closely.

"Well, now," Catriona said, looking up and grinning at me. "You've rejoined the Trackers just in time. I've got your first assignment for you."

I gulped loudly. "Already?"

Catriona cackled at the look on my face. Then she pointed a perfectly polished finger at the targeted Geatgrima on the map. I took a step closer. The triskele that marked its position was pulsing with a powerful glowing energy.

"Pack a suitcase, Ballard. Next stop, Edinburgh."

3

A DUAL MISSION

"OKAY, NOW WHAT'S HAPPENING IN EDINBURGH?"
We were sitting in Catriona's corner of the Trackers office, facing each other from opposite sides of her battered desk. For a woman who was meticulously put together at all times, her workspace was a hot mess.

"What do you know about the city?" Catriona countered, choosing to pose another question rather than answering mine.

I shrugged. "Honestly? Not much. I've never been there. I know it's the capital of Scotland and... there's a huge castle there, I'm pretty sure?" I finished.

Catriona just barely managed not to roll her eyes. "So worldly, Ballard," she drawled.

"Sorry, I haven't had a ton of free time for sightseeing, what with all the times I've had to save our collective asses from the consequences of our own historical actions," I returned dryly.

Catriona flashed a smirk that clearly said 'Well played' before responding. "It is, as you say, the capital of Scotland. It's also the hub of one of the richest, most powerful clans in the world. Clan Rìoghalachd has lorded over Edinburgh for centuries, holding influential positions in politics, economics, and society. There's little of importance in the city that they don't have their hands in. They hold the reins tightly as well and they're obsessed with security; and so, as a result, there's been remarkably little trouble for the Scottish clans over the years."

"If they're so powerful, I'm surprised they're going along with all this Reckoning stuff," I remarked. "It seems like it's usually the most powerful clans who are fighting the changes."

"Oh, they're definitely fighting it," Catriona said. "But they prefer to wage their battles with money and influence, not hastily gathered covens and poorly devised coup attempts."

"So they... aren't happy about the Reckoning, then?" I ventured.

"Oh, quite the opposite. They're livid about it, in truth."

"Well, I'm sure my reception there will be delightful," I said.

Catriona smiled. "Oh, your reception will be a red-carpet spectacle. But we'll get to that." And without any further explanation of this cryptic statement, she reached into her desk and fished out a file folder, which she tossed across the desk to me. I caught it automatically, and flipped it open, scanning the pages.

"Clan Rìoghalachd reached out to us two weeks ago. It seems that something very peculiar is happening to the spirits who approach the Geatgrima in Edinburgh," Catriona said.

"Okay, I'll bite," I said when she didn't continue. "What's happening to them?"

"They're disappearing," Catriona said.

I stared at her. "Isn't... isn't that what's supposed to happen?"

Catriona gave in to the eye-roll impulse this time. "Of course not. I don't mean they're disappearing through it. They disappear on approach, before they can get close enough to Cross."

I blinked. "Okay, yeah, that's definitely weird."

"Too right it is."

"So, what are they thinking? Necromancer interference?" I prodded.

"Frankly, that's unlikely. There are few cities with better Durupinen security than Edinburgh, Clan Rìoghalachd has seen to that good and proper. They've had not a whisper of Necromancer activity within the city limits in centuries."

"Just because they haven't discovered it, doesn't mean it's not a possibility," I pointed out. After all, the Necromancers had been spoken of as a long defunct threat in all my classes at Fairhaven until they damn near took the place when the Prophecy came to pass. Durupinen had been underestimating Necromancers for too long, and we'd already paid a heavy price for it.

"True enough, and I'm certain you will have to convince them to at least consider the possibility."

"You speak about them like they're a totally separate entity from Fairhaven. They're part of the Northern Clans, aren't they? If they're as powerful as you say, they must have a Council seat."

Catriona grimaced. "Naturally, but they rarely deign to fill it in person. The wild amount of money and resources they've devoted to the Northern Clans over the years has afforded them certain privileges, including the ability to vote in absentia and by proxy. You've likely caught a glimpse of their current Council representative over the years, though. Clarissa MacLeod?"

The name rang a bell. I scoured my memory and came up with the image of a tall, slender woman with a curiously blank expression and blonde hair swept into an elegant chignon. I was sure Hannah had pointed her out to me before.

"Yeah, I've seen her," I said. "So, if it's not the Necromancers, do they have any other theories about what might be going on?"

"They've decided that's not their problem," Catriona said, the bitterness sharp in her voice. "Ever since the Reckoning, that city has been even more of a fortress than usual. Clan Rìoghalachd refuses to divert resources from their own personal protection to investigate the matter. In short, they've made it the Trackers' problem to sort out. So, here we are."

"And you think I'm the best person for this job, knowing how opposed they are to all of the changes in our status? After all, it's... pretty much my fault."

"But that's exactly why you're the perfect person for the job," Catriona said, looking quite pleased with herself.

"Is this when you explain that 'red carpet' comment you made earlier?" I prompted.

"Bang on!" Catriona said, slapping her hand against the desk. "You are the only person who can solve two mysteries at once."

"If that was supposed to be an explanation, it was entirely unhelpful," I replied.

"Keep your knickers on, I'm not finished," Catriona snapped. "In sending you to Edinburgh, we hope to discover two things. The first is, of course, what's happening with the Geatgrima. The restoration of the map and the resulting functionality of the Léarscáil has proved beyond a shadow of a doubt that Edinburgh is our most pressing priority. But by sending you, we are likely to discover by what means Clan Rioghalachd is trying to undermine the Council."

"I'm still not following."

"They're going to try to win you over, Jess. They know you're at the center of the Reckoning, and if they can win your loyalty by any means within their grasp, they are going to do it!"

"So... you're sending me in as bait?" I asked.

Catriona considered the matter for a moment before nodding her head. "Looks like it, yeah."

I flopped forward, resting my forehead on the desktop. "I knew this job was a mistake, but I honestly thought it would take a little longer before you proved that to me."

"Oh, for Aether's sake, Jess, all I'm asking you to do is cozy up to them. They're going to try to wine, dine, and bribe you, not throw you off a cliff," Catriona said. "They've watched from afar as other clans have attacked you, and they know that route has never worked. They'd rather keep their enemies closer, so to speak."

"Okay, so you want me to play into it?" I asked, my face still pressed against the desk. "Let them think they're making progress?"

"Exactly. We need to know to what ends they will go, if any, to fight against the Reckoning. They've been too quiet, too standoffish during this transition. But they've always been content to bide their time, to see how the dust settles before they act. Well, the dust is finally clearing and we want to see them make a move. It's the only way to know what we're dealing with."

I picked my head up and sighed. "This is the whole reason you tried to get me to come back to the Trackers, isn't it?"

A slow, wicked grin spread over Catriona's face before she answered, "Not the *whole* reason. I also enjoy ordering you around. I find it soothes me."

A strange battle took place in my brain then, the desire to curse her out warred with the desire to laugh. The laughter won out, and I chuckled, shaking my head.

"Okay, fine. You win. I will go to Edinburgh and cozy up to the ultra-rich Durupinen overlords."

"Excellent. Now let's talk about who you're taking with you."

~

"You'd better believe I'm bloody well going!" Savvy crowed, punching the air.

"I didn't realize you'd be this excited," I said, laughing at her kid-on-Christmas-morning reaction to a work assignment.

"Not just any assignment, mate," Savvy said, leaning in eagerly across the table where we were choking down lukewarm barracks coffee. "This is an assignment *on location!*"

"And... that's good?"

"Of course it is! Jess, think who you're talking to! I've been trapped on babysitting duty at this bloody castle for over a year. It's driving me mad. When I signed on to be a Caomhnóir, I may not have been in the best headspace, right, but I still knew what I wanted. I wanted to get in some trouble, yeah? I wanted to chase some cars and brawl on occasion. Not constantly, I'm not mad, but... just often enough to keep it interesting. And instead, I've been here with my thumb up my arse because you went and removed all the immediate threats."

"Are you saying it's my fault that your job is boring?" I asked, laughing harder now.

"Bang on, mate," Savvy said, completely unabashedly. "Well, not completely your fault. Whenever anything remotely interesting comes along, the leadership passes right over me and hands it to one of the blokes to handle. Seems they don't want to expend too much energy training a mere female."

"Ew, did they actually say that?" I cried.

Savvy shrugged. "They didn't have to. It was crystal clear in the way they looked right past me, mate."

"It wasn't because you're new?" I suggested tentatively.

She smirked. "They've already assigned four Caomhnóir who finished their training after I did. Trust me, it's not the training, it's the tits."

"So you're stuck at Fairhaven, which is boring now because I had the audacity to make it safe?"

"That's about the long and short of it, mate. That's why it's perfect that you're the one coming to me with this opportunity. It's like the apology you didn't even know you owed me."

"This feels like a lame apology. Had I known, I would have brought flowers," I said, batting my eyelashes.

"Oi! Watch it, Ballard. The only one who should be giving her flowers around here is me!" I looked up to see Savvy's girlfriend Rana Patel grinning at us as she plopped down in the chair next to Savvy. She leaned in to kiss Savvy, who pulled away.

"Hang on now, where are my flowers?" she demanded.

Rana winked. "I said I'm the one who should be giving them to you, not that I'm actually doing it."

"A technicality, Patel, but I'm nice enough to let it slide," Savvy said, and accepted her hello kiss this time.

"So what's all this, then? I heard Sav's crow of excitement from the hallway."

I explained to Rana about the Tracker mission to Edinburgh and extended the invitation for her to join us.

"When are you leaving?" Rana asked eagerly.

"In two days. Catriona insists there's no time to waste."

Rana's face fell. "Blast it all. I can't come with you. I've got final exams next week. I can't miss them or I'll be booted from training."

"Well, I think we're going to be there for a while," I said. "You could meet up with us when your exams are over," I suggested.

Rana's face brightened once again; she couldn't help it, the girl's natural state was an almost blinding optimism. "Well, that's all right, then! Sound good to you, Sav?"

Savvy shrugged. "Best we can do, I suppose."

"Don't you dare go having all the fun before I get there," Rana said, poking Savvy in the ribs.

"And by fun you mean dangerous encounters, chases, fights, and all other forms of violent confrontation?" Savvy asked dryly.

"Obviously," Rana replied, flashing a grin.

"I don't see why you're always so eager to throw yourself into danger. You've not even finished your first year of Novitiate training yet," Savvy grumbled.

"So, should I tell Rana how much you were looking forward to the exact same chance for violent confrontations, or is now not the moment?" I asked Savvy in an exaggerated stage whisper.

Rana broke into a bright peel of laughter while Savvy gave me an enthusiastic hand gesture that was anything but ladylike. I snorted into my coffee. Of course, I was happy just to see Savvy happy, regardless of who she was with; but there was something uniquely enjoyable about watching her with a partner who gave as good as she got. They were well-matched, those two.

"Right, well, we're off then," Savvy said, standing up and taking Rana by the hand. "We've got drills in a quarter-hour. Shall I come up to your room when I'm done, so we can hash out the details and all that?"

"Sounds good," I told her. "See you later."

I watched as Savvy and Rana walked out the door right as Hannah came hurrying through it, her expression anxious. She stopped Savvy with a question, and Savvy hooked her thumb over her shoulder in my direction. Hannah spotted me, thanked Savvy, and came scurrying over to the table.

"Is it really true? Are you being sent to engage with Clan Rìoghalachd?" Hannah asked, dropping into a chair without so much as a 'hello'."

"How did you find out already?" I asked. "I hadn't even bothered to text you yet because I thought you were going to be tied up in committees most of the afternoon!"

"I was, but Catriona came in late and when we took a break, she told me all about it," she explained, waving her hands impatiently as though none of this mattered. "But is it true? Did you agree?"

"Yes, I did," I said slowly, "although now that I'm seeing the look on your face, you've got me doubting the sanity of that decision."

Hannah bit her lip. "It's just... oh, Clarissa MacLeod is such a nasty piece of work, Jess."

I raised an eyebrow. "Catriona hinted as much. Is that what has you looking so worried?"

"Yes!" Hannah said, somewhat breathlessly.

"But Hannah, we've dealt with Council members like her before," I reminded her. "I mean, she can't be worse than Marion, can she?"

Hannah pursed her lips before replying. "I'm not sure if 'worse' is the word, but she's certainly just as dangerous in her own way."

I sighed, took a sip of my coffee, and leaned back in my seat, crossing my arms. "Okay. Explain."

"She's... well, she's different from Marion. She doesn't wield her power in the same ways. She doesn't make obvious grabs for things. She doesn't deliver grand speeches or travel in a pack so that you always know exactly how many allies she has. She's more subtle than all that."

"And that's bad?"

"Of course it is! Often you can't even detect her hand in things she's orchestrated almost entirely by herself. She doesn't do it for the glory or the attention. She simply engineers the outcome she wants, the one that will benefit her the most, and she's perfectly happy to let someone else claim the credit for it."

"And you're afraid that I won't be able to handle her?" I asked.

"I... think direct confrontation might be more in your wheelhouse?" Hannah suggested timidly.

I burst out into such a raucous peel of laughter that every Caomhnóir currently knocking around the barracks turned to stare at me.

"I wasn't trying to be funny," Hannah mumbled.

"I know, I know. It's funny because it's true," I said, wiping tears of mirth from my eyes. "But seriously, you're right. So, do you have a solution to suggest?"

"Of course," Hannah said, still looking slightly miffed. "I'm coming with you."

I blinked. "You... you want to come?"

"Is that okay?"

"Of course it is! I would love for you to come! But I wasn't planning on asking you to."

Hannah's face crumpled and she looked positively heartbroken. "Why not?"

"I just thought you had so much going on right now!" I clarified, reaching out to snatch up her hand and squeeze it affectionately. "Between Council stuff and wedding planning, I didn't want to—"

"But that's exactly why I need to go!" Hannah replied, leaning forward eagerly. "The stress is going to drive me mad! I can't sleep, I can barely eat, every time I look at my phone Karen or one of Kiernan's sisters has texted me another link to a caterer or a photographer or someone who handmakes customized wedding underwear! I can't take it anymore!"

"Customized wedding underwear? I didn't even know that was a thing."

"Well, unfortunately for me, it is most definitely a thing and multiple people who have never seen my underwear before seem entitled to have rather strong opinions about it. And so I would like nothing better than to have an ironclad excuse not to answer my phone for several weeks," Hannah said, looking slightly desperate now. "So, I'm begging you, okay? Tell everyone I'm an indispensable part of your team and that you can't possibly manage without me. And then I can pretend to reluctantly agree and we can plan my escape. What do you think?"

"I think it sounds great. But do you think Kiernan will be okay with it?"

"Are you kidding me? He'll pack my suitcase for me! He knows how stressed I am! And anyway, there's a huge restoration project happening in the archives at Skye and they've asked him to attend. He's been working so hard to make that team, and he finally did it. He's going to be gone all next week anyway."

I raised an eyebrow, smirking. "So are you sure your desperation to go with me isn't mostly a distraction from the fact that Kiernan will be gone for a week?"

Hannah had the good grace to blush and grin. "Oh sure, I mean, I guess a little."

"Well, whatever the reason, I'm glad you want to come and I'll be glad of the help. It sounds like you know more about Clan Rìoghalachd than I do."

"That doesn't mean I know how to handle them," Hannah warned.

"Yes, but you do know how to handle me. I imagine having you there to step on my toe or pinch me at the right moment will probably come in handy."

Hannah smiled. "Yes, I think it probably will. More than once." The smile faded from her face as quickly as it appeared, and she looked anxious again. "Do you suppose Catriona has held off sending someone until she could secure you for the job?"

I considered this. "I think the Tracker office is genuinely swamped, but yes, she was holding out to see if she could get me back on the team. And after everything you've told me about Clan Rìoghalachd, I think she was right. There are two problems in Edinburgh and I seem to be the only one relevant to both."

Hannah sighed, looking at me almost pityingly. "Do you ever get tired of being the target all the trouble is aiming at?"

I shrugged. "Oh definitely. But this time, at least, I volunteered to be the target. It's weirdly empowering."

"Have you told Finn yet?" Hannah asked.

"No, but after the events at Castle Island, I know better than to keep him in the dark," I said. "Not that I'd want to, on a mission like this. He knows the powerful clans as well as you do."

"Probably better," Hannah said, nodding. "After all, we didn't grow up surrounded by it."

I shuddered. "Family outings with Aunt Marion and cousin Peyton. God, can you imagine?"

Hannah grimaced. "I'd rather not."

4

JOURNEY AND DESTINATION

THE NEXT TWO DAYS WERE A WHIRLWIND OF PREPARATIONS. Between packing, making arrangements at work and Fairhaven, and broken, anxious sleep, I could cheerfully have murdered someone when my wake-up call came on Friday morning in the form of a gentle kiss on my forehead.

"Rise and shine, love," Finn whispered into my ear.

"I won't be doing either of those things, thanks."

He chuckled and nuzzled my ear with his nose. "And why not?"

"Because I feel like an extra in a zombie movie. And like, not even one of the ones in the front row. I'm like one of those zombies that can't even keep up with the horde."

"Despite never having watched a zombie film, I think I understand the reference," he laughed. "Do try to put a little pep in that undead step, though, because our car will be here in half an hour."

I sat up to find he was not in bed beside me, but already dressed and looking so awake and full of anticipation that it was actually offensive.

"How did I wind up with a morning person?" I grumbled.

"I let you sleep as long as I could," he said, an apologetic note in his voice. "Any longer and you'd be running around in a panic so as not to miss our train."

"How long is the train ride?" I asked, mid-yawn.

"Four and a half hours or so," Finn said.

"Excellent, that sounds like a solid nap to me," I replied. Though now that I was more fully awake, I could already feel the anticipation that had been roiling in my brain and stomach for the last forty-eight hours beginning to ramp up again; and part of me knew I wouldn't sleep a wink on the train no matter how hard I tried.

Hannah poked her head around the door frame. "Oh good, you're up," she said.

"I'm not sure if 'up' is the word I'd use. I'm conscious," I corrected her.

"Savvy's here, and so's the car. Have you got your bags?"

"I already put them by the door," Finn answered before I could open my mouth.

"Great. Coffee's on," Hannah chirped, and disappeared again into the hallway.

"She's awfully chipper, isn't she?" Finn remarked.

"She's even more excited to go on this assignment than Savvy is. She sees it as being rescued from the seventh circle of wedding planning hell."

"Too bad this little demon is coming along as well," Milo said, drifting in through the bedroom wall.

"Milo, you promised," I said, a warning in my voice; but Milo was already batting his eyelashes and drawing halos around his head with his finger.

"I know, I know," he said. "No wedding talk on the trip. I'll be good."

"You'd better. And what are you going to do to keep yourself busy so you don't break that promise?" I asked him.

"Scope out the local haunts, so to speak," he said, cackling at his own joke. "I'm also going to be scouting for real. I hear Edinburgh is a very picturesque city. I'm thinking about launching my next collection with a photoshoot there, so I need to explore."

"Throwing them off your scent, eh?" Finn said with a grin. He found the public quest to discover Milo's identity extremely entertaining.

"That's right! A few cryptic posts and filtered shots from the Scottish capital, and that will take the pressure off the London studio for a few weeks, at least," Milo said.

"Who do they have you pegged for this week?" Finn asked.

"Oh, haven't you heard? Apparently, I'm secretly a member of the Swedish royal family, and I'm concealing my identity for diplomatic and national security reasons."

"Next week you'll be three talented cats in a trench coat, I suppose," I said.

Milo pulled his hands up in front of him like little paws. "Meow, sweetness. Whatever keeps them guessing!"

Thirty minutes later we were loaded with all our luggage into a sleek black SUV and on our way to King's Cross Station. Security and secrecy being of the utmost priority, Catriona had bought out an entire first-class car for the nearly five hour journey, so that we could freely discuss our plans without being overheard by random passengers. Her first choice had been to fly us in one of the Northern Clans' private planes, but I'd rejected those arrangements before she'd even finished her sentence. I'd rather spend three days in a crowded New York subway car than three hours on a plane, thanks to a nearly debilitating case of aerophobia. Luckily, my companions were happy to indulge me, and we piled into the LNER high-speed train at platform five. The car was quiet and meticulously clean. Finn, Savvy, and I settled into a set of four seats that faced each other in groups of two on either side of a wooden table, while Hannah and Milo snagged two single seats set up in the same way on the other side of the aisle. Savvy plugged her phone into the charging port, threw her headphones on, and was soon snoring contentedly with her mouth hanging open. Hannah pulled out a stack of magazines for Milo and turned at once to press her face to the glass like an eager child, waiting for the journey to begin. Other than a pair of chatty women who bustled through the car on occasion offering drinks and snacks off a little rolling trolley, we were completely free to converse about the upcoming assignment. Finn was frowning over the file folder of tickets, itineraries, and other information Catriona had provided us.

"Everything okay?" I asked him.

Finn sighed. "I can't decide if it was brilliant to let Clan Rìoghalachd handle our accommodations in Edinburgh or utterly mad."

"Why would it be mad?"

Finn shrugged. "Just feels a bit like handing over control. After all, Catriona is fairly sure they're going to attempt to bribe you or something, isn't she?"

"Exactly. Letting them make arrangements is like extending an olive branch. It tells them that we trust them."

"But we don't trust them."

"Ah, but we don't want them to know that," I pointed out.

"Hmm. I suppose so," Finn muttered, the lines between his brows deepening. I smothered a smile. Finn didn't like risks, even calculated ones. It was one of the things that made him a top-notch Caomhnóir all the time, and a mildly irritating partner some of the time. Not that I was about to complain. After all, I was no cakewalk to date, that was for damn sure.

"It says we'll be met at Waverley Station by Pippa Barclay."

"Who's she?" Hannah asked, adding her own frown to the mix. "I've never heard of her before."

"It says she's Clan Rìoghalachd, but I don't recall hearing her name either. Still, it's not as though they'd send a MacLeod, is it?" Finn said. He and Hannah shared a knowing smirk.

"What's that supposed to mean? Why wouldn't they send a MacLeod?"

"MacLeods aren't sent, they do the sending," Finn clarified. "But there are a number of offshoots in the family, you know the sort of thing: cousins and second cousins and the like. A family tree like the MacLeods has many branches, and they all wave whatever way the MacLeods choose or they get pruned."

"You make them sound like a particularly toxic royal family," I said, wrinkling my nose.

"That's not a bad way to think about them, actually," Finn said, nodding. "Durupinen royalty. And they expect to be treated as such, so it's good that's the impression they give. There will be less of a chance of angering them that way."

"Oh, I think you underestimate my ability to anger people," I said. "I'm really, *really* good at it, and most of the time, I'm not even trying."

Finn snorted but didn't take the bait. "What's this about a reception?" he asked instead, continuing to scan the itinerary.

"Clan Rìoghalachd wants to welcome us to Edinburgh in style," Hannah said, her lips pursed together like a disapproving old spinster.

"You make it sound like a bad thing," I said.

"Not bad, just... calculated," Hannah said. "I think they mean to dazzle us."

"Dazzle us?" I repeated.

"Oh, you know. Charm us. Lull us into a false sense of security with an over-the-top display of welcome," Hannah said, her eyes narrowed.

"Well, I, for one, cannot wait to be dazzled," Milo piped up, tearing himself away from his stack of magazines. "I only wish I could try the food."

"Posh food is rubbish," Savvy interjected, causing me to jump. I hadn't noticed that she'd woken up. "I worked that clan fundraiser last month at the Lanesborough, remember? Thousands of dollars a plate and you could barely see the bloody food, it was so small! The lads and I had to stop for burgers and chips on the way home, and that was *after* they fed us!"

"So far the only immediate dangers seem to be poshness and starvation. I'll keep some snacks in my purse, okay? To be honest, I'm much less interested in the MacLeods and their scheming than I am in the actual reason for our trip, remember?" I said.

Hannah bit her lip, looking mildly embarrassed. From the look on her face, she'd given very little thought to the Geatgrima which was the subject of our assignment to begin with. As though she'd only just thought of it as well, Savvy spoke up again.

"Oi, what's going on with the Geatgrima anyway?"

I raised an eyebrow. "Didn't you read the file I gave you?"

Savvy grinned sheepishly. "I mean, I definitely glanced at it and all..."

"It has to do with spirits vanishing before they can Cross," I told her.

Her eyebrows shot up in surprise. "Well, I'll be buggered! Vanishing? Just... poof?"

I shrugged. "Seems that way. There's actually very little detail in the report about how it's happening."

"And they have no idea why?" she asked.

"Apparently they aren't very interested in finding out," Finn said, pressing his lips into a grim line that showed just how much he wasn't saying about the situation. Savvy, however, had no such worries about decorum.

"And why the devil not?" she asked, her voice rising like a tide. "Too busy eating gold-crusted fish eggs on kelp tarts or some such buggery nonsense?"

"It's their none-too-subtle way of expressing their anger at the situation," Hannah explained. "They're one of the clans unhappy about the Reckoning, so they've decided to make it everyone's problem but their own."

"Meaning?"

"Meaning the Council supported the return of the Gateways to the Geatgrimas, so they can bloody well deal with any issues that arise from that decision," Finn blurted out.

"That Geatgrima is on their property, isn't it?" Savvy asked.

"Yes, although to be fair, they own half of the city," Hannah said.

"Right, but isn't it their job to look after that Gateway? Isn't that the whole bloody reason we have clans in the first place?"

"As far as Clarissa MacLeod is concerned, they've done their duty. They spotted a problem and they reported it. But yes, it's not really in the spirit of things for a clan to wash their hands of a problem that could be having terrible consequences for the ghosts in their territory."

Milo snorted over his magazine, "In the *spirit* of things. I see what you did there." He looked up to see Hannah staring at him. "What? Can't I enjoy a little ghost humor? This job's got to have perks, you know."

"The point is, their inaction is meant to send a message, and the rest of the Northern Clans have received it loud and clear," Finn went on. "You took our power, you deal with the consequences. That's what this whole thing is meant to say."

"You don't think... oh, never mind," Hannah mumbled, chewing absently on one fingernail.

"Don't think what?" Finn asked, looking curious.

Hannah sighed and pulled her hands into her sweater sleeves with a shiver. "I was just wondering if they—the MacLeods, I mean—well... if they might have caused the problem, whatever it is, on purpose."

Finn narrowed his eyes. "Go on," he encouraged her.

"Well, they're angry, of course, we all know that. And we also know that Clarissa MacLeod is too smart and savvy to wrangle for open rebellion after watching other clans try and fail with that route. And so I just wonder if they might not just be reporting a problem, but causing one."

"What would they hope to gain from doing something like that? I mean, they would make life more difficult for the Council and the Trackers, but I'm not sure that would be an adequate reason to go to so much trouble," Finn said.

"Well, think about it. The Durupinen took the Gateway into their blood-lines to protect it. If we thought the Gateways were in danger again, mightn't we be persuaded to do the same thing again?" Hannah asked, so quietly that she might have been asking herself the question, probing her own mind for an answer rather than posing it to the rest of us.

No one answered at first, everyone seeming to give the question the same moment of contemplation that Hannah herself was giving it. It was clear that none of us had even considered the possibility that Clan Rìoghalachd was actually responsible for whatever had gone wrong with their Gateway. Finally, however, Finn cleared his throat.

"We shouldn't jump to conclusions, but I think Hannah is right in keeping her mind open to all possibilities under the current circumstances. We cannot dismiss the possibility out of hand."

"Which means we'll have to be very careful when dealing with the MacLeods," Hannah added.

I shifted uncomfortably in my seat. The more I learned about the MacLeods, the more nervous they made me. I wasn't naive about the moral ground upon which the Durupinen stood; it was shaky at best, and we seemed to make a habit of pushing each other off what little of it remained. And yet, I found a stubborn part of me that didn't want to believe that we could be responsible, yet again, for some kind of power hungry scheme at the expense of the spirits we were supposed to protect. I mean, couldn't we at least pretend to deserve our position in the spirit world for five minutes?

I let my gaze drift toward the window as the train broke free of its urban restraints like a wild creature running free. Soon, we had traded the graffitied walls and chain link fences for the open countryside which stretched out around us like a patchwork quilt in varying shades of verdant greens and sun-bleached yellows, run through with hedgerows and dotted with sheep and little villages, buildings clustered with their heads together like gossiping old women intent on hearing every sordid detail of the latest local scandal.

The hours slipped by as we traded sweeping landscapes of the emerald-hued countryside for intermittent views of the iron-gray North Sea, battering the coastline under an armor of striated clouds the color of smoke as we crossed over the border from England to Scotland. At last, the train rolled into Waverley Station, and the chipper voice of the conductor came over the loud-speaker, reminding us to take our belongings.

I stumbled off the train, my legs stiff from the journey, and looked up into the arching glass ceiling of Waverley station. It revealed the sky above as a dark mass of clouds that seemed ready to open at any moment. It was only a little after two o'clock in the afternoon, but Edinburgh seemed determined to disguise the day in the trappings of night. We trudged up the stairs and glided up the escalators to reach the ground level.

"Where do you suppose we should—" I began, but a voice rang out.

"Jessica Ballard?"

I turned and saw a young woman waving enthusiastically over her head. She was dressed in a meticulously tailored pantsuit and held a laminated sign with my name on it like an airport chauffeur. She hurried forward as I raised a hand in reply, her face breaking into a tight but genuine smile. She held out a hand and shook mine firmly.

"Jessica, it's very nice to meet you. I'm Pippa Barclay, Clarissa MacLeod's personal assistant," she said. She had sharp green eyes that flashed at me behind a pair of oversized, wire-rimmed glasses and a bright clear complexion spattered with the kind of freckles one usually only finds in a photo filter. Her honey-colored hair was parted down the middle and slicked into a tidy low ponytail. She looked to be in her late twenties.

"Hi, Pippa. You can call me Jess. Everyone does," I told her.

"Very well then, Jess," Pippa replied. She gave a careless little gesture over her shoulder and two men in dark suits emerged from the shadows behind her, hovering expectantly. "Is this all your luggage?" she asked.

"Yes, that's everything," I said.

Pippa nodded to the men, who began, with wordless efficiency, to gather up the bags and place them on a luggage trolley. They gave Finn a silent look of acknowledgment which he returned, confirming my assumption that the men were Caomhnóir. I could hear Savvy's teeth grinding behind me at the slight.

Pippa stepped forward, shaking everyone's hands and making proper introductions all around, while our luggage was wheeled out the door ahead of us.

"I'd like to welcome you all to Edinburgh and, of course, on behalf of Clan Rìoghalachd, to our ancestral lands." She gestured around her, as though the train station itself were the very heart of Clan Rìoghalachd's domain, and the implication couldn't have been clearer: they considered the city itself as theirs. "We're grateful you could make the journey, and appreciate your help with the, ehm... issue we're having," she said the last bit rather hesitantly, as though 'issues' weren't a thing they had much experience with, and therefore didn't even really know how to discuss them. Something else had pulled her up short, too, as she looked over our group once again. "I was under the impression you were bringing two Caomhnóir," Pippa said, glancing back over her notes. "Catriona hadn't notified me about any change to that detail. Do you need me to arrange for further security for you?"

"I'm the other Caomhnóir, mate," Savvy replied, her expression rueful.

"Oh. My goodness. I'd heard they were training female Caomhnóir now. How novel!" Pippa said. The words could easily have been condescending, but they weren't. Instead, Pippa's surprise was tempered with mild delight, and she looked at Savvy with unmistakable respect in her expression. Savvy noticed it, too. She drew herself up and returned Pippa's smile. I felt my stomach unclench ever so slightly. Clarissa MacLeod might still turn out to be a nightmare to deal with, but at least her assistant seemed nice, if super-humanly efficient.

"The car is waiting for you outside. We'll get you situated at your hotel, and you can freshen up for this evening's reception. Ms. MacLeod and the rest of Clan Rìoghalachd are eager to welcome you to Edinburgh," Pippa said, clicking across Waverley Station's tile floor in her high-heeled shoes. While she spoke, she was simultaneously answering a message on her phone and consulting the clipboard in her hand. Everything about her gave off an air of relaxed efficiency and competence, which I found at once soothing but also foreign to me, being the kind of hot mess who would never be capable of exuding such an impression. This woman had her shit together on a level that made her feel like a different species entirely.

A gleaming black stretch limo was waiting for us outside the station as we emerged into Edinburgh itself. The city rose around us, a glorious amalgamation of natural beauty, history, and modern convenience. Above it all, standing sentinel over the city for centuries from its perch on the craggy mountainside, was Edinburgh Castle. I spun on the spot, taking in as much of the view as I could even as Pippa ushered us all toward the waiting car, checking the time on her phone and murmuring instructions to the driver. My gawking and gaping would have to wait. We were on Clan Rìoghalachd time now, and evidently, it did not make allowances for my being a gobsmacked tourist. I repressed the immediate urge to pull out my phone and document everything. There would be time for that later, unless Pippa had scheduled every minute of our stay with the same precision that she had arranged for our arrival.

"Where is it we're staying?" I asked as we all settled into the limo's sleek black interior. There were bottles of water nestled in ice and packets of crisps and individually wrapped cookies tucked into baskets at our elbows. Savvy was halfway through a shortbread biscuit by the time I'd managed to get my seatbelt buckled.

"We've secured accommodations for you at The Witchery by the Castle," Pippa said, handing us each a manila envelope with our names neatly printed on the top corner. "These contain everything you'll need—room numbers, key cards, ID badges, invitations, security protocols, maps, and vouchers for meals. You needn't check-in, as we've made all the arrangements for you, but the front desk can assist you with anything we may have forgotten." She spoke these last words with a quiet confidence that assured us that there definitely wasn't anything that they'd forgotten.

"Is it far to the hotel?" Hannah asked.

"Four minutes or so, at this time of day," Pippa said briskly. "We chose a location to ensure walkability. I realize you are here on a Trackers assignment, but there ought to be some time to explore the city, and we wanted to make sure you were optimally placed in case you chose to do so. Old Town is full of history and, of course, full of ghosts."

"When do we hear more about the Geatgrima?" Finn asked.

For the first time, Pippa's smooth, unflappable smile faltered. "Ms. MacLeod will discuss it with you this evening. Then we will plan to visit it tomorrow so you can see for yourself the... uh, *situation*."

"Can't you tell us a little more about it?" I asked.

"I've been instructed to let Ms. MacLeod handle your initial debriefing," Pippa said, her porcelain complexion warming with just a touch of pink now, and I realized she wasn't allowed to discuss it with us. The knowledge sent a little jolt of nervousness through me. That jolt intensified when Pippa looked up from her clipboard and caught my eye. Her expression, in the unguarded moment before she smoothed it over again, was deeply uncomfortable—like she wished she could be anywhere but in that car with us. But then I blinked, and her former mask of efficiency was neatly back in place.

Well, well. I considered my curiosity officially piqued.

5

MACLEOD MANOR

A FEW MOMENTS LATER WE PULLED UP TO OUR HOTEL, which was located on the Royal Mile, so named because perched at the top of it were the gates of Edinburgh Castle itself. The hotel looked like a relic from an earlier time; a foreboding facade of sandstone crowded with leaded glass windows, and topped with a series of dormers that gave the impression of a crown perched upon its head. Perhaps to enhance the eeriness of the place, the front of the building was also uplit in a bloody scarlet hue, beams of red light reaching up over the sandstone like so many reaching fingers. A wrought iron sign which looked like a medieval shield more than anything else, complete with a coat of arms, thrust outward from the facade on golden posts. As we piled out of the car and onto the sidewalk, all I could do was stare. Milo materialized beside me, his face lit up with excitement.

"Oh, this place is a whole vibe," he whispered.

"And what vibe is that?" I asked.

He considered for a moment, then said, confidently, "It's giving me Bram Stoker chic."

I thought for a moment and then nodded, because he was absolutely right, and the more of the hotel we saw, the more correct he became. The interior was as darkly glamorous as the outside, full of glittering chandeliers, rich dark jewel tones, and lush fabrics set against dark imposing wood and stone.

"If there's nothing else right now, I'll see you downstairs by the front desk at six o'clock sharp, and we'll proceed over to the reception from there," Pippa said. "A reservation has been made for you all in the hotel dining room for high tea, if you're feeling peckish. You can find me in the Sempill Suite. I'll be on-site here for the duration of your stay, in case you need anything at all."

"Wait, you're staying here, too?" I asked.

Pippa turned, eyebrows raised. "Yes. Ms. MacLeod has placed me at your disposal while you're here."

"Oh wow," I said, frowning. "I feel kind of weird about that."

Pippa looked mildly amused. "Weird? Whatever for?"

I shrugged. "I don't know. I guess it seems... kind of crazy to have another person just waiting around to do stuff for you?"

Pippa laughed and then leaned in, lowering her voice conspiratorially. "Not to someone like Clarissa MacLeod. In fact, between you and me, I rather fancy she'd find it weird *not* to have someone waiting around to do things for her."

It was my turn to laugh. "Okay, then. Well, I guess I'll, um... see you later?"

"Six o'clock, at the front desk," she reminded me, all business yet again.

"Right. I'll be there," I promised.

"The dress code for the reception is black tie formal. Is that... going to be an issue?" Pippa asked, an embarrassed flush reddening her cheeks.

I followed her gaze to my shredded jeans and oversized black sweater, through which both of my thumbs were poking by means of ragged holes at the cuff. I chuckled.

"If it was me on my own, it might be an issue; but I brought Milo Chang with me, and I promise he can handle it."

Pippa smiled a little sheepishly. "Very good. I'll leave you in his capable hands, then."

I walked down the hallway to find Finn emerging from one of the rooms. I approached the door, but he shook his head, grinning. "I'm terribly sorry, Ms. Ballard, but that's not your room," he said.

"But then why were you just in there?" I asked him.

"Because that's my room," he said.

"But that's..." He chuckled again as the horror dawned on my face. "They put us in separate rooms?"

"They certainly did," Finn confirmed.

"But we specifically requested... we made it clear that we were... well, you know," I said, lowering my voice as a member of the staff walked by, nodding in welcome.

"I realize that. I think we just got our first taste of MacLeod disapproval," Finn said.

"Meaning?"

"Meaning that they're as old school as it gets, and the idea of Durupinen fraternizing with Caomhnóir is still distasteful to them. I think they took the opportunity to say as much without actually saying it."

My mouth fell open. "Wow." I finally managed.

Finn shrugged, still smirking. "I told you they were a handful."

"You sure did," I said, shaking my head and letting loose an incredulous laugh.

"Did I hear that right?" Milo sailed through the wall and appeared beside us. "Did they actually put you in separate rooms? What is this, a middle school field trip? Where do they find the audacity?"

"My guess is they keep it in the safe, next to their piles and piles of money," I said dryly. "Isn't that generally where rich people keep shit?"

"Like I would know, sweetness," Milo replied, rolling his eyes. "But seriously, this place is doing the absolute most at all times. Have you seen the rooms yet? There are hidden closets behind paintings and bookcases. Chandeliers hanging from the chandeliers. Red velvet everywhere. It's like if Dracula and Moulin Rouge had a baby and then upholstered it. I simultaneously can't handle it, and can't get enough of it. In fact, I'm inspired and now I have to go sketch, excuse me." And with an excited shiver of energy, he vanished again.

"Well, at least someone is happy with the living situation," I pouted. "You aren't going to stay in that other room, are you?"

Finn pulled me against him and kissed me in a way that left me breathless and flushed. "Obviously not," he whispered.

"Well, I'm glad that the MacLeods haven't intimidated *you*, at least," I said. I, however, could feel a gnawing pit of anxiety starting to grow in my stomach. I would have dreaded the evening's reception anyway, just by virtue of the fact that I'd have to change out of my jeans and Docs to go to it, but now I was experiencing dread that had nothing at all to do with the dress code.

What the hell had Catriona gotten me into?

~

Three hours later, I was grumbling much more loudly about what Milo had gotten me into, and by 'gotten me into,' I meant physically.

I stared at my reflection in the elaborately framed mirror in the corner of my room, biting my lip. "Wow."

"I know," Milo chirped, his hands pressed to his face in delight: like I was his baby who had just taken her first steps, rather than his friend that he'd crammed into a cocktail dress. "I can't even stand how chic you look. Why, oh, why don't you let me dress you every day?"

"Because I like breathing. And I hate complicated underwear," I reminded him.

Milo snorted. "A small price to pay to look like *that*, sweetness."

I looked again at the woman staring back at me from the mirror. Her hair was slicked elegantly back off her forehead and worked into a braided crown on the top of her head. Her makeup was smoky with just a touch of sparkle, which picked up the sparkle in the rhinestone cuff earring encasing one ear, and the subtler stud winking from the other. Her body was encased in a sleek black dress with a long sleeve on one side and no sleeve at all on the other, which showed her sleeve tattoo to full advantage. Her toes peeped out from a pair of jewel-encrusted pumps that promised to leave blisters in places she couldn't even fathom. Frankly, she looked just as doubtful as I felt that either of us could pull this off for the entire night. She narrowed her eyes at me as though to say, "You're going to spill something on us in the first hour we're there, aren't you?" Sadly, I thought she was probably right, so I pressed my lips together and said nothing.

A knock sounded on the door and Hannah poked her head in. She took one look at me and her face split into a wide grin.

"You look amazing. And miserable," she said, mirth sparkling in her voice.

"I can confirm the second, and I'll take your word for it on the first," I told her, before turning and getting a good look at her. "Wow," I said, gesturing broadly at her.

She beamed. "Thank you. All Milo's work, of course."

Her hair was down, curls tumbling down her back, and her dress was made of a glimmery pale gold material that seemed to float around her like golden mist when she moved, which she could do much more easily than me, given that her shoes looked like dainty ballet slippers.

I turned to Milo, scowling. "Why does she get flats?"

Milo lowered his voice to a whisper. "Because we are in hostile negotiations and I am making a gesture of goodwill. Three wedding dresses, remember?"

"Right," I said grumpily, snatching a black satin clutch from the throne-like chair in the corner of my room. "Well, let's get this over with."

As I stepped out into the hallway, Finn emerged from the other bedroom, which had turned out to be pretty useful once Milo had kicked him out of ours so he could go all glam-squad on my ass for two solid hours. He had also dressed for the occasion and, in a nod of deference to Clan Rìoghalachd, his formal attire included a kilt, in which he looked horribly uncomfortable. He tugged at the kilt, adjusted a stocking, and then looked up to find me staring at him. He straightened up at once, hoisting one eyebrow as he looked me over.

"You look utterly amazing," he said, causing a flood of warmth and color to my cheeks.

"Thanks," I said. "So do you."

He spun on the spot. "Not my usual attire, I admit, but I can endure it which, I imagine, is the same way you feel about your ensemble."

I toddled across to him in my heels and kissed him. "I love that you just get me."

He leaned in for one more kiss and then looked over his shoulder at Milo. "Well done, you."

Milo took a bow full of unnecessary flourishes. "Thank you very much."

We walked down to the front desk, where Pippa and Savvy were waiting for us—Pippa looking efficient, yet elegant, in a sleek black cocktail dress with a high neckline and a draped back—Savvy voluptuous in a green satin creation of Milo's with a plunging neckline and a matching quilted clutch. Pippa did not comment on our attire, but looked each of us over and gave a satisfied nod, as though she could find nothing amiss. I found myself wondering what would have happened if she *had* found something amiss. Would we, perhaps, have been sent back up to change if we'd worn something that clashed with Clarissa's floral arrangements, for example—or else didn't meet her expectation of formality? The very thought of it was almost enough to send me sprinting back to my room to throw on my holiest jeans and most battered pair of boots, just for fun. I sighed to myself. These kinds of thoughts were exactly why Clarissa was smart to send Pippa as my handler; I clearly couldn't be trusted otherwise.

Hearing my sigh, Finn leaned over. "You all right?"

"Yes," I murmured back. "Just eager to get this over with."

"Agreed," he said, tugging ruefully at the kilt again.

Pippa consulted her phone. "Our car's here. If everyone's ready, let's be off, then."

We clambered into the same limo that had fetched us from Waverley. Savvy lost no time reaching into the nearest basket and stuffing three more shortbread cookies into her purse. Remembering what she said about posh food, I snuck a cookie into my clutch as well.

"What about me?" Finn whispered.

"You should have brought a purse," I whispered back, but pilfered him another cookie, despite his ill-preparation. Couldn't a guy get a kilt with pockets? I opened my mouth to make a joke about it and then, catching the disapproving purse of Milo's lips, closed it again. His expression clearly said he didn't approve of shortbread as accessories, or maybe he was just worried about crumbs. I decided I didn't dare ask him, in case it meant being forced to give up my contraband cookies.

The drive to Clarissa MacLeod's estate took about twenty minutes. Pippa kept up a steady stream of polite commentary about the sights of the city, drawing our attention to various points of interest with the air of a tour guide; but I could hardly will myself to pay attention to what she said. My stomach was beginning to roil unpleasantly as we approached the wealthy suburb of Barnton, in the northwest part of the city. Here the buildings were spread out, rather than crammed shoulder to shoulder like soldiers at attention. Here there were sweeping lawns and manicured gardens.

At last, we pulled up to a wrought iron gate. The driver had a quick word with the gatekeeper and the gates swung silently forward. The driveway curved around in front of a magnificent mansion, built in traditional sandstone like much of the city we'd left behind us. The many tall windows of the house were aglow, sending sharp-edged golden patterns out across the immaculate flower beds, fountains, and topiaries that dotted the sweeping lawns. The breeze carried the muted tones of string music out into the grounds as we stepped out of the car. Two barrel-chested Caomhnóir guarded the entrance, but stood aside without a word, throwing the doors wide as Pippa led our group confidently up the steps.

It was a bit like someone taking my hand and pulling me into a dance that had already begun, the perfectly executed steps whirling around me as I struggled to acclimate to the rhythm. An oily man in a tuxedo was plucking wraps and bags from our hands and replacing them with champagne flutes that floated by on silver trays balanced by waiters so unobtrusive that they might have been invisible. I waited for the next tray to pass and returned my champagne flute to it; I needed my wits about me, and champagne always went straight to my head. Elegant couples drifted up and down the monstrous staircase effortlessly, as though it might have been a well-disguised escalator. An impossibly large swan carved from ice threw rainbows from its slowly melting facets over a table that looked in danger of collapsing under the weight of cheeses, charcuterie, breads, pates, fruits, and vegetables. People milled about the table like skittish butterflies, but no one appeared to be eating anything—perhaps balancing plates and producing crumbs were not an accepted bit of choreography in this particular dance. From every corner of the room, jewels sparkled around throats and perched on polished fingers. A constant buzzing hum of conversation gave the whole affair the air of bees in a wildly glamorous hive.

Pippa, ever the diplomat, allowed us a long moment to take it all in and then close our gaping mouths before gesturing us across the room. She seemed perfectly at ease in this setting, despite the fact that she was only admitted under the auspices of her job. I wondered how many degrees she was removed from this level of wealth herself—probably many, if she had deigned to take a job here. We moved as a single entity across the polished floors, through the main entrance hall and into a great room crowned by one of the largest chandeliers I'd ever seen. A string quartet played in the corner by the windows, filling the air with a lush waltz that almost demanded to be danced to, but the assembled company was not inclined to acquiesce. Pippa stopped in the middle of the room, turning on the spot, a wrinkle of concern appearing between her eyebrows. We all piled up behind her like a traffic jam.

"Something wrong, Pippa?" I asked her.

Pippa smoothed out her face at once. "Not at all. I expected to find Clarissa here, but no matter. Please, enjoy yourselves. I'll track down our hostess and introduce you. She'll only be sorry she hadn't been ready to greet you." And with that, she slipped between two groups of people to speak to a white-haired man.

We stood grouped together as though for safety, and though we hadn't said or done anything to draw attention to ourselves, it was soon clear that we had become the topic of nearly every conversation in the room. All around us, covert glances were being made, heads were bowing together, and subtle gestures were made in our direction.

"Why don't they just stop the music and announce a staring contest? Aren't rich people supposed to have good manners?" I grumbled to Hannah, who nodded in agreement. Perhaps it was her role as a member of the Council, but it was clear she didn't think much of our welcome so far. A moment later, however, a woman swept over to us with a broad smile on her face that revealed very large, very white teeth and a dimple in one cheek.

"These must be our guests from Fairhaven!" she said, opening her arms wide as though she meant to embrace us. At her words, people all around the room pretended to notice us for the first time. "I do so apologize for not meeting you at the door, the time got away from me."

I opened my mouth to greet the woman I assumed was Clarissa MacLeod, but Pippa appeared beside me again out of nowhere and forestalled me.

"Where is Clarissa?" she asked in something of an undertone.

"Just dealing with a minor situation," the other woman said in a dismissive tone. "And in her absence, it is my absolute pleasure to welcome you to MacLeod Manor and to Edinburgh!" The woman thrust out her hand eagerly, taking and squeezing each of ours in turn. "I'm Danica MacLeod. It's our pleasure to have you here. How have you found your accommodations? Acceptable, I hope?"

"More than acceptable," I said, and I managed a smile despite feeling completely wrong-footed. I had been prepared for cold civility at best and haughty disdain at worst, so Danica's friendliness left me reeling a bit. "It's very... um, fancy?"

Danica laughed trillingly. "I told Clarissa the Witchery was a bit over the top, but she insisted. I thought you might be more comfortable in a flat with a kitchen and all that, but Clarissa couldn't imagine anyone wanting to make their own food when you could have someone make it for you. No one ever listens to me, but I'm well used to it by now." There was a lovely lilt to her accent, a kind of musicality that enchanted the listener. I felt my smile widening and had to remind myself that I still had to be on my guard with any MacLeod I met.

"Please don't concern yourself. We're very comfortable where we are," Hannah said.

"Well, it's very good of you all to answer our summons, as it were," Danica said. "If you need anything at all during your stay, don't hesitate to let Pippa know. We are hopeful that your time in our city will be as pleasant as we can make it, despite the reason for your visit. Now let me guess, because I so dearly love to be right: you're Hannah, and you're Jessica. Did I guess right?"

I nodded, still smiling. "Yes, you did."

She snapped her fingers together and winked at us. "I knew it! This one's got a civilized, responsible look about her, so she must surely be the Council member," Danica said, surveying Hannah with satisfaction.

"And this one's got the air of a troublemaker," Hannah finished for her, poking me in the arm.

"Hey, just because it's true doesn't mean you have to say it out loud," I said to Hannah, poking her just slightly harder than she poked me. She smirked at me. It was becoming more obvious by the day that I was a bad influence on her.

Danica dropped her voice, glancing anxiously around the room before she continued. "I'll let Clarissa give you the details, but I just wanted to say we're grateful you're here. This situation with the Geatgrima has been most distressing. I wonder if it isn't best for us to—"

"Danica, perhaps we should let Clarissa handle this particular conversation," Pippa said. Her voice was utterly calm, and yet I heard the warning in it just the same. Danica must have heard it too, for she nodded her head and then pressed her lips together like a small child trying not to blurt out a secret.

"Of course. Silly me, always forgetting myself. You mustn't mind me, I'm the most terrible bletherer, always have been," Danica said, parting her lips to smile broadly again. "Yes, yes, it's best for Clarissa to... that is to say, she's really the one who... who handles everything, you know." Little pink circles were appearing on her cheeks. "Oh Jessica, my dear, no one's given you a drink!"

"No, it's fine, I don't—"

"Nonsense, you need a drink! Clarissa would never forgive me if we neglected you! Ah, here we are," Her hand shot out over my head to snatch a glass from a passing waiter, but I wasn't quick enough to get out of her way and her jingling bracelets snagged on my braid.

"Oh dear!" Danica cried out, the champagne sloshing down over her dress as she tried to disentangle herself. "I seem to have... it's snagged on... oh, for heaven's..."

It took several more seconds, three people, and a painful tug to detach us, and even then, a little clump of my hair went with her.

"Oh, I am so sorry. I'm just the most inept... the clumsiest... I'm always making a mess of everything, honestly. Here, that's yours, my dear," she said, handing me the half-filled champagne flute. "Oh, and so is this!" she added, holding out the little clump of strands to me.

"Don't worry about it. Um, thank you," I said, accepting the hairs and at the same time wondering what she thought I was supposed to do with them. It wasn't as though I could reattach them to my head.

Danica smiled around at us all again, cheeks flushed with embarrassment, and with one last apology, she swept away, the skirt of her pink satin dress swishing loudly as she went to tend to the champagne stain. When she was out of sight, I brushed the hair from my hand and let it drift to the floor.

"Well, while we're waiting for Clarissa, why don't I introduce you to a few other prominent members of the clan," Pippa said. Her expression was one of determined calm. This wasn't how she had planned the evening to go, and it was clear that the unexpected detour had thrown off her usually unflappable composure. It wasn't that she couldn't deal with things on the fly—even in the few hours since I'd met her, it was clear she was a person who could handle almost anything. I had a sneaking suspicion that she was more concerned about how Clarissa would respond.

The next twenty minutes were a whirlwind. Once it became clear that they were no longer waiting for Clarissa to begin the introductions, members of Clan Rìoghalachd began accosting us from all sides, jostling each other for position so that they could meet us. It was a bit like being an exhibit in a zoo, the way they stared openly and without the faintest trace of embarrassment. Hannah's complexion was so red I could actually feel the heat coming off her. I reached back, found her hand, and squeezed it. She squeezed back, and then I heard her take a deep, steadying breath behind me. I reminded myself that she was making a big sacrifice for me, coming to this reception at all, given that she detested crowds and introductions and awkward small talk as much as any introvert. I wasn't a huge fan either if it came right down to it. My mouth kept going dry, and my first reaction was to drink the champagne already in my hand, but after draining the flute in less than ten minutes, I realized this strategy was not sustainable unless I wanted to be staggeringly drunk before the first hour was up, so I caught a passing waiter by the elbow, deposited my empty champagne flute on his tray, and requested a glass of water. He obliged about two minutes later with the tiniest glass of water I'd ever seen; had he misheard me and thought I'd ordered a shot of water? And so it went on, me ordering shots of water and him bringing them until I'd met all of Clan Rìoghalachd and also really had to pee.

I inclined my head toward Pippa, who was speaking in an undertone to one of the waiters. "Where do I go to... um... powder my nose?" I whispered.

"Up the staircase, second door on the left," Pippa whispered back, in such a distracted voice I was surprised she didn't ask me to repeat myself. She had abandoned her attempts to ask the other guests where Clarissa might be and was now enlisting the help of the people whose job it was to know: the servants.

I politely extricated myself from the group and made for the staircase, taking a deep breath. I'd never have believed a person could feel claustrophobic in such a large room. As I rose above the milling crowd, though, I felt my breathing ease and my composure return. It hadn't been simply the physical closeness of the curious crowd, it had also been the boldness of the questions they'd asked, and the comments they'd made.

They don't look at all like I thought they would.

They look exactly like I thought they would.

So, you're a Walker, what is that like?

You went to that Traveler camp, my goodness that was brave of you.

...remember their mother? Trouble from the word go, I've heard.

Never saw a clan fall so hard so fast as theirs did.

I reached the top of the stairs and peered down the hallway to the right. It was deserted, thank goodness. No random guests were lying in wait to ambush me before I could empty my bladder. I made for the second door on the left as Pippa had instructed and had just placed a hand upon the handle when voices from the other side of the door froze me where I stood. Quite unintentionally, I found myself eavesdropping.

"...am not going to ask you again. Put that dress on, get downstairs, and do your duty to your clan!"

This demand was met with a delighted shriek of a laugh. "Duty? Listen to you going on about duty! My God, you're such a hypocrite."

"You'd better take care to watch what you say to me, Maeve, or I swear, I'll—"

"You'll what?! Hit me? Go ahead, Mother. Right across the face, eh, and lay that palm open—I'd like a clear pink handprint to match that horror show of a dress. That way I can show it off to everyone."

There was a long, exasperated sigh.

"Of course I'm not going to hit you. Don't be absurd, please."

"That's right, how silly of me. You prefer subtler means of controlling people, don't you? If bribery and extortion left a mark, I daresay half the assembled company would be comparing wounds over their canapés."

"I might have called that remark clever, if there were any truth to it, but as usual, your ambivalence toward your legacy and your family means you have no idea what the devil you're talking about. Now, are you going to put that dress on and come downstairs, or am I going to have to make yet another excuse for you?"

There was a long pause, as I imagined the glares that must surely be passing between them.

"I'll be down in a few minutes," came the reply at last, much calmer than I had expected. "Who knows, wouldn't want to miss anything fun, right?"

6

ENTER CLARISSA

"Jess."

A hand pressed lightly on my shoulder and it took every ounce of my self-control not to scream at the top of my lungs. I spun around and saw Pippa standing just behind me, her eyes wide, terrified, and slightly magnified behind her glasses.

I opened my mouth, whether to explain or apologize I didn't even know yet, when Pippa's eyes widened even further and she shook her head desperately. The hand on my shoulder slipped down to my hand and she began tugging me away from the door. A sound behind me alerted me to the reason for her haste: someone on the other side of the door was walking toward us with quick, businesslike steps. We only had seconds.

"I'm sorry, I thought that was the bathroom," I hissed.

"No, I'm sorry, I meant to say right, but I was so distracted trying to—"

We managed to get about halfway back to the staircase before the door flew open and a tall, regal woman stepped out. Every muscle in her body tensed and froze the moment she saw us standing there.

"Pippa," she said, in a cryptic tone that was part-question, part-admonishment, and part-greeting. I felt rather than saw Pippa pull her hand away.

"Clarissa! There you are!" Pippa said, with a valiant attempt at a relieved smile. "We were beginning to wonder where you'd got to."

"So you decided to come looking for me upstairs?" she asked, one eyebrow hoisted in haughty disdain. I jumped in, eager to save Pippa any trouble I could.

"That part was my fault, Ms. MacLeod," I said, for some reason raising my hand like I was answering a question in class. I lowered it awkwardly as the woman took me in—it was like being x-rayed and I had to repress a shudder before I could continue. "Please excuse the intrusion. I was looking for the bathroom, and it was so loud downstairs I think I misheard Pippa's directions."

Pippa stepped in to rescue me from my own floundering. "This is Jessica Ballard, Clarissa," she said quietly.

At the mention of my name, I watched Clarissa's entire demeanor transform. The harsh lines of her face softened, her ramrod straight posture melted into an elegant slump of the shoulders, and she glided forward, a smile dawning on her features like the sun over the horizon. The change was so complete that by the time she arrived in front of me, her hand outstretched, I could hardly believe that this was the same woman who had spoken so harshly only a few moments before. The transmutation was terrifying.

"Jessica, it is I who should be asking for your forgiveness. Please, do forgive me," Clarissa said, closing the last of the distance between us and clasping my hand between hers, which were inhumanly soft and decked out with one of the biggest emeralds I'd ever seen. "I had every intention of being downstairs to greet you the moment you arrived, but I was prevented from joining you. The joys of parenting a teenager, not that you'd know anything about that, but you may one day, and you will have my deepest sympathies if you do."

I joined in the laughing, because what the hell else was I supposed to do? She still had my hand between her hands and showed no sign of letting go of it.

"I ought to have been the first to say this when you walked through my doors, but welcome to Edinburgh. I have no doubt that Pippa has seen to your every need since your arrival." It wasn't a question, but I jumped in with my assurances that we had everything we needed.

"I suppose you are anxious to hear about what's happened with our Geatgrima here in the city," Clarissa said, finally letting go of my hand. "Perhaps, Pippa, you could escort Miss Ballard and the rest of her group to the west library. We can speak more privately there," she said, with just the slightest glance over her shoulder at the room where her daughter was, presumably, submitting to her mother's instructions and dressing for the party. "I've just one more tiny detail to see to up here, and I will join you there."

"Very well, Clarissa," Pippa said, and Clarissa swept past us down the hallway and disappeared around the corner. When she had gone, I turned to Pippa.

"I'm so sorry. I thought you said left, and then I was afraid to move in case—"

"No, no, it's my fault. I said left when I meant right. I was so distracted trying to discover where in the world Clarissa could have gotten to that I wasn't paying you proper attention. I realized what I'd said just a minute later and ran up here to find you, but..." she gestured helplessly toward Maeve's bedroom door.

"It's okay," I said. "It all worked out. Luckily, I didn't just open the door and walk into the middle of their...uh, conversation," I finished lamely. Conversation wasn't really the right word, but I didn't want Pippa to feel any worse about the situation than she already did.

After successfully finding the bathroom, we descended the stairs again and tracked down the others. We pulled a reluctant Milo away from an admiring crowd of women who had all heard of his clothing line and were peppering him with questions, and a reluctant Savvy away from the charcuterie table. Then we extricated Hannah and Finn from the same crowd of Clan Rìogha-lachd members we'd abandoned them to a few minutes ago, and we all made our way through a dizzying number of rooms until we arrived in the west library, which I realized inferred the existence of an *east* library. Built-in book-cases lined every inch of the walls except for where the ornately carved fire-place rose to the ceiling. There was a rolling library ladder on a track that ran the perimeter of the room. Good lord, how much money did these people have?

Pippa must have flagged down a waiter at some point in our travels, because we'd barely had a moment to look around the room before several of them arrived, depositing trays of drinks and appetizers on a sideboard table that ran along the back of one of the wine-red leather sofas. I helped myself to something wrapped in puff pastry and let my eyes wander to the space over the mantelpiece where hung an enormous painting of Clarissa herself, looking both regal and academic, a book laying open at her elbow.

"Imagine wanting to look at a giant painting of yourself all the time," I said under my breath. Hannah nodded fervently. Milo, however, snorted.

"Speak for yourself, I'm one gilt-covered frame away from artwork at all times."

I had to swallow my snarky reply along with the puff pastry, for Clarissa swept into the room at that moment. After the obligatory introductions, each accompanied by one of her trademark x-ray glares, she gestured for us all to be seated. She spent an extra long time surveying Hannah down the bridge of her aquiline nose, an undisguised fascination in her eyes. It was an expression I'd seen on many faces before Clarissa MacLeod's when they looked at my sister: a poorly concealed greed for the power that ran in her blood.

When she'd finished her inspection of her guests, Clarissa walked around the room, seeming to be considering her words before she came to a stop directly beneath her own portrait. Savvy did an admirable job of pretending that her resulting chuckle was a choking little cough, and I thumped her on the back to help sell the illusion. I didn't dare look at her or we'd both be in trouble. Savvy was one of those people you couldn't sit next to at serious occasions, like funerals or when a woman stood directly beneath a portrait of herself and unconsciously struck the exact same pose and expression.

"The spirits of our city appear to be in peril," Clarissa began, and all impulse to laugh instantly vanished. "I worried—we all worried—that the transition to using Geatgrimas again might be too swift, too... sudden. But our concerns were not heeded."

"Um, with all due respect, Ms. MacLeod—" I began.

"Please, call me Clarissa," Clarissa replied, and though she smiled, her nostrils flared slightly. I don't think she was at all accustomed to being interrupted.

"Clarissa," I amended, trying to return the smile. "But as to the restoration of the Gateways, we really didn't have much choice. It wasn't something we could choose to slowly phase in. We had waited too long as it was—centuries too long, in fact. We risked the destruction of everything if we waited."

Clarissa nodded, giving every indication that she valued this input. "This may be true," she said, after a moment's consideration, "and I certainly do not mean to cast the blame on you directly. After all, you were put in a terrible position. But the fact remains that here in Edinburgh, we were not ready, and now something is terribly wrong."

I did not reply, because the words dancing on the tip of my tongue ("Clans like yours will never be ready, and are also the reason we reached that crisis point,") were better left unsaid. Hannah placed a restraining hand on my knee, as though she knew exactly what I was thinking, and then I remembered that she probably could—one of the perks of our spirit guide connection was being tuned in to each other's thoughts, or at least the tone of them.

Clarissa continued, "We worried that the infrastructure, neglected for so long, might not be prepared to handle the sudden restoration of the Gateways, and now that fear has become a reality. Something is wrong with the Clan Rìoghalachd Geatgrima, and that's why we've asked the Northern Clans to send the Trackers, to sort out the problem and restore the balance."

I looked at the others before turning back to Clarissa. "That's why we're here, and we'll do anything we can to help."

Clarissa's face slid into a satisfied smile. "I'm delighted to hear that."

"I was wondering," Hannah said, her soft voice nonetheless cutting through the room like a blade, "why we haven't been taken to the Geatgrima yet?"

Clarissa looked mildly bewildered, but there was a disingenuousness to the expression. Clarissa MacLeod didn't appear to me to be a woman who was ever truly bewildered. "But you've only just arrived," she said.

Hannah looked at her watch. "Yes, several hours ago now. Please don't misunderstand me, we are grateful for the warm welcome you've thrown for us here this evening, but we were under the impression that the situation at the Geatgrima was quite dire."

"Dire, yes, but not constant," Clarissa explained. "We've prepared some notes for you. Pippa?"

Pippa leaped into action, handing each of us a manila folder. I have absolutely no idea where she pulled them from; they must have been waiting in the room for us. We opened the folders and found a kind of running document—a timeline of sorts, detailing when the problem had been noticed, and when it had been observed since.

"As I'm sure you know from what we've shared with Catriona and the Trackers office, spirits have been vanishing when they come into a certain proximity to the Geatgrima. What you probably don't know is that these vanishings do not happen around the clock. They only seem to happen between the hours of two and three o'clock in the morning."

"The witching hour," Finn murmured under his breath.

"If we'd taken you to the Geatgrima earlier this evening, there would have been nothing for you to see. From all we have been able to discover, the Geatgrima is functioning as it is meant to for the other twenty-three hours of the day. That is why it took us months to even realize there was a problem."

"What, if anything, have you been able to rule out?" Finn asked, flipping through the timeline, his eyes flashing back and forth as he spoke.

"So far, all we've been able to determine is that the Geatgrima itself seems to be intact, and that the surrounding area seems to be clear—that is, our Caomhnóir have found no signs of intruders in the area, nor of any Castings that should not be present," Clarissa answered. "The Geatgrima security details are well and truly stymied."

"I should think so," Savvy murmured under her breath.

"Those folders contain all of the information we have, aside from what we have already sent along to Catriona for you. I trust you will take the time to review it, and tonight Pippa will see that you are escorted to the site to see the problem for yourselves."

Hannah nodded, satisfied. It was clear she didn't want to waste any time when the welfare of spirits was at stake. And as a matter of fact, neither did I.

"Well, maybe we should head back to the hotel then, get started on all of this, and prepare for tonight," I said, standing up from the sofa. My feet were already aching from Milo's chosen footwear.

"Oh, you can't go yet. We've got a formal welcome prepared for you in the ballroom," Clarissa said. She glanced at a delicate gold watch that dangled from her wrist. "We are scheduled to begin in just a few minutes. Let me see that all is in order, and you can join us momentarily. Pippa? Five minutes?"

The door through which we had come slid open and Danica's anxious features popped through the gap. "Clarissa! There you are, thank goodness. I wasn't sure what to—"

"Yes, here I am Danica, precisely where I am meant to be. The question is, why are you here and not in the ballroom with the rest of the guests, as I directed you?"

Danica's cheeks blazed. "Well, yes. Quite. I just began to worry because the welcome is—"

"Completely under control, as I am the one who arranged the details," Clarissa said sharply.

"Of course, Clarissa. I'm sorry. Silly of me to..."

Danica withdrew, like an abashed turtle into its shell, and Clarissa swept from the room after her. We all stood silently a moment after she left, a distinct feeling of tension draining out of us.

"That was..." Savvy began.

"Intense?" I suggested. She nodded, giving her head a shake as she rose from the couch. She turned to Pippa. "Your blood pressure must be through the roof, mate."

Pippa gave a dismissive chuckle. "I do assure you, one gets used to her."

"That's your lookout, I suppose, but better you than me," Savvy muttered.

We waited five minutes by Pippa's watch. At last, she nodded and we rose to enter the great room once again. Just on the threshold to the library door, Milo stopped so suddenly that I walked through him by accident.

"Gah!" My teeth slammed together in the rush of cold.

"Sorry, sorry," he said, but didn't look at me. He was looking all around him, his eyebrows pinched together in a curious expression.

"You've got to stop d—hey, what's up?" I asked, cutting off my own grumbling at the look on his face. "Are you okay?"

"Yeah, no, I'm fine, it's just..." he continued to look around as though he was watching something invisible flit around above us. "Did anyone else feel that?"

"Feel what?" Savvy asked around a mouthful of chicken satay on a stick.

"I didn't feel anything," Hannah said, though she looked wary now.

"Nor did I. What's up?" Finn asked, a sudden rigidness to his stance which meant he'd shifted into full Caomhnóir protective mode.

"I'm... not sure. It was almost... like an energy surge?" Milo said. "Like, I expected ten more ghosts to suddenly walk in the room and join the party, but then... nothing."

We were all looking around the room now, probing our own gifts, trying to see or sense what Milo had felt. Finn actually walked the perimeter of the room as though a spirit might be camouflaging itself behind the draperies.

"Have you seen any spirits since we've been here?" I asked Milo.

"There are at least a few in the house, yes. Several servants clinging to the servitude of centuries past, that sort of thing. But of course, the property must be heavily Warded, so I wouldn't expect many."

"Shouldn't that have kept you out, then?" Savvy asked.

Milo shook his head. "Spirit guide, remember? As long as one of the spooky twins is here, I can pass through without a problem."

"Ah, right. I thought that might just have been a Fairhaven thing," Savvy replied.

"Is everything all right?" Pippa asked, hovering in the doorway. There was an edge in her voice, and I knew she was anxious for the rest of the night to go smoothly after the rather rough start.

"It was probably nothing," Milo said, but he still looked unnerved.

"Let's all stay on alert," Finn said. "Milo, you'll tell us if you sense anything else out of the ordinary?"

Milo nodded, with a half-hearted attempt at a smile.

Pippa cleared her throat. "Shall we?" she asked, gesturing us through the open door.

We followed her back to the great room, where all the guests had assembled and the string quartet was still playing quietly. As we appeared on the threshold, though, the music came to an abrupt stop and the lights, twinkling brightly around the room, suddenly lowered. Clarissa appeared on the small dais that had been erected for the musicians, and all eyes turned expectantly toward her.

"All hail the queen," came a quiet, sarcastic voice just to my left.

I turned and saw a teenage girl in a pink cocktail dress and equally pink hair pulled into a chic chignon leaning casually against the wall. She caught my eye and rolled hers, which were a startling shade of aquamarine and lined generously in kohl black eyeliner. Then she smirked and raised a champagne flute in my direction. I nodded at the acknowledgment and then turned away. I assumed this was Maeve, Clarissa's daughter; but I couldn't let on that I knew that, or she'd know I'd been eavesdropping.

Clarissa's voice rang out, filling the room. "We gather once again, the great tapestry of Clan Rìoghalachd, here within the walls of MacLeod Manor, to welcome visitors who—"

Her words were cut off in a collective gasp as a bitter coldness enveloped us, as though the whole room had fallen through ice and been swallowed into the freezing waters running beneath. My lungs felt frozen, unable to expand, and whatever exclamation I'd been ready to make was extinguished in breathless shock. The lights flickered, dimmed, and then suddenly brightened again. Every light in the room, including the flames in the candles and in the fireplace, roared to blinding brilliance before exploding one by one (*pop-pop-pop-pop-pop!*) and plunging us into icy darkness. Guests were screaming and Caomhnóir were shouting instructions that no one was heeding as we all groped around in the blackness. But the confusion only lasted a few seconds before a strange, misty glow permeated the room, cutting through the dark, but only deepening the cold. And then with a gust of wind like an angry hurricane, dozens of spirits swarmed the room, shattering the windows and upending the furniture as they shrieked and moaned. It was like being caught in a storm—a storm of pure spirit energy, and that energy was not hard to read. I could taste the electricity, the bitterness, the violence of it: the room was alive with the pure, unadulterated fury of the dead.

The cacophony was deafening, but I resisted the urge to cover my ears in my desperation to comprehend their meaning. At first, I could make out only unintelligible chaos; but then individual voices became clear in the din as I focused not only my ears, but my gift upon the swarm. I opened the connection between Hannah, Milo, and me, and let it all flow through, connecting us in our understanding.

You trapped us here!

Fear us at last, you evil, power-hungry hag!

My daughter! Where is my daughter? What have you done with her?

We are free at last!

He hunts us and you do nothing!

You know where they are! You know, and yet you leave them to their fate!

Even more than their words, it was their emotions that overwhelmed us. The connection became almost like the Gateway itself, a flood of sheer human suffering that flowed in a current. Layered behind it, I could feel Hannah and Milo, their fear and their horror at what had descended upon us, all three of us paralyzed by the unutterable force of it.

Luckily for us and everyone else in the room, Savannah Todd was not paralyzed in the slightest. I felt rather than saw her breaking away from our group and moving around us, crouching low. I felt her tug on my arm, and I obeyed the pressure without really thinking about it. I felt Hannah on one side of me, Finn pressed tightly against the other side; and then, suddenly, the cold dissipated and I could breathe.

It was as though we were in a bubble of safety, an eye in the middle of a paranormal storm. I looked around for Savvy and found her with her arms still outstretched, her breath coming in gasps as she stared in surprise at what she had done.

"Bloody hell," she muttered. "So, that's what it's like to Banish properly."

"Not just properly—brilliantly! Well done, Savvy!" Finn gasped, staggering to his feet. Savvy had pulled him within the borders of the circle as well, but the chaos was still raging, the sound oddly muffled and distorted, outside of our strange little fishbowl of safety. Guests were running for cover, trying to flee the room even as doors were slammed shut with invisible hands. Most of the spirits had converged at the front of the room, where Clarissa had been standing, but I couldn't see her, as about half a dozen Caomhnóir had descended upon her, trying to shield her from the onslaught.

"All right, Sav, grab every spare Caomhnóir you can find and start them all Banishing," instructed Finn. "I'm going to check the doors and windows. Clearly, someone's tampered with the Wards, and we need to heal the breach. The rest of you, stay inside this circle, there is nothing you can do, understand?"

For once, I didn't argue with him. I had no Casting bag of my own with me, and I could feel the spirits flinging themselves against the outer edges of our protection. As little as I wanted Finn or Savvy back out there in the chaos, I knew that was their job. I watched them take off across the room, the barrier of our protection shivering oddly like a haze of heat as they left it behind them. I turned to Hannah, whose face was glazed with tears.

"Are you okay? Are you both okay?" I asked, looking back and forth between Hannah and Milo. They both nodded, though their expressions told another story. Milo looked as though he might be sick, if ghosts were capable of such a thing.

"It's so horrible. The... the *rage*," Hannah whispered. I felt more than heard her words.

I reached out and squeezed her hand. "I know."

I turned my attention back to the ongoing calamity. I spotted Savvy just as she Banished a spirit clean across the room. It soared straight through the wall and out of sight, but returned almost immediately. Finn was trying to make his way to the front door, but it was utter pandemonium. The rogue spirits were targeting Caomhnóir right and left, using their manic energy to slam doors shut to prevent anyone from leaving. I watched in shock as a woman who was trying to escape up the staircase was thrust back down by the ghost of a man in tattered, ragged clothes. She tumbled down at least ten stairs and crumpled into a heap at the bottom, unmoving. By the time I'd torn my eyes from her, I'd lost Finn and Savvy in the swarming crowd.

"It's too much."

I turned to Hannah. Her face was set and paper white.

"What did you say?"

"I said it's too much. They can't control them. There's too many of them, and they're so strong!" she said.

"But what do you—"

But Hannah had gotten to her feet, a look of calm determination on her face. "I have to help. I have to Call them."

At the word, my heart contracted, like one of the rogue spirits had shoved a hand right into my chest and squeezed it. Hannah's Caller powers were strong, and she didn't like to use them if she could help it. I opened my mouth to tell her that she didn't need to, that someone else would handle it, but she was looking me steadily in the eye, waiting for me to come to the same conclusion she had reached: there was no one else. She was the last resort.

I nodded once. Milo, beside me, shimmered with a cold, tangible anxiety.

"It'll be okay, sweetness. If I'm in the circle, it shouldn't affect me... much."

Whether he was placating her or telling the truth, I had no idea, but Hannah knew there was no time to debate the matter. She closed her eyes, inhaled deeply, and blew it out again. When she reopened her eyes, she was in that place, the place where the Calling lived, deep inside of her. If I spoke to her now, I don't know if she could even hear me.

She stepped outside the circle and at once the force of spirit activity began to whip her hair around her face. She raised her arms, her fingers outstretched. Then, with another deep breath, she jerked her hands back into fists.

Everything stopped. Every spirit, frozen mid-action. The lights flickered and returned. The very air in the room seemed to have become tethered to the power Hannah now clenched tightly inside her fists. The screams and cries of the guests fell silent or softened to dull whimperings and feeble stirrings. All around the room people were getting to their feet, peeking out from behind furniture, and gingerly probing at injuries. But even this soon stopped as their focus was drawn to the spirits, still as statues hovering all over the room. And then all eyes were drawn, inevitably, to Hannah, as she brought her hands together slowly, drawing the spirits from every corner of the room into a cluster, hovering over the center of the room and giving off their misty light like a ghostly chandelier. Their faces were blank, senseless, their eyes trained expectantly on Hannah, the puppeteer who now held all the strings.

From behind a wall of Caomhnóir, Clarissa MacLeod was watching my sister with a curious expression, and it was a moment before I could recognize the emotion behind it—and when I did, it disturbed me more than anything I'd seen that night: it was deep, bitter envy.

For a moment, the whole room seemed to hold its breath. Then Hannah spoke, and the words were quiet, calm, and almost detached.

"Finn? Where are you?"

"I'm here!" Finn's voice called out from the front door, which he had managed, despite the spirits' opposition, to force open. I could see the sweeping grounds of MacLeod Manor behind him, framed like a landscape painting in the doorway.

"The Wards. Are they intact?" Hannah asked in the same, detached voice.

"This one at the front door's been tampered with. I'm not sure about the others," Finn called back to her. "But if you give me a moment, I can reinstate it."

"All the Wards need to be checked. I can't let them go until I know they can't get back in." There was a tremble in her voice and I knew that she was fighting against the power, controlling it so that it could not control her. It was a very fine line, and my sister could walk it, but not forever.

"Oi! You heard the woman! Caomhnóir, fan out on the perimeter! You know where the Wards are, see to them!" Savvy barked. It was a mark of the seriousness of the situation that not a single Caomhnóir batted an eye at taking orders from her. They scattered, moving for the windows and doors all over the room, some of them jogging out past Finn to check the Wards outside. What seemed like moments later, they had all returned.

"The rest of the Wards are intact!" one of them panted.

"Finn, I'm going to send them off. Once they've crossed the threshold, seal it," Hannah said.

"Ready!" Finn shouted back.

Hannah leaned forward. Every spirit dangling above her leaned forward too, desperate for the thoughts and words that would direct them, for they had none of their own, not when they were under the spell of a Caller. Hannah crooked a single finger and they drew closer. The order, when she gave it, was a whisper.

"Go."

And with a force like an explosion, they went—shooting out the open door like projectiles into the waiting night. With a flourish and a last slash of chalk upon the floor, Finn repaired the Ward and, for good measure, slammed the door behind them.

Hannah's body sagged. She dropped her hands to her sides, and she began to tremble violently. I scrambled to my feet and out of the circle and reached her just in time for her to sag against me like she'd just run a marathon.

"Are you all right?" I asked her, taking her face between my hands and tilting it up so that I could look into her eyes. As I watched them, the curious distance vanished—the hold of her power—and they sparked again with the familiar warm glow. She smiled weakly and I smiled back.

"I'm okay," she said. "I just... there were a lot of them and they were...intense."

"Nothing my badass sister couldn't handle," I murmured into her ear as I gave her a hug.

But she pulled away from me, craning her neck to look over my shoulder. "Milo?" she called, and her voice cracked.

"I'm here, sweetness, all is well," Milo said, drifting over from the circle. "You directed your energy like a boss bitch. Seriously, barely a twinge."

Hannah's face broke into a relieved smile. "Just like I planned," she replied.

There was a long, drawn out sigh from behind me, and I turned to see Maeve peeling herself away from the wall behind me, looking frankly bored.

"Well, I can't imagine anything my mother might have to say will be nearly that interesting. I think I'll pop up to bed," she drawled. And then, draining her champagne flute in a single go, handed it to a dazed-looking Caomhnóir and slunk up the stairs, not bothering to stifle a rather exaggerated yawn.

7

THE GHOST WALK

"WELL. THAT DIDN'T GO QUITE AS PLANNED, DID IT?"
Milo's question hung like a Called spirit in the heavy atmosphere of the car as it trundled its way back through the streets of Edinburgh to our hotel. No one spoke the answer out loud, but from the slightly dazed expression on every face, we were all thinking the same thing.

No. No, it sure as hell hadn't.

Someone had sabotaged the welcome reception, that much was absolutely certain, though Clarissa MacLeod seemed unable to accept it. Despite a reputation for being unflappable in nearly every situation, she could not hide her shock and fury. As soon as the spirits had been ousted and the Wards restored, she'd risen from the protective circle of her Caomhnóir like an avenging fury, eyes flashing as she demanded shrilly for the grounds to be searched and the guests questioned. Wishing to remain in her good graces, Finn and Savvy had offered their assistance with this process, handing back over the reins they'd so swiftly taken up upon the onset of the crisis, and instead taking orders from the resident head of the Clan Rìoghalachd Caomhnóir, a heavily muscled cube of a man named Rory. Clarissa had stood at her podium, fists clenched, lips white and pressed together while the investigation proceeded, still as a statue and just as cold. It was clear from her expression that this breach of the manor was beyond her comprehension. Someone had defied her. Publicly humiliated her. And all I could think as I watched the fire gleam in her eyes was that I was extremely glad it hadn't been me.

I glanced over at Hannah. She was staring out the car window, her face pale and drawn. It was bad enough she'd had to use her power as a Caller—a power she utterly despised—but she'd also had to use it in front of an audience who already regarded her with a mixture of distrust and awe. Now, after such a public and unfiltered display of what she could do, I was sure she felt raw and exposed. I could also tell that she didn't want to talk about it, so I just put my hand in hers and squeezed.

After she had sent the spirits forth from the manor, she'd asked to speak to Clarissa alone. They had a whispered conversation in the corner of the room, a conversation that left Hannah looking solemn and Clarissa somewhat resentful. But it wasn't until now, as she looked out the window of the car, that she told us what had passed between them.

"While we were waiting for the Wards to be fortified, I was able to get a read on the energy of the spirits that attacked us," she said into the quiet. Every head turned to look at her. "All of those spirits had been Caged."

Milo let out a soft gasp. Finn shook his head, his expression one of disgust.

Caging was a controversial Durupinen practice that involved binding a spirit so that they could not communicate or harm others. On the one hand, if used very temporarily, it could prevent a spirit from harassing or harming living people. However, if abused, it could leave spirits in a state of helpless, tortured silence until it was removed. Years ago, we had seen just how inhumane Caging could be when we'd met and then freed the Silent Child.

"How did you know?" I asked finally.

"It was written in their rage," Hannah said in a voice little more than a whisper. "I could read it like a book in the energy they were giving off. But Clarissa confirmed it when I spoke to her."

"I could feel it, too," Milo added.

"It certainly explains the power of their energy," Finn said. He had his hands clasped together, his elbows resting on his knees, his head hanging down. "It's like water building up against a dam. When the dam finally breaks…"

His voice trailed away with a rueful shake of his head, but he didn't need to finish the sentence. We'd all experienced the breaking of the dam in all its terrifying power.

"What had they been Caged for?" Savvy asked. "And for how long?"

"I don't know," Hannah said. "I couldn't risk loosening my hold on them or delaying their expulsion to find out."

"Didn't you ask Clarissa? Surely she must have an explanation," I said.

Hannah shook her head. "I did ask her, but she wouldn't tell me. She just said that the clan had a right to protect itself. I didn't want to press the matter, in case it seemed like I was questioning her authority."

"I could go back there tonight," Milo said suddenly. "See if I can track any of them down."

Hannah finally tore her eyes from the window. "Would you? I didn't want to ask, I know how hostile they were, but—"

"Oh, I think that hostility was pretty specifically directed," Milo said, raising his eyebrows. "As I'm neither alive nor a member of Clan Rìoghalachd, I think I'll be fine."

I thought back to the words I'd heard amidst the din. Some of them made sense now, knowing that spirits had been Caged:

You trapped us here!

Fear us at last, you evil, power-hungry hag!

We are free at last!

But then hadn't there been other voices in the fray? Hadn't I heard a woman calling for her daughter? And someone else saying something about being hunted? There was definitely more to this attack than Caging could explain. The sooner Milo could find those spirits, the better. If Clan Rìoghalachd saw fit to Cage them once, they would likely do so again as soon as they were able, and then we'd never get the chance to question them.

"I think it's a good idea," I said. "As long as you're careful, Milo."

Milo rolled his eyes. "Obviously. I'm nothing if not careful."

And blowing a kiss to each of us in turn, he vanished from the car.

"What else did Clarissa say to you?" Finn asked Hannah after Milo had shimmered from sight. "Anything that might shed some light on who those spirits were, or who freed them?"

Hannah shook her head, biting her lip. "When I asked her if we could help her identify who was responsible, she just said that she would be dealing with that personally. Then she said, 'It could only be one of us.'"

"One of us as in *us*?" I asked, pointing my finger around the car.

Hannah shook her head. "No, I think she was talking about Clan Rìogha-lachd. She thinks it's an inside job."

"That would make sense," I said. "It would take insider knowledge to even know about those Caged spirits, and then of course, the culprit would need access to the Wards in order to tamper with them."

"Bit odd to unleash a horde of ghosts hellbent on destroying your own clan," Savvy said. "I mean, you'd be putting yourself in danger, wouldn't you?"

"Maybe putting yourself in a bit of danger is worth it, if it means humiliating someone you hate," I said. The sentiment may have been generalized, but I was thinking of someone very specific. My thoughts kept returning to Maeve MacLeod. Not only had she and her mother had a very contentious argument just before all hell broke loose, but her reaction after it was all over was definitely suspicious. Of course, I hadn't noticed what she was doing or saying while the chaos reigned, having been slightly distracted by the murderously angry horde of ghosts; but afterward, when the dust had settled, she'd made a damn good show of seeming not only unbothered, but downright bored by the proceedings. If she had been faking her apathy, she was a damn good actress.

"Either way, we are going to have to tread very carefully indeed," Finn said, and his voice had that brooding quality it always got when he contemplated any dangerous situation. "It was no coincidence that those spirits were unleashed while we were there. We were either the targets, or the intended audience. Either way, we will need to be on our guard. This may not be an isolated incident."

"If we were the targets, wouldn't the spirits have gone for us, instead of Clarissa?" Hannah asked.

"They may have done, if it hadn't been for Savvy's quick Casting work," Finn said. He looked over at Savvy and smiled at her. She merely shrugged.

"What can I say, you trained me well, guv."

By this time, we'd pulled up in front of The Witchery. We thanked the driver, and I pulled out my phone to text Pippa to let her know that we'd arrived at the hotel, as she'd requested.

Arrived safe and sound. Going to get some sleep. I typed.

The answering dots began to bounce in reply almost immediately. *I am glad to hear it. You'll forgive me, but I cannot take you to the Geatgrima tonight. Too much to handle here at the manor, and I can't leave Clarissa. Will meet you at break-fast in the morning at the hotel. Let's say 9?*

I texted back a thumbs up, grateful she hadn't said something ludicrous like 6 AM—she seemed like she was probably one of those unbearably cheerful and productive morning people who had already worked out, show-ered, dressed, and sent a dozen emails before I'd managed to drag my ass out of bed. I told the others about the change in plans as we headed down the hallway to our rooms. Savvy took the news cheerily enough and headed off to bed, but Hannah looked worried.

"That's another night spirits are going to be unprotected at that Geatgri-ma," she said, biting her lip.

I placed a hand on her shoulder. "I know, but I'm not sure what else we can do. We don't even know where it is, and even if we could find it, I don't think it would be a good idea to visit it without a member of Clan Rìoghalachd there."

Hannah nodded her agreement, though she looked less than happy about it, and slumped off to her room, looking defeated. Finn and I closed our door behind us and I flopped into a chair, pulling my shoes off with a groan.

"Well, if that was our welcome to Edinburgh, I'll be interested to see what else Clan Rìoghalachd has up its sleeve," I said dryly.

Finn made a sound that was half grunt, half humorless chuckle, and then grabbed his Casting bag. "If we're staying here tonight, I'm making sure it's been Warded properly," he said, and stumped back out into the hallway.

I changed, washed the makeup off my face, and crawled into bed, deter-mined to wait up for him until he had finished; but the next thing I knew, the exhaustion of the day hit me like a bus, and I never even heard him come back in.

～

The next morning, I was awakened by a very rude beam of sunlight that snuck its way between the curtains and struck me directly in the face. Yawning, I went to the window to close the gap, but found myself opening the curtains wider to see the city shrouded in a blanket of early morning fog—the golden glow of the rising sun slashing through it here and there with long, straight, shining beams that lit the cobbles and warmed the stone faces of the stately old buildings. It was so beautiful that I nearly forgot about the events of the previous night as I watched the morning rouse the sleepy city. But then I heard my alarm go off, and the reality of it all came flooding back.

The Caged spirits...

The faulty Wards...

The look on Clarissa MacLeod's face as her perfectly orchestrated night fell to tatters around her...

I glanced at the place in the bed where Finn ought to be, and found a note on the pillow instead.

Gone for a run. Meet you at breakfast. xx

I rolled my eyes. "Gone for a run" was overprotective Caomhnóir code for "doing a sweep of the perimeter," and I bloody well knew it. Still, after the events of the previous night, I was grateful he was being thorough. If Clarissa's security had been tampered with, I was sure that we, as her guests, were also vulnerable.

I showered, dressed, and threw my wet hair up into a messy knot on the top of my head before heading down to breakfast. The restaurant in the hotel was just as sumptuously decorated as the rest of the rooms, and I felt like a walking insult to the place as I settled into a richly upholstered chair by the window. I'd just ordered a pot of coffee when Hannah appeared in the doorway. She stopped short when she saw me at the table.

"You're... early?" she asked blankly.

I laughed. "Stranger things have happened."

"Not many," she replied, smiling gently as she slid into the chair opposite. "Have you seen anyone else yet?"

I shook my head. "Finn's out on a reconnaissance jog, and I don't think Savvy's awake yet. Have you seen Milo?"

"No, but he said he'd meet us here this morning," Hannah said, pouring herself a cup of coffee as well. "I almost reached out to him through the connection, but I didn't want to interrupt if he was—"

Hannah stopped speaking at that moment, and I followed her gaze. Pippa was walking in the door to the restaurant, looking as meticulously groomed and organized as ever, though her makeup couldn't quite hide the dark circles under her eyes, nor the general pallor of her complexion;. She was exhausted, even if she was trying to hide it.

"Rough night?" I asked her as she arrived at our table. I pulled a chair out for her and she slid into it.

"Quite," she replied, stacking a file folder, a planner, and her phone in a neat little pile beside her plate. "I trust you all slept well? No trouble here?"

"Everything was fine, thanks," I told her, and she breathed a quiet but fervent sigh of relief.

"Clarissa has asked me to extend her apologies again for the unfortunate events of last night, but also wishes me to reassure you that all has been restored to normalcy," Pippa said.

"Does that mean you know who was responsible for the breach last night?" I asked.

Pippa's carefully professional expression faltered for just a moment. "We're still investigating the matter," she said. "But I am confident we will have an answer soon."

Hannah and I glanced at each other, and I didn't need the connection to know what she was thinking: they had no idea who the culprit was.

If Pippa noticed our silent exchange, she didn't let on. Instead, she continued, "And we have rescheduled your trip to the Geatgrima for tonight. A car will arrive here at 1:30 AM to take us over to the site, and then your investigation can formally begin."

"Okay, that's great," I told her. It was hard to believe that we hadn't even begun the investigation yet—so much had already happened.

"You said 'us,'" Hannah pointed out. "Does that mean you'll be accompanying us to the site of the Geatgrima?"

"Yes," Pippa said, "along with two of our own Caomhnóir. After last night, doubling up security seemed... well, prudent."

"It certainly can't hurt," I said.

Pippa nodded briskly. "Precisely." She rose from her chair. "Well, that's all I really needed to tell you. Unless you need anything else from me, I'll just be—"

"Hang on, aren't you staying for breakfast?" I asked.

Pippa blinked, as though it had never occurred to her to stay still long enough to eat an entire meal. "Oh, thank you very much, but I can't. Lots to do today. Oh, and here," she added, placing a neat stack of tourist brochures on the table. "Since you won't be needed until tonight, we'd like to encourage you to explore the city. Here is some information about the more popular attractions and sights. I'm sure you'll find plenty to amuse yourselves, and please remember to expense them to the MacLeods." And with a wave, Pippa was gone again, her phone to her ear before she'd even left the restaurant.

"Thank GUCCI, I thought she'd never leave," came a voice from beside me, and I barely managed not to yelp in surprise. Milo materialized in the chair Pippa had just vacated, looking like he could use a cup of coffee himself.

"There you are, I was starting to worry!" Hannah said, frowning in a motherly way. "Where have you been?"

Milo rolled his eyes. "Back at MacLeod Manor, where else?"

"Why did you wait for Pippa to leave?" I asked him, as I picked up the breakfast menu and began perusing it. My stomach was starting to contribute a little too loudly to the conversation.

"I don't think Clan Rìoghalachd needs to know that I've been snooping around, do you?" Milo asked. "I don't think they'd appreciate it."

"What makes you say that?" Hannah asked.

"Well, to start with, they've got that place locked down like a prison now. I couldn't even get close to the house. They've got new protective circles and Wards set up everywhere, not to mention a virtual army of Caomhnóir swarming all over the place."

"Well, that's not surprising. They'll want to keep the hostile spirits as far from the family as possible," I said.

"Yes, but I also overheard the Caomhnóir getting their orders at shift change this morning. They've been instructed not to let you onto the grounds without prior authorization from Clarissa herself. They were even given photos of you to study."

"Hang on," I said indignantly. "Are you saying they think *we're* somehow responsible?"

"But... but that's impossible!" Hannah gasped. "We'd never been to the manor before last night! When were we supposed to have tampered with Wards, never mind find and Uncage spirits! And anyway, we're the ones who helped end the attack!"

"Maybe they think you staged the attack just to be able to publicly come to the rescue?" Milo suggested.

"To what end?" Hannah asked.

"I didn't say it was logical," Milo said with a shrug. "I'm just telling you what I found out."

"Well, is there anything else, aside from ridiculous conspiracy theories?" I asked, jumping in before Hannah could continue to argue. "Were you able to find out anything at all?"

"Not much. I couldn't find any of the attacking spirits still on the grounds, and the spirits who inhabit the place are a very snooty lot, completely loyal to the clan. Every time I found one, they demanded I leave at once, that I was trespassing, and that they would alert the Caomhnóir to my presence if I didn't. They wouldn't even let me explain who I was or why I was there in the first place. They'd closed ranks, probably on strict orders from Clarissa, and didn't want to be seen speaking to me."

I sighed, frustrated. "Well, thanks for trying, Milo. I'm sorry you wasted your night."

Milo sat up straighter. "Hang on, I'm not finished yet!"

I frowned. "I thought you said you didn't find anything."

"I said I didn't find *much*," Milo corrected me. "You didn't let me finish. I was getting to that part."

"Why didn't you just lead with that part?" I asked.

Milo pouted. "Well, that's not very dramatic, is it? I'm building up to the climax of my story; otherwise, how will you be impressed with my pluck and determination?"

I rolled my eyes just as the server approached the table. Hannah and I both studiously ignored Milo while we placed our breakfast order, and waited for her to leave before turning back to him.

"Okay, Milo," I said with a sigh. "Please proceed to the climax."

Milo leaned forward, lowering his voice theatrically. "Well, I was just about to give up and leave for the night when I came across a ghost out near one of the garden sheds, a former chambermaid. At first, she gave me the same spiel as the others, but then I told her I was visiting from Fairhaven, and suddenly she couldn't stop talking. Turns out she had a sister who worked there, and she was desperate to know if she'd Crossed or if she was still on the grounds there. I made a big deal about promising to inquire after her when I got back, and so she let her guard down a bit."

He paused, looking a bit like a cat expecting a treat and a pat.

"Go on," I said impatiently.

Milo's expectant expression sagged into a frown. "Anyway, she told me that while she had never seen most of those spirits before, several of them were familiar because they'd been Caged inside the manor itself, some of them for decades. They'd been kept in a kind of dungeon in the basement, sentenced to Caging because they refused to stop harassing the family, and also refused to Cross."

"I said that, didn't I!" Hannah said, slapping her hand down on the table in triumph. "I knew their energy was too strong! Caging was the only explanation that made sense!"

"My guess is, when the Wards were tampered with to let those Caged spirits into the manor, the other spirits came with them—like walking right through an open door," Milo said.

"But who were the others, and why were they so angry?" I asked.

Milo shook his head. "Alas, my new friend Alice the chambermaid did not know."

"Well, we definitely know more than we did before," I said. "Good work, Milo."

Hannah sighed. "So, if the MacLeods won't let us help at the manor, and we can't get to the Geatgrima until tonight, what are we going to do all day?"

I smiled and tapped the pile of brochures from Pippa. "Let's go be tourists," I said.

"There's a whiskey museum. A bloody museum. Of whiskey. GOD I love this city!" Savvy announced to the entire Royal Mile at the top of her lungs. Several raucous cheers from passersby answered her.

"I take it you've had fun sightseeing, then," I said with a laugh.

"Absolutely brilliant," Savvy said. "Mind you, it could have been a Tesco's and a crappy pub, and I still would have thrown a bloody parade just to be out of that damn castle."

"You hear that, Finn?" I said, turning to him. "Sign Savvy up for all hauntings at Tesco's and crappy pubs."

"Duly noted," Finn replied, pulling a tiny grubby notebook from his back pocket, and pretending to make a note of it. Sav just chuckled good-naturedly and dug into her chips.

We were sitting at a table outside a cafe, eating a late lunch and resting our feet after walking what had to be miles. We'd toured Edinburgh Castle, wandered the Palace of Holyroodhouse, taken in the sights at the National

Museum of Scotland, and drifted through the vibrant displays at the Royal Botanic Gardens. I hadn't always loved exploring new places, but I'd always been good at it—a skill I'd reluctantly acquired during the many years my mother had dragged me around the country in her quest to escape who we really were. Now that I was wandering on my own terms, however, I loved getting lost and then finding myself again in a new city. Pippa had left us with a whole stack of maps, but we'd left them abandoned on the front hall table in the hotel for someone else to pick up and use. I preferred the 'wander-around-until-you-find-cool-stuff' method of tourism. Besides the major attractions we'd managed to visit, we'd also found a cafe that served one of the best sandwiches I'd ever eaten, a used bookstore that swallowed us up in dusty fascination for over an hour, and an amazing thrift shop that we left with two bags full of finds but without Milo, who announced he would be haunting the place permanently and to forward all his mail.

We finished our lunch and slipped down an alleyway to the Royal Mile again. We were just debating whether to enter a shop dedicated to traditional wool and plaid clothing when Savvy hailed us over.

"What do you suppose that is, then?" she asked, hooking a thumb over her shoulder at a knot of people gathered on the corner of the block, clustered around two men in anachronistic ensembles that made them look like extras in a low-budget production of Great Expectations.

"Next tour begins in five minutes, gather 'round and hear the dark and bloody history of Edinburgh!" the taller of the men called to passersby in a plummy, theatrical voice.

"What kind of tour is that, do you reckon?" Savvy asked.

"A walking one, and my feet are killing me," I said. "So I think I'll take a pass on—"

But at that moment the tall man shifted over to sell a ticket to a patron and I spotted the sign posted on the wall behind him. It read: Experience Edinburgh's Original Ghost Walk! Explore the city's haunted history!

"Oh, you have *got* to be kidding me," I snorted, and turned back to Savvy. "It's one of those ghost tours."

"Ah, class! I love those things. Who wants to do it with me?" Savvy said, perking up at once and thrusting her hand eagerly into her bag for her wallet.

I hoisted an eyebrow at her. "Seriously? Don't you get enough ghosts in your everyday life without listening to some con artist spout off a bunch of legends and ghost stories that almost definitely never happened?"

"Nah, it's brilliant! Who doesn't love a good ghost story, even if you basically live in one? Jolly good fun, listening to someone who's never seen a ghost before try to scare the local tourists. Even better when a ghost turns up, like now."

I swallowed my skeptical retort. "A ghost?"

"Yeah, didn't you notice? Only one of them tour guides is breathing, mate."

Startled, I craned my neck to catch another glimpse of the tour guides. Sure enough, now that I was on the alert for it, I felt the spirit energy of the shorter, stouter of the two men—the way his outline had the faintest of shimmers, the way the patrons looked right past him. The crowd had masked it before, but now I saw him for exactly what he was.

"Come on, it'll be a lark!" Savvy said, pulling on my sleeve like a kid begging for sweets in the checkout line. "Go on."

I looked at Hannah, who shrugged. "I'm game if you are. Finn?"

"And as I can't allow you to go on a highly spooky, possibly dangerous tour without proper security, you can count me in," Finn said very seriously. "Did you even read the sign properly? 'Warning: May cause terror and sleepless nights. Join at your own risk.' I would be derelict in my duties if I let you attend on your own, any of you."

I slumped, defeated. "Okay, fine. Let's do the stupid ghost tour."

"I'll get the tickets!" Savvy crowed, and began shouldering her way through the little crowd so that she could reach the tour guide. The rest of us joined the back of the group.

"Excellent, excellent, madam, I thank you for your patronage, and here are your tickets. That's five pounds apiece," the living tour guide simpered as he dug in his pockets for change.

His deceased counterpart snorted loudly. "Still scrounging in your pockets like an amateur, Lawrence? Never mind the cash box with the carrying strap sitting UNTOUCHED in that box upstairs that I bought for us, but which you refused to use because it 'ruined the effect of the costumes.'" He punctuated the criticism with highly exaggerated air quotes.

Lawrence, hearing none of this, was counting out change from a little heap of coins in his hand. A ten pence piece dropped with a tinkling sound on the cobblestones and rolled away. Lawrence seemed to decide it wasn't worth hunting for, and let it go.

"Incompetent," the spirit tour guide grumbled. I shifted to the left and caught sight of the name tag on his waistcoat. His name was Terry.

"The time to begin our adventure approaches!" Lawrence fumbled with a pocket watch, flipped it open, and frowned at the face. Then he held it up to his ear, swore under his breath, and shoved it back into his pocket. Then he pulled out a smartphone, consulted the time, and hastily hid it back in his trouser pocket. "Yes, gather around, for the witching hour approaches!"

The crowd shuffled awkwardly forward, even as Terry sneered, "That's three o'clock in the morning, not the afternoon, you absolute git."

Savvy's expression was positively gleeful as she munched on the remainder of her chips. Apparently, this was already as entertaining as she'd hoped.

"Gather round, ye of stout spirit, and together we shall peer into the deepest, darkest depths of human folly. Every city is haunted by its past. Every city has its ghosts. But nowhere is the past so alive, and the ghosts so present, as here in the ancient streets of Edinburgh." Lawrence's voice boomed out over the crowd of tourists, who were all exchanging grins, skeptical smirks, and, here and there, that dubious look that clearly said, "Uh-oh, what the hell have I gotten myself into?"

"Is this going to give me nightmares? Why did I let you talk me into this, Nancy?" one middle-aged woman with a Welsh accent and a fanny pack whispered to her companion.

"Ah, don't be such a spoilsport, Mary, it'll be a laugh!" the apple-cheeked Nancy whispered back, squeezing Mary's arm as though to release some of her own unbearable excitement.

"I must ask you all to keep close—very close to me, and not to stray from the path. It is not safe to wander into dark corners or through the swinging gates of a graveyard unaccompanied," Lawrence continued. Mary and Nancy huddled together, shivering deliciously.

"They could get closer to you if you'd stop visiting the pub between tour groups," Terry snapped during what was clearly an attempt at a dramatic pause on Lawrence's part. "You smell like a walking distillery."

Savvy smothered a snort of laughter and Terry gave her a curious look. I nudged her and she nodded to me, trying to straighten her face. Spirits didn't sense our presence as easily now that the Gateway had been removed from our blood, but it still wasn't wise to draw attention to ourselves.

"As we walk, you shall hear about grisly crimes, tragic demises, and supernatural events. Do not let yourselves be comforted by the thought that it is all in the past. In the streets of Edinburgh by moonlight, the past is the present. Be wary, and stay together," Lawrence told us.

"The sun hasn't even set yet. My God, you are going to run this venture into the ground through sheer incompetence," Terry said through gritted teeth as the group began its shuffling progress up the road.

The tour took us off the mile to a place called Greyfriars Kirkyard, where we listened to Lawrence tell the tale of Greyfriars Bobby, a little dog who guarded his master's grave for fourteen years before dying himself. He pointed out a little statue of a dog, its nose rubbed bright and shiny by the hands of many a tourist who simply couldn't resist booping his little snoot.

"And so, as we wander the graves, be on the lookout for a little sniff near your feet, or a soft brushing against your legs. It just might be wee Bobby, here to make sure you pay your respects properly."

"Oh God in heaven," Mary whispered, turning in a complete circle as though sure the little dog was about to nip at her ankles.

"That's so sad," Hannah whispered, looking at the little statue with a wistful expression.

Terry, meanwhile, was fact-checking Lawrence in real time, berating him all the way through the graveyard for mixing up dates and mispronouncing names on the cracked and faded headstones, finally pronouncing that he was "an embarrassment to tour guides everywhere and ought to be made to hang up his boots."

The tour took us through some closes, which we learned from Lawrence were like little covered alleyways that connected the bigger thoroughfares and which, also according to Lawrence, were the scenes of brutal killings and terrible tragedies. Still, despite his insistence that the city was peopled with nearly as many ghosts as living folk, Terry was the only spirit we saw in any of the so-called haunted locations. In one of these closes, Lawrence paused, clearing his throat fussily.

"Now, I've no doubt that you all have heard of London's infamous Jack the Ripper?"

Everyone nodded or murmured their confirmation.

"Well, not to be outdone by our neighbors to the South, Edinburgh once had its own serial killer, even more prolific than the Ripper and just as slippery, for he, too, was never caught."

"Oh no," Mary squeaked.

"Ah, keep your knickers on, Mary, that was hundreds of years ago," Nancy whispered back.

"Indeed it was," Lawrence boomed, making everyone jump. "In fact, Edinburgh's most prolific serial killer predates the more famous Jack the Ripper by more than a century! While Jack the Ripper terrorized the city of London for a summer in 1878—"

"1888, you twit," Terry growled.

"—this killer stalked the streets of Edinburgh for several years, starting in 1756 until 1760, when he seemed to have simply vanished. And as he was never caught, also like Jack the Ripper, he is known not by his real name, but only as," he dropped his voice dramatically to a stage whisper, "*The Collector.*"

He let the silence stretch horribly before he continued, clearly enjoying the effect he was having on his captive audience.

"We stand now on the site where his very first victim was found, a local washing woman by the name of Nellie McBride. She was found in the wee small hours of the morning by some children. She'd been hit over the head and then strangled with a length of brightly colored silk. That silk became The Collector's calling card."

"Calling card?" a teenage boy repeated, looking mystified.

"It was like a clue linking the victims to the killer," Lawrence explained. "It let the local authorities know they were looking for a single man responsible for all those deaths."

"Or a woman," a freckled young woman piped up.

"Pardon me?" Lawrence asked.

"Well, you said he was never caught," she said, lifting her chin and her voice now that she seemed to have everyone's attention. "So, if they never caught him, they don't know that it was a man, do they? It might have been a woman."

"I suppose it is possible," Lawrence allowed, though his tone was indulgent to the point of condescension, "but evidence suggests otherwise. Among the records there are documented eyewitness statements which claim to have seen a man fleeing the scene of several of the killings; and in the absence of an arrest and true identification, history has come to take these statements as proof enough that The Collector was indeed a man."

The young woman 'humph-ed' as though anecdotal evidence from the 1700s hardly excused the possibility of misogyny, but she didn't argue any further.

"Now I'm sure you are all wondering how The Collector got his name," Lawrence said. "And the answer, I am sorry to say, is quite disturbing."

"You're not sorry in the least, you ghoul," Terry said, rolling his eyes. "And frankly, your fixation on this case is what's disturbing."

I caught Hannah's eye and we traded smirks. It was a bit rich for a man who'd made his money off ghost tours to call someone else a ghoul, but I guess even being dead didn't automatically give a person proper perspective, even if it seemed like it was the one thing that should.

"You see, The Collector always took something from his victims, an object that was never recovered. A ring here, a necklace there, once a boot, another time, a hair ribbon. Once, in the absence of anything of value, he took a lock of hair. The grisly collection of souvenirs he must surely have amassed is the inspiration behind his name."

"How many people did he bump off?" asked a man in a green baseball cap.

"Throughout his reign of terror, he is believed to have been responsible for more than a hundred murders in all, each taking place at night, and always in one of the closes. Many of his victims still haunt the sites of their tragic demises."

"Hate to burst that bubble, Lawrence, but they bloody well do not, and I should know," Terry barked.

"Here in this Close, for example, people have reported hearing a woman's voice and feeling tugs upon their clothing. Many believe it is the spirit of Nellie McBride, desperate to communicate to the world the identity of her murderer."

"And they would be wrong," Terry snapped. "It's only Dolores Maguire who died in the flat over the chippy last year, and all she ever tells anyone is that if they see her cheating numpty of a husband, to send him her way, as she's got a few choice things to say to him before she Crosses over."

Savvy had to pull her hood down over her face to muffle her laughter, but earned herself a disgruntled, sidelong glance from Lawrence.

"A skeptic, I take it," he said.

"Not... not exactly," Savvy said, still trying desperately to get her face and voice back under control.

"Well, if you will permit me to quote Shakespeare, 'There is more in heaven and earth, Horatio, than are dreamt of in your philosophy.' I encourage you to open your mind, young lady, to the possibility of the unseen world, for only then will you truly understand the wonders of life... and of death."

"Right, sorry. Yeah. Will do, mate. Carry on, then," Savvy said. She had managed to wrestle her face into a solemn expression, though there was a muscle jumping in her jaw.

I dropped my gaze as well, before I got myself into the same trouble with the now thoroughly offended Lawrence, though it didn't help when Terry's somewhat hollow voice muttered from somewhere behind me, "Wonders my arse."

"And so, as you traverse our fair city, mind yourself in the dark corners and sheltered solitude of the closes like this one; and if you feel a breath upon your neck, or enterprising fingers snatching at your scarf, it may just be The Collector, still stalking the city, still looking for victims and objects to collect."

We continued the tour, the woman called Mary fairly hysterical until we emerged out of the Closes and onto the wide open thoroughfare of the Royal Mile. The tour continued after that, but Mary grabbed Nancy by the hand and dragged her away, muttering furiously about how she was never allowed to plan a trip again, and that she could start making it up to her by buying her a stiff drink.

Terry, meanwhile, was practically apoplectic with rage, having spotted a flask sticking out of Lawrence's pocket. It was hard to hear much of what Lawrence said as we worked our way up the Royal Mile toward the castle, because Terry was now ranting about customer complaints and loss of license through the city if Lawrence didn't clean up his act. I started to wonder if Lawrence couldn't sense Terry in some way. He seemed to be getting flustered, losing his train of thought and flinching at odd moments. He was unable to answer several questions, and at one point looked like he wasn't sure which street to take to their next haunted location, like he'd forgotten the way. It was with a distinct sigh of relief that he deposited us at the gates of Edinburgh Castle, insisting that the castle itself was perhaps the most haunted location of all. Then he shuffled away back down the mile, looking slightly defeated, with

Terry still stalking along behind him, shouting about the importance of a strong social media presence.

I turned to Savvy. "You were right, that was surprisingly entertaining," I said.

"Told ya!" Savvy said, wiping tears of mirth from her eyes.

"Do you think we should follow him? Tell him about Terry?" Hannah asked.

"Or try to convince Terry to stop haunting the poor bloke and Cross already?" Finn added, though he too looked amused.

"I don't think we should be encouraging any spirits to Cross until we know the Geatgrima is safe," I said, which wiped the smile from every face and reminded us why we were here to begin with. I looked at my watch. It was after five o'clock now. Soon night would fall on Edinburgh, and we would make our way to the Geatgrima. The Léarscáil determined this place was the biggest threat in the spirit world, and tonight we would find out why.

8

THE SCREAMING

THE PLEASANT DISTRACTION OF OUR TOURIST ESCAPADES melted away slowly over the course of the evening like one of Clarissa's ice sculptures, dripping and seeping, leaving ample room for the anxiety to grow and expand. By the time we were heading down to meet the car, I was practically bouncing with nervous anticipation about what might be waiting for us at the site of the Geatgrima.

Finn had half-heartedly suggested we try to get a few hours of sleep beforehand, but I just lay there, staring at the ceiling, nerves jangling, while Finn kept sliding off the bed to pace the room, recheck the contents of his Casting bag, and peer repeatedly through the curtains at the window like an edgy cop on a stakeout.

"What are you looking for, exactly?" I asked him the fifth time he did this.

"I have no idea," he said with a sigh, twitching the curtains closed again. But a few minutes later he was doing it again.

Finally, I heard the beeping alarm on Finn's watch.

"It's time," he said.

"Thank God," I muttered, rolling off the bed and pulling on my boots.

Savvy, Hannah, and Milo were already waiting downstairs by the front desk, Savvy yawning broadly—she'd obviously had no trouble getting a nap in.

"Ready?" Hannah asked us all.

Pippa was sitting shotgun as we all piled into the back of the car, a sleek SUV this time rather than the limo—Savvy looked a bit disappointed, but took it in stride. Pippa was dressed more casually than we'd seen her so far, but she still somehow managed to make a pair of jeans, a windbreaker, and a pair of running shoes look almost formal.

We'd only been driving a couple of minutes when we stopped. "Here we are," she said, reaching to unfasten her seatbelt.

"We're here already? What did we drive, three blocks?" I asked with a laugh.

"I suppose so. More like four and a half. Why?" Pippa asked, looking at me curiously.

"Nothing, it's just... you really didn't need to go to all the trouble of the car and driver and everything. We could have just walked."

Pippa looked confused, as though it would never occur to her to walk a few blocks when a car could get her there quicker. "I suppose," she allowed. "Although the car is more efficient."

Savvy was shaking her head. "Posh people," she muttered under her breath.

We emerged from the SUV and grouped together on the pavement while Pippa gave instructions to the driver to wait for us. Then she joined us and gestured ahead.

"Please follow me," she said, and walked right up the steps of a sandstone building, pausing at the front door.

"We're going inside?" Hannah asked, surprise written all over her face.

"Oh yes," Pippa replied. Then, seeing our collective confusion she said, "Clan Rìoghalachd owns this entire block of buildings. It's publicly known these days as the Canongate Collective. They constructed them centuries ago, to protect and conceal the location of the Gateway. They lease out the flats, the offices, and the shopfronts to businesses they hold financial interests in. It keeps it all in the family, and ensures the continued protection for the Geatgrima."

I was sure that we'd be driven out to the craggy mountainsides on the outskirts of the city, or to some remote hill on the sweeping highlands, some-place deserted and remote. Never had I imagined the Geatgrima existing in the midst of all this modern-day hustle and bustle. Something about the juxtaposition of those two things felt wrong to me; but of course, the Geatgrimas existed where the veil between the worlds was thin, and always had. If a city grew up around that same place, it wasn't as though the Geatgrima could be picked up and moved. And so it had to be protected instead—hidden in plain sight from the generations of souls who would one day be drawn to it at last.

We waited while Pippa unlocked the door, using a ring with no fewer than twenty different keys on it, and then followed her inside. The foyer of the building was sleek and modern with white walls and blonde woodwork, and glossy, understated furniture. We passed several frosted glass doors as we followed the hallway to the back of the building. I glanced at each in turn and noted a lawyer's office, an interior design studio, and a realty company. On many of them, the MacLeod name was prominently displayed.

The hallway ended at a plain white door, which Pippa used a second key from her ring to open. The door led to a staircase descending into a dimly lit basement. Here, at last, the age of the building was apparent. The gleaming woodwork and pristine white walls gave way to a narrow passage with rough-hewn stone walls with gas lamps attached by metal brackets. This hallway had doors along it as well, but no minimalist boutiques or luxury goods suppliers made their homes on this level. The doors were all heavy wooden things, with rusted iron hardware and gaping keyholes like tiny open mouths. The smell of the place assaulted the nose—a heavy scent that combined the tang of rusting metal and the deep musky odor of damp earth. Beside me, Milo shuddered.

"You okay?" I whispered to him.

"Is it too ridiculous for a literal ghost to say that this place gives me the creeps?" he asked.

I snorted. "Oh, it is absolutely ridiculous, but in this particular case, I'll allow it," I said. He was right. There was an almost oppressive feeling in the dank basement hallway, like a hundred invisible bodies pressing in on me on the world's creepiest subway car. The air was somehow at once damp and alive with what felt like static electricity. I felt jumpy and confined and suddenly desperate for fresh air.

This hallway, too, ended in a door, but when Pippa wrenched it open, we were met not with a dank earthen chamber, but with a gust of fresh, cool night air. The door opened onto a courtyard, hidden from the street and nestled into a small, rectangular space about the size of a tennis court. Low stone walls—or the remains of them, at least, ran around the perimeter, crumbling into moss covered piles in the shadows of the surrounding buildings. Flat stones were set into the ground like a patio, and though broken and half-buried and over-grown with grass, I could make out the pattern of concentric circles which converged upon a stone dais at the center. And there, upon the dais, was the Geatgrima.

It was astonishing to think it could be here all this time, the city growing up around it, modernity pressing in, smothering from all directions. And yet here it was, as though the protective walls of the surrounding buildings had cut it off from reality, from time itself. An eerie quiet nestled here, an unnat-ural stillness that belied the existence of the vibrant, pulsing lifeblood of the metropolis from which it was separated by only a matter of feet. I realized with a start that we had walked past it a dozen times the previous day and never had an inkling it was here. Now, however, the waves of powerful energy that emanated from its very stones were impossible to ignore, and we all stood for several long moments in silent contemplation of it. It was Hannah who finally broke the spell.

"How was the problem discovered?" she asked.

"Well, as I mentioned, all of the buildings overlooking the Geatgrima are owned by Clan Rìoghalachd, and the flats in the upper levels are used as housing quarters for Caomhnóir and other staff. I used to have a flat here as well, in the east building, before I was promoted to be Clarissa's full-time assistant." She pointed up to a window on the top floor of the building across the courtyard from where we stood. "Anyway, one of the Caomhnóir noticed it first. He'd been out late on a security detail for one of the family and saw it from his window as he was getting ready to go to bed. I asked him to join us here tonight so that you can hear his story for yourself. Malcolm?"

The Caomhnóir who had accompanied us silently from the car stepped forward, his hands clasped in front of him. His face, which was very square with rather severe features, seemed oddly soft as he flushed and cleared his throat to address us. When he spoke, his voice was also unexpectedly soft; frankly, I'd expected a grunt.

"Well, as Miss Pippa says, I had just finished a detail and arrived home very late. It was 2:15 as I got ready to close the curtains—I know the time because I'd just set my alarm for the morning, and I'd been calculating how much sleep I could still get before I had to be up again."

He glanced between us all, as though waiting for permission to continue.

"That makes perfect sense. Go on, please," Hannah said, taking pity on him.

"As I pulled the curtain shut, I caught a movement out of the corner of my eye. It was a spirit moving toward the Geatgrima. I stopped to watch." He flushed again. "You might think that a bit odd, but I'd never seen a spirit Cross through the Geatgrima—the Gateways had only been restored for a few months, and I'd been away on a course to get my certification in combat training. I want to be an instructor, like you, Mr. Carey," he added, nodding respectfully at Finn.

"I'm sure you'll make an admirable one," Finn said, returning the nod. "Please, do continue."

"Well, I stopped to watch because I was curious. The spirit was that of a woman. I was too far away to see her properly, but she looked young. Anyway, she seemed to be drawn forward, in a sort of trance, almost, with her eyes fixed on the Geatgrima. And then, just as she reached the outer edge of the cobbles here," and he pointed to a spot on the ground, about halfway between the building we'd just come through, and the dais upon which the Geatgrima was perched, "she froze. It was the strangest thing. It was as though she had encountered some kind of barrier. I could see her straining forward, but she didn't seem able to get any closer. And then... then she began to scream."

"Scream?" I repeated, and felt the goosebumps rising on my skin.

Malcolm nodded, his expression pained. "It was a terrible sound, miss. Just terrible. And she began to struggle, and I realized she couldn't move—it wasn't just that she couldn't get any closer to the Geatgrima—she couldn't get any further away from it either. She'd been rooted to the spot. And the screaming, it got louder and louder, and then... and then she was gone." His voice shivered and died.

My mouth had gone dry listening to Malcolm's story, and I had to clear my throat and swallow to get any sound to come out.

"How did she disappear?"

Malcolm's eyes went wide. "I've got no idea, I promise. I thought that was why you'd been called here, wasn't it? To answer that question?"

I shook my head. "Sorry, I didn't ask that very clearly. What I meant was, can you describe her disappearance? Like, was it one moment she was there, the next she was gone? Did she blink out all at once, or did she fade slowly?"

"Oh, I see," Malcolm said, his expression clearing now that he understood I wasn't accusing him of anything. Then he frowned for a moment in concentration. "Well... she faded, and as she got fainter, the screaming got louder, and then she was gone. And well..." He hesitated, looking almost sheepish.

"Go on," I encouraged him.

"Well, it almost seemed as though she went... down."

"Down?" I repeated.

He nodded. "Just at the end, it seemed like she sort of... sunk down through the ground."

No one spoke for a moment as we digested that information.

"Well, that's bloody strange, innit?" Savvy finally muttered, giving a nervous chuckle which she quickly stifled.

"What did you do, after you saw that happen?" Finn asked.

"I went down to the courtyard at once," Malcolm said, "and I searched for any sign that anything might be amiss, but I didn't find anything strange. Then I kept watch over the Geatgrima for the rest of the night."

"And did it happen again?" Hannah asked.

"I only saw one other spirit, round about five o'clock in the morning. I tried to warn him as he approached, but he ignored me—he seemed almost hypnotized by the Geatgrima, as though he couldn't even hear me. He didn't need my warning, however. As I watched, he drifted clear across the courtyard without encountering any barriers at all and stepped right up onto the dais and through the Geatgrima. No screaming. No struggle. He just... slipped off peacefully into the Aether, just as I'd expected the first spirit to do."

"Malcolm reported the phenomenon in the morning to his shift commander, and that's when we began to monitor the Geatgrima continuously. That's how we discovered that the problem was isolated to a certain time of night," Pippa added.

A breeze swept through the courtyard, catching at my hair. Beside me, Hannah shivered violently and pulled her jacket more tightly around herself.

"Surely you can just warn the spirits away during the dangerous time, can't you?" Savvy asked. "Sort of like a security guard, yeah? Sorry, no Crossings between two and three o'clock, come back in a bit when we're open."

"We have attempted it," Pippa admitted, "but it's not that simple. Once a spirit has decided to Cross and has felt the pull of the Gateway from so close a proximity, it is extraordinarily difficult to get through to them. We can warn them away, even attempt to expel them, but once the Geatgrima has a hold on them..." She shrugged helplessly.

Finn's expression was grim. Hannah looked very pale.

"What time is it?" I asked, breaking the silence.

Pippa consulted her watch. "About quarter to two."

"So that gives us fifteen minutes. Let's have a look around."

We spread out through the courtyard, taking swift stock of the space, examining the dais, the stones of the Geatgrima, the walls of the surrounding buildings, even the cobbles in the ground.

"Hard to know if we've found anything when we don't even know what we're looking for," Savvy muttered as we worked.

"Just anything out of place—signs of a Casting having been performed, or anything being added or taken from the courtyard," I told her.

"Malcolm, can you show me the place the spirit seemed to get stuck when you saw her from your window?" Hannah asked.

"Of course, miss," Malcolm said, hurrying to her. He looked up at his window, then down at the ground. Then he took several paces to the left of where Hannah stood. "It was almost exactly here," he said, confidence in his tone. "I remember that stone there, the large one, became visible just as she disappeared, so she was standing just in front of it."

Hannah walked over to Malcolm and he stepped aside to allow her to stand on the stone in question. She turned slowly on the spot, examining the ground around her feet, shifting her weight experimentally, and brushing some grass and a few dead leaves away to look for signs of a Casting. Then, looking up at the Geatgrima, she closed her eyes and grew very still. We all stopped what we were doing and watched her. At last, she opened her eyes with a sigh of frustration.

"I'm just not picking up on anything," she said. "Everything seems to be as it ought to be. Anyone else?"

Her question was met with a flurry of shrugs and shaking heads.

"Milo? What about you?" Hannah asked. "If anyone here might sense something amiss, it's bound to be you."

Milo smiled ruefully. "And I'm as stumped as you are."

Finn consulted his watch now. "It's very nearly two o'clock," he said, a sharp note of tension in his voice. "We'd best clear off to the edge of the court-yard, just in case."

We all did so, our tension mounting as the hour drew nearer. And then, at the same moment, Finn's watch beeped and a distant church bell tolled the hour. It was two o'clock.

"Here we go, then," Savvy muttered. She was bouncing on the balls of her feet in an effort to siphon off the tension.

The echoes of the bell died away, leaving a silence that seemed to have grown heavy in their absence. A cloud shifted overhead, obscuring part of the moon and deepening the shadows in the courtyard.

But it was Milo's face that caught and held my attention. He'd spoken barely a word since we'd arrived in the courtyard. He'd been so quiet, so remarkably unobtrusive, that I'd almost forgotten he was with us: Milo was generally notorious for making his presence known.

"Milo?" I asked, and even the gentle murmur of my voice made him jump as though I'd shouted in his ear.

"Huh? What?" he stammered, and turned to look at me in surprise, as though he'd forgotten my presence as well.

"Are you okay? You look... freaked out," I said, unable to hit on the right phrase for the wide-eyed, frozen expression on his face.

"Oh... yeah, I'm...I'm fine," he said, giving the least convincing imperson- ation of "fine" anyone has ever attempted. "It's just... can anyone else feel that?"

"Feel what, mate?" Savvy asked.

"That's a no, then," Milo mumbled and then clarified, "It's just that... well I think you'd know if you felt this. It just... *wow*, it feels really, really wrong in here all of a sudden."

"Wrong?" Hannah asked, alarm creeping into her tone. "Wrong, how?"

"Well, you don't pick up on it at first, because of the Geatgrima," Milo said.

Every pair of eyes in the courtyard turned to watch him, and he struggled for a moment to collect himself, to gather his thoughts.

"I'm less sensitive to the pull of the Geatgrima because Hannah and I are Bound," he explained for Pippa and Malcolm's benefit; the rest of us knew all about the nature of his unusual status as a spirit guide. "But nonetheless, I'm not completely immune. The pull is there, I've been able to feel it from the moment we stepped into the courtyard, but now there's something else, too."

I could see the struggle on his face as he grappled with just exactly how to explain, to describe what defied description.

"I'm not sure the other spirits would pick up on it," he went on finally. "It's subtle and hard to describe. Almost like... a spiritual aftertaste?"

"I beg your pardon?" Pippa asked, politely frowning.

Milo ran a hand over his face. "I'm sorry, I can't think of any other way to describe it. It's like when you bite into something, and at first it tastes just the way you expect, and you're enjoying it, and then just as you swallow, you get another note—a bitterness or sourness that lingers in your mouth. And you know now that something's off or wrong about what you just ate, but you've already eaten it. It's too late. Do you understand what I'm saying?" He asked, looking around at us all eagerly.

I nodded. "I think so. You're saying the spirits are so drawn to the Geatgrima that they don't recognize they're in trouble until it's already too late. And that the call of the Geatgrima is powerful and all-consuming enough for them that they don't notice the... the wrongness... until it's too late?"

Milo clapped his hands together. "Exactly. And as a spirit guide, I've got a more refined palate. Like the way a sommelier can taste the subtle notes and differences between wines, I'm able to pick up on the same differences in energy." He shrugged, looking a bit sheepish.

"Oh, I see," Pippa said, her expression clearing as understanding finally took hold. "It's like concealing the taste of a poison with something that overwhelms it. The Geatgrima is so overwhelming that it masks the threat."

Milo's face broke into a smile, though it quickly faded. "Yes. Exactly."

My mind, meanwhile, had wandered not to poisons, but to booby traps. Lost in the woods, you see a cabin ahead, and you're so eager to reach it that you rush forward and suddenly find that you've fallen into a pit concealed with leaves and sticks to look like the rest of the forest floor, a pit you likely would have noticed if you hadn't been so focused and intent on reaching the cabin.

"It's a trap," I murmured.

"What did you say, Jess?" Hannah asked.

I cleared my throat. "I said, it's a trap. Whoever or whatever is causing this, it's using the Geatgrima as bait to ensnare the spirits."

"Surely not," Pippa said, looking genuinely alarmed. "We were quite sure it was simply a matter of the Geatgrima itself not functioning properly after so many centuries of dormancy."

Milo looked grimly at me, and I knew he shared my view. "I think Jess is right. I think you're dealing with something more sinister than that," he said. "Something is at work here that has nothing to do with the Geatgrima."

"Oh, no!" Savvy cried out, making us all jump and tear our eyes from Milo. She was pointing with a shaking finger toward the far corner of the courtyard, where the spirit of an old woman had appeared. Her form was feeble and faded, but as she edged closer to the Geatgrima, she seemed to brighten and solidify around the edges, like a dying flame that suddenly finds an influx of oxygen. Her expression transformed from fear to wonder, until she suddenly looked younger. Savvy made a strangled sound beside me, a kind of half-swallowed sob.

"We can't let her... are we just going to let her..." she whispered.

"But that's why we're here," Pippa said, her brow contracted in confusion. "At this time of night. So that you can see the phenomenon for yourself."

Savvy looked at the rest of us. "And you lot are okay with that, are you? We're gonna sacrifice someone's little old nan just so we can get a proper look?"

Finn looked grim. "Sav, she's just told us they've tried everything to prevent—"

"Tried everything they could, I'm sure, but we've got a Caller, haven't we?" Savvy said, gesturing to Hannah.

Hannah's eyes went wide. "That's right! I... I didn't even think... has anyone tried Calling a spirit away from the courtyard?"

Pippa shook her head. "I'm afraid we haven't got a Caller in Clan Rìoghalachd at present, or I'm sure we would have done."

Hannah looked at me, biting her lip. "Do you think it would work?"

I opened my mouth to answer but Savvy's increasingly hysterical voice cut in.

"We've got to at least try!" Savvy said, her voice creeping higher on the tide of her rising panic. "We can't just let this happen, if we don't know what's going to become of her... come on now! Are you lot actually going to let this happen?" She looked around at all of us and then froze. "Where's Milo?"

I turned, startled to discover he was no longer standing beside me. I whirled around, scanning the courtyard, my heart pounding, and spotted him; but Hannah was a step ahead of me.

"Milo, stop! What are you doing?" Hannah cried out.

But Milo wasn't listening. He was already calling out to the spirit of the old woman as he sailed around the outer edge of the courtyard, keeping himself pressed to the perimeter, as far from the source of the trouble as he could get.

"You can't Cross now!" he was shouting as he flew. "You have to come back later when it's safe!"

If the woman could hear him, she paid him no mind at all. Every fiber of her being seemed fixed on the Geatgrima, hypnotized by its silent, irresistible melody. She moved toward it slowly but purposefully, deliberately, and without hesitation. Milo called out again.

"Please! Come back! It's not safe!"

I heard a quiet curse and then Hannah took off after Milo, skirting the edge of the courtyard. My heart in my throat, I tore off after her. I lost sight of the old woman as I ran, one side of the Geatgrima blocking her from my view. By the time I could see her again, she was a mere step or two away from the edge of the cobbles, the very spot from which—according to Malcolm—she would be unable to escape once she had set foot upon it.

"Hannah, she won't listen to me. Call her, just Call her, make her turn back!" Milo cried out.

Hannah stumbled to a halt and closed her eyes, gathering her power. When her eyes opened again, they had that empty, hypnotic quality that meant she was within the grip of the Calling. She held out a hand and, very slowly, curled her fingers inward in a come hither gesture.

I saw, rather than heard, the words she whispered.

"Come to me."

There was just the slightest hitch in the woman's step, a brief moment of hesitation, but she kept moving, the cobbles mere inches from the toe of her battered old wellies.

Hannah said the words again, and this time they were not an invitation, but a command.

"Come. To. Me."

The woman's form shuddered with the force of the words. Her forward progress stalled and she stumbled a little, her balance thrown off by the strength of the forces now locked together, vying for control of her next step.

"That's right," Hannah said, soothingly. "Come away. Come here to me, where it's safe."

The little old woman's face, curiously blank a moment before, twisted with what looked like sudden pain. She looked at Hannah, then back at the Geatgrima. Her fluttery breeze of a voice replied. "But I'm meant to go. I can feel it."

"You mustn't, not yet," Hannah replied. "Come away from the Gateway, come to me."

But the woman shook her head with a force that startled me. "I've stayed too long because I was afraid. I ignored the call. But I can't anymore. I must go."

"No, please," Hannah cried out, but the Call was not strong enough. The little woman shuffled forward another step.

And the screaming began.

I understood now why Malcolm had been unable to find the words to describe the screaming. And I knew, too, that that sound—that torturous screaming, at once inhuman and the most human thing I'd ever heard—would live in the darkest corners of my nightmares for the rest of my life. I flung my hands against my ears in a desperate attempt to deaden it, to prevent it from infecting me like a virus, but it defied the rules of living senses. It only grew louder, burrowed deeper into me as we watched, utterly helpless.

A blurred shape darted toward the woman, and then, just as suddenly, darted away from her. It happened so quickly that it took a moment for me to realize that the shape had been Milo. Desperate to help the woman, he had attempted to reach her; but Hannah had used her Caller ability to force him back, and now he stood pinned against the wall of the nearest building. They struggled against each other, Milo desperate to surge forward, to help the woman, and Hannah desperate to keep him exactly where he was. But the standoff was brief. Before Milo could do more than fling out a few strangled curses, the woman's form faded, like layers of her energy were being stripped away, piece by piece; and then, at last, when she was a mere suggestion of herself, she seemed to slip down through the ground at her feet, leaving behind her a yawning emptiness and a silence weighted down with unadulterated horror.

Hannah dropped her hand and both she and Milo slumped to the ground like mirror images of each other.

"What... were... you... doing?!" Hannah panted, her words strangely slurred like she was fighting to stay conscious.

"I'm sorry," Milo was sobbing. "I'm sorry, but I had to do something. I couldn't... couldn't just watch her..."

"You wouldn't have been watching anymore! You would be *gone!*" Hannah replied, managing to sound angry even as her eyes fought to stay open.

"I know, it was dumb, but I just couldn't... I'm sorry," Milo said, each word sounding as though it cost him great effort.

"We'll have time for apologies and explanations back at the hotel," I said. "For right now, I think we need to get out of here. Hannah, no offense, but you look like hell, and Milo, you don't look much better. You've both depleted yourselves, and you need to rest."

Hannah managed to frown, but it looked like hard work. "But the Geatgrima—"

"...will still be here tomorrow, and you've just proven that the only weapon we have won't fix it. Certainly not right now. You couldn't Call a cell phone after that, let alone a spirit."

I looked over at Milo, who swallowed his objections like a dose of bitter medicine and nodded once. "I'm going to blink out, to save energy," he said.

He caught my eye as he faded out. I tried to smile at him, but I didn't have a smile in me.

Together, Malcolm and Finn lifted Hannah to her feet, where she wobbled unsteadily for a moment before Finn just reached down and scooped her up into his arms.

"I tried," I heard her say. "I tried, but I couldn't Call her."

"You did all you could. Don't blame yourself," Finn told her, his voice low and soothing.

We turned to cross the courtyard again and I spotted Savvy, standing just beyond the border of the cobbles. She could have reached out and touched the spot where the old woman had just disappeared. She must have felt my eyes on her because she looked up and met my gaze.

"I don't know what the bloody hell is happening here, but we've got to stop it, Jess."

I nodded my head. "I know."

We had crossed the courtyard and were just about to disappear back into the dank basement hallway when a movement up above the courtyard caught my eye. It happened so quickly, I couldn't be sure, but I thought I saw a face vanish behind a curtain.

A face framed by shockingly pink hair.

9

BOUNDARIES

Back at the hotel, we all gathered in Hannah's suite. Finn had insisted that we put her to bed at once and let her recover from the draining ordeal that was the Calling. Milo insisted he, too, needed to rest, and though I could feel him nearby, he chose not to manifest. Pippa stayed only long enough to see that we were all settled, and then she went to her own room to get some sleep. Finn, Savvy, and I sat up in the sitting room with a fire blazing in the grate and a tea tray called up from the front desk.

"Is she sleeping?" I asked Finn as he emerged from Hannah's room, easing the door closed behind him.

He nodded. "Almost before I settled her on the bed. She tried to talk to me, but the words kept getting lost. Once I pulled the duvet over her, she couldn't fight it anymore."

"She doesn't usually get like this when she Calls, does she?" Savvy asked, sounding edgy.

"That's just it, though, Sav, she doesn't usually Call," I explained. "Like, ever, if she can avoid it. She's only ever done it in times of great need, and it's always exhausted her, even if the adrenaline managed to carry her through. But now she's done it twice in two days. It's not surprising that it's worn her out."

"It's possible she'd get better at it, with practice," Finn added. "But of course, she's Hannah, so it's not the kind of thing she'd want to practice, is it?"

I caught his eye and smiled. If there was one thing I adored about Finn, it was that, after all these years, he understood my sister almost as well as I did.

No one spoke for a long time. We sat with our tea cups, not really because we wanted to drink, but because it was nice to have something to hold. The pot went cold and the sandwiches grew soggy on their little silver tray and we just sat, each of us processing what we'd seen in our own way, knowing that it wouldn't be much use to discuss it until Hannah woke up. Several hours passed this way, and before long, the sun was poking rosy fingers through the curtains, probing at the darkness.

I'd seen a lot of things that disturbed me in the Durupinen world—things that still reared their ugly heads in nightmares and left me to shriek myself awake, drenched in cold sweat and shaking from head to foot. You couldn't live with one foot in the world of the dead without paying a price for it. I'd honestly thought nothing I'd see in Edinburgh could hold a candle to what I'd already experienced.

But I'd been wrong. Terribly, terribly wrong.

I could still hear the old woman's screaming. The faintly distant echo of it was still living in my head, taking root like a living thing. And there was something truly awful about the way she had disappeared—like she was being stripped from the courtyard piece by agonizing piece. Seeing it once had been enough to wreck me, and yet...

It was as though the rest of my thought came right out of Savvy's mouth.

"They've been letting this go on for months," she said in a hoarse whisper.

"Nothing in the file could have prepared me for seeing that. For *hearing* it." I said.

We all shuddered at once, as though the same cold wind had just touched us.

"Catriona can't have known," Finn said. "She can't have known how bad it was or she wouldn't have waited even a day to get someone from the Trackers over here."

"She gave us the file. We all read it. That was everything she had. Not once in the notes did it give any indication that spirits who weren't reaching the Geatgrima appeared to be... tortured," I said.

"Seems like pretty bloody relevant information, if you ask me," Savvy muttered. Her expression was as dark as a storm cloud, and I knew that she was already filled with the anger I could feel brewing beneath the shock.

"Says a lot about Clan Rìoghalachd , doesn't it," Finn agreed. "I'd have thought no Durupinen could witness that and not do something to stop it."

I nodded grimly. "Looks like you were wrong about that."

The door behind us opened and Hannah peeked out.

"Hey, I thought you were sleeping!" I said to her. The sternness in my voice made her flinch.

"I heard you all talking," she said. Her voice was still thick with sleep.

"I'm so sorry, we didn't mean to wake you. Do you want us to leave?" I asked.

I was already halfway off the couch before she could shake her head. "No, no, please stay. I can't sleep anymore, and I don't want to be by myself right now."

"Come sit," Savvy said. "Do you want something to eat or some tea? This lot's gone cold now, but we could—"

"No, thank you. I'm fine, I promise," Hannah said. She padded across the room in her too-baggy sweatshirt,—which I recognized as Kiernan's because it had the name of his favorite rugby team on it,—and sank onto the sofa beside me, curling up like a cat in that fluid way she had.

"How are you feeling?" I asked.

"Tired," she said, and then, before I could launch myself into protective mama bear mode and order her back to bed, she clarified, "Not sleepy. Just mentally tired."

I narrowed my eyes at her but didn't argue.

"Where's Milo?" she asked in a tiny voice.

"He promised to stay close, but he blinked out. He was feeling pretty drained too, I think," I said.

Hannah dropped her head into her hands. "It's my fault. It's all my fault."

I blinked. "Excuse me? What's your fault?"

"Milo... If I hadn't... if I didn't..." The end of her sentence was lost in a shuddery sigh.

"Why don't you talk to him? Just open up the connection and—"

Hannah shook her head violently. "No. I'm not forcing myself on him. If he wants to talk to me, he can come to me. And I understand if he doesn't. I'd understand if he never wanted to talk to me again."

"Nah, Milo's not like that!" Savvy said, in as soothing a tone as she could wrangle her boisterous voice into. "You're getting yourself all worked up over nothing."

But Hannah's head was still shaking. "You don't understand. You couldn't feel the way he was fighting against me. It was awful, struggling against him like that…"

She was still trying to put it into words as I silently opened a tiny mental window into the connection, probing ever so gently, until I found Milo's steady pulse of energy. It was strong but not bright, a sign that he was as weary from the night as Hannah was.

"Milo?" I tried.

"I'm here," he replied.

"Hannah's awake. She's… she's scared to try to talk to you."

Milo's energy lit up with surprise. "Scared? To talk to *me*?!"

"She thinks you're mad at her."

I felt rather than heard the sigh, and a moment later I felt the distinctive sizzle of displaced energy as Milo manifested into the chair closest to the fire.

"What's this I hear about someone avoiding me?" Milo asked, tucking the specters of his legs around each other.

Hannah glared at me. "I told you I didn't want to bother him."

"Who's bothered? Certainly not me," Milo said, shrugging. "The queen of unbothered right here."

Hannah took a deep breath and turned to look at Milo. "Milo, I owe you a huge apology. There's no excuse for what I did in that courtyard."

Milo let out an incredulous laugh. "Of course there's an excuse. You were trying to protec—"

"No! Don't defend me, Milo, it only makes it worse. I can't…" Hannah pressed her lips together and took a deep breath through her nose. I recognized her trick for trying not to cry. "Please, just let me say this. Let me get it out. You are Bound to me in ways that neither of us understood when it happened, and I know you don't think I should feel bad about that, but I do. Your choices are limited because of me. And it is absolutely unpardonable that I would do anything that would limit them further."

Milo looked ready to burst with replies to all of this, but he also knew how important it was to her to say it out loud, so he just listened quietly, keeping his face neutral even as a muscle jumped in his jaw.

Hannah went on, "I took your agency from you. It's not the first time I've done it, but it is the first time since I understood how Calling truly works that I did so without your permission. It's everything I hate about this gift... or curse, depending on how you look at it." Her voice was low but fervent. "No one should be able to do that to another soul, living or dead. If I could tear this gift out of me and toss it away, I would. It's not who I want to be."

A short pause blossomed after these words before Milo ventured, "Can I speak now?"

Hannah nodded.

"Well, first of all, no one's gift is who they *are*, sweetness. It is only something they can *do*. Jess doesn't think of her sister as the Caller. Kiernan could list a thousand reasons he wants to marry you, and being a Caller wouldn't even make that list. The only people who think of you as a Caller first are ignorant people who don't really know you. I need to make sure you understand and acknowledge that before I keep talking," he said.

Hannah chewed the inside of her cheek for a moment, and then nodded grudgingly.

Milo nodded. "Good. Now second of all, I'll admit I was upset in the moment. I was trying to do something and you were stopping me. I wanted to help. You wouldn't let me. That was hard."

Hannah's eyes filled with tears but she still didn't speak.

"But the only reason you stopped me with your gift—yes we are still calling it a gift, regardless of your disillusionment—was because you couldn't stop me physically. You didn't have that choice. But if Jess had run for that spirit and tried to stop what was happening, you would have tackled her to the ground."

Milo looked at me for confirmation. I nodded. "'Though she be but little, she is fierce.' She could totally take me," I said.

"And if you did that, wouldn't you be taking away *her* agency?" Milo asked.

Hannah scowled. "That's not the same thing."

"Of course it is. When you see someone you love about to do something that could get them seriously hurt, you stop them. By whatever means you can. Those were the means you had. You used them. It's okay."

"But you were mad," Hannah said.

Milo shrugged. "For about a minute. I'm over it."

"Well, whether you're over it or not, I'm sorry Milo. I'll never do it again, no matter how much I think you're being a self-sacrificing ass."

Milo's mouth curved gently into a smile. "Thanks. I accept your apology. And if it makes you feel any better, I'm only a self-sacrificing ass, like... *very* occasionally."

Hannah's face broke into a tiny smile, and Milo flew at her, making her gasp and laugh with the sudden onslaught of cold.

"Ugh, get a room, you two," I scoffed, before officially making it a group hug.

"Can a ghost get squished? Because you're squishing me," came Milo's muffled voice from underneath us.

"If you want me to move, you'll have to get Hannah to tackle me," I said seriously.

"Jess!" Hannah cried.

"Too soon? Fine, too soon," I said. And I relented, releasing them both.

The laughter had been a temporary light in the room. Now that it had gone out, we were all left again to contend with the darkness left behind.

"We have to do something," Milo said into the emptiness. "We can't just let that continue, not even for one more night. How do we stop it?"

"Until we know what it is, how can we?" I asked.

Milo shook his head fiercely. "I'm sorry, but I just don't believe there's nothing we can do to prevent more spirits from... *that*." He gestured vaguely, helplessly, but of course we knew all too well what he meant, and it was no wonder that he was at a loss for words. "There has to be something; and from what I've seen so far, I'm not convinced that Clan Rìoghalachd gives a shit."

"They aren't even attempting to keep spirits away from that courtyard. They've simply been letting it happen until we came along to clean up the mess," Finn added.

Savvy made a growling sound that we all took to be in agreement with the sentiment.

"I think we should talk to Clarissa, see what resources we can get from her," I said.

"Resources? You mean like, Caomhnóir?" Hannah asked.

"Anything!" I said. "They may have been content to let this happen, but I'm sure as hell not; and if they want Fairhaven help, then they have to play by Fairhaven rules."

"I'm sure Queen Clarissa will just love that," Milo drawled.

"Yeah, well, whether she loves it or not isn't actually something I give a shit about." I stood up, checking my watch. "Do you think Pippa's up yet?"

Sav snorted. "Probably. She strikes me as one of those 'early bird catches the worm' types."

"I'll be right back," I said, heading for the door.

"What is it?" Hannah called.

"I just want to ask Pippa something." As I looked back toward the sofa my eyes fell on the dawn light creeping across the floor. The red curtains through which it was filtered had given it a bright pink hue, which jostled loose another memory of the previous night. "Actually, two things. I'll be right back," I repeated, and ducked out into the hallway before any of them could question me further.

The hallways of the hotel were empty aside from some housekeeping staff —I knew it was early for people to be up, but I was beginning to realize I hadn't seen any other guests in the hotel since we'd arrived, other than in the restaurant, and that was open to the public. I was starting to think Clarissa had actually rented out the entire hotel for our stay. I stopped outside Pippa's room and knocked softly on the door. I heard quick, efficient steps on the other side, and it swung open in a matter of seconds.

Pippa's face betrayed mild surprise. "Jess! I wasn't expecting to see you so early. Is everything all right?"

"Yeah, sorry for the early hour. I couldn't sleep," I said.

"I got precious little sleep myself," Pippa said with a knowing grimace. "Is everyone quite well this morning? How is Hannah? I was concerned about her."

"She's okay now," I assured her. "Calling takes a lot of energy, and she hasn't done it in a long time. It just drained her."

Pippa nodded, looking relieved. She stepped back and gestured for me to come in. "What can I do for you, Jess?"

I stepped inside. The room was spotless—the bed made, each cushion placed with artistic precision. There wasn't a personal item to be seen apart from Pippa's laptop and bag on the table by the window. It was hard to believe she was actually staying here.

"I was hoping you could tell me a little about Maeve."

Pippa blinked. "Maeve?"

"Yeah, Clarissa's daughter?" I clarified, though I knew she knew full well who I was talking about. "I was just wondering, does she live at the Canongate Collective? Or have an office there, maybe?"

Pippa gave an incredulous laugh. "Certainly not! Maeve lives at MacLeod Manor and attends private school. She's on holiday at the moment, of course."

"And would she have any reason, that you can think of, for being there last night?" I asked.

Pippa looked quite alarmed now. "None at all, that I can think of. But why are you asking me this?"

"It was just something I saw last night. It was probably nothing," I said.

Pippa looked for a moment like she wanted to ask me what I'd seen, but then seemed to decide she didn't want to know. Instead she said, "Maeve is... well, she's going through a bit of a trying age, at the moment. But she's a good lass... deep down."

I smiled, trying to put her at ease. "We've all been there. Well, I have, at least. It's kind of hard to imagine you as a rebellious teenager—no offense."

Pippa laughed, and the tension in her face eased a bit. "None taken. You're quite right. I was a bit of a goody-two-shoes, as the saying goes."

I grinned at her. "Well, it's never too late. You can always start rebelling now. Just say the word and I'll take you to get something pierced or tattooed."

Pippa's cheeks flushed. "I'll... think about it."

"Good. And in the meantime, what do you think my chances are of seeing Clarissa today?"

10

CONFRONTATIONS

MacLeod Manor looked sterner, more austere in the daylight, without the twinkle of lights in its windows and the milling, thrumming life of a crowd inside. Today it reminded me more of a monument to a clan past than the bustling seat of a current one. Nonetheless, when we walked through the door, the place was deceptively busy. A maid was arranging an enormous vase of fresh flowers on an entryway table. Another was carefully sweeping an area rug in front of the nearest fireplace. Two women dressed in identical cream pantsuits were working together to carry a clothing rack full of impossibly expensive-looking dresses up the main staircase. And of course, the ever-present security of the Caomhnóir scowled at us from every corner.

Pippa had offered to come with me, but I declined her offer. In fact, I'd declined everyone's offer. Hannah, Milo, Finn, and Savvy had all been perfectly ready and willing to accompany me, and Milo had even offered to bring popcorn, but I wanted to do this on my own.

In the first place, Catriona had been insistent that Clarissa and the rest of Clan Ríoghalachd were interested in me, specifically. She had some kind of idea that they wanted to influence me in some way—recruit me, as it were, to their side of the debate. I assumed, then, that there were things Clarissa would say to me that she might not say in front of the others. Secondly, I had a few choice things I wanted to say to her as well, and I didn't want anyone else trying to soften the edges. Both Finn and Hannah were far too diplomatic to have the kind of conversation I intended to have with Clarissa. Milo and Savvy would definitely back me up—Savvy probably too much so—but I didn't want either of them to wind up in Clarissa's crosshairs, no matter how willingly they stepped into them.

The man who opened the door for me—the butler, I guess? Do people actually have butlers anymore?—showed me down the corridor past the rooms we'd mingled in for the party and into a small sitting room to wait. I'd barely been there a minute or two when a grim-faced woman in a starched apron came in and set a tea tray wordlessly on the table. They must just have tea trays lined up in some secret pantry ready to go, kettles constantly on the boil just in case someone might be in danger of going a full five minutes without being handed a cup of tea. By this time, I was very used to the omnipresent cuppa across the pond, but this was next-level.

The door over my shoulder slid open and Clarissa sailed into the room, all ruby lips and flowing silk jumpsuit, and shining golden hair. She smiled broadly when she saw me sitting there, but I'd realized by now that her smiles, as gleaming and perfect as they were, never quite reached her eyes.

"Jessica. It's lovely to see you. I see you've been brought some tea. Can I offer you anything else?" she practically purred.

"No, thanks, I'm good," I said.

Clarissa nodded, then settled herself elegantly into the chair opposite mine. She peered at me expectantly from across the coffee table, the steam muddying the air between us.

"To what do I owe the pleasure of this visit?" she asked.

With difficulty, I let the word "pleasure" pass without comment. No point in opening hostilities this early.

"We visited the Geatgrima last night," I reminded her.

"Ah, yes, of course. Pippa did leave a message for me regarding that," Clarissa said, and she sighed, letting her face fold down into a sad expression. It looked odd on her face, as though her muscles weren't used to working in that way. "It's truly terrible, isn't it?"

"It certainly is," I agreed, watching her face carefully. It was like watching a dancer mark through carefully plotted choreography.

"Heartbreaking," Clarissa said, nodding her head. "You can see now why we called you here. I wish the restoration of the Gateways was the smooth and simple process we all hoped for, but clearly you can see what we've known for months: things just aren't that simple."

I took a sip of tea. She was watching me carefully now, her elbows resting on her knees as she leaned forward to scrutinize my expression.

"I'm sure you must feel dreadful, knowing that you were the one who restored the power to the Geatgrimas, only for them to malfunction like this; but you mustn't blame yourself. The Geatgrimas have been dormant for so long. We ought to have known their reactivation would be fraught with difficulties our ancestors could not predict."

Her face crumpled with pity, but her eyes sparkled maliciously. Wow, this woman really was a piece of work. With an audacity that was actually breathtaking, she reached out and patted my hand.

"I'm quite eager to hear what you make of the situation," she went on, giving my hand a little squeeze. Her skin was abnormally smooth and cold, like a mannequin's.

My whole body stiffened as rage shot through it, and it took every ounce of my self-control not to slap her touch away. Instead, I reached down, picked up my teacup, and took a long sip.

"Are you?"

"Indeed, I am. What did you make of it?"

I set the teacup down. "Before I answer that question, I have one for you."

Clarissa looked mildly surprised, but gestured for me to go ahead.

"Have you personally been to the courtyard where the Geatgrima is?"

Clarissa snorted as though the question was silly. "Naturally. Many times."

"Have you been there since this phenomenon began?" I asked.

"Of course."

"During the period of time when the spirits are disappearing?"

"You can't seriously think I would not observe the situation for myself?" Clarissa said with a humorless laugh. "What kind of head of clan would I be if I didn't even bother to see it with my own two eyes?"

"It's interesting you say that," I replied, keeping my voice pleasant. "Because I was just wondering what kind of head of clan would be able to witness such a thing and just allow it to continue for months on end?"

Clarissa's expression froze, giving her face a temporary waxen quality.

"I beg your pardon?" she managed through tight lips.

I stood up and paced around the back of my chair. "I keep going over it in my head—I had a lot of time because I haven't been able to sleep—and I'm trying to understand how a woman whose calling it is to safely guide spirits to the other side could watch them being torn violently out of existence without raising a hand to stop it." I stopped pacing and looked at her. "Can you explain it to me?"

Clarissa had gotten her bearings now and was looking at me with imperious disdain. "You seem to have forgotten that the reason you are here is because we are trying to stop it. We filed a report. We requested Tracker assistance."

"I read that report. The whole thing. And do you know what I noticed? It was sanitized."

"What exactly do you—"

"Oh, come off it, Clarissa. There's no way that report made it out those doors without your stamp of approval on every last syllable. I've only been here for two days and even I know that. There was no mention of the extreme suffering being inflicted on the spirits who get trapped. No description of what is truly happening to them. The screaming, the stripping away of their being, piece by agonizing piece. Didn't you think that was relevant information?"

"Your complaint is that we did not offer enough descriptive language for your taste?" Clarissa asked, smirking now. "You would prefer for a Caomhnóir report to read like a page-turning suspense novel, perhaps?"

"I would prefer it to read like the *truth*," I said. "Catriona would never have sat on it for weeks if she'd known the torture being inflicted in that courtyard. She would have been here the next day with a legion of Trackers bent on putting a stop to it. And she certainly wouldn't have wasted time sweet-talking me into coming back on board. And I think you knew that."

Clarissa quirked an eyebrow but did not answer.

"I think you want things the way they used to be," I continued. "I think you liked the power and the perks that came with having the Gateway in your blood. And I think you wanted this problem with the Geatgrima to get as bad as possible, and I think you wanted to bring me here to make me feel guilty about it. And maybe, just maybe, if it was bad enough, I could be persuaded that I'd made a mistake about the Reckoning."

"And do you always make such wild claims to know other people's thoughts and motivations, or is this a privilege you reserve for those you barely know?" Clarissa asked archly.

"You can scoff all you like," I replied. "But people really aren't that hard to read, and anyway, I found out what I could about you before I got here. I have no doubt you did quite a bit of research on me as well. I bet you knew how I'd be likely to react to the scene in that courtyard, especially if I wasn't expecting it. I bet you were counting on me to do whatever I could to help those spirits, even if it meant reversing everything we've worked so hard to build since the Reckoning. And if the true problem here was the Geatgrima itself, I might do exactly that."

Clarissa frowned. "*If* the true problem was the Geatgrima? Are you saying it isn't?"

"That's exactly what I'm saying. The danger in that courtyard isn't the Geatgrima at all. The Geatgrima is simply being used as bait to lure spirits there."

"For what possible purpose? And by whom?" Clarissa shot back.

For a moment we glared at each other, and I felt sure that she knew what I was thinking this time. I didn't need to accuse her out loud, but it could not have been clearer to me that someone in Clan Rìoghalachd was responsible; and who more likely than the woman perched right at the top of their power structure? Who would dare to act without her approval? And who could possibly benefit more from the fallout than Clarissa herself? Still, if I said all of this now, she'd just deny it. I needed proof, and I didn't have it yet.

"I don't know yet. But I'm damn sure going to find out," I said instead. "And until I do, I'm certainly not going to let more spirits be sacrificed."

"Is that so? And how do you intend to do that?" Clarissa asked. "From what Pippa told me, even your sister, the great Caller, could do nothing to stop it when it happened right in front of your eyes."

Was I imagining it, or was there a badly suppressed note of triumph in her voice? It was several seconds before I could be sure that my voice would not shake with my own badly suppressed rage.

"That's true. And so, until we know how to stop it, we intend to do what you failed to do yourself. We're going to keep ghosts out of that courtyard until we know it's safe for them."

"Keeping spirits from Crossing?" Clarissa said, tutting disapprovingly. "That's quite the opposite of our intended role in the world, isn't it?"

"They will still be able to Cross. Twenty-three hours a day, they will have unfettered access to that Geatgrima. But between the hours of two and three o'clock, we're going to keep them out. Something you should have been doing all along."

"It's not our job to stand between the Gateway and the spirits who want to Cross," Clarissa said.

"It is when that Crossing could be a trap," I said. "But since you brought it up, that's exactly what we were doing for centuries. Standing between spirits and the Gateway, only allowing them to Cross at our whim, at our convenience. Not anymore. We're going to sort this out, and the spirits of Edinburgh will have free access to the Gateway once again, just as they were always meant to have."

"How very gallant of you," Clarissa said, her voice dripping with sarcasm.

I ignored the dig. "We need manpower during the time in question. What can you give us?"

Clarissa held up her clenched hands and unfurled them, to show they were empty. "Nothing at all, I'm afraid. Our Caomhnóir are stretched to their limit with family security details."

I ground my teeth together. "You might not be so short-staffed if you'd hire a few female Caomhnóir to fill out your ranks. Fairhaven is anxious to place them, and as Savvy demonstrated two nights ago, they are more than up to the job."

"I think you'll find Fairhaven is ahead of the curve, so to speak, when it comes to its new policies on gender roles," Clarissa said frostily. "Here in Edinburgh we are, forgive us, dreadfully old fashioned."

I snorted but managed to keep my retort to myself. "Fine. I'll be calling in reinforcements from the Fairhaven Caomhnóir, then. I'll send you the bill."

Clarissa simply waved a hand in a dismissive gesture. Money was no object, clearly.

I stood up. "Okay, then. If there's nothing else to discuss, I'll update you when we have anything to report."

Clarissa continued to stare at me appraisingly. "You are very much how I expected you to be," she said finally. It didn't sound like a compliment.

"So are you," I returned, smiling as pleasantly as I could. "Glad to see us both living up to our reputations, earned or otherwise. Please don't bother getting up. I'll see myself out."

And without waiting to be dismissed, I strode from the room.

Once out in the entryway again, I took a deep breath. My hands were shaking. I clenched and unclenched them a few times, and then shook them out. I hoped I hadn't betrayed to Clarissa how intimidated I had been. I talked a good game, but I wasn't an idiot. I knew how powerful Clarissa MacLeod was, and to make matters worse, I was on her turf. But I had to make it clear where I stood, and I didn't regret it.

Okay, well I regretted it a little when I stepped outside to make a phone call.

"Jess! I was wondering when I'd hear from you! How is it going?"

"Well, you were right about Clarissa MacLeod. She's... a lot."

Catriona laughed. "I did warn you. But tell me what's happening!"

At her invitation, I launched at once into a detailed description of what had happened at the Geatgrima. When I had finished, there was such a prolonged silence on the other end of the line, I thought I'd dropped the call.

"Cat?"

I heard the delicate clearing of a throat. "Yes, I'm still here. That... almost none of that was in the report they sent to us. I never... I can't... oh my God!"

I just nodded along to the sounds of her indignant, horrified spluttering until it was over. Then she asked, "How is Hannah?"

I was taken aback for a moment—Cat had grown on me over the years, but she wasn't exactly the most sympathetic person in the world. I felt gratitude surge up inside me as I answered, "She's shaken up. You know how much she despises having to Call, and then for it to not even work..." I sighed. "We're all shaken up, honestly. And pissed. Really pissed."

There was a loaded silence for about three seconds and then...

"Jess? What did you do?"

"I told Clarissa MacLeod that I'm calling you to send Caomhnóir from Fairhaven to help us patrol the perimeter of the courtyard and keep spirits out of it during that dangerous window between two and three o'clock."

"Oh." Catriona sounded intensely relieved. "Okay, well, that's not too bad, considering what I thought you might have said to her."

"Well, that was after I told her that she was basically evil and let spirits suffer needlessly for weeks on end just so she could guilt me into coming here and reversing the Reckoning."

Catriona's initial response was merely a long, deep groan.

"Ballard," she said, "we did have a conversation about Clarissa trying to recruit you to her cause, right? We discussed letting her think she was influencing you? We talked specifically about letting her lead you along, so that we could find out what quiet plans she had to undermine the new system? Is any of this ringing a bell?"

"Yup," I said.

"And you decided to abandon that plan in less than two days by insulting her to her face in her own house?"

"That is correct."

"And the reason you chose to do this is because you, and I quote, 'got pissed?'"

"Also correct."

"And am I to understand this in the American context of 'getting angry' as opposed to the UK context of 'getting spectacularly drunk?'"

"Correct again," I told her. "You're really on a roll today."

"I suppose I should be glad of that at least. Better than stumbling off the whiskey tour and slurring at her," Catriona sighed. "How bad is it?"

"I mean, I don't think we've reached mortal enemy status, but I definitely called her on her bullshit," I said. "Look, Cat, I'm sorry, I know you wanted me to play along. I gave her the out. I asked her if she'd seen it happen for herself, and she admitted without hesitation that she had. I know I should have kept my cool, but if you saw and heard what I did last night and you knew she was just letting it happen..." My voice shuddered and died.

A moment's silence. Then, "I understand. I probably would have done the same thing."

I hadn't expected that. "Thanks."

"Jess, do you think there's any chance that—"

"That she's behind it all herself?" I finished for her. "I'm not sure. It's possible, but if that's the case, then she's definitely not the only one who's up to something around here."

"What do you mean by that?"

Quickly, I backtracked to the previous night's reception and told her all about the spirits who attacked during what was supposed to be Clarissa's big speech.

"And you're sure Clarissa didn't stage that herself? More proof that things were out of control and needed to be restored to the way they were before the Reckoning?"

"I can see why you'd ask, but I really don't think so. If she was faking her shock and outrage, someone should just hand her an Oscar right now, because she made Meryl Streep look like a hack."

"Fair enough. It seemed a distinct possibility," Catriona said.

"There is definitely someone around this clan who is behind all of this. I just need more time to figure out who. God, it's just so disgusting, using spirits like that. Do you ever get the feeling..." I began, and then hesitated.

"Go on."

"Do you ever get the feeling that, to some Durupinen anyway, spirits stop being human in their eyes? Like, they're less than, just because they've left their bodies?"

Catriona didn't answer right away, but I could imagine the litany of examples she must be turning over in her mind. Caging. Leeching. Calling. Warding. All of them necessary in their place, and yet, in the wrong hands...

"Yes. I reckon you're right about that," she said finally.

"The point I'm trying to make is that she sees the spirits here as bargaining chips... acceptable collateral damage. She's not going to help us solve this. She's going to sit back and hope we fail so that she can point to it as a reason to reverse the Reckoning. Did I mention the problem isn't even with the Geatgrima itself?"

"Wait, seriously?" Catriona asked. She sounded stunned.

"Seriously. The Geatgrima seems to just be the bait used to lure the spirits there."

"It's a trap," Catriona murmured.

"Exactly," I agreed. "And we need to keep spirits away from it while we figure out what kind of trap and who set it. Can you help us?"

"I'll put together a team right away and send them up. We may need to use some Novitiates to find enough manpower. It's going to cock up the exam schedule, but we can deal with that later."

"I think utilizing Novitiates would be fine," I said, thinking of Rana. "In fact, it might be the perfect field training for them. All we need them to do is patrol the outer perimeter of the buildings that enclose the courtyard between two and three o'clock in the morning, and warn off any spirits they see

approaching. And Clan Rìoghalachd can house them right in the buildings
that surround the courtyard. They'll be right on site."

"Right then. Well, I'd better get a bloody move on if we're going to have the
people you need in place before tonight. Do me a favor and try not to piss off
Clarissa any more than you already have?"

"Yeah, I'll try," I said, knowing I couldn't very well promise.

"And Jess..."

"Yeah?"

"Good work."

She hung up and I let out a long sigh. Somehow, despite losing my temper
with Clarissa, I'd avoided landing myself on Catriona's shit list. Miracles were
possible.

I pocketed my phone and started down the front steps when I heard raised
voices from around the corner of the manor house. Well aware that I'd be in
major trouble if Clarissa caught me snooping anywhere on her property, I
tiptoed my way as quietly as I could toward the sound.

A tall hedge ran in close proximity to the corner of the house, and I kept
myself behind it where I could stay hidden. From there, the hum of lowered
voices resolved into words.

"...not really sure what you expect me to do about it," said a man's voice.

"You must be able to do something! Ask for a different shift or a different
assignment!" This voice belonged to a young woman.

"I can't do that. I'm on thin ice as it is!"

"Everyone's always on thin ice with my mother. Thin ice is all we've got!"

With a start, I realized who the young woman was, and that I was eavesdropping on her for the second time in two days. This time, however, rather
than sneaking away before she could catch me, I decided to take the opportunity to speak to her. As quietly as I could, I backed away from the hedge
and then started whistling to announce my presence. The voices stopped. I
walked right around the hedge, pretending to be scrolling on my phone,
and gave what I hoped was a convincing start of surprise at the sight of
them.

"Oh! I'm sorry, I didn't realize anyone was out here," I said.

The Caomhnóir merely grunted and turned to walk toward the back of the
house, throwing Maeve one last look as he did so. Maeve arranged her look of
surprise into a thin-lipped smile.

"You're all right," she said by way of forgiveness, and brushed past me in the direction of the front of the house.

"It's Maeve, isn't it?" I asked, calling after her.

She froze and then turned, looking frankly startled that I knew her name. "That's right."

I caught up to her and extended a hand. "I'm Jess Ballard. I'm here from Fairhaven about the—"

"I know who you are," Maeve said bluntly, cutting me off. She didn't take my hand, choosing to cross her arms protectively across her chest as though she'd suddenly taken cold. "Everyone knows who you are."

"Glad to know my reputation precedes me," I said with a half-laugh, but Maeve didn't even crack a half-smile in response. Tough room.

"I was hoping you might be able to help me with something," I said.

Maeve's eyebrows came together in a sharp 'v'. "Me?"

"Yeah," I said, still keeping my tone light. "We went over to the Geatgrima last night, to check out what's been happening there."

"Okay."

"And I was just curious if you could tell me what you were doing there?"

Every muscle in her body tensed. For a second, I thought she was just going to turn tail and flee. Then she cleared her throat and tried—too late—to assume a posture of nonchalance.

"I have no idea what you're talking about," she said. "I wasn't in that courtyard last night."

"Oh, not in the courtyard, no," I said, smiling as though it was all a silly misunderstanding. "I meant upstairs, in one of the flats? Top floor of the East corner, if I'm not mistaken. I saw you looking down at us."

She crossed her arms tighter across her chest. "That wasn't me."

I cocked my head to the side. "You sure about that? That hair color is pretty distinctive."

"Of course I'm sure!" she snapped, doubling down. "Besides, plenty of people have pink hair. It's all the rage at the moment. You're certainly no stranger to bold hair colors, I see." She nodded her chin in reference to my own hair, which had purple highlights in the underlayer.

"I know what I saw," I said, "and before you get all defensive again, I'm not accusing you of anything. I don't know you, and I don't give a damn where you go. I was just hoping you might be able to help me with—"

"I'm sorry, but you've made a mistake," Maeve said, cutting me off with an angry snap in her voice. "And I can't help you. I'm sorry."

She turned on her heel and marched back toward the front doors. I called after her, but the sound of her name only made her break into a jog.

"Well, well, well," I murmured to myself. "That was interesting."

I'd have to do a bit more digging on Maeve MacLeod.

11

INSIDE THE ARCHIVE

"**D**O I EVEN WANT TO HEAR ABOUT IT?"

Pippa was standing outside the hotel when I pulled back up, looking like she might pace a hole clear through the pavement.

"Probably not," I told her, and then sighed. "I'm sorry. I probably made your job more difficult today. But after what we saw last night, there were things that needed to be said, and I said them."

Pippa sighed, her shoulders slumped. "I expected as much. I was told you were rather a wild card."

I put up some jazz hands. "That's me! Anyway, I expect you'll hear from Clarissa, but we're going to have a crop of Caomhnóir coming in from Fairhaven later today, probably about a dozen of them. They'll need lodgings in Canongate Collective. Do you think you could arrange that for us?"

"Of course," Pippa said, pulling out her phone and looking frankly relieved to have something productive to do. Then she suddenly looked up at me. "For what it's worth, I didn't know." She swallowed convulsively, like the thought of the previous night made her feel physically ill. "I didn't know how bad it was. I hadn't seen it for myself until last night. I'm not saying I could have done anything about it if I *had* known, but I would at least have warned you."

I didn't know her well enough to know if she was telling the truth, but the words felt genuine, so I said, "Thanks. I appreciate it."

Pippa nodded once, and then put the phone to her ear and turned away. I left her to the logistics and turned to walk into the hotel when my own phone rang. It was Finn.

"Are you back yet?"

"Yeah, I just got here."

"We've just set out for the pub around the corner, MacCreary's. You want to meet us there? We were going to wait for you, but Sav was getting hangry."

I laughed. "No problem, I'll be right there."

Ten minutes later, we were all crammed into a worn leather booth. The place was packed and very loud, even on a weekday afternoon, and there was live music playing, so we were able to speak freely without worrying about being overheard. I wasted no time in filling them in on all the gory details of my conversation with Clarissa, not bothering to gloss over the encounter like I did with Pippa. By the time the food had arrived, everyone was weighing in.

"Well done, mate. That woman needed to be told some things. Bet she's never heard the word 'no' her entire bloody life," was Savvy's assessment as she attacked her fish and chips. "Would have paid good money to see the look on her face, though between the Botox and the Leeching, there may not have been much to see."

Hannah's reaction surprised me. "I never liked that woman. Every Council meeting she ever attended she's been haughty and dismissive of everyone, even Celeste."

"Isn't this the part when you scold me for losing my temper and blowing half the mission?" I asked her, raising a skeptical eyebrow.

"I suppose I should, but remembering what we saw last night, I find I can't quite manage it," she said with a suggestion of a smile.

"That's my girl," Milo crowed, leaning in to give her what must have been a very chilly peck on the cheek. "I, for one, am only sad I wasn't there to help add drama to the proceedings. I have a few choice words I'd like to sign, seal, and deliver directly to her face."

I looked at Finn. "And you? What do you think of your rash and irresponsible girlfriend?"

To my delight, he leaned across and kissed me. "I think you've forced Clarissa to drop the pretense, which keeps us safer. We already knew we couldn't trust her, but now at least we won't have to tolerate weeks of her pretending otherwise. I'd rather face her wrath dead on than have to sniff it out under a hundred layers of pleasantries, fancy hotel suites, and expensive champagne."

"Hear, hear!" Savvy roared.

"That said," Finn continued, "now that we know what she was hiding from us, I think we need to consider another possibility."

"What possibility?" I asked.

"Before we got here, we all acknowledged that Clarissa was likely using this situation with the Geatgrima to further her own ends. But now we should consider that it was Clarissa herself—or someone close to her—who set this trap in the first place."

Hannah looked startled, but she was the only one.

"I'd already thought of that," I admitted. "In fact, one of the only things I managed to stop myself from saying to Clarissa was an outright accusation. Even Catriona seemed to think it was a possibility, when I called her to request back up."

"It seems like an awfully big chance to take," Hannah said. "If she gets caught, she'll be dragged up in front of the International High Council. She'd be stripped of her Council seat without a doubt, and frankly, she'd be lucky to avoid a lengthy term in a *príosún*."

"Probably can't imagine she'd get caught," Savvy said. "She's the type isn't she? Thinks she's smarter than everyone else."

Hannah shook her head. "The thing is, though, that she really *is* smart. Smart enough to know how much trouble she'd be in. Refusing to solve the problem herself is one thing, but causing it in the first place? I just can't see it."

"People at the top are known for delegating their dirty work," Finn said. "We can't rule her out, but we should be looking at the whole clan."

Milo groaned. "Awesome. There's only about a million of them. Where do we start?"

"I've got a suggestion," I said, and told them all about Maeve.

"You never mentioned seeing her last night!" Hannah gasped indignantly.

I rolled my eyes. "We were just a teensy bit preoccupied, Hannah."

"What did she say when you confronted her?" Savvy asked.

"She denied it, of course, but what else would she do? Told me lots of people have pink hair."

"Actually, pinks are very last season. It's all about the cool colors this year," Milo declared, with the undeniable air of Elle Woods clinching a court case.

"Well, regardless of whether she's on trend or not, I think it's more likely to be her than Clarissa," Hannah said. "But just because she was there doesn't mean she had anything to do with it. Those buildings were full of people, and all of them connected to Clan Rìoghalachd."

"Even so, it's worth investigating, don't you think?" I pressed.

I suppose, but how do you propose to investigate it? After your confrontation today, I doubt she'll talk to you voluntarily again," Hannah said.

"I think it would be smart to have one of the Fairhaven Caomhnóir tail her," I said.

Savvy perked up. "You should have Rana do it! I bet it would never occur to Maeve she was a Caomhnóir—they still haven't hired any female ones around here."

"Really? Is Savannah Todd suggesting we place her Novitiate girlfriend on a dangerous solo mission?" Finn asked, grinning playfully.

Savvy threw a fry at him as she snorted. "Dangerous? Following around that wee pixie of a thing? Rana can handle it. Besides, if we wanted to talk about Caomhnóir who are overprotective of their girlfriends, we could be here until last call enumerating your offenses, mate."

The two of them threw the fry back and forth until Sav caught it in her mouth and swallowed it, effectively ending their impromptu food fight.

"Okay, well, if you two are done acting like middle schoolers in a cafeteria, I think that's a great plan. You're right, Sav. Maeve definitely won't suspect Rana of being a Caomhnóir," I said.

"Will that leave us enough people to guard the courtyard?" Hannah asked, gnawing at her thumbnail. I glanced at the rest of her nails. They were all bitten to the quick.

"Plenty," I assured her. "It's not a large perimeter, and Catriona will send as many as she can. But I think we need to be in that courtyard again tonight. We need to investigate properly."

"Hard to investigate while you're super busy being traumatized," Milo muttered. Hannah nodded vigorously in agreement.

"If we know that no spirits are going to be wandering through, we can spend some real time trying to understand the nature of the trap in the courtyard. The more quickly we find out what it is, and how it works, the more quickly we can destroy it before it claims any more souls," I said.

"I just wish we had any bloody idea where to start," Savvy said.

"I've already started," Hannah said, and she set her copy of the *Book of Téigh Anonn* on the tabletop with a muffled thud. "I've been leafing through it all morning, because if this is an intentional trap and not some kind of natural malfunction, then a Casting is the most logical conclusion."

"And?" I asked.

"Nothing yet," Hannah said with a sigh. "Not that I expected to find anything in here. What we witnessed last night couldn't possibly be an official, sanctioned Casting, could it? But I thought maybe I could find something else, something that was meant to counteract what we witnessed."

"What we really ought to be searching out is Necromancer magic, I expect," Finn said. "Not that I think a Necromancer is involved, necessarily," he said hurriedly, as a hush of fear fell over the table. "We all know they're in disarray and well in hiding at this point. It would be lunacy for them to attempt an attack on a Geatgrima now, especially one surrounded by such a powerful clan. But that doesn't mean that someone else couldn't borrow one of their sick experiments for their own gain, does it?"

I shuddered, but nodded. Every Necromancer I'd ever had the misfortune to interact with had been utterly deranged. And what we'd seen last night? Only an equally deranged individual could have been responsible for it. I wouldn't be at all surprised if that was exactly what we were dealing with: a Necromancer Casting repurposed.

"I'm sure we could find all the information we need back at Fairhaven, but without access to the library there..." Hannah began.

"Hang on, though. That room we met in two nights ago at MacLeod Manor, that was a library," Savvy pointed out. "And a lot of those books looked really old. I bet a clan like that would have loads of books about Necromancers."

Hannah blinked. "I think you're right, Sav."

Savvy frowned. "No need to look quite so surprised. It does happen, on occasion."

I had already pulled out my phone.

"Jess?" Pippa's voice was wary before I'd even said a word.

"Hi, Pippa. I was hoping you could do me a favor?"

"I'm not sure how many favors I'll be in a position to do, given your confrontation with Clarissa this morning, but I can certainly try," she said, somewhat wearily. "What is it?"

"What do you think are the chances of us accessing the MacLeod Manor library today?"

"Oh!" Pippa exclaimed. Clearly this was not the kind of favor she had in mind. "Which one?"

"Uh... I don't know. Are there a lot of them?"

"Three in the manor and an archive in the Canongate Collective," Pippa said promptly. "If you know what you're looking for, I can better direct you to which collection will be the most useful."

"Oh wow. Okay, well, we're thinking we may need access to whatever the clan has on Necromancers and Necromancer Castings."

"In that case, you'll want the archive," Pippa said, "which will be easier to manage access to, as it doesn't require you to go back to the manor which would be... awkward, at present, I think."

"Yeah, I don't think I should become a regular house guest after this morning," I said. "When do you think we can get into that archive?"

"Just let me make a few quick phone calls, and I'll let you know," Pippa said, and she hung up.

"There's an archive at the Canongate Collective where they keep all their documentation on Necromancers. Pippa's working on getting us in there," I told everyone.

"That's brilliant!" Finn said. "We can be on site."

I nodded. "I say we all head over there together to investigate the courtyard some more. Then, when we hear from Pippa, Hannah and I can just head inside and start the search in the archive."

Everyone agreed it was a good plan, though no one looked very happy to be going back to that courtyard. The memories of what had happened there the previous night were still too fresh in our minds to feel anything but trepidation about entering that space again. For me, at least, it felt like returning to a scene of a particularly violent and horrific crime. I knew it had to be done, but I definitely wished it was someone else's job rather than mine. Then I reminded myself of the sad truth: I'd actually volunteered for this.

~

When we pulled up to the Canongate Collective, Pippa was standing outside waiting for us. I hadn't expected her there, but she explained as we climbed out of the car.

"I was able to get you access to the archive," Pippa said. "I was already down here arranging it, so I decided to stay and let you know in person."

"That's great," I said, peering at her strained expression. "I was half-expecting Clarissa to refuse after our little... uh... conversation this morning."

Pippa's smile was tight. "I didn't ask Clarissa. It didn't seem wise to ask for favors on your behalf today. So I went around her. Fortunately, there are several senior members of the clan who have the power to grant access to the archive, and they were more than happy to comply with the request."

I returned her smile. "Thanks."

I turned to the others. "How should we handle this?"

It was Finn who answered. "Why don't you and Hannah start in the archive? Savvy and I can walk the perimeter, figure out the best places to station the other Caomhnóir when they get here." Finn turned to Milo. "What about you, Milo, where would you like to start?"

Milo didn't hesitate for a moment. "The courtyard. I can explore it in ways you can't. The same can't be said for the archive."

"Fair point. Milo will start with us," Finn said, nodding.

We all shared a grim look that said, "Here goes nothing," and then turned to follow Pippa into the building. We parted at the top of the stairs and watched Finn, Savvy, and Milo disappear into the damp darkness at their base.

"We're headed this way," Pippa said, gesturing us along another hallway and up a flight of stairs to the second floor. She stopped in front of a frosted glass door that read, "MacLeod Interiors" and knocked briskly.

I heard muttering and a bit of commotion, and then the door swung open, revealing a frazzled-looking Danica MacLeod.

"Yes, can I... oh, hello Pippa," she said, and then her gaze traveled over Pippa's shoulder to where Hannah and I stood. "Oh! And the Ballard sisters! Please, do come in."

Danica stepped back and ushered us into the space, which was bright and white and looked like a showroom for glittering knick-knacks. The walls were covered in shelves that housed lamps, candle holders, small abstract sculptures and the like. I glanced at one price tag as I passed and almost choked on my gum.

"What can I help you with? I imagine you aren't here to spruce up your flat, given that you're staying in a hotel!" She let out a shrill peal of laughter that sounded mildly hysterical. Pippa's answering chuckle was perfunctory but convincing—she must have a lot of practice laughing at decidedly unfunny things in her constant quest to stroke egos and smooth over crises.

"No, and we apologize for bothering you at the studio. Jessica and Hannah need access to the archive, and I was hoping you could let us in. Your cousin Leah approved the access, but was unable to meet us here. She couldn't leave the golf club in the middle of a fundraising tournament."

Danica looked between Pippa and us as though she couldn't understand what was being asked of her. "You want me... to open... the archive?"

"That's right."

"Me? Why not Clarissa, or—"

"We don't want to inconvenience Clarissa, dragging her down here when you've also got the keys," Pippa said smoothly.

Danica's eyes went wide. "Oh, no! Of course not! No we mustn't... So you want me to...?"

"Yes, if you don't mind. It should only take a moment. Do you have a client coming in? We can come back in a little while if—" Pippa began, but Danica waved her off with another trilling laugh.

"No, no, I can... I just need my... hold on a moment."

It was like watching a slightly manic tropical bird. Danica's brightly patterned caftan flapped and swirled around her as she hurried over to the desk in the corner and began to rifle through the drawers. She muttered furiously to herself, scolding herself for being disorganized, before shrieking with delight and raising a set of keys into the air like a trophy.

"I've got them! Such a scatterbrain, you know. Can't trust me with anything, Clarissa's always saying so, and I must say she's quite right," Danica said.

"Nonsense," Pippa said, smiling again. "You run a whole business all on your own, don't you?"

Danica glanced around the shop with a dubious expression, as though she wasn't quite sure that was the case, and then bustled toward the door. "It's right this way, just follow me," she said.

We followed her up another set of steps to the third floor. There was a door to the left of the landing that had a keypad installed beside it. Danica hummed a little tune to herself as she put in the code. The door opened with a strange rushing sound, like it had been airlocked. I glanced edgily at Hannah, who smiled reassuringly.

"Temperature and humidity controlled," she murmured. "It helps protect the integrity of the older documents."

I nodded and let out a shaky breath. "As long as someone can hear us if we scream," I murmured back. After what we'd seen last night, I didn't trust these MacLeods as far as I could throw them. Well, Danica seemed harmless enough, but I wouldn't put it past her to lock us in the place and then forget all about us.

We followed Danica down another long corridor, narrower than the last, with square flickering lights set into the ceiling that gave everything a cold, sterile appearance, and reminded me of hospitals. At the end of the hall there was a white metal door with a tiny window set high in its face. Danica tapped her fingers against a second keypad. It beeped three times, and then a little door slid open beneath it, revealing a lock. Danica inserted her key and turned it. There was a loud click, a muffled thrumming hum, and the door slid open.

We stepped through into a room full of neatly organized stacks, dark wood work tables, and glass-topped display cases. The tables all had an impressive collection of implements for research, including cups full of pens and pencils, small blank notebooks, boxes of latex gloves, and oversized magnifying glasses attached to the tabletops on flexible metal arms. As anxious as she was, I could tell that Hannah, who spent half her life in libraries, was impressed with the set-up.

"Is there anything else you need? Only I'm expecting a phone call from a client," Danica said, hovering in the doorway.

"No, thank you, I think we should be fine," I told her.

"The door will lock behind you when you leave, so no need to find me to lock back up," Danica said. "Oh, and please sign the log book. Clarissa likes to keep a thorough record of everyone who uses the archive."

I looked where she was gesturing. A leather book lay open on a little pedestal just to the left of the door we'd just come in. One at a time, Hannah and I added our names to the short list already on the page, along with the date and time.

"Do let me know when you've finished, though, just so I know the archive is empty before I set the alarms for the night," Danica added.

"We will. Thank you again for your help," Hannah said, already starting to drift along one of the stacks, examining the contents.

"Do you mind my asking what you're looking for?" Danica asked. Her expression was mild, curious. "I might be able to point you down the right row. I haven't spent a lot of time in here, as I've always been a dreadful scholar, but enough to know the layout, you know."

"It's all part of the investigation. We were looking for any resources you might have on Castings and Necromancer magic," I told her.

Danica's eyebrows disappeared into her curly fringe. "Really?!" Her eyes filled with tears. "Do you really think the Necromancers are involved? Oh that's too horrible! I thought they were routed after the Reckoning! Clarissa never said a single thing about suspecting Necromancers!"

"We're just trying to cover all the bases," I told her in a calm and even voice. There was something about Danica, a wide-eyed innocence and deference to her sister that was almost childlike. I found myself, without meaning to, talking to her the way I would talk to a child—trying to reassure her even as I reminded myself that she was a high-ranking member of a clan I had no business trusting.

"Well, I hope you find what you're looking for. There's a full catalog of the archive contents for your reference, right there on that table," Danica said, pointing. "It ought to speed things up for you." And with that, she left us to our task, muttering quietly as she hurried back down the hallway.

"Do you require anything else?" Pippa asked as I set my bag down on an empty chair.

"No, I think we're good for now. Thank you for making this happen, Pippa. I know we aren't making your job any easier this week."

Pippa gave a smile, slightly strained, perhaps, but genuine. "My job is never easy." And with a parting nod, she followed Danica back down the hallway, letting the door shut with a loud click behind her. Hannah and I looked at each other, shared a deep breath, and got to work.

It was tedious. Like, mind-numbingly tedious. Hannah consulted the book on the center table that Danica had indicated, so we had no trouble finding the section of materials we were looking for, but once we sat down with them... ugh. After three hours of poring over page after nearly illegible page, I was contemplating just slamming my head against the desk and letting unconsciousness claim me.

"Nothing," Hannah said with a frustrated sigh, closing another book and adding it to the stack on her left, before picking up another tome from the stack on her right. She smirked at me. "How are you holding up?"

"Excellent. This place is great. They should offer birthday party packages."

Hannah giggled. "You didn't expect it to be fun, did you?"

I sighed and stretched my stiff legs out straight under the table. "No. I guess I just hoped we would find something quickly. Or at least, that they'd find something outside and rescue us from having to do this."

"Sometimes there are no shortcuts. No smoking guns," Hannah said, nodding sagely. She opened the book and started turning the pages slowly. "Even if there is something here, it could take us days to find—"

She stopped mid-sentence, a delicate page still held carefully between two gloved fingers.

I glanced at her expression and then sat up straighter, my pulse quickening. "Hannah? What is it?"

"There are pages missing," she whispered.

"What?" I stood up and moved around to the other side of the table to look over her shoulder. "How can you tell? That book looks old, is it possible they just fell out?"

Hannah didn't answer, but gestured pointedly to the open book in front of her. Someone had cleanly sliced several pages out of the book, probably with a razor or a utility knife, leaving a mere half inch of each page still woven tightly into the binding.

"Guess not," I murmured, running my finger down the cleanly sliced edge. "Well, well, well, that's interesting, isn't it?"

"Indeed," Hannah said, examining the previous page, and then flipping forward to investigate the table of contents. "The chapter is meant to cover a Necromancer attack in Edinburgh in the mid-1700s, but the entire account of the attack has been removed."

"I know I wasn't exactly a model Apprentice back in the day, but I don't remember reading about that in Celeste's Durupinen history class, do you?" I asked, trying to drag up fuzzy memories of tests and papers I hadn't thought about since I'd handed them in.

"I don't think so, no," Hannah said, her brow furrowed in concentration, and as far as I was concerned, that settled the matter. If Hannah didn't recall it, we hadn't learned it.

"We can't leap to conclusions, of course. This book could have been in this condition for years," Hannah said.

I blinked at her. "You don't actually believe that, right?"

"Not even a little, but it felt like the reasonable thing to say," Hannah admitted.

"What should we do?" I asked. "Alert Clan Rìoghalachd that someone is desecrating their priceless artifacts?" Already I could imagine Clarissa glaring at me, demanding proof that we hadn't ruined the book ourselves.

"No, definitely not," Hannah said, looking horrified at the thought. "We can't tell them what we've found until we know what these pages contained." She reached for a pad of sticky notes and began scribbling. "I certainly wouldn't put it past her to cast blame at anyone other than her own precious clan."

"What are you doing?" I asked her.

She'd flipped to the front of the book. "I'm copying down the publication information. If there's another copy of this book anywhere in Durupinen hands, we need to find it."

"And by 'we,' do you mean your super-nerd Scribe fiancé?" I asked, grinning.

A fleeting smile drifted across Hannah's face. "That would be correct." Then she pulled out her phone and snapped a photo of the sticky note, as well as a few of the book itself. She pocketed the note and her phone and sighed, a very serious look coming over her features. "You know what this means, Jess. If those pages contain what we think they might, this is definitely an inside job. No one but the most senior members of Clan Rìoghalachd can grant access to this room, which means they are well aware of every person that's been in here in the last year. They may even have a record of it. CCTV footage, even." She threw a cursory glance around the perimeter of the ceiling, looking for security cameras. "Ah-ha! See? Right there! I knew they'd have state-of-the-art security in here. After all, they have state-of-the-art everything else."

"Do you suppose anyone actually monitors that footage? And how long do they keep it before they wipe it?" I said.

Hannah shrugged. "Only one way to find out. We'll have to speak to Pippa again, see if she can—"

But the rest of Hannah's sentence was swallowed whole in the sudden, wailing shriek of a siren.

12

TARGETED

HANNAH JUMPED AND YELPED, almost falling back off her seat in surprise. I flung my hands up over my ears, staring around the room for the source of the sound. A fire alarm in the far corner was flashing.

"It's the fire alarm," I shouted, though I don't know how I expected Hannah to hear me when I couldn't even hear myself. She nodded, though, and we both hurriedly collected our bags and ran for the door. I pushed on it. The lock disengaged but the door didn't swing open.

"It's not opening!"

"What?! What do you mean?"

"I mean I can't open it!"

I shoved. I yanked. In panic, I flung my shoulder against the door. It made no difference. The door wouldn't budge.

"What do we do?" I shouted.

"The windows!" Hannah mouthed back.

"It's too high!"

"But we can call down for help!"

We tore across the room toward the windows; but before we'd made it halfway across the room, the lights began to flicker madly and an enormous book flew off a nearby shelf, whizzing past our heads and missing us by inches. A second book followed, and then a third. Hannah managed to duck behind a table, but I wasn't so lucky. The fourth book caught me on the side of the head, just above the temple, and I fell to the floor, momentarily stunned.

"Jess! Are you—aaah!"

Hannah tried to reach me, but had to fling herself behind a chair as another book launched itself at her, hurled with such force that it rent the pages from the covers, which lay splayed open and empty on the floor between us.

"I'm okay," I tried to say, but the words sounded thick and wrong in my head. There was a ringing in my ears, and my vision was blurry. The fluorescent bulbs continued to blink on and off like a strobe light, making the entire scene like a stop-motion cartoon. I struggled to get my bearings even as another book flew at me, slamming into my back between the shoulder blades. I cried out from the blow but still managed to struggle unsteadily to my feet, my hands thrown up in front of my face just in time to block a magnifying glass hurled with deadly force.

"It's a ghost!" I shouted. "It has to be! Can you—HANNAH BEHIND YOU!"

I don't know how she heard me over the blaring alarm and her own frightened shouts, but she turned just in time to fling herself out of the way as an entire shelving unit tipped and came crashing to the ground, landing exactly where she had just been crouching a moment before.

"Milo! MILO!" Hannah screamed through tears, and I started looking frantically around for him until I realized what she meant. My thoughts were choked with fear as I struggled to find the concentration to open the connection, but luckily Milo came bursting clearly through at that very moment.

"Where are you two? Can't you hear the fire alarm?" Milo's energy hummed with an anxiety that set my teeth buzzing.

"We're trapped in the archive with a really angry spirit! Whoever they are, they're attacking us and we can't get out!"

"Shit! Okay, we're coming! Can't Hannah—"

"No, no, we're too busy trying to protect ourselves. Hurry up!" I shrieked, both in my head and out loud as another giant metal shelving unit started teetering forward with an ominous creaking sound. I only just managed to throw myself out of the way as it, too, came crashing down, landing on one of the work tables, which splintered and collapsed.

I crawled across the floor and made a lunge for my backpack, which I had dropped when the first book hit me—I had a Casting bag in there, if I could just reach it. As though I'd spoken the thought out loud, our ghostly attacker got hold of the bag. It shot across the floor out of my reach, propelled by an unseen force. As it did, I felt the spirit's energy assault my senses as thoroughly as its owner was assaulting my body: a cold that burned like fire, a strange, disorienting scent of sulfur, and the sweetish stench of something rotting away to dust.

Suddenly, there was the pounding of footsteps in the hallway and the chaos in the room just...stopped. One moment, the lights were flashing and books and furniture were being hurled through the air, and the next, utter stillness.

"Jess! Hannah! Hang on, we're going to get you out!" It was Finn's voice.

At the same moment, Milo came sailing through the wall, his arms raised defensively in front of him like he was about to engage in hand-to-hand combat with our invisible attacker. He dropped them, though, when he saw us huddled on the floor.

"Oh my God! Are you all right? Are you hurt?" he squeaked, blinking out only to reappear right beside Hannah, who was attempting to crawl out from under a half-crushed table.

"I... I think I'm okay," Hannah said, her voice shaking madly. She made to stand, but thought better of it, as her legs were trembling as violently as her voice.

"Jess, are—shit!" Milo gasped. "You're bleeding!"

He was pointing at my forehead. I reached up with numb fingers and was surprised to see them come away from my hairline red and sticky with blood. "I... I got hit with a book."

"This is... I can't believe... *one spirit* did this?!" Milo cried, staring around at the wreckage of the room.

"I don't know. I don't... I *think* so," Hannah muttered dazedly. "It all happened so fast and so violently, it was all I could do to protect myself."

There was a babble of deep voices outside of the door, and then there was a click and a beep and the door swung open. Finn barreled into the room, his Casting bag swinging from his wrist, his arms raised, ready to Expel a spirit that seemed already to have vanished. Behind him came another half-dozen Caomhnóir and, behind them, Danica's pale, horrified face peeked hesitantly around the doorjamb.

"What in the world's happened in here?!" she cried, her voice shooting up an octave.

Finn took one look at me and dropped his hands, closing the distance between us with two long strides. "You're hurt."

He caught me gently into his arms and then raised one hand to probe at my hairline while I winced.

"Ouch," I said in mild surprise, as the shock began to wear off and the pain set in.

"You're going to need stitches," Finn murmured. He reached into his pocket and pulled out a bandana. He pressed it firmly against my head. "Can you walk?"

"Of course I can—" I began, but swallowed the rest of the declaration as the room seemed to give a heave. I fell into Finn, who caught me at once around the waist.

"I expected as much. Probably a concussion. Let's get out of here. Can't someone turn that blasted alarm off?" he roared back over his shoulder toward the Caomhnóir crowding the doorway. Two of them broke away and jogged off down the hallway.

"We've got to get you both outside. I don't think there's a fire, but we don't want to risk it," Finn said. "Malcolm, could you—" Finn gestured toward Hannah, and the Caomhnóir named Malcolm rushed forward at once, helping Hannah to her feet and keeping an arm under hers in case she was as unsteady as I was.

"Milo?" Finn said.

Milo looked up from fussing over Hannah and caught Finn's eye. "Oh! Yeah, I'm on it," he replied, and shimmered from sight.

"What's Milo doing?" I asked.

"What none of the rest of us can do: search the building safely for your attacker," Finn explained as he half-carried me out of the room. Now that the adrenaline of the attack was wearing off, I realized how dizzy and off-center I felt. That book had hit me harder than I'd realized. In fact, now that I wasn't distracted by a violent spirit attack, I was aware of just how many places were starting to ache. I'd lost count of how many books the ghost had managed to hurl at me, but it seemed that more than a few of them had hit their mark.

It was a slow, laborious process down the stairs and outside onto the sidewalk. From what I overheard pass between the Caomhnóir, they had managed to avoid the police and fire services showing up with a few well-placed phone calls—Durupinen in Edinburgh had enough clout to make that happen. As we stumbled out onto the sidewalk and Finn deposited me on a low stone wall to rest, the alarm inside the building finally stopped screeching into the gathering twilight. We joined dozens of people out on the pavement waiting for the all-clear to head back inside. My eyes roved over them and landed on a slight figure in shredded jeans and an oversized sweatshirt. She peered out from under the shelter of the hood and we locked eyes. I nodded at her, and her eyes widened. She shook her head once, sharply, almost pleadingly, and then dropped her gaze to the pavement, letting the hood obscure her once more.

There was Maeve MacLeod again, exactly where she shouldn't be. Interesting.

"Caomhnóir Carey?" a gangly young Caomhnóir approached, looking nervous.

"Yes?"

"I think we found what set off the alarm, sir." And the young man held up a cigarette, burned nearly down to the filter, which had been placed carefully in a plastic bag. "It had been taped to the wall underneath one of the alarm sensors."

Finn took the bag from the young Caomhnóir's hands, staring at it with a very dark expression. "Thank you. I will make sure it is properly investigated."

The young man nodded, looking relieved to no longer be in charge of the damning bit of evidence, and hurried away.

A sleek black van pulled up right in front of us and two white-coated women climbed out, each carrying a black bag. The taller of the women had a quick whispered exchange with one of the senior Caomhnóir, and I watched as he turned and pointed directly at me. My brain felt sluggish, spluttering away in my head like an old car being coaxed to start; and it wasn't until the woman sat beside me, and wordlessly pulled out a pair of latex gloves, that I realized she was a doctor.

"Miss Ballard? I'm Dr. Stewart, Clarissa MacLeod's personal physician. With your permission, I'd like to examine you—get that nasty cut cleaned up. Does that suit you?" The woman had the kind of brisk, efficient voice that calmed me at once. Everything from her expression to her bearing spoke of competency. I nodded gratefully, and she helped Finn get me to my feet again and over to the van. The back of it was flung open, revealing the interior to be almost indistinguishable from that of a standard ambulance. Hannah was already sitting inside it, having a small light flashed in her eyes.

"Is she okay?" I asked, as Dr. Stewart sat me on a small seat that folded down neatly from the inside of the open door.

The other doctor answered the question without looking at me. "A few bumps and bruises, nothing worse. I'd worry about yourself, love, your sister's just fine."

I let out a shaky breath and then sucked it back in again sharply as Dr. Stewart applied an antiseptic to my head.

"Sorry, it's going to sting a bit. I'll numb it up before I stitch it, though," she said with a small but genuine smile. "What caused the injury, if I may ask?"

"A book," I said.

She frowned. "A book?"

"A big one," I said defensively.

"Well, that's a first," she muttered, shaking her head.

I didn't bother to explain any further. I had no idea how much this woman knew about the MacLeods. It was likely that she was handsomely paid not to ask any more questions than were strictly necessary to do her job. I sat quietly and winced through her ministrations, and about fifteen minutes later she pronounced me all patched up, with seven fresh stitches in my scalp and a clean dressing wrapped over them.

"You have a mild concussion," she told me. "So you'll want to take it easy for a few days. You may find you are nauseous, dizzy, and sensitive to bright light and loud noises. If any of those symptoms worsen after a day or two, please have Clarissa contact me. You can sit here for a few minutes while I speak to the head of security."

"Thank you, doctor," Finn said, reaching out to shake her hand. She took it, gave it a firm shake, and set off toward a knot of Caomhnóir hovering near the front doors. They hadn't yet given people the all-clear to re-enter the building. Passersby were gawking, peering up at the building for signs of smoke or fire.

"Jess! Hannah!"

Pippa was pushing her way through the crowd on the sidewalk. She arrived beside me slightly out of breath and very pale.

"What in the world happened?" she asked.

"Yes, I'd like to hear this myself," Finn said, crossing his arms over his chest.

Hannah climbed down out of the van to sit beside me, and together we pieced together the story of what had happened inside the archive. I found the details to be a bit confusing, and a few times I lost the thread of what I was saying; but fortunately, Hannah was there to fill in the gaps.

"What I don't understand is why we couldn't get out," Hannah said, when we'd told all we could remember. "Did the alarm trigger the door to lock or something?"

"I can answer that," Finn said, and pulled something out of his pocket. It was a zip tie. "I cut this off the door handle."

I wouldn't have thought Hannah could look paler than she already did, but she managed it. "But that means…"

"Someone trapped you in there with that ghost on purpose," Finn answered for her. "And this," he held up the cigarette in the bag, "is proof that they intentionally set the alarm off as well."

Pippa dragged a hand over her face, looking bewildered. "I just can't comprehend why someone would do that," she said.

"Pippa! Oh, Pippa, thank goodness you're here!"

Danica was hurrying toward them, flapping like a deranged butterfly, her eyes red-rimmed, streaks of mascara staining her cheeks.

"It's terrible! I was on the phone with a client and then suddenly the alarms were all going off. No one can seem to tell me if there was a fire, although I can't for the life of me see any smoke to speak of. And did they tell you? They were attacked! By a ghost! I can't understand it!" Danica was wringing her hands. "Have you called Clarissa? Someone needs to call Clarissa! Someone needs to tell her what's happened! Oh, she's going to be so very distraught!"

Personally, I thought Clarissa would be ambivalent at best, hearing I'd been attacked by a spirit, but I kept that assessment to myself.

"Danica, does this building have CCTV?" Finn asked.

Danica nodded, eyes like saucers. "Oh, yes. The whole of the Collective is fully wired up. Clarissa insisted on it. She's very particular about security."

"We saw a camera in the archive," Hannah added.

"We need access to that footage. Can you get it for us?" Finn pressed.

"Oh, heavens, I wouldn't even know where to start!" Danica fluttered. "I suppose Caomhnóir Murphy would be able to help you' He's the one in charge of building security, so I imagine he can provide you with what you need. Shall

I fetch him for you? I know I saw him here somewhere." She turned and began scanning the crowd for him.

"That's all right, I know who he is. I can speak to him myself," Finn said. "We appreciate your help."

"No need to thank me. I'm simply useless, aren't I? Clarissa's always saying so, you know. I feel just awful. Imagine, a violent spirit in our own archive! It just doesn't make any sense, none at all. First, the spirit attack at the manor and now this! Why, it's quite terrifying! We've had nothing of this sort happen until you came here!" Her tone wasn't accusatory—more wondering, like she would find it all rather fascinating if it weren't so dreadful.

"Yeah, we seem to have that effect," I said dryly.

Finn stood up. "I requested a full list of everyone who was on the premises when the alarm went off. They're doing a full sweep of the building now, in case the perpetrator chose to hide inside while everyone else vacated. Pippa, do you think you could take Hannah and Jess back to the hotel? I don't want to leave until I've been debriefed by the Caomhnóir in charge."

"Of course," Pippa said, looking relieved to have something productive to do.

"Where's Savvy?" Hannah asked. "I haven't seen her since we got out here."

"She and five other Caomhnóir are still patrolling the inner courtyard," Finn said. "We thought at first that the alarm might be meant to interrupt our investigation outside, before we realized it was really meant to interrupt yours up in the archive. I wanted them to stay and make sure no one fled out the back door while everyone else was distracted by evacuating out the front."

"Oh, that was clever!" Danica whispered, looking almost comically impressed.

"Uh, thanks," Finn said, slightly nonplussed, before turning back to me. "I'll see you back at the hotel. Stay in the room until I get back, but check the Wards first. We don't want any more uninvited visitors tonight."

I was too tired and sore to make a snarky comment about house arrest, and instead just nodded. Finn kissed me on the top of my head and jogged off to confer with the other Caomhnóir.

"Do you need assistance getting to the car?" Pippa asked. "It's just here."

"I've got her," Hannah said, helping me to my feet. She smiled at me. "I've always got her."

13

TAKING CONTROL

I THOUGHT THERE WAS A RULE ABOUT SLEEPING AND CONCUSSIONS, but I had no idea what it was—and I was too sore and exhausted to look it up. So I said screw it, and fell into my bed the moment we got back to the hotel. If Hannah objected to my plan, she kept her objections to herself. Instead, she curled up next to me, unlaced my boots, and drew a crushed velvet throw over me to keep me warm. Then she fished a bottle of water and a slightly smushed granola bar from her purse, and watched me like a hawk while I consumed both, along with a painkiller Dr. Stewart had given me. I didn't really want to take the meds, because I was afraid they'd make me loopy and useless for the foreseeable future; but as the pain mounted from my various injuries, it became clear that I was pretty useless anyway, so I swallowed the pill without argument. I decided just to close my eyes for a few minutes.

Fifteen hours later, I woke up.

I'd slept so deeply and so soundly that when I came to, I thought I'd missed the school bus. I had no idea where I was for a solid thirty seconds. Then my bewildered gaze fell on the pill bottle by the bed, and everything came crashing back. I shot up into a sitting position, then sank back onto the pillows with a groan.

"Well, hello there, sleeping beauty," Finn said, jumping up out of a chair by the window and coming over to sit on the edge of the bed. "How are you feeling?"

"Like someone hit me with a library full of books," I groaned. "Is there anything I can drink?" My mouth felt and tasted like sandpaper.

He handed me the bottle of water, from which I drained the last few sips. "I already called for breakfast. Coffee is on the way."

"Breakfast?!" I cried, and then winced at the volume of my own voice. "What time is it?"

"Nearly ten o'clock. You slept straight through. And don't look at me like that—you were ordered to rest," he added sternly, correctly interpreting the meaning behind my answering glare. "I certainly wasn't going to be the one to wake you when you were snoring so soundly."

"I don't snore," I grumbled.

"Of course you don't," Finn agreed solemnly.

Before I could decide which pillow to throw at him, there was a knock on the door and Finn got up to answer it. A timid-looking woman in a black and white uniform set the breakfast tray on the coffee table, and scurried out again without a word. Hannah slipped in before the woman could close the door.

"Sorry, I heard the knock and came to see how you're feeling," she said, helping herself to a little scone from the tray.

"Forget about me, I'm fine, it's just a few stitches," I snapped, still grumpy.

"And a concussion," Hannah added.

"And several contusions," Finn piled on.

"Whatever! The point is, how I'm feeling should be the least important thing right now! I've been unconscious for the better part of a day! What's happening at the Geatgrima? Do we know who pulled the alarm? Did Milo track down our spirit attacker? Did the Fairhaven Caomhnóir get here yet? And what about last night? Did we manage to keep any more spirits from being victimized?"

Hannah poured out a cup of coffee and handed it to me. "Drink this, and we'll fill you in."

Never one to refuse coffee, even under duress, I accepted the cup quietly.

Finn sighed, "If we seem reluctant to talk about it, it's because there's hardly anything to tell. Whoever pulled that alarm and locked you into the archive did a damn good job of making sure they wouldn't be found out."

My heart, beating rapidly a moment before, sank with disappointment. "You can't be serious! Nothing? Not even on the CCTV?"

Finn's expression darkened. "The CCTV footage had been wiped. All of it. They don't have anything from the last six months."

"But how is that possible?!" I cried out, ignoring the ringing in my head. "I thought Clarissa was some kind of security nut, isn't that what Danica said? How could no one notice that months of footage was just gone?"

"Because they only check the footage when there's something specific they want to review. They've had no cause to review it in recent months."

"Which means, not only is there no footage from today, but there's no footage to help us figure out who took the pages out of that book in the first place," Hannah said.

"Damn it!" I hissed through clenched teeth.

"We interviewed every single person who'd been on the premises at the time," Finn said. "Upwards of fifty people, mostly Caomhnóir who live in the flats there. Not a single person saw anything suspicious, and, of course, they all deny involvement."

"Did you interview Maeve MacLeod?" I asked.

Finn frowned. "Yes."

"And what was her story?"

"Said she'd only just gotten there. Had come to see her aunt Danica, and hadn't even gone upstairs yet when the alarm started sounding," Finn said, closing his eyes and pinching the bridge of his nose as though that would help him remember the details of what she'd told him.

"And did you buy any of that?" I asked.

"Not a word," Finn said. "There was a Caomhnóir there with her. They seemed to be trying a little too hard not to look at each other."

"Hmmm," I said, still sipping the coffee. "That means she's been present at all three major spirit events we've had since we arrived here. I'm sorry, but it's hard for me to believe that that could be a mere coincidence."

"Well, we'll soon see whether it's a coincidence or not," Finn said. "The Fairhaven Caomhnóir arrived late last night, and I've already given Rana her assignment."

"You would have thought she'd won the lottery," said Hannah, grinning.

Finn managed a smile, too. "Ah, well, she's still just a Novitiate. She's unlikely to realize how tedious a task surveillance can be, but I wasn't about to tell her so. She's just happy to be of use and, truth be told, I'm glad to have someone I trust to do a thorough job. She can't watch Maeve 24/7 of course, but there are two other female Caomhnóir in the mix, and they'll be taking it in shifts. If Maeve MacLeod is anywhere she oughtn't be from now on, we'll be the first to know."

I felt a tiny bit of the tension leave my body. I trusted Rana, too, and it was comforting to know there was one less thing to worry about. But then my brain turned to my other still unanswered questions, and the tension mounted again.

"You said the Caomhnóir arrived late last night. Did they arrive in time to patrol the courtyard during the... disturbance?" I asked, unsure what else to call the dreadful events that occurred between two and three o'clock in the morning.

"Oh, yes. And I am happy to be able to report at least one piece of good news. They were successful in warning away every spirit who ventured near Canongate Collective during that time. Whatever dark mischief is at work there, it claimed no new victims last night."

"Well, thank goodness for that," I breathed, and then drained the rest of my coffee. I made a motion as though to get up and refill my cup, but Hannah thrust out a warning hand. Then she snatched the cup from my hands and tutted at me while she filled it.

"Rest!" she demanded as she handed it back.

"I've been asleep for fifteen hours! How much more rest am I supposed to get?" I grumbled, but I leaned back against the pillows as I accepted the cup from her. After a sip, I turned back to Finn. "What about the spirit that attacked us?"

Finn shook his head. "Milo spent nearly all of last night searching in ways we never could, but he came up empty. Well, nearly empty..."

"Nearly?" I prompted eagerly.

"I'll let him explain it to you, as I barely understand it myself. He should be back pretty soon. In the meantime, how would you feel about trying to get up and dressed?" Finn asked.

"Yes, please!" I exclaimed. "I'm all for sleeping in on a random rainy weekend morning, but if I have to spend one more minute just lying in this bed when there's so much going on, I think I might lose my mind."

While Hannah left to update Pippa on my condition, Finn helped me out of bed and into the shower. The hot water felt wonderful on my stiff and aching muscles, but seeing my body in the mirror was something of a shock. I had several very large, very colorful bruises on my arms, legs, and torso. There was hardly a movement I made that didn't ache somewhere, and my head still felt strange, like someone had removed half my brain and replaced it with cotton balls. The painkiller Dr. Stewart had given me had long since worn off, but I was hesitant to take any more, afraid they would render me even more groggy and useless than I already felt. I compromised on the max dose of some over-the-counter stuff I had in my suitcase, hoping it would take the edge off and help me achieve at least borderline functionality.

When I'd dressed and eaten something, Hannah returned, this time with Milo in tow. His form was a bit pale and flickery.

"Are you okay?" I asked him. "You look about as good as I feel right now."

"I don't know what the spirit equivalent of a nap is, but sweetness, I need one," he replied, sinking like a feather down onto the couch beside me.

"What did you find out?" I asked, unable to stop myself from getting right to the point.

Milo frowned. "Well, as I'm sure Finn told you, I wasn't able to track down the spirit from the archive. But that said, whoever it is, they didn't vanish without a trace."

"Okay, I'm listening," I prompted a little impatiently.

"Before I tell you what I found, I need to ask you... did you sense anything at all about the spirit who attacked you?" Milo asked, leaning forward and fairly glowing with sudden interest. "I know it was fast and frantic and all that, but still. Did you get any sort of impression at all?"

I cast my mind back to the previous evening, which was harder than it should have been thanks to my newly acquired head injury. I sorted and sifted through the memories, alternately sharp and fuzzy, searching for the impressions I'd had of the spirit during the attack. All at once, it surfaced.

"Cold," I said stupidly, then made a second attempt at eloquence. "It wasn't the kind of cold that always accompanies spirits. It was painful and deep and..."

"Dark," Hannah said. I glanced over at her to see her eyes glazed over, as if lost in the same memories I was attempting to access. She nodded, gave her head a little shake, and met my gaze. "I don't think I even would have remembered it if you didn't say it, but you're right. I've never, ever felt a cold like that."

"There was something else, too," I said. "An awful smell."

"I don't think I ever noticed that. Can you describe it?" Hannah asked.

Again, I had to think harder than usual. "It was rotten and sweetish and musty. And familiar, although I can't think of where I... the mausoleum!"

The sound of my own shout was as sharp as a blade in my head, and I winced before continuing in a lower voice. "It reminded me of when I was in the mausoleum at Fairhaven, the one where Eleanora Larkin was buried. Remember when we had to break in there, to retrieve her diary?"

"I'm not likely to forget your brief foray into grave robbery, am I?" Hannah asked dryly.

"When I opened her tomb, there was such a distinctive smell from inside, and that's exactly what I smelled last night when that spirit was attacking us." I turned to Milo, who was looking grimly satisfied. "I'm guessing from the look on your face that something I just said rang true."

Milo nodded. "I can't explain why or how, but that spirit—whoever it is— leaves a fleeting but distinctive trail behind them."

I sat up straighter, ignoring the way even that small movement hurt. "Go on."

"Well, I first noticed it when the attack was still happening, but of course, I didn't experience it the same way you did, because... well, the five senses aren't really something I can rely on the way that I used to now that I'm traveling light, corporeally speaking," Milo said, a little ruefully. "But I felt something very strange nonetheless, like the air was harder to move through, and it was... charged up, somehow. You know that feeling you get right before an electrical shock? A sort of building up of potential energy—it was kind of like that. And when the spirit fled, which it did almost as soon as I got there—there was a kind of... trail behind them, like the surrounding air held on to the impression of them." Milo's face crumpled and he shook his head before dropping it into his hands. "Sorry, I'm explaining this so badly. It's just... I've never experienced anything like it before, so I don't have the words for it."

"Don't be ridiculous, you're explaining it just fine," I told him. "Go on."

"Well, that... energy, or impression or whatever it was—lingered behind that spirit for just a few seconds. When I took off to find them, I actually picked up on it briefly, almost like a trail. Unfortunately, it didn't last long, and I didn't realize what it was until it had already faded away. Does that make sense?"

I hesitated for a moment. "I'm not sure if it makes sense or not, but I'm not sure if that matters, really. The important question is whether you would recognize it again—this energy trail thing—if you felt it?"

Milo lifted his face. "Oh, I definitely would! And that's what I'm saying! Now that I know what I'm looking for, I think I could track that spirit if I ever got close to them again!"

"I don't want anyone getting close to that spirit again," Hannah said with a shudder. "Not until we know why it's so powerful and angry."

"And until we know who's controlling it," I added. "Because one thing is for sure: that spirit didn't tape a lit cigarette to the wall or zip-tie us into that archive. Only a living person could have done that. That said, we may not have a choice. As we keep investigating, we are going to get closer to the truth and there's clearly someone who will go to desperate measures to prevent that from happening."

"It seems strange," Hannah said slowly, "that Clarissa would invite us here to investigate if she's the one behind it." She raised a fingernail to her mouth to chew on it, but Milo gave a gasp of disapproval and she reluctantly dropped it to her lap again. "I mean, it's like she's asking to get caught."

"That's true, unless she's one of those people who considers herself far more clever than everyone else around her, which tracks, honestly," I said, a clear vision of Clarissa's face in my mind, it's even and flawless features rendered quite beauty-less when twisted into her smug look of superiority.

Milo nodded. "I wouldn't put it past her either."

Hannah looked like she might argue, but then shrugged halfheartedly and bit her lip instead of the aforementioned fingernail.

"Well, I can't just sit here anymore, I'm going to lose my mind," I announced into the several seconds of silence that followed. "What's the deal? Am I being kept on house arrest, or am I allowed in the field again?"

Hannah rolled her eyes. "No one's going to force you to sit it out, Jess, as long as you don't martyr yourself. Just take it one step at a time. As long as you feel okay and don't push yourself past your own limits, no one's going to baby you."

It was my turn to roll my eyes, and I took it, relieved that *that*, at least, wasn't painful. "Good luck getting Finn to agree to that approach."

"Finn's not as bad as he used to be," Milo said fairly. "A couple of years ago, he'd have already had you on a train back to Fairhaven encased in bubble wrap. Give the guy some credit."

I didn't reply, partly because I was annoyed that he had a point. Instead, I said, "Okay, well in the spirit of taking it one step at a time, I'd like to get out of here and do something productive. What's the plan today?"

Hannah sighed. "I sent the photos I took in the archive off to Kiernan, and he's going to try to track down any records of that book while he's at Skye. If anyone can find another copy—or another account of the same events—it's him. There's no point in going back to the archive, because someone literally tried to kill us there; and anyway, the information we need is gone."

"Meanwhile, Maeve's rebellious little self is being tailed by Rana, so if she's involved, we'll know it," Milo said confidently. "Other than planning to go back to the courtyard later on tonight, we're in a bit of a holding pattern. Or at least, you mere mortals are. I plan on doing more ghostly reconnaissance this afternoon."

"Why don't we go back to the courtyard now?" Hannah said. "Between last night and this morning, the Caomhnóir have been combing it for clues. We could go over there and see what they've found, if anything."

"Yes, please," I said. "Anything to get out of this room."

I stood up too fast and swayed a little. Hannah narrowed her eyes at me as I plastered on a too-bright smile. "Taking it slowly," I promised, with more bravado than I felt. And then, to distract from my less than optimal physical state I added, "Where's Savvy? Is she going to come, too?"

"She's off with Rana this morning," Hannah said. "They're both off duty for a bit, so I think they wanted to spend some time together."

As we walked over to Canongate Collective ten minutes later, I had to admit that I was shaken. The attack in the archive had not only brought home the danger of this assignment, but it had also left me with an injury that made me feel vulnerable—like a superhero suddenly stripped of their usual powers. Granted, the only superpowers I possessed were my knack for attracting trouble and my utter lack of filtering my own thoughts before blurting them out. But still, the analogy stood. I was lucky the concussion wasn't worse, but if that spirit decided to come back for round two, I'd be at a serious disadvantage in defending myself.

The courtyard, when we walked at last into it, looked like an FBI crime scene from a true crime tv show. Every inch of the place was crawling with

Caomhnóir engaged in every kind of traditional investigative technique I could think of—dusting for fingerprints, examining footprints, photographing everything—and a good deal of untraditional ones as well. I was pretty sure Olivia Benson and Elliot Stabler never whipped out a Casting bag full of candles and crystals to check for traces of paranormal presences; but then again, I was admittedly a few seasons behind. They were also doing what looked like yard work: mowing, digging, and literally leaving no stone unturned.

Milo halted on the outer border of the space, closing his eyes and assuming an air of intense concentration. A few seconds later he sagged, shaking his head.

"Nothing," he said dully. "Not that it was likely that spirit could be here without being sensed or spotted by a dozen Caomhnóir." And he shot off across the courtyard to confer with a young man who was dropping precious stones into the grass around a lit candle.

I spotted Finn squatting in the grass near the Geatgrima, contemplating the structure with such intensity that it looked like he was trying to shoot laser beams out of his eyeballs. We'd nearly reached him before he spotted us.

"How's it going?" I asked him.

Finn stood up and dusted his hands off on the fronts of his pant legs. "Whatever's causing this phenomenon, it hasn't left a bloody trace within these walls, at least not that we can find."

My heart sank. "Nothing at all? How is that possible?"

"I'm not sure, but we've been combing this space for hours now, and we've turned up sod all. I can't understand it. If it's a Casting, how can there be no trace of it, even while it's active? And if it's not a Casting, then what in the name of the Aether is it?"

We didn't answer because we couldn't.

Suddenly, Hannah gasped. "I see we've got an audience today."

Finn and I turned in the direction she was looking to see that Clarissa MacLeod was standing in the doorway leading out to the courtyard, Pippa on one side of her and one of the Clan Rìoghalachd Caomhnóir on the other. The latter had leaned in close, his lips practically to her ear as they conferred together.

"Well, well, well, the Queen has deigned to grace us with her presence," I muttered before turning to Finn. "Did you know she was going to be here?"

Finn shook his head. "No, but I'm not surprised. With so many Fairhaven

Caomhnóir here, I'm sure she's eager to save face and make it look like she's still in control of the situation."

"Isn't she?" I asked.

"Not anymore," said a smooth voice from behind me.

I turned to see Catriona walking toward us, impossibly graceful as always in a pair of shoes wildly inappropriate to the terrain. She closed the distance between us in three long strides and placed a hand on my shoulder.

"I was going to come and see you over at the hotel if you hadn't turned up soon. How are you feeling?" Her tone was as disinterested as ever it was, but her eyes were fixed intently on my face, and there was a gleam of worry in them.

"Cat! I didn't realize you were staying. I'm great," I told her and then, when she continued to stare at me with narrowed eyes, I sighed. "Okay, well, I'm not great, but I'm okay, seriously. The concussion is minor. I'm taking it easy. Walking over here was the first thing anyone would let me do since yesterday." I was not entirely successful in keeping a petulant grumble out of my voice.

Catriona nodded once, as if the sound of my petulance satisfied her, and then said, "I'm not staying. Or rather, I'm not staying long. I just need to deliver this order to Clarissa and make a few arrangements, then I'll be catching the train back to London." She held up an official-looking envelope made of thick cream paper and sealed with the official wax seal of the High Priestess of the Northern Clans.

"What is that?" I asked, pointing to it.

To my surprise, Catriona's face broke into a wide smile. "Follow me and you'll find out," she said.

Hannah and Finn and I traded looks before falling into line behind Catriona as she strode across the grass, heading straight for Clarissa. Clarissa watched us approach with an inscrutable expression on her face.

"Catriona. A pleasure, as always," Clarissa said as we halted in front of her.

"An odd sentiment under the circumstances, but I thank you all the same," Catriona shot back.

Clarissa tilted her head, peering around Catriona to look at me. "Jessica, I was profoundly disturbed to hear of what befell you and your sister while examining our archive. Dr. Stewart assures me you were not seriously injured."

"I've had worse," I replied curtly.

"Regardless, my private physician remains at your disposal. I hope this unfortunate encounter has not affected your decision to stay on and continue your assignment here in Edinburgh."

"I'm sorry to disappoint you, but I don't give up that easily," I said.

Clarissa's lips twitched as though she might smirk, but she managed to keep her expression smooth. She turned back to Catriona. "Is there anything else that you require before you depart, Catriona?"

"Only to see that this is delivered directly into your hands," Catriona replied, and she held out the envelope.

Clarissa looked down at it. Did I imagine it, or did she turn just a shade paler when she spotted the official seal?

"And this is...?" she asked languidly, reaching out and plucking the envelope from Catriona's hand.

"A Council-approved order to suspend your jurisdiction over this case and ban all members of Clan Rìoghalachd from this property until the investigation is complete."

Clarissa was halfway through unsealing the envelope when her head snapped sharply up.

"I beg your pardon?" she hissed.

"Based on the reports from our Tracker team, there have been several very unpleasant incidents since their arrival, incidents that have targeted them and put them in danger. All evidence thus far suggests those incidents were planned and carried out by a member of Clan Rìoghalachd ."

"How dare you!" Clarissa gasped. "That is an utterly unfounded accusation and an intentional slander of the very—"

"Save your grandstanding for someone who gives a shit," Catriona cut in, her voice somehow managing to sound both sharp and bored at the same time. "Read it. It's all in there, the whole report. We aren't dealing with a malfunctioning Geatgrima. We are dealing with a Geatgrima that has been sabotaged, and until we know who has sabotaged it, we are taking over the property. You have twenty-four hours to vacate the premises and turn it over to Tracker control."

"That is ludicrous! These buildings are in constant use, not only for Caomhnóir housing, but also for a number of other clan related business purposes—"

"None of which trump the first and most sacred purpose of your and every clan, which is to protect the Gateways and the spirits who Cross through them."

Clarissa's mouth twisted up into a little knot like she'd just sucked a lemon. "And what am I meant to do with all of the Caomhnóir housed here, throw them out in the street?" she snapped.

"Perhaps you could house them in one of the other hundred properties you own within walking distance of this one," Catriona suggested. "Clarissa, you own half this city. Please don't pretend you lack the resources to deal with this temporary inconvenience. You'll only embarrass yourself."

"Inconvenience, indeed! It's an insult, that's what it is!"

"You are, of course, more than welcome to lodge a formal complaint, in writing, as soon as you've complied with the terms laid out in that order," Catriona said with an absolutely beaming smile. I dropped my gaze to the ground at once in an attempt to hide my own smile.

Clarissa opened her mouth and closed it again, her eyes positively burning with rage. She seemed to be struggling internally, trying to decide whether it was worth it to keep arguing so publicly—every person in the courtyard had now halted in their various tasks to turn and gawk at the raised voices. Beside her, Pippa's face was so starkly white, I thought she might faint.

"I am going to make every Council member who voted for this order deeply regret her decision," Clarissa said, in a soft voice that nevertheless held all the menace of a vicious, feral snarl.

"Oh, I do so look forward to it," Catriona said dryly.

Clarissa handed the order to Pippa, who took it with a slightly shaky hand. "See to this," she said stiffly.

"Yes, of course, Clarissa," Pippa replied. "Consider it done."

In that moment I felt my one and only pang of regret at the Council's decision. As far as I was concerned, nothing could be more welcome than any opportunity to bring Clarissa down a few pegs; but I did feel bad that it had now become Pippa's problem to clear Canongate Collective. I knew it would be no easy task to organize.

"Thanks so much for your cooperation!" Catriona chirped, smiling broadly once more. "When we've finished the investigation, of course, all can be returned to normal."

Clarissa only glared in answer, and then turned on her heel and stalked back through the door and down the corridor, Pippa and the Caomhnóir trotting along behind her like obedient pets.

"Well, that was fun," Catriona sighed, turning to look at us.

"Best part of my day so far, and I'm including coffee in that," I agreed.

Hannah was trying not to smile, but failing spectacularly. "I must admit, I enjoyed it more than I should have," she muttered.

"I don't know why you get to have all the fun, though," I said to Cat, pouting at her. "I've been the one dealing with her bullshit all week. Why do you get to deliver the order?"

"Because I'm the boss," Catriona said, somewhat indignantly. "Do you honestly think I'm going to delegate one of the only enjoyable parts of my job?"

I grinned. "I guess not."

"Besides, if I was going to confer the honor, I'd give it to Hannah, not you. Hannah's had to deal with that woman in Council meetings for years."

Hannah gave up trying not to smile and grinned as well. "Cheers, Cat!"

I glanced suddenly around us, realizing whose commentary on the subject I was sorely missing. "Where's Milo? Don't tell me he missed the fun!"

Hannah glanced around, too. "He was here a few minutes ago. I saw him over there."

"Well, he did mention needing to do some 'ghostly reconnaissance' earlier, so he must be off doing that. I guess we'll just have to reenact the whole thing for him later," I said. "I call dibs on being Clarissa. I've been working on my resting bitch face."

For the next few hours, we watched the Canongate Collective get cleared out. An army of black SUVs showed up to transport the Caomhnóir to their new lodgings, wherever they might be. We also watched the exodus of other members of Clan Rìoghalachd who used the buildings for a variety of business and personal ventures. I spotted Danica wandering out to a car parked across the road with a cardboard box full of items, and a bewildered expression on her face.

"I daresay, is this necessary?" she asked Finn as she passed him.

"Unfortunately, we believe it is," Finn replied. "And we apologize for the inconvenience to your business."

Danica shrugged and waved an airy hand. "Oh, it's not so dire as all that. I don't meet many clients here anyway. But do you suppose it will do any good?"

"We certainly hope so," was Finn's careful reply.

Danica sighed. "Well, Clarissa must have thought so too, or she wouldn't have agreed to the arrangement, I expect. She knows best, after all."

No one bothered to enlighten her that Clarissa hadn't, in fact, been given a choice at all.

"Oi! Jess!"

We all turned to the sound of my name and saw Savvy and Rana crossing the street to join us. Savvy was wearing a bright red t-shirt that said "I survived The Real Mary King's Close!" and carried several shopping bags with the names of local shops on them.

"Hey Savvy! Rana!" Hannah replied, waving.

"All right, Hannah?" Rana said, smiling. Then she turned to me with more of a grimace. "All right, Jess? I heard about the attack. How are you feeling?"

I waved off her concern. "I'll live. What are you all doing? I thought Rana was supposed to be tailing Maeve."

"We're taking it in shifts, me and two other female Novitiates," Rana explained.

"Anything suspicious yet?" I asked eagerly.

Rana shook her head. "Not yet. But I'm back on duty in half an hour, so I'll let you know what I find out at shift change."

"Thanks. What's with all the tourist swag?" I asked.

"Well, since Rana's had a few hours off, I've been showing her the sights," Savvy explained.

"What's 'The Real Mary King's Close?'" I asked her, squinting at her t-shirt.

"Oh, it was brilliant!" Savvy cried. "Wasn't it, Rana?"

Rana rolled her eyes. "It was a bit cheesy."

Savvy waved a dismissive hand at Rana. "Ah, don't listen to her, it was class! It's one of them closes, right, like those little alley-like side streets that you see all through the city—but it got built over hundreds of years ago and it was, like... preserved in time, just the way it had been all those years ago! And it's supposed to be haunted as well!"

I laughed. "What is it with you and haunted attractions? Your life is a haunted attraction."

Savvy shrugged. "This one wasn't just about ghosts. It was like finding a time capsule big enough to walk through and explore!"

"It was pretty interesting," Rana admitted, "even if they did lay it on a bit thick with the ghost stuff. I, for one, didn't see a single proper spirit the whole time we were down there."

"How do you just... build over a whole street and then forget about it?" Hannah asked with an incredulous little laugh.

"Apparently it's not all that unusual in cities that have been around so long," Savvy said. "Especially one like Edinburgh, with all these blasted stairs."

This, at least, made sense. I'd never been to a city that was so... vertical. My leg muscles had been on fire ever since we'd gotten here.

"Where are you two off to, then? Fancy doing the tour? I'd do it again!" Savvy said eagerly.

"We're actually looking for Milo. You haven't seen him around in the last few hours, have you?" Hannah asked. She was doing her best to sound unconcerned, but I could hear the edge of worry in her voice.

"Oh, yeah, we have, actually!" Savvy said brightly. "We bumped into him right after we left the tour, didn't we? So what was that, maybe two hours ago?"

"That's right, yeah," Rana said.

Hannah let out a relieved sigh. "Thank goodness. Did he happen to mention where he was going?"

Savvy's eyebrows drew together in concentration. "Lemme think. He asked us what we'd been up to, and we told him all about the museum, and the castle tour, and the tour of Mary King's Close. Then he got this look on his face like he'd just thought of something, and said he had to go. Disappeared like that," Savvy added, snapping her fingers together.

Hannah threw her hands up. "Well, that clears it up!" she said sarcastically.

"Sorry," Rana said again with a guilty grimace.

"It's not your fault," I told her, smiling. "Hannah has a hard time functioning without Milo. He's like her emotional support ghost."

Hannah threw me a withering look, but I noticed that she didn't contradict me, probably because she knew it was true. She and Milo were basically inseparable, and had been almost from the moment they met. If he hadn't met her first, I'd have been jealous.

Without any more to go on, we gave up looking for Milo for the moment and headed back to the hotel.

"He's not a lost puppy, Hannah," I reminded her as she continued to chew anxiously on everything from her nails to her bottom lip to the strand of hair that kept blowing into her face. "He's off on his own all the time. You remember what he said, right? Ghostly reconnaissance. He's probably just trying to concentrate. If that nasty ghost can be tracked, Milo's going to need all his wits about him to do it, and that means no twins jabbering away inside his head distracting him."

"I know, I know, you're right. I'm just... this whole situation has me on edge. We're being hosted by a hostile clan that we've now kicked off of their own property, and we're no closer to figuring out what is happening to the spirits in that courtyard. If I thought we were making some headway, I'd probably be able to stay calm, but..." she trailed off with a helpless shrug.

"I know. But I think we just need to be patient. Kiernan needs time to track down that book. The Caomhnóir need time to investigate the courtyard. It's frustrating to wait, but I'm not sure what choice we've got."

Hannah looked up at me with a very skeptical look on her face. "I'm sorry, have we slipped into an alternate universe here? When did you become the reasonable, rational twin?"

I shrugged. "It's probably the head injury. Don't worry, I won't make a habit of it."

But as the night wore on, the silence in the connection chipped slowly away at my calm rationality. I couldn't think of any time, in all the years we'd been Bound, that Milo had gone radio silent for so long. I found myself tuning into the connection every fifteen minutes or so, and becoming more agitated every time I found it empty. Had Milo gotten himself into some kind of trouble that meant he couldn't communicate with us, or was it possible he was just trying to concentrate? And if it was the latter, why hadn't he at least given us a heads-up that he was going silent? It seemed like the kind of thing he would remember to do, knowing Hannah the way he did. He must have known she'd be going out of her mind with worry. I was having a harder and harder time believing that he'd put her through that if he had another choice.

To kill time, I tried to comb through some documents Kiernan had scanned and sent over to us by email. He hadn't tracked down any other copies of the book that had been tampered with, but he had found others that focused on Durupinen history in Edinburgh. My progress through the material was slow and agonizing. My head was both swimming and pounding, and my eyes felt like I'd been rubbing them with sandpaper. I kept at it for longer than I should have, and finally gave up, slamming the lid of my laptop down rather more aggressively than I meant to. This concussion was making everything feel impossible. I was just digging through my bag for some pain meds when my phone buzzed. I snatched it up, my heart in my throat, and saw Rana's name on the screen.

"Hey, what's up? Did you find Milo?" I asked before she could say so much as hello.

"Milo's still missing?" was Rana's mystified reply.

My heart sank. "Yeah. I was hoping you might have—"

"Jess, I don't mean to cut you off, but Maeve just showed up at Canongate Collective and forced a window."

14

CAUGHT

"WAIT, WHAT?!" I CRIED. "You can't mean she broke in!"

"That's exactly what I mean," Rana confirmed. "I just watched her with my own two eyes. What should I do?"

"Don't do anything! I'm coming down there right now," I said, leaping up from the bed and stepping into my shoes, trying to ignore the way my head swam. I grabbed my Casting bag and shoved it into the crossbody bag that I had slung over my shoulder, and hurried out the door.

It would take more time to request and wait for a car than it would just to walk over to Canongate Collective myself, so I set off on foot. The city was vibrant at night, with lights gleaming from building windows and music streaming into the night from pubs, and people teeming in the streets. And I marveled, as I had a dozen times since I'd come here, at the juxtaposition of the ancient and the modern; a medieval castle gazing down over the raucous 21st century night life of a bustling and thriving city. Ubers clattering over cobblestones. People taking selfies.

Rana was waiting outside of Canongate Collective and started toward me as I rounded the corner. She wore a dark gray hoodie with the hood pulled up, and winked at me as she closed the last few steps of distance between us.

"All right?" she asked, eyes sparkling with excitement.

"Where's Maeve?" I asked without preamble.

Rana jerked her head over her shoulder. "Come on, I'll show you," she whispered.

I followed Rana at a jog to the east-facing building. Rana silently pointed out the open first floor window. Marks on the sill suggested the window had been forced.

"She took a car from the manor, but had the driver drop her off two blocks away," Rana explained in a hurried whisper. "She pretended to be headed in the door of a pub, but when the driver pulled away she backtracked and came here. Then she used a crowbar to force the window."

"Why didn't any of the Caomhnóir on duty see her?" I asked. "Aren't they patrolling?"

Rana shrugged. "It's easy enough to slip past them if you're quick about it, which she was. The alarms would alert them if anyone was inside, but if she knew the code to disarm it, they'd be none the wiser."

I looked up at all five stories of the building and groaned in frustration. "We'll be lucky to find her in there," I said.

"Oh, I don't think we'll have to look too hard," Rana said with a smirk, and pointed toward the top corner window. A moment later a flash of light skittered across the shade which had been pulled down over the window.

I snorted. "Not exactly a professional, is she?"

Together Rana and I entered the building using the keys Rana had been given as part of the security team. I waited, bouncing anxiously on the balls of my feet as Rana entered the alarm code, and then we made our way as stealthily as we could to the fifth floor, which consisted of one long hallway with doors to the flats at regular intervals along each side. Rana pointed silently to the last door on the left. We approached it slowly, working to keep our breathing quiet after climbing five flights of stairs.

Maeve had pulled the door closed behind her, but she hadn't locked it. Rana looked deeply disappointed at this discovery.

"I was hoping I'd get to try my hand at picking it," she whispered, a lock-picking tool kit halfway out of her pocket.

I grinned. "Maybe next time."

I pressed my ear against the door and listened, but heard only distant rustling, which made me feel sure she wasn't about to come bursting out. Carefully, I eased the door open, holding my breath lest it creaked and gave us away; but it swung inward smoothly and silently on its hinges. It opened into a small but neat one-bedroom flat. The main room was a combination sitting room and kitchen. To the left was an open door through which I could see a shower curtain. To the right, an open door led to the only bedroom, and it was in this room that I caught a glimpse of the wildly swinging beam of light from Maeve's flashlight.

I looked over my shoulder at Rana, who nodded and followed me closely across the sitting room, the dim light spilling from the hallway just enough to ensure we didn't trip over the furniture. We skirted the sofa and pressed ourselves against the wall so that we could approach the bedroom door unseen. I took one last deep breath, blew it out, and stepped into the doorway, pressing the light switch on the wall.

"Hello, Maeve."

The petite figure bent over the dresser gave a shriek of surprise and dropped her flashlight, which was actually just her phone. It landed with the beam pointing at the ceiling, casting Maeve's pale and terrified face in a ghostly circle of light.

"Crivvens!" Maeve gasped, her hand pressed to her heart. "You nearly scared me to death! What do you mean, sneaking up on people like that?"

"I think the better question is, what are you doing in this building when the High Priestess of the Northern Clans and the Council have ordered all members of your clan to vacate the premises until the end of our investigation?" I asked.

Maeve's mouth snapped closed. She did not reply.

"You know what, you don't need to tell me," I said with a sigh. I pulled my phone from my pocket and pulled up my calls. "I can just call right over to Fairhaven and see if they'd like to question you there."

"No! No, please! It's..." Maeve swallowed hard. "It's not what it looks like."

"I certainly hope not," I said. "Because it looks like you're hoping to get arrested for defying a Council decree."

"I'm not!" Maeve gasped, and there were frightened tears brimming in her eyes now, threatening to spill over onto her flushed cheeks. "Please, please don't report me!"

"If you don't want to get reported, you better have a damn good reason for being here," I said. "Because if you have anything to do with what's happening down at that Geatgrima, you'll have a lot more to worry about than a petty trespassing charge."

"I don't, I swear it! I would never... I don't know anything about it!" Maeve cried, her voice creeping higher and higher toward hysteria.

"I need the truth, Maeve."

Maeve pressed her lips together and dropped her chin, letting her shoulders slump. When she looked up again, there were tear tracks on her face, but her voice was calmer. "It's Reilly."

I blinked. "Who the hell is Reilly?"

"The Caomhnóir who lives in this flat. We're sort of... seeing each other," Maeve whispered.

"Sort of?" I pressed.

"We're in love," Maeve said. Then she drew a shaky breath, as though it had cost her much to say it out loud. "We didn't mean to. But he was assigned to my security detail last summer and it just... happened. We've been dating each other ever since."

"Let me guess: your mother doesn't know," I said, my tone softening now.

Maeve's head snapped up, abject terror shining in her eyes. "No! And she can't ever know! Please, she'll... she'll..." Maeve's voice choked off and she cast her eyes around the room, as though searching for the words for just how horrific her mother's response would be.

"It's not illegal anymore, you know," I told her. "There's no Durupinen law against it."

Maeve barked out a bitter little laugh. "As if that matters to my mother. She's always made her own rules, and everyone in her orbit has always followed them. I've tried to assert myself—I'm eighteen now, after all, but it's no use. She threatened to stop paying my tuition at university just for this." And she pulled out a strand of her petal pink hair. "If she knew about Reilly and me, she'd probably disinherit me or lock me in the dungeon or something."

I raised an eyebrow. "Your mother has a dungeon?"

Maeve smiled ironically. "Two, actually. One at the manor, and another under this building somewhere, or at least that's what I've heard. And she'll send Reilly away, I know she will, and we'll never see each other again." Maeve's mouth twisted up and her voice was swallowed in tears again.

"I'm really sorry you're having to deal with all of that, but it still doesn't exactly explain what you're doing here," I pointed out.

In answer, Maeve reached down and picked up a backpack that had been open by her feet. "I had to come back and get my stuff. I was afraid they might search people's flats, and if they did, and found out I had a drawer of my own..." she shook her head. "Please, you can look through it if you want. It's just clothes and some toiletries and a hair straightener."

I glanced at Rana, who nodded sharply and sprang forward to look through the bag.

"Sorry," I said to Maeve. "It's not that I don't believe you, but this way I can clear you of suspicion before you leave."

Maeve just nodded, as though she didn't have the strength to argue. She looked at me hesitantly, as though trying to decide if she wanted to say something. Finally, as Rana rose from her inspection of the bag with a nod that said "All clear," Maeve finally spoke.

"I heard a rumor that you and the Caomhnóir that accompanied you here are together," she blurted out.

I was too surprised by the sudden exclamation that I didn't answer right away.

"Is it true?" Maeve added somewhat breathlessly.

"Uh... yeah, it is," I said. "We've been together for a few years now. We had to hide it at first, but now that the rules have changed, we don't have to anymore."

Maeve looked close to tears. "And how did you bear it, when you had to hide it?" she murmured.

"It was rough, for a while," I said. "And when we were found out, they sent Finn as far from Fairhaven as they could." The memory hit me rather harder than expected and I found an unexpected lump in my throat. "And it was awful."

"That's what I'm most afraid of," Maeve said, "that my mother would send Reilly away."

"I can't promise that won't happen," I said. "Knowing your mother for even the short time I've been acquainted with her, I can tell that she's..." I paused trying to come up with the right tactful word choice.

"A monster?" Maeve supplied bitterly.

"I was gonna say something like 'harsh' or 'strict', but you know better than me, I suppose," I said with what I hoped was a sympathetic smile. I felt it slip from my face as a realization dropped into my head like a bucket into a well. "Is that why you messed with the Wards at the manor on the night of the welcome reception?"

Maeve's eyes widened, and I watched her struggle for a moment before deciding to tell the truth. At last, she sighed. "How did you know?"

"I guessed."

Maeve's bright and eloquent face darkened as though a cloud had passed over it. "She's always going on about how she knows better than the whole rest of the Council, how if she was in charge, everything would be so much better. Mother was always controlling, but since the Gateways were restored, she's become frankly tyrannical. Stripping the Gateways out of our blood was like stripping my mother of her crown, and she's acting like the dethroned despot on a daily basis. You aren't to know that, of course, because you aren't around her all the time, are you?" Her tone was bitter with envy.

"I'm sorry it's been difficult for you," was all I could manage as I grappled with a sudden onslaught of guilt.

Maeve just shrugged, as though an apology was hardly necessary. "The worst part is the way she treats me now, like I've somehow depreciated in value. I'm her only daughter, you see, with five older brothers. She was positively desperate to produce the next Gateway, utterly terrified that one of her sisters or cousins would beat her to it and steal all the glory of carrying on the line. And then, after all that, to have to let go of it anyway." Maeve sighed a sigh that seemed to dig right down into her shoes. "I just couldn't take it anymore. Someone had to teach her a lesson. So, I waited until I had the biggest audience possible and tampered with the Wards when I came down to join the party."

"You couldn't have done that on your own," I pointed out.

Maeve shook her head. "No. Reilly helped me. He slipped away just before my mother's scheduled speech and released the angry spirits, so that they'd be ready to attack at the right moment. In retrospect, it was a stupid thing to do. The spirits were far angrier and more destructive than I had anticipated. I'd hoped for a bit of hostility aimed at my mother, and instead, I unleashed a full-on assault on the whole crowd." She smiled ruefully at me. "I'm sorry you were caught up in it."

"It was definitely not the welcome I was expecting," I said.

"And I do feel bad about that," Maeve said. "But I knew her humiliation would be at its absolute peak if she lost control of her own city while the Fairhaven contingent was here."

"But she'd lost control of it already," I reminded her, "when the trouble began in the courtyard downstairs."

"My mother's never lost control, as long as she sees a way to turn a situation to her advantage," Maeve said. "She was unsettled about what was happening in the courtyard, of course, but only at first. Then she began to see it as an opportunity, I reckon. I think she might have wanted to use it as leverage to get the Gateways back in our bloodlines. I don't know that for sure, you understand," Maeve added quickly. "I've never been allowed in family Council meetings, and my mother doesn't discuss such matters with me. But I know her well, and between that and the snatches of conversation I overheard from other family members, I'm confident it's a reasonable assumption."

"Maeve, I need to ask you one more question, and I want you to consider it really carefully before you answer. I know you're well and truly pissed at your mom right now, but do your best to leave that out of it. Do you think your mother might be causing the crisis in the courtyard on purpose to reverse the Reckoning?"

Maeve looked startled at the prospect, but she shook it off and settled into about ten seconds of serious contemplation. At last she said, "I think it's possible. My mother is capable of almost anything to get what she wants, and there's nothing she wants more than to maintain her power. But I remember, when it first came to light, she *seemed* surprised. And even if she didn't cause it in the first place, I think she's used it to her advantage ever since. So, I suppose, do with that what you will."

I looked into her solemn face, and I believed her.

"Thanks, Maeve. Have you gotten what you need out of here?" I asked.

"Oh! Um, yes, I think so. Wait, hang on…"

She trotted away into the sitting room and disappeared into the bathroom beyond. A few seconds later she returned, holding up a toothbrush.

"That's everything, I expect." She bit her lip, twisting the toothbrush between her fingers. "You aren't going to report me, are you? I'll understand, if you have to, but I'd appreciate a warning, if I'm going to have to face my mother about it."

I looked at Rana, who winked back. I turned back to Maeve. "I think we can let this one slip our minds. But for what it's worth, just be a little patient. Things worked out in the end for Finn and me, and I bet they will for you and Reilly. And please, lay low until all this is over. It's dangerous over here, and besides, Rana doesn't want to have to keep tailing you all over existence."

Maeve looked momentarily startled, then smiled sheepishly. "Of course. And thanks. For the advice, and for not ratting me out."

I rolled my eyes. "Do I look like a snitch?"

Maeve laughed softly and then slipped out the door as quietly as a shadow.

I returned to the hotel to find Hannah practically vibrating with worry over Milo, who still hadn't shown up or contacted anyone. The plan had been to try to get some sleep before returning to the courtyard, but I could tell when I met Hannah in the hotel lobby at 1:30 that she hadn't slept a wink either. We didn't mention Milo out loud, but he weighed as heavily on our minds during our walk over to Canongate Collective as if he'd been right there with us, chattering away.

When we arrived in the courtyard, it was empty except for Finn and two other Caomhnóir. They had taken the time during the day to mark out a perimeter in yellow tape of what Finn was now calling "the danger zone." It was concentric with the Geatgrima dais, with the Geatgrima at its center. Inside it, the Gateway's gently pulsating energy could be felt, luring spirits toward it with its irresistible pull. I had never felt anything but awe and wonder when in the presence of a Geatgrima, but now I felt a sense of foreboding dread. I knew the Caomhnóir around the perimeter would warn the spirits away before they got too close—expel them, even, if they had to—but I still couldn't shake off the shivers that kept running riot through me, raising the hairs on my arms and making me jump at every movement out of the corner of my eye. Finn spotted us from across the courtyard and came to greet us.

"Rana filled me in about Maeve," Finn said, as he pecked me on the cheek by way of greeting. "Do you really think we can take her at her word?"

"I do," I said. "As convinced as I was yesterday that she had something to do with what's happening down here, I'm now even more convinced that she doesn't. It was just a case of being in the wrong place at the wrong time."

"That's good enough for me, then," Finn said, looking satisfied. Then he turned to Hannah, confronting her miserable expression. "Still no word from Milo?"

"Not yet," I said, intentionally brightening my tone and hoping Finn would catch on. "But I'm sure we will soon."

Finn nodded gravely, taking the hint. "Oh, I have no doubt. Milo can certainly take care of himself. If he's gone quiet, I expect it's for a very good reason."

Hannah sniffed but didn't reply. I half expected her to burst into hysterical tears right then and there, but she held it together. She knew how important it was to have our wits about us when the clock struck two.

"What's the plan?" I asked Finn.

"Well, the building's been searched again, after Maeve's little stunt, and it's truly empty this time. Have you both brought your Casting bags?"

Hannah and I both held them up, and Finn nodded his satisfaction.

"After conferring with Catriona, she suggested we try a Revelation Casting. It's a bit obscure and bloody complicated, but if performed correctly, it will reveal the nature of any Casting already at work."

I perked up at this. "I've never heard of that before!"

"Well, as I said, it's obscure. It also requires six Durupinen working in tandem with each other to pull it off," Finn said.

"But where are we going to get the other four?" Hannah asked. "We can't possibly trust any member of Clan Rìoghalachd to help us."

"Catriona has delayed her return to London to assist us, as she's the only one of us who has attempted this Casting before. Rana, Savvy, and another Novitiate, Clara, will be joining us to round out the necessary number of participants," Finn explained.

"That's going to mean fewer eyes on the perimeter outside," I pointed out. "Is that safe?"

"It's not ideal, but we have no choice. We just need to perform it as quickly as we can and hope that it works," Finn said. His expression was grim, and I knew he didn't like the idea of the reduced security any more than I did. But he was right. We had no choice.

At that moment, Catriona, Rana, Savvy, and Clara walked into the courtyard, each of them clutching a Casting bag in her hands. Rana took a moment to introduce Clara to us. She was a tall, lithe girl with an athletic build and dark, careful eyes. She smiled at us as she shook our hands, but the smile faded quickly as her eyes darted around the courtyard. She was bouncing a bit on the balls of her feet, and I could tell she was trying hard to disguise how nervous she was to be there.

"Right, well, here are the instructions for the Revelation Casting," Catriona said, handing a sheet of paper each to Hannah and me. "I've already gone over it with the others."

I read through the instructions and let out a low whistle. "There are about a hundred steps here, Cat."

"I know. That means a hundred different things that could go wrong, so we'll all need to be on our toes. This requires perfect synchronicity among the casters. The most important thing will be to keep our eyes on each other and not to lose focus," Catriona said. "But if we're successful, the Casting will be forced to reveal itself."

"How will that work, then?" Savvy asked. "What does it mean for the Casting to reveal itself?"

"No bloody idea," Catriona admitted. "The *Book of Téigh Anonn* just says 'and the nature of the Casting shall reveal itself to you.' How exactly it does that, we'll just have to wait and see. I reckon it may be different for each Casting."

"You don't suppose it will be dangerous, do you?" Hannah asked. "After what we've seen happen to spirits in this courtyard, I worry what could happen if we force this particular Casting into revealing its nature."

"That's why we've had the perimeter marked so carefully," Catriona said, hitching a thumb over her shoulder where the yellow tape flapped in the light breeze. "If we all be careful not to tread inside it, we should have enough distance to witness the Revelation without getting caught up in it. Again, I must stress, I have no idea what that will look like. Are you still sure you want to help with this?"

I watched all four of the other girls nod emphatically before doing so myself, and the commitment was made.

"I've divided out the steps, and what order we're to do them. I've also marked out who says which part of the Casting and when. Does anyone want to review the Gaelic before we start?" Catriona looked pointedly at me.

"I'm good," I said, a little snappishly. She'd never let me live down how much better Hannah was with the language than I was. To this day, my pronunciation left much to be desired, but this was hardly the moment to remind me of that, with so much at stake.

Cat grinned and then gestured to us all to gather together. One by one, she handed us gemstones, different colored stubs of candles, bundles of dried herbs and a few other small artifacts—a silver charm, a braid of hair, and a small white piece of something that might have been bone. I shuddered as she dropped it into my hand, wondering to whom—or what—it had belonged.

We fanned out around the courtyard. Because Durupinen Castings often required directional instructions, the courtyard had been designed with stone markers that designated north, south, east, and west; and so it was easy to be sure we were in the appropriate positions. I took the position due north, standing directly on top of the stone marker. The feeling of it beneath my feet helped me wrangle a little of my anxiety—at least I knew I was in exactly the right spot. Catriona took a few extra minutes with a compass to ensure that Rana and Clara were positioned correctly, as due southwest and due northwest had no stone markers to designate them. Then, she took her own place due east, and nodded her head toward Finn, who shooed the Caomhnóir present into the doorways and out of the perimeter of the Casting. When she was sure they were all clear, she lifted a lighter into the air.

"Oh, one last thing. We only get one shot at this. A Casting cannot be forced to reveal itself twice."

"No pressure," I heard Savvy mutter.

"Right, then, light them up!" Catriona called, and we all lit our candles in unison.

A hush fell over the courtyard and we all waited, hearts pounding for the moment when the church bells shimmered their ancient call out over the city.

One... two...

The effect in the courtyard was instantaneous. A ripple of strange, dizzying energy swept through it like a wind, and I felt the enigmatic pull of the Geatgrima falter and then fade, as though an invisible barrier had gone up between us. A wave of nausea rippled through me as the memory of screams echoed in my head—the strange and multitudinous screams of the spirit we had seen caught up in the terrible power of whatever evil had gripped the courtyard. I had to shake my head to clear it, and even then, that queasy feeling of wrongness remained.

Cat raised a hand again, to signal the official commencement of the Casting. Each of us held our candles aloft. She called out in a clear, resounding voice that echoed around the courtyard, and we joined ours to hers in the chorus.

> *"Chrochaimid scáthán chuig an draoíocht seo ,*
> *Scáth d'aghaidh atáimid ag lorg.*
> *Éilímid a h-ainm agus fógraímid é don Aether.*
> *A nádúr a nochta, lig dhó a bheith."*[1]

We repeated the words, over and over, as each of us took our turns in the ritual: scattering gemstones, tying and cutting knots, plucking the fragrant leaves from bundles of herbs, and letting them fly from our fingers on the breeze. Our voices did not falter, not even when the perimeter we had carefully marked in the center of the courtyard began to glow as though an alien sun was about to burst through the ground, its brilliant fingers of light pushing and prodding through the cracks.

I think I sensed more than saw Finn's sharp movement in my periphery. I turned to see him a mere step from the grass. Beside him, another Caomhnóir had his hand pressed warningly against Finn's chest, a silent reminder. I held his eye and nodded once, as though to say, 'It's okay,' and continued to chant the incantation. I was just as alarmed as he was about the sudden appearance of the glowing circle, but we couldn't lose our heads now. It might be our only chance to find out what was really going on here. He seemed to understand and, with a jerky nod in reply, retreated a step further back into the safety of the doorway.

The light dimmed to a dull, pulsing golden glow, still in the outline of a perfect circle, concentric to the circular perimeter of the courtyard itself, with the Geatgrima at its center. It was unmistakably some kind of Summoning Circle.

This thought barely had time to crystallize in my brain before the air was rent with a nightmare of a sound. It hit each of us like a physical blow, and it was a near miracle that no one broke from the chanting. It was, I realized once the initial shock of it had passed, the same sound that had echoed in my head a moment before—the sound of the spirit's screams from that first night in the courtyard.

Or, wait. No. Not exactly the same. Now there seemed many voices twisted together in the multitudinous scream, the pain within it a palpable thing, a cold ice in our veins.

Or was it on our skin? I just knew that suddenly I was cold—colder than I'd ever been in my life. I felt every muscle in my body tense with the shock of it, and I thought the candle in my hand would snap with the force of my grip; but luckily, I neither broke it nor caused it to go out.

Should it be this hard? Had we done something wrong? I didn't think so, somehow. The cold coursing through me wasn't new—I'd felt it before, for a fleeting instant during the spirit attack in the archive. It had only been for a moment, but I knew the ache of it at once. And so I had to conclude that the screaming and the light and the intense cold meant, rather, that we had done something right. We were experiencing the nature of the Casting. I forced my brain and my body not to be distracted, but to pay as much attention as I could to everything around me. The moment I did so, I took a deep breath and my nostrils were filled with the same sweet, rotting, musty smell that I'd smelled in the archive. My stomach heaved, but I forced myself to keep chanting.

And then suddenly, from within the multitudinous screaming, I heard something that made my heart stop. A voice, screaming with the rest, and yet I could faintly make out the words hidden in the cacophony of shrieks.

"Jess! Hannah! Help us! We're down here! He's got us trapped down here! He's—"

A very different scream echoed across the courtyard, and suddenly everything just...stopped. The golden circle of light vanished. The wailing chorus died away, as did the smell and the bitter, biting cold. Every one of our candles extinguished as if one mighty breath had blown them all out.

There was a beat of silence, and then Hannah's voice cut through the night. I didn't need her next words to understand the meaning behind her scream, because I was fighting against the same rising horror of realization that had now driven Hannah to her knees in a torrent of tears. I dropped my Casting artifacts and ran to her, sinking to my knees beside her.

"Jess..." she sobbed.

"I know."

We knew the voice that had cried out to us. Somehow, the evil in the courtyard now had Milo in its grasp.

1. *"A mirror we hold to this magic,*
    A reflection we seek of its face.
    Its name do we claim and proclaim to the Aether.
    Its nature revealed, let it be."

15

NO STONE UNTURNED

"HANNAH, BREATHE. Come on now, going to pieces isn't going to help him."

Finn's deep, soothing tones were the only sound in the courtyard, apart from Hannah's near hysterical sobbing. Everyone was huddled in a small knot in the southern corner of the courtyard, clutching the now meaningless artifacts of the Casting and staring helplessly at each other.

"This is my fault. It's all my fault," Hannah was gasping. "I should never have let him go off on his own, I never should have—"

"Hannah, you're not his mother!" I cried, exasperated. "And anyway, we have no idea how this happened. Beating yourself up and blaming yourself isn't going to fix it!"

"Nothing can fix it!" Hannah's voice was a harsh roar of pure unadulterated pain, and the very sound of it cut straight through me like a knife. "You saw what happened to that spirit the first night we were here! And now it's happened to Milo and I... I can't..." and she dissolved again into a storm of crying.

I didn't know whether to slap her or hug her, but it was clear I couldn't talk to her, not yet. Instead, I looked over her head at Finn.

"What do we know?" he asked me, still rubbing a hand absently over Hannah's back.

I took a shaky breath and tried to steady myself, no easy feat with my sister howling in such abject misery right between us.

"The spirit that attacked us in the archive is wrapped up in this," I said firmly. "The bitter cold and the rotting smell I experienced in the archive, I felt them again." I looked over at the others. "Did you all feel that, too?"

Clara nodded with a violent shiver.

"I still can't feel my fingers," Rana confirmed.

"Smelled like a bloody corpse," Savvy agreed. She was so pale she looked almost green in the moonlight.

"And we know there's been a Summoning Circle cast in this courtyard," Catriona added. "I have no bloody idea how, as we can't see a trace of it with the naked eye, but it's here, the Revelation Casting proved that."

I nodded, my brain working rapidly. We'd asked for the nature of the Casting to be revealed, and the circle itself appeared. "So spirits are entering the courtyard, lured into the Summoning Circle by the pull of the Geatgrima, and then..."

"Then that other Casting gets hold of them," Catriona confirmed, nodding. "But I'm damned if I understand what that Casting *does*."

"Whatever it is, it isn't bloody pleasant," Savvy muttered.

"Did any of the rest of you hear Milo?" I asked. Below me, Hannah's sobs redoubled at the sound of his name.

Everyone shook their heads. I nodded, expecting it.

"I think we may only have heard him because of our connection. It's been silent since he disappeared, sort of cut off. The Revelation Casting was able to override that, at least for a moment," I said.

"What was it he said, exactly?" Cat asked.

"He said our names, then he said, 'Help us. We're down here. He's got us trapped down here.' He was about to say more, I think, but that was when H— I mean, that was when the Casting broke off." Shit, that was close. I'd almost said, "and that was when Hannah broke the Casting," and the last thing she needed was another reason to pile guilt onto her own head.

"Who is 'he?'" Rana asked, more to herself than to anyone else.

"It's obvious, isn't it? He must have meant the spirit that attacked you!" Savvy said.

But I was shaking my head. "Or the living person using that spirit as a weapon. Remember, a spirit couldn't possibly be responsible for the Casting we just revealed. Only a living person could have done that." It was a basic tenet of Durupinen magic, and an important one. If spirits could work Castings the way we could, it would have made our job as Durupinen practically impossible, not to mention even more dangerous than it already was.

"Right," Savvy said, drooping. "Thinking too quickly there, sorry."

Catriona was repeating Milo's words aloud. "'He's got us trapped down here. Where's 'down here?'"

"Absolutely no idea," I said, a badly suppressed note of desperation in my voice. "That doesn't make any... hang on. I remember that when we saw that first spirit become trapped by the Casting, she seemed to disappear *downward*. Did anyone else notice that?"

In unison, every face dropped to our feet, as though expecting the ground beneath us to split like the maw of hell and swallow us up. It was Finn who spoke up first.

"I did notice that, but there's nothing below here. He stamped his foot. This is just... the ground. We've even had a bit of a dig, looking for signs of a Casting. Nothing but dirt, I'm afraid."

I growled with frustration, jumping to my feet and beginning to pace. I ran my hands over my face and looked up into the sky, willing my brain to come up with something... anything. Then my eyes fell on a window on the top floor of the nearest building and something clicked. Something Maeve had said to me...

"There's a dungeon here," I whispered.

"Come again?" Catriona said sharply.

"A dungeon. Maeve mentioned it. She said there's one right in the basement of the buildings here. And also one at MacLeod Manor."

This was the first word anyone had spoken that seemed to cut through Hannah's misery. She suddenly swallowed a sob and scrambled to her feet. "We have to search them! Both of them!"

Catriona looked at me, and we shared a very grim smile.

"This is going to get ugly," I said.

"Clarissa may actually breathe fire," Cat agreed, nodding.

"We're doing it anyway, right?" I asked.

"Oh, gleefully. I'll bring the fire extinguisher," Cat replied. Her phone was already to her ear. "Caomhnóir Carey, can I count on you to assemble the troops and divide them up? We'll leave half here to search below Canongate Collective and the other half can come over to MacLeod Manor with me."

"Consider it done," Finn said, leaping into action at once.

Hannah was calmer now that things were happening. I put a hand on each of her shoulders and turned her to look me in the eyes.

"Hey. It's going to be okay. We won't stop until we find him."

"What he must be going through... that screaming..."

"Don't. Don't think about it. Shove it away, Hannah, and just keep telling yourself: he's still here. He reached out to us. He gave us a clue. We will follow it to him, and we will rescue him. It is the only outcome I will accept, do you understand?"

Hannah nodded. I pulled her to me, burying my face in her vanilla-scented hair. I said what I'd said to convince myself as much as to convince her. I could feel my own self-control fraying at the edges with every passing minute, and I couldn't afford to go to pieces now, not when Milo needed us. So I choked it down—every fear, every sob, every worry, stuffed it into that handy box I kept in the back corners of my mind. It didn't get a lot of use these days, but today I was glad my unhealthy coping mechanism remained. In this moment, in this crisis, it might just save my sanity... and my friend.

My friend. Who could have imagined how much Milo would come to mean to me after our oil and water beginning? He was as much an indispensable part of who I was as Hannah or Finn or Karen was. I'd finally reached a place where it felt like all the pieces fit together, and it had taken a long time to get there. If I lost that piece now... *no.* I pushed that feeling away, too, and locked the box up tight. It was time to focus.

I extracted myself from the hug and took Hannah's hand instead, tugging her over to Catriona, who was finishing with the arrangements for MacLeod Manor. She ended her call and looked at me expectantly.

"Where will we be the most useful?" I asked her.

"Help with the search here, both of you," Catriona said. "If there really is a dungeon here, it's the most likely location. Besides, things are ugly enough between you and Clarissa without you bursting in unannounced to search her house. Let me deal with that."

"What if she won't let you in?" Hannah asked, wringing her hands together.

"She won't have a choice. Even Clarissa MacLeod can't refuse an emergency search warrant handed down from the High Priestess herself, which I've just managed to secure. Anyone who tries to deny us entry or interfere with our search in any way will be arrested on the spot. And we can't risk them getting tipped off somehow. If someone from that clan is behind this—and I'm having a hard time seeing how that's not possible—we can't give them the chance to cover it up or hide the evidence."

I nodded, satisfied. I trusted Cat to lead a thorough search, and as much as I wanted to be everywhere at once, she was right. I'd be of more use here.

"You'll call me?" I asked her.

"The moment I know anything," Cat promised. There was no trace of her usual coolness. Her eyes burned with the sincerity of her promise. She reached out and placed a hand on Hannah's shoulder and squeezed it. I felt Hannah's body relax by a degree, a sign that she shared my trust in Catriona.

Trust in Catriona. My God, the difference a few years could make.

Cat left the courtyard, joined by the Caomhnóir Finn had assigned to her, and Hannah and I joined the remaining knot of people. Finn was dividing the troops, so to speak, assigning a group to each of the four buildings that enclosed the courtyard.

"We don't know which building houses the dungeon, so we spread out and search all of the basements," Finn said. "I want everyone to be on the lookout for traces of Castings, or even a trace of spirit energy. If anything feels even slightly off, report back and I'll join you." He held up his walkie-talkie before clipping it to his belt. "We are also searching for any recurrence of what we just experienced in the courtyard: the smell, the screams, the cold. I reckon none of us will forget any of that in a hurry. If you experience even a passing trace of any of those things, you must alert me at once. Is that clear?"

"Yes sir," came the resounding answer. Every face was pale and set, determined.

"Good lads... uh, that is, good... folks," Finn said awkwardly, throwing an apologetic look at Savvy, who winked at him.

"Rome wasn't built in a day, mate. 'Lads' works as good as any, I reckon," she said.

Finn nodded and then handed a ring of keys to each group. "These are the master keys to each building. There shouldn't be a single room you don't have access to, but if you encounter one, alert me at once on your radio. Be prepared to Expel or Cage as necessary. The spirit we are looking for is dangerously powerful and will not hesitate to harm you. Be vigilant. Look out for each other."

And with that, we broke apart and scattered to the four sides of the courtyard. I watched Rana, Sav, and Clara disappear into the north-facing building before Finn called my name.

"Jess?"

"Yeah, I'm coming," I said, and hurried after him and Hannah, who was already hovering in the nearest doorway.

I was grateful to have Finn with us as we walked back through the gloomy basement passage we had entered from. The air was musty and damp, but I caught no whiff of the dreaded mausoleum smell. Finn carried the ring of keys for the south building in his hands, and we began, door by door, to search the basement.

The first three rooms off the hallway were used only for storage. Moldering cardboard boxes, discarded furniture, and a collection of outdated office equipment. We squeezed between teetering piles of typewriters and rotary phones, fax machines and ancient desktop monitors. It was almost funny to think of the basement of a Durupinen-owned building to be as mundane as that of any office building. We searched each room thoroughly, opening closets, knocking on walls, and pushing against panels, lest one should pop open to reveal a secret passage or a long-locked door. We found nothing but more junk. There were two more rooms filled with row upon row of filing cabinets we didn't bother to open, and then two rooms after that containing absolutely nothing at all. Every room we entered was coated from floor to ceiling in a visible layer of dust. No one had been down here, not for ages.

Hannah was bouncing on the balls of her feet, her tension mounting higher with each dead end. Finally, we reached the door at the end of the hallway, by far the oldest looking of the doors, with a rusty old handle and a keyhole that gaped like a toothless mouth. Finn pulled out the only key that could conceivably fit in it: a rusty skeleton key at least three times as large as any other on the ring. He worked it into the lock, ignoring the squeaks of ancient protest from the metal inside. It took a solid minute of effort before he could finally get the thing, grudgingly, to turn. Then he pushed the door inward, revealing the yawning black hole of the passage beyond.

The floor was dirt, the walls an ancient, crumbling stone. It was only perhaps twenty feet long, with two doors set down either side of it. All four doors hung open, hanging crookedly and rotting away on their hinges. It was unnaturally quiet, save for the steady drip, drip, drip of water coming from somewhere near the end.

"Milo?" Hannah's voice was cracked with fear as she called out for him, but no answer came save for the silvery whisper of an echo.

"This... seems to be the dungeon, but I don't think anyone's here," Finn said. He stepped closer to the first door on the right and inspected it more closely with the light from his cell phone. The faint outlines of a Warding were still etched into the planks. He shined the light into the narrow, almost cave-like chamber, which was little more than a hole gouged out of the earth. It was empty.

He examined each in turn. Each of them was empty.

"This can't be it! How can this be it?" Hannah cried, her voice edging toward hysteria again. And without waiting for an answer, she began probing at the walls and doors with her hands, as though a touch in the right place would cause it to crumble away and reveal something beyond.

Finn caught my eye and shook his head. My heart, already aching, now sank into my shoes. Whatever Milo had meant by "down here," it hadn't been this forgotten dungeon.

"Hannah?" I asked gently, after allowing her to grope around fruitlessly for another minute or two. "Hannah, let's get out of here. This isn't it."

"It has to be it!" she cried. In frustration, she kicked the wall.

"It's not, and we are wasting time!" I replied, with more snap in my voice than I meant; but my nerves were like live wires too, sparking with fear. "Let's get out of here and back up to the courtyard to see what the others have found."

She opened her mouth, her expression electric with a dozen wild emotions, but then she closed it again, along with her eyes. She took a deep, steadying breath, and then blew it out slowly.

"Fine. Let's go," she said, the words stilted. She brushed past us and stalked back up the hallway toward the courtyard.

"I really thought we might find something here," I murmured, watching her retreat into the shadows.

Finn nodded. "I was hopeful as well. But we mustn't give up. Come on, let's go see what the others have found."

But the other three buildings turned up nothing. No other building had anything like the dungeon we'd found. Nobody stopped her when Hannah reached out wordlessly for the other three sets of keys, they just handed them over and watched her stalk away.

"She's not going to find anything, mate," Savvy said to me as Hannah marched resolutely into the west building. "We scoured it from top to bottom."

"I know, but just let her try," I said with a sigh. "She'll be calmer if she has something she can do."

It was heartbreaking, watching Hannah enter and then emerge from each of the other three buildings in turn, each time looking more dejected, each time the tears flowing more freely until at last she stumbled out of the last one, sank to her knees, and dissolved into incoherent sobs again. No one tried to calm her down, though Rana went over and sat beside her in the grass and silently held her hand.

My phone buzzed in my pocket, making me yelp, and I fumbled to extract it.

"Cat, give me some good news, I am begging you," I said as I put the phone to my ear. I felt rather than saw everyone around me tense and turn their attention to me.

"I wish I could," Catriona said. "But we've come up empty. Not a sign of Milo or anyone else being held captive."

"And there's no chance they knew you were coming?" I asked, grasping at the last remaining glimmer of hope. "If they were tipped off, they could have—"

"They hadn't been tipped off. Even Clarissa isn't that good of an actress," Catriona said firmly. "She tried to keep us out of the house, of course, kept calling the order a 'personal insult and an abuse of power,' but there was nothing she could do. In the end, she had to simply step aside, and the few minutes she spent trying to deny us entry wouldn't have been enough time to hide something like what we heard in that courtyard."

"So you found nothing," I said, and felt the disappointment roll like a wave over everyone around me. Savvy swore under her breath. Finn ran his hands through his hair in a characteristic gesture of pure frustration.

"Nothing," Catriona confirmed. "That space might have been a dungeon once, but it's more of a museum now. All of the cell doors are permanently held open, and each one is like a historical display. They're using it to house all of their clan-specific artifacts. I imagine they bring important visitors from other clans down there on tours now, yet another way to prop up their own power and mystique." Catriona listened to my silence for a moment. "I'm guessing from the desperation in your voice when you picked up that you haven't found anything either," she added.

"No," I said, dropping my voice so that it wouldn't carry over to where Hannah was sitting. "We've checked all the basements. Nothing. Wherever Milo was referring to, it doesn't seem to be here."

"What's your next move?" Catriona asked. I appreciated, even in the extreme duress of the moment, that she trusted me enough not to take the case she'd assigned to me right out of my hands, but I almost hoped she would. I was starting to feel desperate and out of ideas.

"I'm not sure, yet," I hedged. "I think we may head back to the hotel to regroup and figure out what's next. Do you want to meet us there?"

"Sure. I've got some things to finish up here, mostly damage control, but then I'll be over," she replied.

"Thanks, Cat."

I pocketed the phone and turned to Finn. "Another dead end."

He nodded, his eyebrows pulled together into a deep, scowling 'v.' "Right, then. To be honest, I didn't expect there to be anything at MacLeod Manor, not with it being so far from the Geatgrima, but it was necessary to make sure."

"Finn, do you have any ideas on where to try next? Because I am starting to freak out here, and if we don't have a game plan, I might seriously lose it like Hannah's already losing it," I admitted.

"I do have one thought. It might be a long shot, but it's the only shot I can think to take. Clan Rìoghalachd owns dozens of properties in this city. If we can get a list of them, we can search them all."

The thought of breaking down more doors belonging to Clarissa was a satisfying one. "Yes, okay. That's a good idea. Can we do that?"

But Finn had already pulled out his cell phone. "I'll call Catriona back right now and find out what the first step is."

I reached out and caught his hand. He looked down at it, a little surprised.

"Thank you. I'm pretty sure I'd go crazy if you weren't here right now," I said. I could see Hannah over his shoulder, still sunk down in the grass, Rana rubbing her back as she watered the courtyard with her grief. "Do you think there's any chance—"

"—of getting Kiernan here?" he finished the thought. "He'll be my next call. Nothing at the Isle of Skye can be more important than this."

"Thank you." I kissed him, quickly but passionately, then turned to Savvy.

"Can you help me get her back to the hotel?"

Savvy didn't answer. She just took my hand.

I'll never know how we managed it. Hannah was so deeply hysterical that she couldn't even answer us as we talked to her about going back to the hotel. She seemed to have no concept of what we were saying, or what any of it meant. She allowed herself to be lifted from the ground and carried to a waiting car. We laid her across the backseat, her head in Savvy's lap, and were back in front of our hotel in what felt like seconds, a distance we could easily have walked, even carrying Hannah, but chose not to. The last thing we needed was to draw outsider attention to our crisis.

Back in my room, Savvy and I got Hannah settled into the bed. She'd reached the point in her panic that she seemed to have become almost catatonic. Tears still streamed silently down her face, but she said nothing, acknowledged no one, and seemed not to hear or understand a single word that was said to her. Rana covered her with a blanket, and sat beside her, stroking her hair until, miraculously, her eyes slid closed and she slept.

"Thank God," I said into the silence a few minutes later. "I thought we were going to have to call Dr. Stewart to come and sedate her. Do you think she's okay?"

I directed this question at Rana, who I knew had some medical training from a brief stint as a paramedic. "She's in shock, and she's gone into self-preservation mode. But she's physically okay. Her breathing is slow and deep, her pulse regular, her heartbeat strong and even. This is exactly what she needs and her body knew it, even if her emotions didn't. She may be confused or hostile when she wakes up and realizes we let her sleep, but otherwise, she'll be all right."

"And probably easier to manage and reason with after a few hours of decent shut-eye," Savvy added. "We've got to keep a clear head, all of us."

With Hannah asleep at last, some of the fear and grief I'd locked away in my mind slipped out. Before I quite knew what was happening, I was fighting back tears myself. I gave into the inevitability of them. I let them roll down my cheeks, though I did not submit to the loud, snotty, ugly-cry I knew I probably needed. It was like releasing a pressure valve, letting off just enough steam that I didn't explode completely. I allowed myself that, and no more. Savvy pulled me toward her.

"Come here, then, have a good ol' cuddle. God didn't give me these spectacular tits just for show, you know. They're downright cozy."

Somehow, impossibly, a laugh bubbled up from beneath the tears. I cuddled in, and let a friend comfort me—something that would have seemed impossible to the girl I'd been before hauntings and Crossings had become my life. When I finally lifted my head, it was with a sigh and swollen but dry eyes.

"Sorry. I needed to get that out before Hannah needed me again."

"Yeah, I get it," she returned, a tremble in her voice. "Jess, I'll not lie, mate, this whole thing has me scared to death."

"I know. Me, too," I said. "But I'm not giving up."

"Abso-bloody-lutely not!" Savvy said, and her expression turned fierce. "Milo never gave up on me when I became a sentinel! None of you did, come to that, so you'll not see me throwin' in the towel. I'll crawl under every inch of this city if I have to, just try and stop me. I've done it once already just for fun!"

Something in my brain clunked into place. "What did you say?"

Savvy blinked. "Huh?"

"About already being under the city. What did you mean?"

Savvy's expression cleared. "Oh, I'm talking about Mary King's Close. Remember? I took Rana there. I've got the t-shirt on!" She unzipped her hoodie to reveal the bold scarlet t-shirt with the words "I survived The Real Mary King's Close" in a lurid, jagged font.

My body was several steps ahead of my brain, and so I jumped up out of my seat before I'd even fully processed her words.

"Jess, what are you—"

"Parts of this city are built over other parts, isn't that what you told me?" I asked.

Rana's eyes widened and she slid off the bed to walk over to us. "I'm not sure if it's happened in any other part of the city, but that's how Mary King's Close came to be preserved. They just built another building right on top of it."

"We need to get down there," I said.

"Jess, it's a tourist attraction. We've just been all through it, and there was no sign of—"

"But you didn't know what you were looking for, did you?" I said. "You were just having a bit of fun! But if we could get back in there—" I was already halfway to the door of my room.

"Jess, slow down! I'm not saying it's not a good idea. I think it's worth another look, but it's five o'clock in the morning. Nothing's open yet," Savvy said in a logical tone that sounded antithetical to her entire being.

A sound ripped out of me that was half-growl, half-scream of frustration, but I sat back down. Rana shushed me, flapping her hands and looking anxiously over at Hannah, but Hannah didn't stir.

"This is normally where I'd pour someone a strong one, but you're on pain meds for that head injury, aren't you?" Savvy said.

I ran my fingers through my hair, gripping it at the root. "I don't need a drink, I need a fucking time machine! It'll be a miracle if I don't put a fist through a wall or a piece of furniture through the window," I ground out.

"Well, at least you know that if you do, Clarissa MacLeod will have to pay for it," Savvy said with a weak attempt at humor. "Seems reason enough to smash up the whole bloody place, if you take the notion. Need a hand?"

And without so much as a moment's hesitation, she picked up a vase off the side table beside her and started testing the weight of it, as though trying to decide if it could be thrown through a window. The thought of it flying imminently through the air unearthed just enough reason and sanity in my head that I took a hand out of my hair and put it on her shoulder.

"Sav, I appreciate the solidarity, but we probably shouldn't get ourselves arrested for property damage today."

"Fair enough," Savvy said, setting the vase back down again with a clunk of finality. "It is a brilliant way to let off steam, though," she added, somewhat wistfully.

"As an alternative to the property damage plan," Rana said, holding up her phone, "I've just searched the website for Mary King's Close, and the first tour starts at 9:30 this morning, with the admissions desk and shop open half an hour prior. What do you say to heading over there and being first through the doors?"

"Okay," I said. "Okay. Yes. Fine. That's... that's the best we can do."

"Nah, I'm pretty sure we could break in, if we took the fancy," Savvy said.

"Savannah Todd we are NOT breaking into a tourist attraction that we can freely enter in a few hours!" Rana said severely.

Savvy had the good sense to look a bit sheepish. "Right, yeah. Just a bit carried away."

"I appreciate the spirit of the offer, but Rana's right," I said. "We'll go just before nine."

And with that very mature but deeply unsatisfying decision made, I settled in on the couch to wait, probing gently into the connection every few minutes and breaking my heart over and over again each time at the silence waiting for me there.

16

HATTIE

I F I EVER SPENT A LONGER FOUR HOURS OF MY LIFE, I couldn't recall them. Hannah slept on, so soundly that I kept going over and holding my hand in front of her face to make sure she was still breathing, until Savvy slapped me on the wrist.

"Stop doin' that! You're going to wake her, and she won't thank you for that!"

"Ugh, I know, I'm sorry," I groaned. "Anyone want to do me a solid and just clock me so I can be unconscious, too?"

"Mate, if you hadn't already sustained a head injury, I'd punch you in a heartbeat," Savvy said, her soothing tone an odd contrast to the violent, yet well-meant sentiment. "But I can't risk it since you're already concussed, so you'll just have to wait it out like the rest of us."

Waiting it out grew worse and worse, as we got updates from Finn about MacLeod properties all over the city being searched, each yielding absolutely nothing but a steadily rising ire from the MacLeods themselves. The searches would continue throughout the day, but I was placing less and less faith in them as the hours ticked by. The more I thought about it, the more foolish it seemed for the MacLeods to use one of their own properties to house their misdeeds. I was still convinced someone in the clan was involved, but I also knew they were a savvy and clever group. It would be a challenge to out-maneuver them anywhere, but on their own turf, in a city they all but owned, it would be close to impossible.

At last, the clock had crept close enough to nine o'clock that we all agreed we could wake Hannah. Watching her face as she roused from her sleep was like watching a five-act tragedy condensed into a few seconds. Her expression worked first through a deep confusion at where she was and how she had gotten there, then the devastating memory of the previous night that made every pore eloquent with sorrow. And finally, it lit up with the kind of manic energy only true panic can impart.

"How could you let me sleep like that?" she demanded of me, her expression furious. "What if he'd tried to contact me? What if the connection had opened up? What if—"

"Hannah, please calm down. I've been checking the connection constantly while you were asleep. There's been nothing at all. And I let you sleep because you had basically gone into shock. I bet you don't even remember how you got here in the first place."

She tried to contradict me, but she couldn't. I could see in the brief flash of bewilderment that darted across her features that she had no memory whatsoever of leaving the courtyard.

"Besides, we've barely gotten any sleep since we arrived here, and we need to be as sharp as we can be. To help Milo."

"How?! How can we help Milo if we can't even find him?" Hannah cried. Every inch of her was trembling and she was twisting her hands violently together.

Savvy tossed me a look that clearly said, "Shit, maybe we should have sedated her, she's falling apart at the seams." I began to doubt the decision too, but there was no chance in hell she'd just go back to sleep, not now.

"We have a plan—or at least, the beginnings of one. Drink this water, and I'll explain it to you."

"I'm not thirsty, I don't have time for—"

"DRINK!" I interrupted.

Hannah glared at me and then snatched the glass of water out of my hands. She took a shaky sip, half of which dribbled down her chin and into her lap. Then she stared at me as though to say, 'Happy now?!'

"Good, thank you, just... keep doing that," I said. While she continued to sip and glare, I filled her in on what Finn and Catriona were doing all over the city. "Now Rana and Savvy and I were talking, and they reminded me that there is at least part of this city that is completely underground, and it seemed as good a place as any to try next."

Hannah frowned. "What are you talking about? What's underground?"

"Right out there on the Royal Mile, there's that tourist attraction, The Real Mary King's Close," Rana said tentatively.

"I don't know what that means!" Hannah snapped.

Briefly, Rana and Savvy tried to explain it. Hannah scowled through it, looking dubious.

"I still don't understand how you can just... build over a whole street," she said.

"Several streets, actually, with houses still mostly intact," Rana said. "We thought we'd go have a look down there, find out what we can about any other places like that."

"You think that whoever took Milo has him trapped in a tourist attraction?" Hannah asked, her tone quite scathing.

"Look, Milo said, 'down here,' didn't he?" I asked, feeling a bit defensive, even though I knew she wasn't really angry at us. "And that's a well known 'down there' that might give us information about other possible 'down there's' so it's worth a damn try, isn't it?"

Hannah's glare lasted only another second before it melted before my eyes into an expression of bone-deep sadness and exhaustion.

"Yes, of course," Hannah said, running a pale hand over her face. "I'm sorry, I'm just... I just can't believe that..."

"Nobody's apologizing today except the psycho behind all of this," I said, rising to my feet. "Now change into some clean clothes and let's get out of here. The longer it takes us to find him, the more wedding dresses he's going to force you to wear when we finally get him back, and he's got something to hold over your head." I held out my hand to her. "Now, come on. We've got a spirit guide to rescue."

Hannah looked at me, lips trembling, and then something hardened behind her eyes. I watched the determination spread through her and I was reminded, yet again, that my tiny, fragile-looking sister was the strongest person I knew.

She took my hand. "Let's go."

∽

We walked over to The Real Mary King's Close and entered the front door the moment the staff member unlocked it. Rana had purchased our tickets for the first tour of the day online during the interminable wait for the place to open, and she went over to the admissions desk to redeem them while the rest of us looked around the gift shop. There was lots of merchandise meant to lure tourists—t-shirts and mugs and the like—but there was also a fairly large selection of books and guides about the city and, more helpfully, about the close itself. While we waited for the tour to start, we thumbed through them, learning a bit about how the place had come to be unearthed.

"A whole section of the city, frozen in time for more than three centuries," Hannah murmured to herself. "What a shock they must have had when they uncovered it." She dropped her voice to a whisper and asked, "Do you sense anything? Any of the telltale signs of that attacking spirit?"

I shook my head. I'd been on high alert since we'd arrived, but no bitter cold had assaulted me, no screams had reached my ears, and the only unpleasant smell was the chemical tang of whatever they used to wipe down the counters. But that was no more than I had expected. If we were going to experience anything, it would be on the tour, deep under the city.

Savvy and Rana had done a full sweep of the accessible area under cover of perusing the shop offerings, and by the time they rejoined us, they confirmed what we'd already determined. A handful of other people filtered in through the front door, doubtless the other people scheduled for the first tour of the day. Savvy had suggested trying to book a private one, but we'd decided against the idea. If there were more people on the tour, the tour guide would have to divide their attention among more people, and we could use their distraction as cover in case we found anything down there that we wanted to investigate more closely.

At last, a tour guide in period costume gathered us by the inner door and announced the beginning of the tour. We joined the other people grouped around her as she began her scripted introduction. I barely heard a word of it, my own racing thoughts crowding out her voice. I knew I ought to be listening to see if anything in her rote recitation might be helpful in some way, but all I could think was that we needed to get through that door and down those damn stairs.

Finally, the door was opened and we descended behind our guide, who took the stairs slowly in her voluminous skirts as she told us about Mary King, the woman after whom the close had been named.

"It was quite a mark of importance to have a close named after you, and in the case of a woman, it was very rare, a sure sign of great respect and social stature," she called over her shoulder.

I missed the rest of it, as I was trying to take in my surroundings. We appeared to be at the end of a long, narrow street, with tall tenement buildings rising to the ceiling on both sides. The walls were whitewashed and crumbling, the windows narrow and gaping like empty holes where eyes ought to be in the face of a skull. I stared upward, and saw lines strung across the narrow alleyway, with scraps of laundry hanging on them to dry. Flickering lamps, meant to imitate the ones that might once have lit this street when it was above ground, were set into the walls, casting writhing shadows on every surface. Beyond the laundry lines, darkness loomed where a gray strip of morning sky ought to have been. If I hadn't been so wild with anxiety, I would have found it all extremely interesting.

"They'll start taking us through some of the... well, I'd hardly call them houses... dwellings, I suppose," Savvy whispered to me as we shuffled forward up the steep incline. "They'll start talking about all the supposed hauntings as well. We didn't spot any spirits down here the other day, but that don't mean there aren't any hanging around."

"Remember, the spirit we're looking for has a pretty distinctive calling card," I murmured back. "The smell, the cold, and the..." I trailed off.

"The screaming," Savvy finished for me. "Yeah, mate, I promise, I can't unhear that."

I leaned over to Hannah this time, who was bent over peering into one of the tenement windows. They had set up a sort of scene inside, with a life-size figure of a man at work at a table with all manner of tools. The sight of him, as I turned, caused my heart to leap into my throat. I couldn't help it. I yelped in shock.

The tour guide couldn't have been more delighted with my reaction. "Ah, and have we spotted one of our wee ghostly friends, perhaps? Or has the sight of one of our mannequins given you a turn?"

I made an attempt at a laugh. "Yeah, sorry about that. Just... wasn't expecting that."

The tour guide started up about the tenement room in question, which was apparently called, "Chesne's workshop," but I had already stopped listening.

"Do you think we should keep the connection open while we're down here?" I asked her. "If we're any closer to where Milo is, we might have a better chance of hearing each other."

But Hannah was too distracted to listen to me. The face she turned to look at me was so tense it looked like a mask, or the face of one of the mannequins behind her. "Jess, I'm starting to worry this is a waste of time. It would be foolish to use something as public and popular as a tourist attraction to cover up a crime you want to hide."

I didn't answer right away, partly because I was so desperate for this to be the right answer, and partly because I knew she had a very good point. It was ridiculous for the perpetrator of this Casting to use a place where so many people came and went, a place that was only open during certain hours, and which always had a number of staff walking around making sure everything was in order. But at the same time, something in my gut was telling me not to give up on this place quite yet, and I wasn't ready to ignore it.

"We're here now, so let's not leave this stone unturned. The tour won't last long, and if it doesn't pan out, we won't have lost much time. Besides, there may be something to find here yet," I said.

Hannah's face lost not an ounce of its tension, but she nodded and continued tagging along at the back of the tour group, eyes raking desperately over every new corner and crevice of the place.

We followed our tour guide through a series of chambers, each one like a windowless cave with low rounded ceilings and flaking white brick walls. Bare bulbs hung from the ceilings, giving the whole place the air of an abandoned prison. In some of the rooms, there were other scenes set up. I was prepared for the mannequins now, thank goodness, or the one of the plague doctor with his birdlike black mask would surely have sent me screaming up the passage and back above ground.

It was in this room, while the tour guide was cheerfully enumerating the many horrors of the bubonic plague era, that I felt the first fleeting...*something*.

It wasn't the spirit we were looking for, I knew that right away. There was none of the stench, the horror sounds, the utter cold. It was more of a chill breeze that swept the room, a little shiver-inducing breath along the back of the neck, a hair-raising tickle on the back of the hand.

"Someone's here after all," Savvy muttered, sounding more amused than anything. "Well, well, well, who would have thought it? The haunted attraction is well and truly haunted."

"I felt it too," I whispered. "But it isn't who we're looking for."

"Yeah, but it's someone, nevertheless, and someone who might know a bit about the underside of this city, yeah?" Savvy whispered back. Her eyes were bright. She was excited for the first time since we'd gotten here, and that excitement was enough, in my desperate state, to cling to.

"I'm going in search of... her," I said without intending to; and yet, I knew I was right. I was looking for a girl... a young one. Where this information came from, I couldn't have said any better than I could say how I knew what colors looked like or how a sound made me feel. It was just in me, solid and knowable, inherent in the energy she had left behind that still clung to me like cobwebs.

While everyone was facing the great wooden bed where the plague doctor was bending over his doomed patients, I crept back a few steps from the group, holding my breath, begging my shoes not to scrape over the rough floor and give me away. I managed this tiny scrap of luck, and backed out of the room without anyone even glancing my way. I stood in the now deserted hallway and held very still, waiting.

A silvery whisper of a laugh raised goosebumps on my arm. I turned and followed it, but it was almost impossible to tell which direction it had gone. Some chambers, no doubt part of the tour, were open, but others were roped off. I chanced a glance behind me, but I was still alone. Did I dare wander into one of the roped off areas? I didn't want to get thrown out before the tour was even over, but this might be my only chance to learn something I couldn't learn from the tour script.

Another snatch of voice—a little tune or a musical sigh—reached my ears from the other side of one of the ropes, and I abandoned my caution. I stepped over the rope and entered a chamber that was completely empty save for a small antique writing desk pushed up against the wall, with a small, rickety-looking chair placed behind it. I stood on the threshold, letting the energy of the room settle over me before I attempted to communicate.

"Hello?" I said, in barely more than a whisper, unsure of how far my voice would carry. I didn't want to be given away. "I heard you laughing a minute ago. What was so funny?"

Silence, and then... Did I imagine it? Another faint giggle. I eased my face into a smile, hoping to put the spirit at ease. She was still being coy with me.

"Come on. I'd love a reason to laugh. What's the joke?" I tried again.

"It's the faces," came the answering murmur. A figure was starting to emerge in the shadows behind the writing desk—a small, slight figure.

"What faces?" I asked, letting my smile widen. Act friendly Jess, don't scare the poor kid.

"Didn't you see them? On the wax figures." The girl was quite distinct now, though her features were still hazy. I could make out long stringy brown hair and a white summer dress. Wide eyes. Bare feet.

"Oh, right, yeah. I, um... didn't really get close enough to see them," I admitted.

"Oh, they're so funny! Tongues all lolling out and eyes all—" She tilted her head to the side, and I could make out enough of her face now that I could see she was sticking her tongue out and crossing her wide brown eyes. The expression was so comical that I laughed in earnest now only to have to stifle it with the back of my hand.

"That does sound funny," I told her, dropping my voice again. "I'll have to go get a closer look."

"You can see me," the little girl said suddenly. She tilted her head the other way, and her hair swung like a curtain down toward her bony shoulder.

"I can," I confirmed, nodding.

"And you can hear me."

"Yes."

"That's very odd," the girl decided. "Is there something wrong with you?"

I had to fight to keep a straight face. "I'm not sure," was the answer I finally decided on. "But I'm not the only person I know who would be able to see you. Haven't you met anyone else down here who could see you?"

"Once in a while," the girl seemed to consider for a moment, "but mostly there are a lot of people who *want* to see me. They're forever calling out to me and leaving me toys and things. Some of them even carry strange metal boxes with flashing lights and strange black ropes coming out of them. And they ask me to come talk to them a lot."

I smiled, recognizing from her description what a modern day ghost hunting team must look like to someone from a bygone era.

"And do you? Go and talk to them, I mean?"

"Oh, not like this, no," the girl said dismissively. "They couldn't hear me like you can, and I don't like shouting. And besides, they call me by the wrong name. They all do."

"Is that so? What name do they call you?"

"Annie," the girl said, wrinkling her nose. "Not that it's such a terrible name, mind you, I'm sure it's a very nice one to have when it is *yours*, but it's just not *mine*, you see."

I did see, and I told her so. "So, what is your name, then, if you don't mind me asking?"

"Hattie," the girl said, pronouncing it in a very exaggerated manner. "I try to correct them but, as I already told you, they can't hear me that well. And now that everyone's been told that's my name, they *will* insist on thinking that's what I've said." She sighed, as if the whole thing were very vexing and made her tired. "Perhaps you could tell them for me?"

I nodded. "Sure, I'll try. And do you think you could do something for me?"

Hattie frowned. "I'd not like to promise before I know what it is."

"Oh, you don't have to promise," I assured her. "I just have a few questions. If you don't like them or don't want to answer them, you can just tell me so."

"Oh!" Hattie's face brightened once more. "Well, that's all right, then."

"Hattie, do you know this underground place very well?" I asked.

"Oh yes, indeed! I've been here for ages. I could draw it like a map, if, well..." she gestured toward the writing desk and shrugged, to indicate the futility of her attempts to use a quill in her current state.

"And is the part that they show us on the tour—is that the whole of it? What I mean is, are there other Closes or buildings that they aren't showing us?" I asked, trying hard to keep the desperation out of my voice. I'd finally gotten to the heart of the matter, and I didn't want to scare Hattie off now.

"Oh, goodness no, there's a good bit still beyond what they show you. It hasn't all been deemed safe, you see. They've had ever so many important people down here, with special machines and more lights, but it's all too unsteady, I've heard them say. They have to wear funny helmets when anyone goes back there. I've seen them at it."

My heart was pounding so hard now that I feared she could hear it. *Don't get your hopes up*, I told myself. *Don't jump to conclusions.*

"Could you show me how to get to those places? Is there an entrance from down here?"

"Well, yes, but you haven't got one of those funny helmets. You'll get into awful trouble if they catch you," she said in a wide-eyed whisper.

"That's all right," I said, smiling what I hoped was a reassuring smile as opposed to a manic one. "I can handle a little trouble, I promise. And of course, I'd never tell them you told me. It will be our secret, I promise."

Hattie gave me an appraising look, as though she would decide just how much trouble I could handle, but I seemed to pass the test. Crooking a tiny pale finger at me, she drifted along past me and back out into the hallway. I followed as quietly as I could, eyes peeled and heart pounding in case the tour came around the corner and spotted me off on my own.

Hattie floated along ahead of me, skipping and humming to herself like she was walking to school on a sunny day rather than leading a complete stranger through a labyrinth of haunted underground tunnels. Finally, she skidded to a halt at the mouth of another hallway, this one wrapped in darkness save for the flickering orange light of a nearby lamp that throws just enough light to reveal that it ends in a door some thirty feet away. The hallway was roped off right across its entrance, and a small plastic sign affixed to the wall beside it read: "Danger: No Admittance Beyond This Point."

Hattie lifted a hand and pointed. "That's the hallway that leads to the other rooms," she said. "I shan't go down there with you, though." And she shuddered.

The reaction stopped me cold and I looked at her carefully. "Why not? Surely it's not dangerous for you?"

"It's dangerous for everyone," she said solemnly. "That's what the lady told me."

"What lady?"

"The lady. The other one who saw me, like you can."

"I thought you said other people can't see you?" I said.

"No, I said *most* people can't. You really ought to listen more carefully," she said with a somewhat disapproving scowl.

"Sorry about that," I replied hastily. "Could you tell me a bit more about what that woman said to you? Was she on one of the tours?"

"Oh, no. She was down here all by herself at a very odd hour indeed. I don't know how she got in, but she came from that hallway." Hattie pointed down the very forbidden hallway she'd brought me to see. "And then she spotted me and she said, 'Oh, you sweet darling, you mustn't ever go down that hallway, all right? It isn't safe for the likes of you.' She made me promise," Hattie added indignantly.

"And did she say why it was dangerous?" I asked.

"No, but I didn't need her to. Can't you feel it? There's something... *wrong.*"

The word, no more than a frightened whisper, fell like a physical blow on my ears. It was the very same word Milo had used to describe the feeling in the courtyard, spoken in the same disturbed and fearful tone.

I heard voices behind us, and I suddenly realized we had but moments before the tour would catch up with us.

"One last question, Hattie," I hissed. "This lady, do you know who she was? Can you describe her?"

Hattie frowned. "She was a bit older than you. And she spoke properly, not in that funny way that you do."

"But did she—"

"You said one more question, and you're going to be in so much trouble if you're found here! Hide!" Hattie hissed reprovingly at me and, with a twirl of her skirt, vanished from sight.

Because there was nowhere else to hide, I ducked under the rope and retreated along the forbidden corridor, backing myself into the shadows so that the group would not see me as they walked by. I'd only made it about halfway down when a terrible, creeping cold began to steal over me, accompanied by a smell that turned my stomach and froze my blood.

A sweet, rotting, corrosive smell...

I pressed my hand over my nose and mouth and fought like mad against the urge to run while I waited for the tour group to meander past my hiding place. Just as the last few of them disappeared past the entryway, I tiptoed out of the corridor, ducked under the rope, and tucked myself into the back of the group right beside Hannah.

"Jess! Where did you—"

But I shook my head, dropping my hand from my mouth and sucking in a breath of musty air that smelled as clean as a breath of air in the highlands compared to what I'd just left behind me in that corridor.

"And now, if you'll all follow me up the stairs, that concludes our tour of The Real Mary King's Close!" the tour guide called. "Please watch your step and use the handrails!"

We didn't say another word as we passed the tour guide at the top of the stairs. She gave an energetic click on her little handheld counter, making sure that no one had been left behind somehow, and then slipped it back into her pocket and closed the door behind us. I made a beeline for the front door, and the four of us spilled out onto the Royal Mile.

"Jess, what the—"

"I found it," I said, surprised to find that my excitement and fear had left me quite breathless.

"What do you mean?!" Hannah asked. "Found what?"

"I met a ghost down there, a ghost of a little girl—"

"Was it Annie?" Savvy piped up excitedly. "The tour guide was going on and on about Annie, but I honestly thought she was having it on!"

"Well, she wasn't. Annie is real, only her name isn't Annie, it's Hattie," I said impatiently before launching into everything Hattie had told me, and also what she had shown me.

"Who was the woman, do you reckon?" Rana asked eagerly.

"All she told me was that she was older than me, and that she 'talked normally' which I'm guessing means she's Scottish. And if she could see and communicate with Hattie the same way I did, then she's surely a Durupinen."

"And a member of Clan Rioghalachd ," Savvy added.

"I knew this was an inside job," Hannah hissed through her clenched teeth. "I knew it, I knew it, I knew it!"

"But this is brilliant!" Savvy said. "Let's get back in there and—"

"And what?" I asked. "Break into an unsafe restricted area of a popular tourist attraction? Get ourselves arrested for trespassing or worse? Even Catriona will have a hard time getting us out of that, and after how we've basically declared open war against them, I doubt Clan Rioghalachd will be wielding any of their considerable clout to help us. No, we have to find another way to do this."

Hannah turned a gaze on me that nearly broke my heart. Fear and anger blazed in them in a way that would haunt my dreams for weeks.

"One hour," she said. "I'm giving us one hour to come up with another plan, or I will break back into that place, legalities be damned."

"Did she just say damned?" Savvy whispered to Rana.

Yes, she had. And we had one hour before she damned this whole mission.

17

WALKING BENEATH

W E ALL SAT AROUND A PRIVATE PARLOR BACK AT THE WITCHERY: Finn, Hannah, Catriona, Savvy, Rana, and me. Milo's absence was in itself like a presence, hovering over us in a constant reminder of the one of us who should be there, and wasn't. If we couldn't get him back... If it was too late...

Nope, Ballard. Absolutely not. Do not go there. Does not compute, my brain screamed at me as it shoved that particular thought way down to the bottom of the box.

I distracted myself by keeping up a steady, almost manic stream of talking as I filled everyone in on what had happened down in the Close. By the time I was finished, Finn was pacing like a caged jungle cat and Catriona was releasing a stream of expletives fit only for a Scorsese movie.

"To think she called us here, draining our resources, flaunting her wealth, and she's been behind it all along!" Catriona growled.

"We don't know for sure that Hattie was talking about Clarissa," Hannah said, in a hollow voice that betrayed her utter disbelief in the words.

"Who the bloody hell else could it be?!" Savvy retorted. "No one in that clan dares wipe her nose unless Clarissa hands her a hankie first. Of course it's her!"

"Whoever it is, she's unleashed something evil on the spirits of this city, and she needs to be stopped. And punished," Rana said, her dark eyes flashing with the fury we all felt.

"So, what do we do? We can't break into the place, much as that would be the easiest thing," Catriona said. "It would take me a day at least to get access to alarm codes and the like. We don't have that kind of time."

Hannah just snorted with disgust. No one else had paid much attention to her ultimatum of an hour, but I knew better than to underestimate her. If we didn't come up with something better, she'd be back down the Mile before we could stop her, caution and legalities be damned.

"The thing is," Rana said slowly, her brow furrowed in concentration, "whoever the woman is... let's say for argument's sake that it's Clarissa—"

"Because it *is*," Savvy interjected.

"If Clarissa really met Hattie down in those tunnels, she had to have gotten in from somewhere. It was the middle of the night, or so the child claims. How could Clarissa have been in the close itself all that time, unnoticed?"

"What are you saying?" Finn asked, stopping his pacing.

"I'm saying that there must be another entrance to those tunnels, another way to get in. And Clarissa used that entrance and then followed the tunnels where they led and found herself coming out at the other end, into Mary King's Close. Didn't you say they own half the bloody city?"

"More or less," Catriona said, sounding intrigued now.

"Then one of their buildings must contain that other entrance. No other explanation makes sense, unless you really think Clarissa MacLeod crouched in a filthy underground chamber for eight hours at a time, hiding from tourists behind mannequins."

We all looked around the group, the conclusion clear on every face: there is no way Clarissa MacLeod would ever subject herself to anything so demeaning, no matter the goal.

"Haven't you been searching MacLeod properties since last night?" I asked, turning to Finn.

He nodded, a grimace twisting his features. "It took some time to obtain the records of the properties, of course, and we still don't have a full listing. Clarissa must have told the lawyers to obstruct us, because they're dragging their feet as much as they dare. We have a partial list, and the searches have begun, but we're sure there are other properties we don't know about yet."

Catriona nodded, an ugly expression on her usually angelic face. "They'll have hidden many of their assets under the names of shell companies and other such nonsense—it's one of the ways the wealthy avoid paying taxes like the rest of us mere peasants."

"And so, while we're digging around to sort that all out, we've started searching the ones we know about so far," Finn said. "There are a few within a block or two of the Royal Mile, but nothing that could lead you into those tunnels... at least, I don't reckon so. Surely they can't go on for... how far do you think they go?"

"We have no way of knowing for sure," I answered, "but I felt the presence of that attacking spirit, felt it looming strongly at the far end of that hallway, and I don't think that would have happened if they were miles away. I think it's close. I think this MacLeod property must be on the Mile itself, or right off it."

"I agree," Finn said. "Catriona, we've got to turn up the heat on those lawyers, make them give up the rest of the files."

"I'm on it," Catriona said, pulling a phone from her jeans pocket and pressing a few buttons before putting it to her ear.

Hannah stood up. Every eye in the room followed her movement, the tension rising.

"I can't wait for lawyers and files. Milo is missing. Something terrible is happening to him, and I won't make him endure it a single second longer for the sake of some red tape. I'm going back to Mary King's Close, and I'll do it myself if I have to."

"Hannah, wait!" I said, jumping up from my seat on the couch. "Just... just hold on a minute."

"A minute! Jess, Milo might not have a *second,* do you understand that?"

"I promise, I do. But if you go charging off into those tunnels, undefended and unprepared, that spirit is going to kill you."

"If Milo is gone, he might as well kill me!" Hannah shrieked.

The room was silent. I stared at her, at the unshed tears trembling in her eyes.

"You don't mean that," I said softly.

Hannah just stared at me defiantly, the tears breaking their bounds and rolling freely down her cheeks.

"No one is dying, not for Clarissa MacLeod's hollow, evil scheme, whatever the hell it may be." I said each word slowly, watching each of them land on my sister, breaking down her defiance like blows. Finally, she slumped her shoulders and nodded, once.

"Okay, then," I said. "Now that we're all on the same page, I agree with Hannah. We can't wait for these lawyers to run out the clock. Clarissa is stalling and she's going to use every extra moment to her advantage. We have to work around her, take her by surprise."

"I agree that would be ideal, but how do we do it? We can't send somebody down into those tunnels without knowing what they'll find at the end!" Finn said.

"How about the 'some' without the 'body?'" I asked.

It took him a moment before the realization set in.

"No."

"Now, don't you start."

"Me? Don't YOU start!"

"It's a good idea and you know it, that's why you're so mad."

"No, I'm mad because you insist on putting yourself into these maddeningly dangerous situations!"

"Hang on, hang on, what am I missing here?" Savvy broke in, her confusion echoed in every other face in the room.

"Nothing, just a mad notion of Jess's that we're ignoring," Finn growled.

"It's not mad! It's the only thing that might work!" I growled back.

"Will someone please just tell me what the devil you're talking about?" Savvy roared.

"NO, because we're not—"

"WALKING!" I shouted over him, and he seethed into silence. "I'm suggesting that I Walk down into the tunnels and investigate in a way a living person couldn't."

A moment's silence and then Rana said, "Yeah, sorry, I must be missing something, because I don't know what the blazes is happening. What's all this nonsense about walking?"

"Not that kind of walking, love," Savvy said, and pulled Rana aside to whisper an explanation.

A few moments later, Rana, her eyes round, expelled a breath. "Oh! Oh, I see! Right! Well, now that's... that's certainly... not what I was expecting."

Finn and I had been glaring each other down during this exchange, and he had finally pulled his gaze away, realizing we were at a stalemate. He turned to Catriona for support.

"Cat, tell her this is mad, go on."

But Cat was surveying me through narrowed eyes, fingernails drumming furiously on her upper arms. "Now that's an idea," she finally said.

I felt my stomach unclench. If Cat was on board, convincing the others just got a whole lot easier. I felt rather than saw Finn shift his attention to Hannah, for I turned that moment to look at her, too. She was looking at me with a curiously blank expression, as though nothing of what we'd said so far had even registered fully in her brain. Then, through stiff lips, she whispered, "You would do that? For Milo?"

"Of course I would!" I cried. "Don't you realize, he's as much a part of me now as you are!"

"He'll be so mad at you," Hannah murmured.

"Not half as mad as he'd be at you if you got killed before he could dress you up like Bridal Fever Dream Barbie!" I said. "This is the only way to keep everyone out of danger."

"Jess, *you* will be in danger!" Finn ground out.

"No, I won't," I said, and though I'd meant it to be a soothing sentiment, it came out rather snappish. "I won't have a body down there to get hurt, remember? I'll be fine."

"Yes, I do remember, but there is more than one way to be in danger, Jess!" Finn shot back. "You're going down there to confront someone who's been capturing souls. Not bodies. *Souls.* Your spirit is in just as much danger as your body would be, surely you know that?"

"I'm not planning on getting caught," I said, dodging neatly around the question.

"No one plans on getting caught. That's LITERALLY how getting caught works!" Finn cried, throwing his hands up in exasperation.

"Well, whatever, you know what I mean. I'll be careful," I said.

"Oh, is that it? You'll be careful? You think Milo wasn't careful? Did you... can you possibly... didn't you hear that screaming?!"

His words cleaved the room like an ax, and silence fell wholly and completely. And in that silence we all heard it again, dredged up from our own memories where each of us had failed to repress it: the screaming.

"Don't worry, I won't let that happen to me," I said when I was sure I could control my own voice again.

Finn's answer was nothing more than a snort of disgust, and I couldn't blame him. Telling him not to worry was like telling him not to breathe. But there was no time for coddling right now. No time to hesitate.

"Give me a better solution, Finn," I said quietly. "Give me a better plan, and I'll gladly take it."

For a second time, a heavy silence fell—a silence I patiently waited through while Finn struggled for an answer and then, as I knew he must, give up on it. My victory was in the sag of his shoulders as he sighed.

"Are you sure you can still do it?" he asked in a hollow voice.

"Like riding a bike," I said, though nothing had ever been less like riding a bike.

"Do we have what we need?" was his next question.

"No, but Pippa can get it for us, I have no doubt," was my ready answer.

Finn's mouth twisted like he'd just sucked a lemon. "This is a reconnaissance mission. Nothing more. You stay hidden. You avoid detection. You find out what you can without anyone seeing you, and you get out."

I gave him a jaunty little salute, which earned me another scowl. I remembered with a pang that Milo had announced he was going to do some "ghostly reconnaissance" right before he vanished, but this seemed like an extremely foolish time to mention it, especially now that Finn was cooperating.

But as dark as Finn's face now was, Hannah's expression was lightening for the first time since Milo had vanished. There was something approaching hope burning in her eyes, a light which brightened when a knock sounded on the door, and Finn opened it to reveal Kiernan on the threshold.

"Kiernan!" Hannah cried out. She stumbled her way across the room and practically fell into his arms. His face was such an eloquent combination of joy and distress that I found myself once again awed in the presence of the love they had for each other.

"You ought to have called me sooner, darling," Kiernan murmured into her hair, the words coming between the kisses he was planting there like seeds.

"I didn't want to... the Skye project... it's your dream," Hannah blubbered against his shirt as he held her.

"Nonsense," Kiernan said. "You're my dream. That's just a job."

Hannah looked up into his eyes and managed an actual smile through her tears, and the sight of it bolstered me.

"Thanks for coming, Kiernan," I said, and then noticed the stack of crates on a dolly that was still standing out in the hallway. "What's all that?"

"I heard you needed some help filling in the gaps on Clan Rìoghalachd, so I brought every book in the Skye collection related to that clan," he said. I stared at him and he reddened. "Sorry, but 'thoroughly' is the only way I know how to research things. I realize it may be excessive."

"It's not excessive, it's amazing, thank you," I told him. "Trying to get information out of the MacLeods has become a bit like slamming repeatedly into a brick wall."

"Oh dear," Kiernan said, still stroking Hannah's hair. "Yes, I've long known they were a difficult lot. Fortunately, clans as powerful as theirs are well documented, and not just by their own Scribes. We ought to be able to find something that will help us in here."

"Skye really just let you walk out with all of those?" Rana said, eyes wide as she took in the crates Finn had now taken upon himself to wheel through the door.

"Not exactly," Kiernan said. "I had to sign them out and complete roughly a hundred waivers taking responsibility for them. Mind you, they were a nightmare to travel on the train with, but we got here in the end."

"Okay, so then, it looks like we've got a plan," Catriona said, breaking up the discussion that had been thrown off course by Kiernan's arrival. "Jess, contact Pippa for what you need to complete the Casting for Walking. I will continue to put pressure on the MacLeods for the full listing of properties, but I won't wait for them. I'll head straight down to the public records office and see what I can dig up there. We may be able to narrow things down that way."

"We can stay connected to Jess through the connection while she's Walking," Hannah said, finally extracting herself from Kiernan's arms. "She won't be alone down there."

"I don't know if that will work, Hannah," I told her. "We haven't been able to connect with Milo in that place. I'm not convinced the connection works right now. And anyway, we've had issues with it in the past when I've Walked. We just can't count on it. We'll have to set a time limit. Give me two hours to Walk, to find out what I can, and I'll come back."

"One hour. And if you're not back by the end of it, we go in after you, felony breaking and entering be damned," Finn said, his words nearly unintelligible through clenched teeth.

"One hour? Finn, that might not be enough time," I argued.

"Move. Quickly."

I rolled my eyes but let it pass. He was just trying to protect me. I crossed the room to him and put my arms around his neck and stayed that way until he finally gave up and looked at me.

"You would do this for Milo, if you were the one who could Walk instead of me," I said, and it was a statement, not a question.

He sighed. "Of course I would."

"And you wouldn't let my worries stop you."

"No, I wouldn't."

"He's my spirit guide. He's sacrificed a lot for me—for all of us. I can risk a bit of danger for him in return. And you can let me."

Finn's jaw was still tense, but his eyes had softened. "Yes, I can. But I don't have to like it."

I kissed his nose. "No, you don't. You can hate it and be as curmudgeonly as you want."

Was that a tiny twitch at the corner of his mouth? "You better be careful, Ballard," he said. "I can be very curmudgeonly."

"Do your worst," I whispered with a grin, and kissed him again.

And this time, he kissed me back. Ha. Curmudgeonly, my ass, you big faker.

Pippa was rather startled when she received my list of necessities for the Casting, but she assured me, without hesitation, that she could procure them for me.

"The Clan Rìoghalachd store rooms are plentifully supplied with anything a Casting might call for. Give me an hour," she said.

She was back in half that time, with everything I needed. She handed me the bag, her face bursting with a hundred unasked questions that I couldn't answer anyway, because we weren't supposed to tell anyone in Clan Rìogha-lachd what we were doing. For once, though, her perfect composure couldn't hold.

"Do you think... will you be able to fix it?" she blurted out.

"Fix it?"

"That... that awful scene in the courtyard. I can't stop thinking about it. That screaming, I can't get it out of my... can you fix it?"

Her face was so aghast that I almost gave her the answer she needed to hear just to wipe that expression from her features. But I couldn't. Now wasn't the time for lies, but for hard truths.

"I don't know. But we're going to try."

Pippa pressed her lips together and nodded once, accepting that she would hear no better. "And you're sure there's nothing else I can do to help you?" she added.

"You've just done it. Thanks, Pippa. I'd like to tell you more, but I can't."

"I understand," she said stoically. "Good luck, whatever your plan is. I hope it works, truly. And..." She swallowed convulsively, and her cheeks reddened. "And I hope you catch the culprit, no matter who it is." There was a defiant expression in her eyes as she spoke what I'm sure must have felt like something akin to sacrilege to her, but which I understood perfectly. She thought, as we did, that Clarissa was behind this; and she wanted her held accountable, regardless of what that meant for Pippa and her career aspirations.

I left Pippa by the front desk and returned to my room, where everyone was waiting. Hannah, Kiernan, and Rana were spread across the bed, having cracked open the first crate of books with a crowbar they had to borrow from the front desk, which had to borrow it from the pub next door. They were flipping feverishly through the volumes, occasionally causing Kiernan to stifle a whimper of concern at how the books were being handled. Catriona and Finn had managed, against all odds, to start a fire in the ornate old fireplace. I handed the bag Pippa had given me over to Catriona, who snatched it and began feverishly laying out materials in the order we would need them. She was rather giddy about being involved in this particular Casting, having never learned it nor witnessed the effects of it.

"Ready?" Finn asked.

"Ready," I replied.

His lips curled up at the edges in just the smallest suggestion of a smile. "Bugger all. I was hoping you'd answer 'no.'"

"No such luck, pal," I replied with a wink. "But I'm still determined to be very, very careful."

"That'll have to do, I suppose," he sighed, and we began the preparations. I hadn't brought any of my stash of Soul Catchers with me, having not the slightest inkling that it might be possible that I would need one on this mission. All the ones I had stuffed into my bedside table drawer back in London had been made for me by the Traveler Durupinen, and most of those had been made by Flavia, who had been kind enough to teach me how to do it as well, "in case I ever ran out."

The idea that I could run out was ludicrous, in light of the fact that Walking was something I had only ever done to prevent a spirit apocalypse and a hostile Necromancer takeover. It wasn't, like, a *hobby.* In fact, I'd been looking very much forward to never doing it again, ever. But the Durupinen world had me eating my own words yet again, and using the skills Flavia had taught me to weave together my own Soul Catcher. Again, having never expected to need this skill, I hadn't paid as close attention as I probably should have, and I had to restart twice when I miscounted or used the wrong kind of knot. But twenty minutes later, I finally had a functional Soul Catcher tied around my wrist, and a backup one in my pocket, just in case.

I stood up. "Okay. Let's do this."

Hannah slid off the bed and hugged me fiercely. Then she pulled away, not meeting my eyes. "Jess, Finn and I were talking and we were thinking... you know, unless you want me there, of course I'll—"

"I told Hannah I thought it was a good idea if she stayed here and helped aid the search through these books," Finn said, rescuing Hannah from her own dithering. "We both thought she might be calmer if she had a task to focus on."

I caught Finn's eye and I understood the subtext. He was afraid to have Hannah come with us to the Close. He thought her heightened emotional state might make her behave rashly, and therefore unable to stick to the agreed upon plan. In short, she was a liability. I turned my gaze on Hannah again, and decided he was absolutely right.

"Hey," I said, chucking Hannah under the chin so she was forced to look at me. "I will be fine. There's no reason for you to sit cooped uselessly up in a car when you could be making a breakthrough in one of those books that might finally give us all a hint about what the hell we're facing here. Whoever's behind all of this took those pages for a reason. They risked killing us rather than allowing us to find out what was in that book, so it must be important. That's the best way to help Milo and the best way to help me."

Hannah gave me a watery smile, another almost painful hug, and then returned to the bed to resume her feverish study of a leather-bound tome.

We decided to drive over to The Real Mary King's Close attraction and park on the street as close to it as we could get. Up until this point, we'd been chauffeured around by Clan Rìoghalachd , but Catriona had decided that was no longer safe. She didn't want a driver loyal to the MacLeods overhearing our plans, nor did she even trust them to provide us with a vehicle free from surveillance equipment. She had tracked down a sleek rental for us, and wherever she'd gotten it didn't seem to care about the various legalities surrounding heavily tinted windows. My body would remain behind in the car, guarded by Finn and Catriona, and my spirit would slip down into the hidden city below. One hour was all I had before the two of them would come charging after me, so I would need to be quick. Finn enlisted two of the Fairhaven Caomhnóir to follow us over, providing extra protection outside the car, and providing my body with protection if he and Catriona had to tear off after me in a hurry. The plan sounded simple enough: follow the tunnels wherever they may lead, gleaning whatever clues I could along the way, then find the other entrance and get out. It was only three o'clock in the afternoon now, which meant the mysterious Casting wouldn't be active, but we still had to be cautious. Just because it wasn't the witching hour didn't mean that examining the place as a spirit wouldn't be dangerous. That evil spirit, whoever they were, may well be roaming the place at any hour, and the same was true for the living person in league with them.

We found a parking space on the side of the building that didn't run along the Mile—it was quieter, with less chance of detection. Catriona threw the car into park, killed the engine, and turned around in the driver's seat to look at me.

"You about ready?" she asked, checking her watch to glean an accurate time.

"Yes, but I've just thought of something," I said. "How am I supposed to know when an hour has passed? I'm not going to have a functioning timepiece once I shuffle off this mortal coil."

Finn frowned. "I hadn't thought of that either. Should we just forget the whole—"

"Absolutely not, don't be absurd," Catriona snapped impatiently at him. "Just estimate the best you can. And keep an ear out for the church bells. I realize you'll be beneath the city, but those bells are loud. You may yet be able to hear them."

There was little point in trying to explain the intricacies of processing sensory information in spirit form, as it would have taken most of the day and approximately three phone calls to Flavia to make it clear, so I just nodded my agreement. I'd do my best and hope that my spirit self could figure it out.

The aforementioned church bells struck three, eliminating the chance for further debate. I smiled at Finn, who did his damnedest to smile back.

"See you in an hour," I told him firmly.

"Until then, love. Please be careful."

"Always."

I closed my eyes, trying to ignore the way my heart was pounding, and my brain was screaming at me not to do this. And yet, just as I put the edge of my pocketknife to the Soul Catcher, I felt a fleeting thrill of joy, as though something inside of me knew it was about to be free. I whispered the words to the Casting and then, holding my breath, I sliced through the Soul Catcher and with it, the strings that held me to my body.

I was up and away from it, drifting with an unbearably delicious lightness. What I'd said about riding a bike hadn't been such a terrible analogy after all— this was easy. I'd forgotten how natural it was, how the ease of it was a lure and a trap, and how simple it would be to cast off my body forever. No more pain from my injuries, no more fuzzy feeling in my head. Everything was wonderfully, effortlessly clear. Without a body to contain it, everything expanded, and I found that I could count the seconds ticking by with just a tiny sliver of my consciousness, allowing the rest to take in everything around me. I allowed myself approximately six and three-quarters seconds to enjoy the sensation of floating in the air like an untethered balloon before resigning myself to the task at hand. Just for good measure, I swooped through the car's interior on my way down, eliciting a chuckle from Finn and a sort of envious groan from Catriona.

"Show-off," I heard her mutter as I passed through the other side of the car and on through the wall of the gift shop above Mary King's Close. I'd forgotten the strange sensation of passing through things—the compression that wasn't quite painful, but somehow still unpleasant. The gift shop was crowded with milling tourists, including a knot of them by the door, about to begin their descent into the underbelly of Edinburgh. I slipped past them, past the costumed guide already well into her scripted introduction, and down the stairs into the close below.

I wasted no time exploring the spaces I'd already been through, sailing straight toward the back of the attraction to the forbidden corridor with its rope across the entrance and the cautionary sign. In my current form, these attempts to keep people out looked almost comical, and I allowed myself a chuckle.

"It's you!"

I spun in the air to find Hattie staring at me, her eyes saucer-wide.

"Hi, Hattie!"

She frowned at me. "I asked you to tell everyone my real name and now instead you've gone and died, haven't you?" she demanded.

I laughed again at her indignation. "No, don't worry, I'm not dead."

She narrowed her eyes at me. "But you're a ghost."

"Only temporarily."

She pulled a skeptical face. "I don't think that's how this works."

"Well, you'll just have to trust me. As long as things don't go wrong down there, I'll be back here tomorrow, body intact, demanding your requested name change from the tour guides, all right?"

She remained unconvinced. "If you say so. But why are you going down there? Haven't I told you it's dangerous?"

"Yes, I know. That danger is threatening the spirits of this city. That's why I need to go down there. That's why I've taken this form. I'm going to try to stop it."

"How are you going to do that?" Hattie asked bluntly.

"Haven't figured that part out yet," I admitted.

"Well you really ought to, don't you think?" she said.

"I'm working on it," I said. "In the meantime, please do what that other woman told you and don't come down here, whatever you might see or hear, all right? She was right. It's dangerous."

Hattie didn't reply. She just kept staring at me with an intent expression.

"Wish me luck?" I suggested.

"I daresay you'll need it," was her inspiring reply.

"Thanks," I muttered, and then turned my back on her and proceeded down the hallway.

The energy coming from the other side of the door was palpable in a way it hadn't been when I was encumbered with my body or, as Irina used to refer to it, 'my cage.' The wrongness that both Milo and Hattie had mentioned finally made complete sense to me. What had manifested as extreme cold and a terrible smell before felt entirely different now. I thought back to Hattie, and how her presence had felt: cool, bright, a little sharp perhaps, but *normal*—a perfect reflection of who she really was, at her essence, because essence was all she had left. The energy of the presence I was feeling now was warped some-how, like spirit energy being filtered through one of those funhouse mirrors that distorts everything. It made me almost dizzy, the wrongness of it, and for the first time since taking on my Walker form, I was nervous.

The door loomed ahead of me, and the energy that emanated from the other side of it was almost enough to send me shooting back down the hall like a comet. I hesitated.

I did not want to face what was on the other side of that door.

I did not want to subject myself to the danger, the fear, the possibility of loss.

And then I reminded myself, there was something I wanted that eclipsed all of these: I wanted Milo, safe and sound. And I wanted the person who'd taken him to pay for what they had done.

So, I did the only thing I could do. I approached the door and stepped through it.

18

THE UNDERNEATH

P ERHAPS I OVERSOLD THAT BOLD ENTRANCE. It was more like prodding carefully at the door, then sticking barely enough of my head through it to ensure there was no malicious presence directly on the other side. Having ensured myself an empty tunnel beyond, I stepped the rest of the way through.

Here on the other side of the door, the energy of the spirit was stronger, but not strong enough to worry me that they were close. Milo had mentioned a sort of trail that the spirit left behind as it fled the archive, and I believed I was experiencing a concentrated version of that trail right now. I was like a predator, tracking my prey and stumbling onto its empty lair, where its scent was strong from repeatedly occupying the space. The spirit used this hallway—used it often. I was on the right track.

I continued down the corridor, which was less a corridor than it was a roughly hewn tunnel. Debris littered the floor, bits of rock and moldering old remains of wooden beams. There were no more bare bulbs strung here to light the place, but fortunately I didn't need light to see. I was able to perceive the space more clearly and completely than my body could have done with the aid of a floodlight.

I drifted along carefully, probing out in front of me for traces of any new or unfamiliar energy. The tunnel narrowed, then ended in a solid wall. Though to my left, another opening was revealed, large enough for an average-sized person to duck through and enter. I sailed through it and looked around me to find that I was in a second Close, with a roughly cobbled floor and the shells of tenement buildings rising upward on either side like broken teeth in a ruined mouth. The air was thick with dust motes, and an oppressive, moldy dampness that surely would have made me cough if I'd brought my actual lungs down here with me. A dark spot on the nearest wall caught my notice, and I moved closer to examine it. The lettering was barely visible, but I could pick out the raised shapes of them beneath the centuries of grime: they read, "MacLeod Close."

It was only fear of discovery that stopped me from whooping at the realization. Despite my wandering attention during our recent ghost tour, I knew that Closes were often named after the important people who inhabited them; and so it was natural that the MacLeods would have one of their own. And here it was, buried in the dark, the pathway to one of their deepest secrets. If I'd had even a shred of doubt left at all that the MacLeods were involved in this scheme, it was eradicated now.

I realized now that I had to tread even more carefully. The buildings on either side of me were full of windows and doors, through which anything could be watching me. I still didn't sense the immediate presence of the spirit I was seeking, although the trail of its energy was stronger than ever. But I couldn't become complacent. I'd promised Finn I'd be careful, and I didn't intend to break that promise. My anticipation rising like a tide, I began my search of the ancient close with the building to my right. I drifted and felt my way through the upper chambers behind that crumbling wall. It was full of old artifacts that would probably make a historian wet himself with excitement, but which held no interest for me. Remnants of furniture, scraps of fabrics, buckets, blackened fireplaces, collapsed bed frames with rotted out mattresses —I passed by all of it with only a fleeting sense of curiosity. None of these things would help me now—they were as useless to me in this moment as they were to the long-dead people who had left them behind.

It wasn't until I started searching the building on the other side of the close that I noticed anything out of the ordinary. All of the upper rooms were clear, but in the lower rooms, I started to notice signs that someone had been here recently—someone alive.

It started with a few clear footprints in the dust. In one room, it appeared a chair had been moved, dragged across the floor so that it left long dark trails in the grime. One of the fireplaces had been lit. I sank through the floor to get as close to the grate as I could and saw that someone had tried to burn a twisted bit of newspaper. Whether they had been interrupted, or else the paper wouldn't catch and burn, it was hard to tell; but the browned corner of it revealed that the paper was only six months old. I peered further into the grate and was met with the rich, smoky scent of sage. A Casting perhaps? I looked around the room more carefully now, but I didn't find anything more upon this inspection than I had on the first, and so I moved on to the next room.

Here, there was no doubt. A metal folding chair sat in the middle of the room, an empty Styrofoam cup on the floor beside it. I was so intent upon these mundane, unmistakable signs of life, that it took me a moment to notice that the spirit energy I was tracking was much stronger in this room than it had been anywhere else, though I could tell it was still just a trail and not the presence of the spirit itself. The next thing I noticed was the walls. Wallpaper had been stripped away in great curling sheets which dangled to the floor. In other places, it had been painstakingly scraped, bit by bit, so that it lay in plaster-dusted little heaps on the floor. I had just enough time to marvel at the idea that wallpaper had existed so many centuries ago, until I forgot about the wallpaper altogether.

For the wallpaper was nothing—*nothing*—to what had been revealed behind it.

If I'd brought my heart along with me, it surely would have given me away, beating like a drum echoing through every cracked and forgotten corner of this place. Every inch of the exposed plaster was covered in jagged, manic scribblings and markings. I drifted closer to the wall, both wanting to understand the writing and yet somehow feeling repulsed by it as well. The words, where I could decipher them, were in Gaelic—Scottish Gaelic, mostly, if I wasn't mistaken, but I could also see words I recognized. Scattered between and around the words were any number of other strange markings—some of them drawings of moon cycles, plants, and human bodies, laid out with dotted lines upon them, like something a surgeon might draw. Others were simply tally marks, not just drawn but literally gouged right into the wall.

"What the *hell*..." I whispered.

I followed along from one wall to the next, from one wildly composed image to another, following words that scuttled like beetles up and down and around and between renderings of plants and maps of constellations and a single, staring eye. When I reached the fireplace, I began to see that not every-thing was drawn upon the surfaces, as I had first suspected.

Some things were nailed there. Dozens of objects, each one secured to a rustic iron nail by a tiny, colorful scrap of fabric. My eyes sought out and snagged on four in particular, like fabric snagging on a splinter.

A ring...

A necklace...

A boot...

A hair ribbon...

Something stirred in me, the very edge of a memory. Why did I feel like I'd known what I was going to see before I saw it? Why did I expect those things to be here, somehow? Like someone had simply told me...

I drifted right up to the hair ribbon, and noticed another snatch of writing.

Forgotten parts made whole again.

And then...

Immortality.

"Well, my stars. You found my little secret hideaway."

I spun so quickly the room almost didn't come with me, and I lost just a moment of control over myself, like I had blinked out of existence or forgotten where I was in space. I was so startled to hear a voice that I reacted instinctively, forgetting I no longer had a body that would respond in the way I expected. The room blurred, the sounds warped as I tried to remind myself that I had no eyes, that I wasn't hearing with my ears. When at last I got my bearings back—the matter of perhaps two seconds, but which felt like an eternity to me, I found myself staring into the mildly surprised face of Danica MacLeod, lit by the wavering glow of a lantern she held in one hand.

"Well, it isn't *really* mine, is it now? It's his. But as I'm the only living person to venture here in several centuries, I like to think of it as mine as well. I'm terribly sorry if this is an impertinent question, but have you died?" Danica asked politely.

I had to dig deep to find my voice in my shock. "Danica, what are you doing down—"

"Was it the concussion?" Danica pressed on, looking a bit mournful. "They can be dangerous, you know, if you don't look after yourself properly. I expect you didn't rest up as you ought to have done."

"Danica, I'm not dead!" I finally had to blurt out just to get her to stop talking.

"Oh! Well, that's a relief. I did think someone would have let us know about a thing like that. But then," she frowned, "If you're not a ghost, then whatever are you...oh! Oh, I see!" Her eyes went wide. "You're Walking aren't you?"

"Yes, I am," I told her, because all I could think to do in my disbelief was to keep answering her questions. My mind was absolutely reeling. Danica MacLeod involved in this? There was no way, unless Clarissa or someone else had dragged her along, or else demanded her participation.

"Oh, I do find that fascinating!" Danica said, clapping her hands together, her eyes lighting up with a childlike curiosity. "Truly, I do. And I should have remembered that," she said, her tone suddenly dark and scolding. "Whatever will Clarissa do with me if I can't even remember a simple thing like the fact that you're a Walker." And then, just as suddenly, her face brightened again. "Well, never mind. I wouldn't have known how to keep you out even if I had remembered. I don't know if Wards and other Castings work on Walkers the same way they work on other spirits."

She gave me a hopeful little glance, like I might be kind enough to enlighten her, but I said nothing. I still didn't understand what was happening. I decided I needed to start asking some questions as well.

"What is this place?" I asked.

"It's MacLeod Close!" Danica said eagerly. "It was named after our family in the 1600s and—"

"No, I figured that out already. I meant, what is *this* place?" I gestured around the room impatiently. Why was this woman talking to me like we were two old friends having a cuppa together? Was she really so detached from reality?

"Oh," Danica's face fell just a little, evidently disappointed that she wasn't going to be allowed to give me a full history of the Close. "Well, this is Alasdair's room. It's always been Alasdair's room."

"Who is Alasdair?" I asked.

Danica's eyes went wide again. "Why, he's a genius. Truly, a genius." There was another sharp shift in her voice and face, like a dark cloud passing over her. "People didn't understand that about Alasdair. They just thought he was mad. But they were wrong."

Speaking of mad, I thought to myself, staring at Danica, but I kept the thought to myself. I needed answers, and I wouldn't get them by pissing her off. I opted to ask more questions instead, anything to help me figure out what the hell was going on here.

"And is Alasdair... is he... dead?" I asked.

"Oh, but you already know Alasdair!" Danica said, looking frankly shocked that I hadn't already put that together. "You've met him before, in the archive at the Collective."

My mind was reeling, not the least because she was talking about a violent attack that had left me with a head injury as though it had been a friendly introduction over coffee. "You mean to say that the spirit who nearly killed my sister and me... that was Alasdair?"

"Well, he really oughtn't to have done that," Danica said in an indulgent tone, as though Alasdair was a precocious toddler or a poorly trained puppy. "But he's just terribly enthusiastic, you know. He always does a thing thoroughly. I suppose he just got a bit carried away, but then, he didn't want us to be found out, so I'm sure you can understand why."

No, I could not fucking understand, I thought. Aloud, I said, "And how did *you* meet Alasdair?"

Danica's entire face lit up, just positively beaming. "Thank you for asking me that, because I haven't been able to tell anyone and it is such an interesting story. I haven't got many interesting stories. Clarissa's always telling me so. It was just after the Reckoning. I was here, working late. Everyone was avoiding the manor, because... well, because Clarissa was very... very upset." Her voice was shaking, and all I could imagine was Clarissa in a towering rage over the loss of her Gateway, raining down terror on everyone around her. Danica bit her lip, then shot a glare at me that chilled me straight through to the body I'd left behind in the car. "You ought to have heard the things she said about you. You're very lucky, you know, that she prefers to keep up appearances."

I did not reply to this veiled reference to a previous threat. It didn't matter now. It only served to distract from the moment we were in, and I needed her to get on with it.

Danica gathered herself, shaking off the image of her enraged sister. "Anyway, I happened to look out the window into the courtyard as I was pulling the blinds, and I saw him. Still as could be, like a statue, standing before the Geatgrima. I stood there, curious to see him Cross. I had never seen anyone use that old Geatgrima before, you see. But he just stood. He stood there for so long that I started to wonder if there might be something wrong with him. I might not have had the Gateway in my blood anymore, but there still might have been a way I could help. So, I went down and approached him."

Danica closed her eyes, as though playing it all out again like a favorite movie. I took the moment to concentrate on Alasdair's energy, but I was still quite sure—wherever he was, it wasn't this room, not right now.

"If you could have seen his face, Jessica," Danica went on, her lip trembling now, though her eyes were still closed. "It was just... oh, it was the saddest, most frightened face I'd ever seen. I asked him what was wrong and if I could help him at all. And he looked at me and he said, 'No. No one can help me.'

"I'm an Empath, Jessica. Since I can remember, spirits have filled me up with their own sadness, but never have I come so close to drowning as I did in Alasdair's sorrow. It consumed me. I couldn't bear it. I begged him to tell me, to let me help him. But he fled. I followed the trail of his unusual energy, back through the dungeons and then on through the tunnels to this place."

"We searched the dungeon in the Collective," I said. "There was no sign of any tunnels."

"You searched the *new* dungeons, the ones that were built when the Collective itself was constructed," Danica explained patiently, as though anyone could have gone into those dungeons and thought of them as "new" in any sense of the word. "But the Collective was not the first building on that site. The old dungeons, just like this Close, were built over centuries ago. Now you can only reach them through a sewer grate in the ground near the south building. Of course, that way of reaching it was terribly unpleasant," she added with a shudder. "That's why I went exploring, to see if there was an easier way, and found that they connected to Mary King's Close."

She clapped her hands delightedly, and then shook her head. "But you've distracted me, you cheeky thing. I was telling you about Alasdair. I followed him here. I didn't understand what this place was, or why he would flee to it instead of going through the Geatgrima, so I asked him. And then he turned to me with eyes that flamed and he told me a story that was both new and familiar at the same time. *His* story."

She was slowly circling the room now, the hem of her caftan dragging along in the dust behind her. She was trailing her fingers along the curls of wallpaper, like she could read this story on the wall with her fingertips.

"Centuries ago, when MacLeod Close was the bustling heart of the Old

Town district, our family had already established great status and wealth. We had a hand in everything, from business to law-making to the shaping of the city itself. Alasdair was there in the thick of it all, a wealthy and influential Caomhnóir who enjoyed great respect from the clan. But he had a fatal flaw, Alasdair did: he feared death."

Danica paused in her stroll around the room to look at me, as though trying to gauge whether I was as captivated by the story as she had been. Whatever expression was frozen on the specter of my face, I had absolutely no idea, but it seemed to please Danica, and she dove back into her tale with a renewed sense of drama.

"I know what you must be thinking. Surely it's not a flaw to fear death? Certainly, we must all fear it a little, even those of us who know that there is something beyond this life. The difference is that we all accept death as an unavoidable eventuality. Alasdair was too frightened to do so. He was vulnerable, most vulnerable indeed, to the message of the Necromancers.

"He knew all about them, of course. He'd studied them, been taught to combat them, and therefore knew a great deal about their ideas and their experiments. The difference was that while the rest of his classmates loudly rejected those ideas, Alasdair quietly thrilled to them. He wondered how the others could not see the possibility, the power that they held? How could they calmly agree to be guardians of a gate that they themselves weren't even allowed to open and peek through? It drove him mad, their complacency. And so he sought them out."

"Sought who out?" I asked.

"The Necromancers. He had followed the whispers of their whereabouts in the seedy underbelly of the city, and he found them. He listened. He learned. He began to think that the Durupinen had it all wrong. Why would we be given this gift if we weren't meant to understand it and to use it, to wield it in any way we chose, and to glean every last drop we could from it? But neither were the Necromancers bold enough for him. He wanted to push boundaries. What possible progress could they make toward achieving immortality if they didn't take some real risks? Oh, what's the phrase? 'You can't make an omelet without breaking some eggs?' Is that it?"

"I don't follow," I said.

"The Necromancers cared only about the Prophecy," Danica said indulgently, like I was a small child who was accustomed to not understanding things. "They talked about preparation for it, spent so much of their resources on learning how to predict when it would come, and what they would do if it did. They saw the Prophecy as the preordained moment they would come into their power. But Alasdair didn't want to sit around for a solution that might not come for five lifetimes. He wanted to evade death himself, not just sacrifice himself for the cause of others who might one day achieve it where he had failed. And so, unbeknownst to both the Necromancers who knew him and the Durupinen who thought they did, Alasdair began his experiments."

"He believed the answer was in the spirits themselves. He began playing with the natures of souls, probing their strengths and weaknesses. He wanted to dissect them. He wanted to pull them apart and put them back together again until his understanding of spirits was perfect. The spirits he saw not as people, but as tools, placed there for his utility. Why else should he be able to see them, to communicate with them, if not to use them to his advantage in the furtherance of his great cause? After all, it was too late for them." Danica paused and let out a long, sad sigh. "I can see your horror, Jessica."

I had all but forgotten that we were in a room together, so spellbound was I by her narrative. Luckily, she required no answer, and before I could attempt to formulate one, she went on.

"He was just so frightened, you see. You can understand that, can't you? Fear can drive a good person to such dark places."

There was no chance that someone who experimented on spirits as if they were cadavers had ever been a good person, but Danica looked so pleadingly at me that I certainly couldn't say 'no' without upsetting her, and I didn't want her upset. I wanted her to stay focused on telling me as much as she could, because I still didn't know where this was going.

"Sure, I get that," I said, my teeth only slightly gritted around the lie.

"I knew you would," Danica said, smiling as though I had passed some kind of test. "In any case, he began to formulate a plan. You see, as a Caomhnóir, he knew about Leeching—knew about it, but was unable to participate in it. He could glean none of the youth, the beauty, the longevity that the Durupinen could when they Leeched. In the short term, he hoped to find a way—a Casting—that would enable him to Leech as well. This would buy him time to bring the experiments further for, as useful as it was, even Leeching did not go far enough for him. Leeching was not enough to achieve immortality. He would take the concept of Leeching a step further. He would devise a method by which he could absorb the life force of a spirit, and use it to prolong his life. If he could absorb enough life force, surely he could live forever?"

"Oh God," I muttered under my breath. This man wasn't a genius. He was an absolute lunatic, a madman.

A madman whom Danica continued to gush about as she went on, "This flat was where he came to conduct his work in secret. The important members of the clan had become prosperous enough to move out of the close and build their own family seat, and the Close, though named after the MacLeods, was no longer home to any of them. Alasdair buried himself here, in the under-belly of the city, where no one knew him and no one cared where he went or what he did. He needed spirits for his experiments, but while they were easy enough to find, they weren't nearly as easy to trap, and the longer he tried, the harder it became. He began to suspect that the ghosts of Edinburgh were starting to warn each other about the man who stalked them at night and tried to lure them into traps. He began to grow desperate—and then another idea struck him.

"Now, this idea," Danica said, her face darkening, "was a very naughty one indeed, and I've told him so, several times, since we met. But he does repent of it now, so we must forgive and forget, mustn't we? Anyway, the idea that came to him was that he needed a freshly released spirit—a spirit too disoriented and confused by its sudden freedom from its body to understand its new state, and therefore how to use it to escape from him. And so he began... extracting spirits from living bodies."

Her voice faltered over the words and for good reason. I couldn't help it. I let my mask of polite interest slip with a humorless bark of a laugh.

"Danica, if you're going to tell this story, tell it. He didn't 'extract spirits from bodies.' He murdered people. I mean, that's what you're saying, isn't it?"

Danica's eyes filled at once with tears that seemed to magnify her dark irises. "Oh, please don't say it like that. I know it's true, but it's just so awful to hear it spoken so."

"Tell me how," I said, somewhat impatiently.

"He devised a Casting—it was really quite clever of him. I've been through his notes over and over again, and I've never been able to understand how he managed to figure it out," Danica gushed, gesturing again to the mad scrib-blings all over the walls. "But figure it out, he did! He went about Old Town at night, using the dark corners of the Closes and wynds to do his work. The Casting required a lot of preparation on Alasdair's part, but in the moment, when the soul was leaving the body, he would bind the soul temporarily to himself and then bring it back here, where he would bind it permanently to an object he took from the body."

She gestured now to the array of moldering objects hanging in a ghastly constellation on the wall. Now that I knew what they were—the twisted trophies of a murderer, I could barely stand to look at them.

"The object he would take became the host for the soul," Danica continued to explain in a politely detached voice, like if she could just treat this information like a boring passage from a textbook, I might not notice the murder bit. "This is where the stroke of genius came in. You must know, I am sure, that spirits sometimes attach themselves to familiar objects from when they were alive."

A vivid memory played across my vision like a flickering old movie: a crowded lecture hall, a porcelain doll, and the face of a little girl appearing as if by divine inspiration on a page in a notebook. What Danica spoke of, was one of the first things I'd ever learned about spirits.

"The spirits he chose, they were frightened and confused," she went on. "It calmed them to be near a familiar object, something they recognized as having been a part of their mortal life. He bound them to those objects and kept them here, a collection of souls with which he could do his great work."

There was that sense of déjà vu again. Danica said that Alasdair's story was familiar before he had told it to her, and I was beginning to wonder if I'd heard it before too.

"But it all came unraveled, of course," Danica said, her face drooping almost comically in her sorrow as she continued to walk the perimeter of the room. Her fingers trailed close to the objects hanging on the wall as she passed by them, and I turned on the spot to watch her, careful to keep her in my line of sight. "He could not complete his experiments. Somehow, word of what he was doing in the squalor and solitude of MacLeod Close reached the ears of Clan Rìoghalachd . They ambushed him in the night, arrested him, and put him on trial." Here, Danica seemed to swell with rage, her eyes fairly bugging out of her head in her indignation. "They called it a trial, but really it was just a chance for them to publicly humiliate and shame him. He was allowed no defense, not even the chance to speak for himself, to explain! And then they locked him away in our dungeons and left him there to rot; and even when he died, his soul was still trapped, Caged for eternity in the dungeons. That was his punishment for being afraid, for daring to dream of immortality!"

Every particle of my being wanted to scream at her that Alasdair was a monster, but I refrained. I was very close to finding out where Milo and the others might be, I just knew it. I had to keep her talking, keep her explaining.

"When I found him that night in front of the Geatgrima, he had been freed from his Casting. The return of the Gateway to the Geatgrima had disrupted the integrity of the Castings that had held him prisoner down below. Our clan had all but forgotten him, a shameful secret locked away and scrubbed from our history. We were so ashamed of him that we hid his crimes even from the rest of the Northern Clans, choosing instead to deal him our own warped justice without reference to the Council or the High Priestess. The only accounts of his history can be found in our own books, in our own personal archives here and at Skye. You would have found it that day if I hadn't already removed the pages."

"You cut those pages out of the book?" I asked.

"Oh yes. Once I knew of him, I knew I had to protect him. Someone might catch on to what we were doing otherwise," Danica said solemnly.

"And what is it you are doing, exactly?" I asked, the tension vibrating through me so hard now that I was sure my form must be flickering and pulsating with the force of it. "Alasdair is dead, his quest for immortality is over. So what are you doing?"

"I think it best if I show you," Danica said, her walk around the room now bringing her back to the doorway. "I think you'll be amazed, and you can meet Alasdair for yourself."

"Danica, I'm not going anywhere with you, and I have no desire to meet the spirit who already tried to kill me once," I said.

"I was afraid you might say that," Danica said with a regretful sigh. "And that's why I took steps to make sure you wouldn't have a choice."

I stared at her. "What are you talking about?"

"I couldn't take the chance that you'd leave, not when you still don't understand," Danica said. "You must hear it all, must see it for yourself, and then you'll see, like I've learned to see."

"You can't stop me from leaving, Danica."

"Oh, Jessica. I do apologize, but I'm afraid I already have."

"What the hell do you—" But my voice trailed away. Danica was looking down at her feet, where she dropped a single purple stone. Suddenly, the energy in the room seemed to contract, to press in upon me like it would squeeze the life from me. If I'd had lungs, they wouldn't have been able to draw breath. I stared at the stone in the dust, and then turned, looking all around me. Danica's overly-long dress, trailing along the floor, had created a Circle traced into the dust and grime of centuries. Her muttering, which I had taken to be just another one of her eccentricities, had been a Casting murmured under her breath. All along the perimeter of the circle, she had been surreptitiously dropping stones at intervals, each one landing silently in the soft rot of ages. And with the dropping of that last stone, her Casting was complete. Every moment I had spent listening, captivated, to her story was a moment I was complicit in my own capture.

"There now, no more arguing, pet," Danica said, in what she evidently thought was a soothing voice, but which sent waves of revulsion rippling through me. "Now that you understand what happened here once upon a time, it's time for you to understand what's happening now. It's time you met the Collector."

19

THE COLLECTOR

THE COLLECTOR.

The words cleared away the last of the fog that had obscured the memory, and I finally understood why it all felt so familiar. Like Danica, I had heard this story. And like her, I had not recognized it, at the time, for what it really was.

The Collector: an urban legend rooted in horrifying truth. The serial killer who had stalked the shadows of Old Town, selecting and murdering victims before choosing an item off the bodies like a trophy. When I'd heard the story, I had thought of him as a man, an ordinary man committing extraordinary evil. But he had not been an ordinary man, and the evil he had been committing was even more extraordinary than anyone could have conceived of. And now, when tour guides in costumes led trailing groups of wide-eyed tourists up and down the streets of the city, they wove a story that missed the crucial pages, like that book upstairs in the archive. They knew *of* him, but they didn't *know* him.

But now I would. And I would be lucky if I had the chance to live to regret it.

I couldn't move or speak. Whatever Casting Danica had used on me, it was powerful. She was watching me with interest as I struggled against it, delight spreading slowly over her face.

"Do you know, I wasn't at all sure that it would work!" she exclaimed, clapping her hands together in apparent glee. "It seems your Walker form is close enough to a true spirit form to be subject to the same Castings. Well, that will make everything much simpler, won't it?"

Danica would never know the extensive litany of expletives I was silently hurling at her because whatever Casting she had used had stolen my voice. Desperately, I focused all of my frantic energy on a place just outside of the Circle, envisioning myself occupying not just that space, but every space along the route between where I stood and where I wanted to be, just as Irina had taught me long ago. And though I willed myself forward, I could not move from where I stood, as though the air around me had become a solid substance that I was now encased in. Danica watched me for a few more seconds in fascination before giggling and pulling a length of silk from her pocket. It was similar to the lengths of silk upon the wall behind me, with which all the various trophies from Alasdair's victims were tied, dangling like travesties of holiday ornaments. I remembered our tour guide had called the silk the Collector's calling card. When he said it, of course, he was thinking about murder weapons. As I stared at it now, I knew it for what it was: the tool for Casting.

Murmuring her incantation, Danica wrapped the silk once, twice, three times around her own wrist. Then she took a lighter from her voluminous pocket and used the flame to melt and burn the edges so that they fused together. She hissed once when the flame danced a little too close to her wrist, but she did not let go, nor hesitate in her words. Then she reached into her pocket once again and pulled out something I could barely see. She held it up to the light and smiled.

"I hope you don't mind, but I saved one when your hair caught in my bracelets. I knew you would be investigating the matter, and I thought there was a chance it might come in handy. I'll have to remember to tell Clarissa that part. I rather fancy she'll be impressed." She grinned at me like a child who'd just been awarded a gold star.

All I could do was stare and struggle helplessly as Danica wrapped the hair around the silk, and as she did, I felt as though needles were being pressed into me at various points along the body I no longer occupied. Then Danica gave an experimental flick of her wrist, and the needles turned to hooks, pulling me forward. Danica gave a shriek of delighted laughter.

"I've never tried it before!" she cried, before flicking her wrist again, harder this time, and I was jerked cleanly through the barrier of the circle and floated just above the ground, like some sick puppet or a pet on a leash.

I was distracted from my plight for a moment by the slightest suggestion of a sound in the room and the merest shift in the balance of energy. It was barely a whisper, like an intake of breath, and then nothing at all. Had I imagined it? Was someone else here? I couldn't so much as turn my head to look.

"Well, come along then. Alasdair will be so eager to meet you, and there's still so much to show you!" And with that, like a wee girl who'd been handed a balloon of her very own, Danica turned and led me out of the room and into the close again, looking back at me every few seconds to check that I was still following her—as if I had a choice.

We traversed the length of the close and ducked through a building that had all but collapsed in decay. The back wall was nothing but a gaping hole, and Danica climbed carefully through it, swearing quietly under her breath as she tried to keep her footing. The sweeping folds of her caftan kept snagging on debris, and several times she stopped to untangle herself before we could continue.

"I really do mean to get this cleaned out, but I've just been so busy!" she said, with the air of a harried mother showing someone into her toy-strewn living room. How had I ever thought this woman anything but completely off her rocker?

We moved laboriously through tunnels that threatened to collapse at any moment. The danger of the ruins revealed itself in the rotted remains of several skeletons—both human and animal. This passage, too, was saturated in Alasdair's uniquely foul energy, and a wild fear began to claw its way through me, knowing that I was about to face, in some form or another, this entity that poisoned every place it had traversed, both living and dead. That fear climbed to a fever pitch as that energy began to swirl and grow. It infested every particle of my being until I felt I would scream at the violation of it. By the time Danica came to a breathless stop in front of a door, I thought I would go mad.

"We're here!" she announced, and placed a hand on the door to knock politely. Then, without waiting for any kind of answer, she pushed it open.

The room on the other side of it was a perfect circle of stone, with a cobbled floor, smooth polished stone walls, and—I could just barely get a glimpse of it without being able to turn my head—a smooth stone ceiling carved with half a dozen concentric circles. There were niches carved into the walls, each containing a lantern that blazed with a warm orange glow, and between them, dark recesses with barred entrances, like cages. I could see nothing of what was inside them, but looking at them made me feel queasy and dizzy. Danica set the identical lantern she had been carrying back into the only empty niche, to the left of the door we'd just come through. There were also several long, marble tables, crowded with all manner of Casting tools, scrolls of parchment, stacks of books, and deadly-looking weaponry, including a wickedly curved dagger that glinted in the lantern light. All of this I took in within the first instant, but none of it mattered an instant later as my eyes were drawn to the very center of the room, to the most disturbing thing I'd ever seen.

At the center of the room there was a swirling, glowing mass—a great globe of seething, writhing energy. As I stared at it in a sort of trance of horrified fascination, the globe pulsated and shifted. It expanded and contracted like a great beating heart. Something moved within it—many somethings.

No. No, no, no. Many some*ones.*

The cry I could not release vibrated through every particle of my form so that I felt I would be shaken apart by the force of it. There were hands and faces and bodies undulating through the mass, pressing against its borders with desperation, totally silent but with mouths open in what I knew, even without hearing it, to be the multitudinous screams.

Danica was circling the room, staring at the same abomination that I was staring at, but the look on her face was one of reverence rather than disgust. "Every artist has his masterpiece. This is Alasdair's," she whispered.

I couldn't focus on her words. I was too busy scanning the pulsating monstrosity for some sign of that familiar face, aching to see it and yet terrified that I would. If Milo was in there, how the hell would we ever get him out? Was getting out even possible? Were the spirits within that thing even spirits anymore?

"What do you think of it?" Danica asked breathlessly and then slapped herself on the forehead with astonishing force. "Oh, good heavens, what am I on about? Of course, you can't speak, can you, and it's all down to me. Here, let me just…"

And she fiddled with the silken band tied around her wrist, loosening and retying one of the knots, and there was a sudden, whooshing relief as I felt a sliver of my own agency return to me. The words that were rocketing around inside me, desperate for release, would, at last, find it.

"What the actual fuck am I looking at?!" I managed to gasp.

Danica opened her mouth to tell me, but another voice answered instead.

"Jess, no! Oh my God, no!"

If anything could have torn me to pieces in that moment, it was the sound of that voice.

"Milo!" I cried, my eyes frantically roaming the glow of the orb for some sign of him.

"What did you do to her, you absolute ghouls!" Milo shouted, and I realized with a cry of relief that his voice was not coming from the orb at all, but from one of the cells that was set into the walls. He emerged from the shadows, paler than I'd ever seen him, but angrier too.

"I swear to GOD when I get out of here, I'm gonna—"

"Milo, it's okay! I'm Walking!" I cried out to him.

Relief flooded over his features, and he let out a strangled sob.

"Are you okay? What have they done to you?" I asked him, but Danica held up her wrist, looking fiercely disappointed.

"Jessica, I've returned your voice to you, but I can very easily take it away again," she said severely. "Forget about the spirit guide, he's part of something bigger now, something you told me you wanted to understand. And now here I am trying to explain it to you, and you aren't even paying the slightest attention!"

She tugged once, ferociously, on the silken band and I jerked upward toward the ceiling, a psychic sort of pain coursing through me. I pressed my lips together against a scream, not wishing to give her the satisfaction of knowing she'd hurt me. Danica, however, took it as a sign of my obedience.

"That's right," she said encouragingly, in another dizzying shift of mood. She mimed locking her lips and throwing away the key and then waggled a finger at me.

"You mad bitch," Milo was whispering. "You mad, sadistic bitch."

If Danica heard him, she didn't acknowledge it. All her attention was on the swirling mass again and she cleared her throat, signaling her intention to speak. But instead of answering my question, she called, "Alasdair, please come out. There's someone I'd like you to meet. Come along, love, it's all right."

If I'd been in my body, every pore would have shrunk against the onslaught of cold that followed this invitation, my stomach heaving and my being recoiling against the overpowering stench of death itself. As it was, I felt like I would be torn apart struggling against the bonds that held me in place as every fiber of my being tried to take flight from his arrival.

But arrive he did. Like shadows coalescing into shapes, and then the shapes into a single form, and then that form into a man. Alasdair. At first glance, he could have been a typical spirit. He appeared in what must have been his prison attire, a collection of rags that barely managed to cling onto his bony frame. He moved with a strange loping grace, like a lion, a comparison made even more apt by the absolute mane of filthy, tangled hair that sprang out from around his sunken, bearded face. His eyes, deep-set above hollow cheeks, burned into me from across the room, and each step he advanced sharpened his gaze, so that, by the time he had moved only ten paces toward me, I would have gouged out his eyes just to stop them from looking at me—through me—the way they did.

"She is different," he said, his voice the hollow rattle of a death knell. "What is she?"

"It's the Ballard girl, the one I told you about. She's a Walker, that's why she's in this form," Danica explained eagerly. "She found your room in the Close, so I brought her here."

"You should not have brought her," Alasdair said. "She is no use to me in this state." His tone was cold and dismissive, but I felt relief nonetheless. Did that mean he didn't think he could collect me, the way he did the others? I sincerely hoped that was so because otherwise, I was screwed. I wasn't sure how much time had passed, but I knew that it couldn't have been a full hour. Finn and Catriona would not be looking for me yet; and even if they were, it would take them ages to find this place, and by then it might be too late.

Danica looked like Alasdair had just slapped her. "I brought her here because she would have revealed our plans to the others. Whether she is useful to you is irrelevant. She cannot be allowed to leave."

"Then put her in one of the cells and be done with it," Alasdair said with a dismissive wave of his hand.

Danica turned back to me and shrugged sheepishly. "I thought he'd be a bit more interested to meet you, but you mustn't be offended. Alasdair is singular in his focus, and he is not easily distracted from it."

I could not have been happier to be of little interest to Alasdair. I, however, was burning with interest to understand what the hell was happening here.

"Danica, what is that... that *thing*?" I asked, nodding my head toward the great pulsating ball in the center of the room. The more I looked at it, the more it reminded me of the Elemental, whose form was like a constant flickering film of rapidly shifting images.

"Isn't it beautiful?" she whispered. "Alasdair and I made it together. It's our Collection, you see."

"No, I don't see at all," I said, and it was hard to keep my voice steady while choking back rage. "And it isn't beautiful. It's monstrous."

"Oh, that's only because you don't understand it," Danica said eagerly. "I told you I would explain. Unless... Alasdair, would you perhaps like to explain? After all, it really is due to your life's work that we've managed to create it."

But Alasdair snorted with disgust and turned his back on us, turning instead to his tables full of notes and equipment.

Danica shrugged and rolled her eyes as though Alasdair was a slightly disobedient child. "Apparently not. Well, no matter, I can explain. After I followed Alasdair back to the Close, after he told me the story of how he had come to be trapped down here, I began to wonder. Clarissa was so devastated by the loss of our Gateway—"

"You didn't lose it, it was right back here where it be—"

"Don't interrupt me!" Danica shrieked, and then immediately laughed like she'd just told a hilarious joke. "I do so hate to be interrupted. Clarissa is always... but Clarissa is right to do it, of course. She always knows what's worth saying. Now, where was I? Oh, yes. Clarissa was inconsolable. I was at my wits' end on how to help her. I'd spent weeks wondering if there was a way I could fix it, to cheer her up again; and when I heard Alasdair's story, I thought I had found it at last."

I bit back my words. Cheer Clarissa up, by colluding with the ghost of a homicidal maniac? How had I ever thought this woman harmless? Every moment I'd spent with her in the underbelly of the city had chipped away more of her facade, and the woman who now stood before me scared me almost as much as Alasdair did.

"I helped Alasdair uncover all of his research—you saw it, behind the wallpaper in MacLeod Close. I asked him to explain it to me, and, after a bit of coaxing, he did. I admit that I could not understand a lot of the theory behind it all—I was always a dreadful student, barely scraped by, but I understood enough. And I could hardly contain my excitement."

"Clarissa made a very public display of her concern for the Gateways, that they wouldn't be safe if they were no longer protected in our blood-streams, but I knew her better than that. I knew that what she was really concerned about was the loss of her power and her control. She feared what she would become if she was simply a normal woman. No more Leeching to help her look and feel young and powerful. No more status to hold over the other members of our clan. She didn't know who she was without the Gateway in her blood. She had lost her purpose. And you did that! You did it!"

Danica's face twisted suddenly with ferocious anger, and she gave a violent tug on the silken band around her wrist so that I, too, was yanked sharply upward with the feeling that every part of my body was being squeezed in a vice.

"And to think, you haven't even apologized!" Danica said scathingly.

"I... I didn't... I never tried to..."

But Danica wasn't interested in my excuses. She tugged the silk again, and I let out a yelp of pain.

"What are you doing to her?! Leave her alone!" came Milo's muffled voice from the cell.

"Shut up!" Danica shrieked, then turned back to me. "I don't care whether you're sorry, because I've fixed it! I've cleaned up your mess, and my sister will finally see that I'm worth something! She'll finally see what I've done for her, and she will be proud of me!"

She released the silken band, and I felt the crushing pressure vanish, leaving me drooping and depleted.

"It was too late to carry on Alasdair's work for his own sake, but it wasn't too late to carry it on for Clarissa. And so I told him, if he wished to continue, I would help him. I would gather what he needed. I would help to gather the spirits he needed, but I wasn't yet sure how. After all, I could hardly go around the streets after dark, trapping them the way he used to do. Many of the spirits in the city know us, and I'd be caught for sure. And I wasn't going to kill anyone either," Danica said, pouting. "I'd already told Alasdair that was a no-no."

I heard Alasdair muttering mutinously from his place at the table, but Danica ignored him.

"And then, when I was reading everything I could find about Alasdair in our family collections, I made the discovery that changed everything. I discovered that this old dungeon where he'd been trapped for so many years ran right underneath the Geatgrima itself. That was why the Castings that had trapped him here had been disrupted."

She looked up at the ceiling and I followed her gaze. The carvings in the ceiling were concentric circles, marked with runes—it looked like an ancient pagan calendar or some kind of astrology chart. Except I knew those runes, and I knew the one carved into the very heart of the circles, right at their center. It translated to "safe passage."

It was also the rune that stood for the Gateway itself.

"They drew on the power of the Gateway to strengthen the security of the dungeon," Danica explained. "It kept their prisoners secure and their whereabouts secret. It also allowed the dungeons and the Geatgrima to be guarded at all times simultaneously—two birds, one stone and all of that. Wasn't that clever? I thought that was very clever." She sighed happily as she reflected on the brilliance of her ancestors. "Once I realized this, I knew how we would collect our spirits, but we still had to be careful. We couldn't be greedy and collect every soul that approached the Geatgrima, or we'd be caught. So we chose Alasdair's old hunting time of two o'clock in the morning as the time to activate our Casting for a single hour every night. It seemed unlikely that anyone would be in the courtyard at that time, and even someone looking down from a window would only see a spirit disappear, which frankly is nothing unusual around here." She cocked her head to one side thoughtfully. "I didn't anticipate the screaming. If I'd known trapping spirits was so noisy, I might have reconsidered."

"You are sick," I muttered to myself. "You are really, really sick." Aloud I said, "I still don't understand what any of this has to do with Clarissa."

Danica's face lit up like the morning sun had just broken over the horizon. "That's the surprise! With these spirits, Clarissa can get her power back! She can use their life force as she did before! She can stay young and beautiful and powerful! She can be the most powerful, the most important again! She can reign forever over this city, building her wealth and influence. It's everything she's ever wanted, and I'm going to be the one to give it to her!" Happy tears were gushing up out of her eyes and running down her face, baptizing her lunacy.

"And Alasdair? What does he get out of it? Why would he agree to give Clarissa what was denied to him? Shouldn't he want to punish the Durupinen who imprisoned him?" I asked, glancing over at Alasdair, who was still bent, muttering incessantly, over his table of warped experiments.

"Oh, he doesn't hold that against us," Danica said, waving a dismissive hand. "And anyway, it isn't just for Clarissa that he's agreed to work with me. He has his own goals now. His plan is to come back to life."

She said this so simply, so matter-of-factly, that at first I thought I must have misheard her.

"He what?"

"He doesn't want to stay in spirit form, and he doesn't want to Cross," Danica said, as though this was all a simple mathematical equation. "So what choice does he have, really, but to return himself to a corporeal form?"

"That... that's not possible," I said.

Danica put her hands on her hips and looked at me sternly. "Now, how can you say that after everything that I've shown you? Don't you see? *Anything* is possible if you're bold enough. *Anything* can be achieved if you are sufficiently determined. I never believed that before I met Alasdair, but I believe it now."

"But he doesn't *have* a body," I said, trying to inject a note of reason into this absolutely off-the-rails conversation. "He's dust and bones now. And even if his body was here, he couldn't just... jump back in it."

"Of course he can't," Danica said with a trilling little laugh. "He doesn't plan to revive in his own body. He plans to revive in another."

I blinked. "I... what?"

"Oh, he hasn't really told me much about the how-tos," Danica admitted. "That's his special pet project, isn't it, Alasdair? But he assured me that building our collection would be necessary to that as well. So he's helping me, and I'm helping him, and we'll both get what we want in the end, I expect."

"And what is it you want?" I asked. "What have you done all of this for that could possibly be worth the destruction you've wrought?"

Danica looked innocently surprised. "Why, I've told you. I want to make Clarissa happy. I want to solve the problem she could not solve. I want her to be proud of me."

It was so simple. So human. I would have felt deeply sorry for the woman if she wasn't so totally deranged.

"And I really can't allow you to get in the way of that," Danica said, sighing sadly. "I'm sorry, because I do like you. I think you meant well, in what you did to bring about the Reckoning, but you made my sister unhappy, and so I can't allow that to continue."

In the absence of a racing heart, my spirit form was vibrating with tension. I felt like an elastic band pulled tight, about to snap.

"So what? You're going to add me to your collection?" I cried out.

"Goodness, no!" Danica said, as though the suggestion were ludicrous. "Of course, it would be by far the easiest solution to this little quandary we find ourselves in, but you can't be collected, not when you're still tied to your living body. No, I'm afraid I'm just going to have to imprison you here indefinitely until Alasdair can figure out how to dispose of you. He's frightfully good at figuring things out, so I daresay he'll be able to manage it. Alasdair, would you like to keep her here, or shall I find another place for her?"

Alasdair looked up at this point, his hypnotically evil eyes latched onto me, as though he was considering my possibilities for the first time. His gaze was like a physical sensation, a violation.

"Keep her here. I may find a use for her," he muttered.

"Just as you like, my dear," Danica said, and began working at her silken band again, murmuring her incantations and tying and retying her knots. She pulled me forward with a force that was useless to struggle against, though I did my damnedest, and placed me into the cell beside Milo's. Then she shut the barred door and tied the silken band to the bars, ensuring the security of my prison. And sure enough, when I tried to breach the walls or the door of the tiny cell, I was met with an impenetrable barrier.

"All snug and cozy, then?" Danica said, peeking through the bars and smiling at me, as though I was a budgie in a cage. I'd never wanted to spit at someone so badly in my life. "Excellent. Well, do excuse me. Alasdair and I have some work to get on with."

She traipsed away from the cell, humming cheerfully to herself.

"Jess, I'm sorry, I'm so sorry," Milo whispered from the cell beside me.

"Don't you dare apologize!" I told him. "I'm just glad you're not in there!" I pointed to the writhing, glowing collection.

"I will be, before long," Milo said, a note of hysteria in his voice. "The only reason I'm not already is because they were so busy trying to figure out how to keep you and the others from finding this place."

"How did they catch you?"

"I made it pretty freaking easy for them," Milo said through gritted teeth. "I ran into Savvy and Rana, and they were telling me about some tour they'd just done of one of the underground Closes, and it just...clicked. The spirits were disappearing downward, so it made sense to search underneath the courtyard. If one part of the city could be underground, why not another? But I went alone and Alasdair was lying in wait, and..." He shuddered.

"We heard you," I said. "When we did the Revelation Casting up in the courtyard, we heard you calling out to us."

Milo nodded. "I knew something was happening. The circle on the ceiling lit up gold, and Alasdair and Danica were panicking, and I just... I took a chance and opened the connection. It was the first time it opened for me since I got down here. Something about the Castings in this place had cut it off."

"It used to be a dungeon," I told him. "It's where Alasdair was locked up for centuries. It was designed to trap prisoners, living and dead, so it's no wonder there's some Casting on it that would make it impossible for you to communicate with us."

"What are we going to do, Jess?" Milo whispered.

"I don't know," I whispered back. "I'm so sorry, but I just don't know. The others will be looking for me, but I don't know if they'll find this place in time."

"I'm so scared."

"Me too."

The fear rising in me was threatening to take over, and I staved it off with another question. "What have you learned about... *that*?"

I gestured toward what Danica called "the collection." Looking directly at it made me feel ill.

Milo's voice was hollow as he answered. "They use the Casting to strip the spirits into pieces, and then collect the pieces in that... that thing," he said. "Then they extract the pieces to... to experiment with."

"My God." No wonder the screaming was so terrible. The spirits were being torn to pieces right before our eyes and we didn't realize it.

"He's crazy, Jess. Like, out of his mind. And she might be worse." He shuddered. "I can't believe I thought she was so harmless when we first met her."

"She fooled me, too," I said. "We've got to find a way to—"

But I was distracted by Alasdair. He had begun to slowly circle the collection, Danica trailing behind him with a candle. He nodded at her, and she lit the candle, murmuring a Casting I could not hear, and would not have understood if I had. The screaming began, but it was a distant echo of the sound I heard before, a memory of suffering. The Collection's smooth, spherical shape started to bulge on one side, and I was reminded sickeningly of a baby moving around in its mother's body. The bulge pulsed and twisted and grew, and burst the boundaries of the rest of the orb and formed its own, smaller orb; and in the same moment, the faint screaming stopped. The orb was drawn to the candle like a moth, and then suddenly, it was as though the candle had absorbed it. The flame, a warm and dancing orange a moment before, turned bluish-white and still, like a flame that had inexplicably turned to ice. Alasdair reached out and touched his finger to the flame, and—

"Holy shit, he's on fire!" I cried out, horrified in spite of the fact that I'd gladly watch him burn to ash for what he'd done.

But Alasdair seemed not at all concerned about the fact that the blue-white flame had engulfed him from the point the fire had touched him. In fact, he seemed to revel in it. He let out a sound that was half shout of pain, half triumphant cry of ecstasy. He threw his arms wide and his head back, giving all of himself that he could give to the flame. And then, suddenly, the fire seemed to be sucked into a tiny, concentrated point of light in his chest. It pulsated there for the length of a breath, and then vanished.

"What the f-" I began, but even I couldn't find the will for a snarky remark when Alasdair opened his eyes, and we could see the cold blue fire burning in them.

What had we just witnessed? The 'taking in' of the life force that Danica had told us about? And if so, what good could it do Alasdair, as one who was already a spirit himself? But Milo had an answer for me.

"He does it to strengthen himself. He's trying to turn himself into a... some kind of mutant super-spirit or some shit."

A wave of energy rolled through the room, and it smelled of rot and decay and sulfur, and it felt like being dropped beneath the surface of a frozen lake. That was what we'd been experiencing all along—the energy that came from absorbing pieces of other ghosts. If I could have been sick at that moment, I surely would have been.

"Is it my turn?" Danica said into the tense silence that followed.

Alasdair barely acknowledged her, just waving a hand over his shoulder as though to say, 'Do what you will.'

Danica lit the candle again. She turned to look at me as she held it up. "Clarissa will be so pleased!"

"Danica, what in the name of the Aether are you doing?"

I watched as all the color drained from Danica's face because the voice that had spoken wasn't mine or Milo's, or even Alasdair's. We all turned to the door on the other side of the room.

Clarissa MacLeod stood framed, incandescent with rage, on the threshold.

20

A PROMISE KEPT

Danica's face, exultant a moment before, drooped like a wilted flower.
"Clarissa!"

Clarissa's face, by comparison, was a thundercloud foretelling a storm. She was filthy, her cream suit smeared in mud and dust and other unspeakable substances, and her usually meticulous hair had escaped her bun and was hanging in limp, damp strands on either side of her face. Her eyes darted from her sister to Alasdair, to the great pulsating glow that dominated the room. She watched it for a moment, transfixed, before she was able to tear her gaze from it and look at her sister again. As she did so, she stepped into the room properly, and three figures were revealed in the shadows behind her: Finn, Catriona, and, barely visible peeking around the doorframe: Hattie. All three of them were staring, frozen in horrified fascination, at the Collection.

"No, you can't be here! You'll ruin the surprise!" Danica cried, making shooing gestures with her hands.

"Don't you dare tell me where I can be! What is happening here? I demand you tell me at once!" she boomed. Her voice, though angry, also cradled a note of terror in its depths, and I knew that she was just as scared as I was.

Alasdair gave a low, animal growl, coiling himself like he was about to spring at Clarissa, but Finn was too quick for him. He used the circle above his head to trap Alasdair inside the boundary of it. Alasdair snarled and snapped, but didn't seem able to break out of it, though I could feel the force with which his energy was testing the strength of its perimeter; and it was formidable. Danica shushed him as he paced, a caged animal.

"Don't you do that, Alasdair! That's my sister!"

"Danica! Answer me!" Clarissa practically shrieked. She was holding on to her self-control by a thread. Her fists, clenched at her sides, trembled violently.

Now that Alasdair had been neutralized, Catriona was scanning the room with her eyes, no doubt looking for some sign of me. She spotted Milo first, and then me. She mouthed the next words under the cover of the sisters' continued argument.

"Are you okay?" she silently asked.

I nodded, and sensed Milo do the same beside me.

Catriona returned the nod and seemed to release a sigh of relief. The relief didn't last. Finn was struggling to keep a hold on Alasdair, and Danica was getting edgy as she observed her new audience. But at her sister's persistent plea for information, she had no choice but to comply.

"Danica! Answer me!"

"Oh, all right, although you really weren't meant to know about this yet," Danica said, shifting nervously from foot to foot. She had dropped her candle in surprise upon Clarissa's entrance, and it had extinguished itself with a little hiss on the damp ground. It sent a little slithering trail of smoke up into the air. She took a deep breath and then, unbelievably, smiled. "I've done it, Clarissa. I've solved it for you."

Clarissa just stared at her, fists clenching and unclenching. "I don't understand," she finally said.

"You were so sad, so angry when the Gateway was taken from you!" Danica explained patiently. "I've never seen you so... lost. It broke my heart, Clarissa. It broke my heart and I had to fix it." She gestured proudly to the Collection, like a child showing a parent their art project. If she was expecting gushing applause and compliments, she was disappointed. Every eye in the room was drawn, once again, to the Collection.

Clarissa pointed a shaking finger at it. "And what in the name of all that is holy is *that*?"

Danica's eyes smiled broadly. "It's for you. It will restore all the power you've lost."

But Clarissa wasn't even listening. She was stepping cautiously forward, staring into the orb. All of the others took a moment to examine it in earnest now, and I knew from the widening of everyone's eyes that they were seeing the same thing I had seen—the dismembered parts of the spirits floating around, held together by their mutual destruction.

"Is... are those... those are spirits in there, Danica," Clarissa whispered. Then she looked up at her sister, her face chalk white. "What have you done?"

Danica's broad smile faltered for a moment, but she hitched it back into place almost at once. "I collected them for you. Well, Alasdair helped me." She pointed at Alasdair, who was still struggling against the walls of the Casting Finn had placed on him.

Something clicked in Clarissa's head. "These are the spirits who have been disappearing from the courtyard."

It wasn't a question, but Danica answered it anyway. "Yes! How did you—"

"Danica, I don't know what you've gotten yourself tangled up in, but we need to... I have to... we need to fix it!" Clarissa cried, sounding on the verge of losing it.

Danica's face had fallen now, tears sparkling in her eyes. "You don't need to fix anything Clarissa, that's what I'm trying to tell you! I've fixed it! If you'll just listen, you'll underst—"

"Danica, where is Jessica Ballard?" Clarissa's question cut through Danica's protests.

Danica didn't answer at first, though two angry red spots had appeared on her cheeks. Her eyes darted toward my cell, and I took the only chance I would be likely to get.

"I'm here, Clarissa! I'm here in this cell!" I called out.

Danica turned and stared at me with such venom in her look that I recoiled. Across the room I heard Finn, still struggling with Alasdair, give a cry of relief.

"Are you all right, Jess?" he called.

"I'm okay, and so is Milo!" I called back.

Clarissa took a step closer to me. If she looked horrified before, it was nothing to how she looked now, seeing me in Walker form behind bars.

"Danica! She has been sent here from Fairhaven! What are you doing, locking her up?!"

Danica was looking flustered now. This clearly wasn't going the way she'd hoped. "Well, I didn't want to, obviously, but she kept snooping around, so—"

"Of course she was snooping around! She was here to investigate! I invited her to come!"

"Yes, but I couldn't let her tell everyone what was happening!"

"But what *is* happening?!?" I still don't know what—"

"Because I'm trying to explain it to you, but you won't listen! You never LISTEN!"

The words burst from Danica like an explosion, and she clapped her hand over her mouth in horror. Clarissa looked like she'd just been slapped in the face. It was clear that Danica had never raised her voice to her, and Clarissa was looking at her sister like she'd never seen her before.

"I... I'm s-sorry, Clarissa. I didn't mean to shout. But you have to understand that what I've done here... it's for you! It's my... my gift to you, to make things better, like how they were before!" Danica's voice was thick with suppressed tears now, try as she might to hold herself together. "These spirits, they can help you! They can make you powerful and strong again. Just watch how—"

Clarissa dropped her face into her hands. "Oh my God, Danica. Do you understand, it does not matter what it is you are trying to do! You've ruined everything!"

Danica's face went oddly blank, the tears brimming in her eyes, threatening to overflow.

"Whatever this is, whatever you think you've done..." Clarissa stared down at the Collection again, shaking her head in mute disbelief before she could find the rest of the words. "I need you to release them, all right? Just release them, and maybe we can—"

But Clarissa's words shook Danica loose from her shock and she burst out, "No! No, I can't just release them. It's too late for that!"

"You must! Whatever Casting you've used on them, break it!"

"I can't! They've already been taken apart. They're ready to be used!"

"Bloody hell," Catriona whispered. Her complexion had gone almost green.

"Used?! Spirits aren't meant to be used, they're meant to Cross! That's what they were all trying to do, and that's what you ought to have let them do!" Clarissa said sternly.

It was Danica's turn to look like she'd been struck. "But you used them."

"I never—"

"Yes, you did. You used them for Leeching. You took their life force for your own benefit."

Clarissa snorted. "That was different. That was a sanctioned practice, for centuries."

"It was sanctioned for when you were ill or dying. Not the way you used it," Danica pushed through stubbornly.

But Clarissa waved her off. "Nonsense. Everyone did it. It was common practice."

"But then the Council outlawed it, and you still did it. You didn't care about breaking the rules then," Danica said.

Clarissa's cheeks reddened and her eyes darted to Catriona before she said, "Danica, I will not listen to this absurdity. What I did, and what you've done, they are not the same!"

"They are the same! You stole spirit energy to help yourself. I've stolen spirit energy to help you! You haven't even seen what it can do! Let me show you!"

"No! Danica, stop! I've seen enough!" Clarissa shrieked. "I refuse to be party to—"

"You have to see it, Clarissa, and then you'll understand! Look, just watch!" And she bent to reach for the candle on the ground, but it had landed in a puddle of moisture gathered in a crack between the cobbles. Cursing, she darted for the table, upon which several more stubs of candles lay. Clarissa moved to overtake her.

"Danica, stop! I don't want to see what it does. I don't care what it—"

"No, I have to show you! When you see it, you'll—"

Danica's hand closed around a candle, but Clarissa knocked it from her grasp. Danica cried out in frustration and lunged for a second, but Clarissa was too fast for her and pushed the other candles from the tabletop with a swipe of her arm.

"Clarissa, stop! You're not listening, you won't—"

"Danica, enough of this!"

Danica's scrabbling fingers found another object and closed around it. Finn was the only one close enough to see what it was, and yelled out, breaking his hold on Alasdair and lunging for the two sisters instead. He had not yet closed the distance between them, however, when Danica raised the curved dagger that had been resting on the table and drove it straight into Clarissa's chest.

Everything stopped. Danica and Clarissa stared down at the dagger, wearing identical expressions of wide-eyed disbelief.

"No! No, no no!" Danica cried, and reached for the dagger again, as though she could pull it out and undo what she had done; but Finn reached her first, catching hold of her arm and yanking it behind her back to restrain her. At the same time, Catriona rushed forward just in time to cushion Clarissa as she sank to the ground, still staring at the dagger in a bemused sort of way, as though she had no idea how it had gotten there.

It was Milo who cried out, "Where's Alasdair? Where did he go?"

I looked around frantically, but Alasdair was nowhere to be seen. It was Hattie who answered.

"Oh, he's gone. Vanished, he did, just as soon as that man let go of him."

What anyone else may have said, I would never know. The words were lost in the midst of Danica's howls of abject misery.

～

An hour later, we were all huddled together back at the hotel, leaning on each other as the adrenaline of the afternoon wore off and the shock and trauma set in.

Danica was in Caomhnóir custody and on her way to Skye Príosún. I thought what she really needed was a mental hospital, but Finn assured me that they would assess her thoroughly before deciding what to do with her until a trial could be held. Clarissa had been whisked away to the nearest hospital, accompanied by Catriona, who, together with Finn, had carried Clarissa through the grimy tunnels under the city and back up through the grate to an ambulance. Danica had been a hysterical wreck the entire way up, making no attempts to flee or even protest her arrest.

"I've killed her! I've killed my sister!" were the only intelligible words amidst her wracking sobs as she climbed voluntarily into the waiting Caomhnóir vehicle.

Catriona was able to free us from the cells by cutting through Danica's silken bindings on the bars. Milo wasted no time opening the connection the moment we were outside of the boundaries of the dungeon's Castings.

Hannah's shrieks of relief filled our heads like an explosion, but there couldn't have been a more welcome sound in the world than her voice, no matter how loud. She fairly flew the several blocks from the hotel and was there to meet us when we rose up through the grate and into the street. Back at the hotel—and back in my body—I asked Finn to explain how in the world they'd found us.

"It had only been about forty-five minutes, but I was starting to get on edge," he said, his arms wrapped tightly around me. "Catriona was trying to convince me to stick to the timetable we'd agreed upon when that little girl appeared on the sidewalk outside The Mary King's Close attraction. Her anxious energy permeated right through the car and I climbed out at once, sure it couldn't be a coincidence that a ghost had appeared there at that moment. When I approached her, she told me that she had followed you through the tunnels—"

"Which I specifically told her not to do, so thank God that child doesn't listen," I interjected.

"And she overheard everything that passed between you and Danica. She was able to tell me exactly who was responsible, because you had called Danica by name several times while she was listening. Once Danica had trapped you, she knew she had to go for help, although I didn't really understand what she said about why."

"What did she say?" I asked.

"She said something to the effect of, 'You have to rescue her, she's the only one who can explain to them about my name,'" Finn said with a shrug.

I laughed. "Of course she would think that was the most pressing reason."

"What was she talking about?" Finn asked.

"Never mind, I'll explain later," I said.

"And so we followed her to the sewer grate, leaving your body in the custody of the Caomhnóir," Finn continued, "whom I threatened with a slow, gruesome, and agonizing death if they didn't protect you from any and all possible dangers."

I laughed. "Your threats were effective. One of them didn't even want to let me back in my body until he got your permission first. But what I don't understand is how the hell Clarissa found out?"

"That part was pure luck," Finn said. "Clarissa had come down to the Collective to hand-deliver more records of Clan Rìoghalachd properties to be searched."

"Hand-delivered?" Savvy snorted. "That doesn't sound like the kind of thing she'd stoop to. Hasn't she got minions for that?"

"Catriona reckons she was anxious to appear to be cooperating. She was starting to worry that further obstruction on her part would be bad for politics. And she wasn't wrong. Apparently, Celeste was hours away from a formal censure," Finn said.

"So, you told her Danica was down there? What did she say?" Hannah prompted. She was nestled between Milo on one side and Kiernan on the other, and she looked like the happiest little sandwich I'd ever seen.

"She demanded to come with us. She didn't even balk when she saw we had to climb down through the sewer grate. I couldn't believe it. But the strangest part was how quickly she accepted it. Like she knew her sister was somehow capable of it, even though she insisted loudly the whole way that there had to be some kind of mistake." Finn shook his head sadly.

"I still can't believe it myself," Hannah said. "Danica, of all people! She just seemed so... harmless."

"I thought there was something a bit off about her," Savvy said, eyes narrowed shrewdly.

"Oh, come off it, you did not!" Rana cried.

"Hand to heart!" Savvy insisted. "It was the way she always talked about her sister, like the sun shone directly out of Clarissa's arse. No well-adjusted adult talks like that. I can't even imagine what kind of mental gymnastics it takes to hero-worship someone who's so demonstrably awful to you. I'd feel bad for her if she hadn't... well, you know."

Yes, we all knew now. The horror of it was its own looming presence in the room.

"What do you think will happen to her?" Hannah asked.

Finn's expression was grim as he answered. "Her crimes rank among the more horrific I've seen, even from Necromancers. The Council will assess her mental state, but whether in a *príosún* or a hospital, I doubt she'll ever walk free again, and that's assuming her sister doesn't press charges."

Our joy and relief at escaping the bowels of the city and the atrocities being committed there was tainted by the knowledge that the danger wasn't over. The Collection was still writhing and pulsating beneath the Geatgrima, and we had no freaking idea what to do about it. And of course, even more disturbing, Alasdair had escaped.

"I can't believe I let him go," Finn kept saying through clenched teeth.

"You had to make a choice, Finn. You were trying to save Clarissa's life. It's the same choice any of us would have made," I told him.

"And it didn't matter, did it! I didn't get to them in time, and Clarissa will be lucky to survive," Finn growled.

Catriona's last text had told us that Clarissa was going in for emergency surgery. It would likely be hours before we heard anything else, and the waiting was awful. None of us cared for Clarissa—and some of us actively hated her—but that didn't stop us all from praying she pulled through. After all, despite our suspicions, she hadn't been the one behind the scheme at all, and she had done all she could to stop Danica when she'd discovered it. It was more than I would have expected of her, and it reminded me that humanity exists mostly in shades of gray. The villains do not always act as such, and the sweetest temperament could easily hide the darkest of motives.

Alasdair was an exception to this observation. He was a being of darkness now, whatever else he might have been in life, and the world was measurably less safe with him in it.

Over the next two days there would be much work to do. MacLeod Close would be excavated, and Alasdair's research photographed and collected. Hannah was deeply unsettled by this prospect.

"It should be destroyed, all of it, at once," she said, her eyes alight with righteous indignation.

"Normally, I'd agree with you," I told her. "But without it, we won't have a chance at understanding the Collection, or how to undo it, if undoing it is even possible."

And there was something even more vital within that research. Danica had told me that it wasn't only Clarissa who stood to benefit from the Collection. Alasdair had a new obsession: bringing himself back to life in a new body. It ought to be impossible. Everything we'd ever learned about the spirit world and how it worked forbade the reality of such a feat. But all I had seen over the last few days had taught me that there were no rules Alasdair would not break, no boundaries he would not cross, and that made the impossible seem, suddenly, all too possible. Wherever he was now, Alasdair was plotting his next move, and we would have to do the same. I'd seen the look in Finn's eye. He wouldn't rest until he had rectified what he believed to be his mistake in letting Alasdair slip through his fingers, and that meant I wouldn't rest either. There was work to be done.

It was nearly midnight when we finally heard from Catriona. Clarissa had come through surgery. The dagger had missed her heart by a fraction of an inch, and while she was not out of the woods yet, Clarissa was stable in the ICU, and the doctors were hopeful she would recover. Maeve and Pippa had been keeping vigil over her, a woman with whom they both had a complicated relationship, and yet a woman to whom they were loyal. Theirs would be the faces she would see when she woke, and I hoped Clarissa would learn to better appreciate them both. Danica would be relieved to hear her sister's prognosis although, I thought bitterly, I hoped no one told her too soon. Let her torture herself a while longer with what her lunacy might have wrought. It was the least of what she deserved.

It was just before two o'clock in the morning and the moon was high and full over the courtyard, bathing the Geatgrima in a glow as ancient and magical as the Gateway itself. I had slipped out of the hotel and walked down here alone, leaving a note for Finn in case he woke and found me missing.

There were a few Caomhnóir patrolling the perimeter of the buildings, but they let me pass with a nod of acknowledgment. I sat myself down in the grass and waited. The Collection still languished beneath the surface, and it broke my heart to know that, but we would do everything we could in the coming days to help those spirits. But above ground, I had to know that all was well now. I had to see it for myself, that we had accomplished that small bit of good, at least.

I didn't have to wait long. A spirit wandered into the courtyard just a few minutes after the church bells sang the hour, and I recognized him: it was the tour guide Terry, his name tag still visible on the ghostly specter of his shirt.

He spotted me there, and recognized me, for he gave me a nod and said, "So this is it, is it? The place all the others have told me about?"

"This is it," I agreed.

He looked at the Geatgrima, and I recognized the combination of emotions that ran riot over his features: the awe, the fear, the bewildered wonder.

"And I just... just walk through it, is that it?" he asked. He licked his lips nervously, a holdover habit from his living days.

"That's all there is to it," I confirmed.

He let out a strange little laugh. "You make it sound so easy."

"It's meant to be."

"But you don't really know, do you?" he said, shuffling his feet and taking half a step backward. "You can't tell me where I'm walking to."

"Not your final destination, no," I said. "But I have walked beyond that veil, just once."

Terry turned a desperate face on me. "And?"

"And I could have stayed forever, if someone hadn't called me back," I told him truthfully.

A clarity came into his eyes. He let out a shaky breath. "That... doesn't sound so bad."

"No."

He turned again, and this time, the hesitation was gone. He strode purposely forward, right through the remnants of the cautionary tape that had marked the perimeter of Alasdair's Casting. There was no screaming, no fear, no trap. Just a sense of peace that intensified on his features with each step closer to the dais. He stepped up onto it and turned one last time, his face transfigured with wonder.

"I can feel it. It's calling to me."

I smiled. "Then you'd better answer it."

And he did. He met his fate the way we all wished we might—by holding out a hand to greet it with a smile.

Tears blurred that last glimpse I had of him before he vanished, and I blinked them away.

"Whatever are you crying for?"

I laughed because I knew who I would see sitting beside me before I even turned. It was Hattie, and she was eyeing me with a skeptical expression.

"Oh, I'm not sad," I told her. "It's just... that was beautiful."

Hattie quirked her mouth and looked at the Geatgrima to decide for herself. Finally, after a few seconds of contemplation, she said. "Yes. I suppose you're right. But I'm not sure why you have to cry about it."

I laughed again. This kid was a trip. "Fancy taking the trip yourself?" I asked her.

She shook her head decidedly. "Not quite yet."

"Fair enough," I said. "But it will always be ready for you. Remember that."

She nodded, as though she had already known it.

"I'm glad you came here," I told her. "I was going to come find you and thank you for saving my life."

She shrugged. "You're welcome. I couldn't very well let you go and die down there. You're the only one who knows my name."

"Not for long," I told her, and pulled a folded paper from my pocket. "I had planned to deliver this to one of the tour guides tomorrow. Maybe you'd like to read it first?"

She shook her head. "I can't read."

"That's all right. I'll read it to you," I said, and unfolded it. Hattie leaned in and followed the progress of my finger across the page.

To Whom It May Concern:

I was a recent tourist through your attraction. I also happen to be sensitive to spirit activity. I thought you would want to know that one of the spirits currently haunting this close has a bone to pick with you. She is the spirit of a little girl who you have been referring to as 'Annie.' She has asked me to inform you that her name is actually 'Hattie', and she would very much appreciate it if you would refer to her as such. If you do, she may just reward you with a bit more ghostly activity to entertain your visitors.

Respectfully,

Jessica Ballard

Hattie looked up at me with a little smile. "That ought to do the trick," she said, but then her face fell. "What if they don't believe you?"

I smiled back at her. "You're the ghost. *Make* them believe me."

Her smile spread into a devilish little grin. "I fancy I can do that," she said, and vanished from my side with a little pop.

I laughed as I tucked the paper back into my pocket. It seemed I'd banished one terror from beneath the streets of Edinburgh only to unleash another. The first would have to be chased to the ends of the earth, and I knew it would be my job to lead that chase.

But the second? Well, she could take care of herself.

ABOUT THE AUTHOR

E.E. Holmes is a writer, teacher, and actor living in central Massachusetts with her husband, two children, and a small, but surprisingly loud, dog. When not writing, she enjoys performing, watching unhealthy amounts of British television, and reading with her children.

To learn more about E.E. Holmes and *The World of the Gateway*, please visit www.eeholmes.com

Printed in Great Britain
by Amazon

40546809R00152